STEEL

A NIGHT REBELS MC ROMANCE

CHIAH WILDER

Editing by Hot Tree Editing
Cover design by Cheeky Covers
Cover model: Dan Pearson
Photographer: Al Gonzalez
Proofreading by Daryl Banner

Chapter One

BREANNA QUINE FOLLOWED the red and blue lights as they flashed in the dark night. Tears welled in her eyes as images of the teen flitted through her mind. When Breanna had received the anonymous call telling her the address where she'd find Chenoa—one of her clients—she rushed out of her house, not even thinking of any possible danger. And when she'd entered an abandoned building on the outskirts of town, junkies huddled in corners, whispers wrapped around her, and the semiconscious body of Chenoa McVickers had greeted her. She'd rushed over to the young woman and noticed a syringe, rubber tubing, and a dirty spoon strewn around her. Breanna checked the teen's pulse, then dialed 911.

She gripped the steering wheel as she turned the corner too sharply, St. Joseph's Hospital looming ahead of her. By the time she parked her car and went through the security check, she was a basket case. Her insides twisted as she opened her purse, took out an antacid, and popped it in her mouth. She ran her hand through her long blonde hair as she walked in circles around the emergency waiting area. Breanna took out her phone and dialed Chenoa's mother for the sixth time, and again, it went to voicemail. She didn't have Chenoa's father's number in her case file, so she took a deep breath and dialed the only other number she had—the teen's paternal grandmother.

"Hello?" a shaky voice said.

"May I please speak to Mrs. McVickers?" Breanna crossed her fingers, hoping the number she had in the file was still the correct one.

"Speaking," the woman said slowly.

"Mrs. McVickers, my name is Breanna Quine and I'm your granddaughter's caseworker. I've been trying to contact her mother for the last hour without any luck. There's been an accident. Chenoa is at St. Joseph's Hospital." Her stomach lurched when she heard the older woman's gasp over the phone. She always hated this part of her job— informing family members that their loved one was hurt, or worse, dead. "I just need to contact one of her parents. Do you have her father's phone number?"

"Is she going to be okay?" Sadness and fear seeped through the phone.

Breanna exhaled. "I don't know. I need to have one of her parents here."

"I'll call my son." The phone went dead.

Breanna stood staring at the black screen, wondering if she should call back.

"Ms. Quine?" a strong voice boomed out.

She whirled around and saw a man in a white coat with a folder in his hands. "That's me." She went over to the middle-aged man.

He extended his hand. "I'm Dr. Sanchez." She took it and nodded. "Have you been able to contact Ms. McVickers's parents?"

"Not yet. I've just spoken to her grandmother and she told me she'd call her father. How is Chenoa?"

"We've stabilized her. You got to her in time, but it's too early to tell if there will be any physical or mental issues. We're monitoring her."

"I really thought she was making progress with her addiction. She's a really good kid." Breanna blinked rapidly.

The doctor nodded. "You can go in and see her. We're waiting for a room to transfer her to. Since you're her caseworker, you can stay with her until one of her parents gets here."

Breanna followed Dr. Sanchez through the double steel doors and down the sterile hallway until he stopped in front of a door that was slightly ajar. He pushed it open and gestured for her to go in. Breanna muttered her thanks under her breath and walked into the dimly lit room.

Chenoa lay in the bed wrapped in white sheets and a blanket with tubes stuck in her veins and nose. Several machines hissed and beeped as bright numbers in lime green and red displayed intermittently on their monitors. Breanna padded over to the bed. The teen looked so peaceful, yet Breanna knew a storm was brewing inside her. She ran her hand gently over the young woman's cheek while her gaze fixed on the angry red lines on the girl's thin arms. Anger wrapped itself around the social worker's spine.

I want to kill whoever sold Chenoa heroin. How did it get to the reservation? Why isn't the sheriff doing anything about this?

To Breanna, it seemed as if heroin had started appearing in the county late the previous year. She could pinpoint the date based on when her brother had started showing up at her house begging for money. She shook her head. She'd been hoping that law enforcement would've had a handle on it before it made its way to the reservation.

The door banging against the wall startled her and she looked up, then sucked in her breath. Before her stood a tall, broad-shouldered man who exuded blatant virility and rebelliousness. The leather vest he wore clung to his bare, toned chest, revealing menacing inky images. Outlaw patches filled his leather cut. On his face, a wicked scar paled against his tanned skin, a silent testimony to the world of violence in which he lived. It looked out of place amid his high cheekbones and sculpted nose, which momentarily captivated her.

He had long black hair that he wore loosely around his shoulders, and several silver earrings in both ears gleamed under the light. Her gaze dropped to his corded legs, encased in black denim, and then to the bulge in his crotch. She quickly raised her eyes, meeting his dark green ones, and she gasped. His eyes were the color of the forest right before sunset; they were the kind of green that distracted a person from everything around. They were simply gorgeous. And at that moment, they glared at her. His whole expression was fiercely arrogant, and there was an aura of danger about him.

She smiled weakly.

He crossed his arms, his biceps bulging. "Who are you?"

She took a few steps forward and shoved her hands in her gray hoodie. "I'm Breanna Quine. Who are you?"

He took a few steps toward the bed, his eyes softening when they landed on Chenoa's body. In two strides he was near her, bending down and placing a kiss on her forehead, whispering to her in a language Breanna couldn't understand. After several minutes, he looked up. "I'm Chenoa's father. Steel."

"It's good to meet you. I'm so glad you're here. I couldn't get a hold of her mother." She extended her hand. "I'm Breanna Quine, your daughter's caseworker."

Ignoring her hand, he stiffened. "Her caseworker? Where the fuck were you when this happened?" He glared and jerked his arm over his daughter.

Anger prickled her skin as she lifted her chin and glared back. "Where the fuck were *you*?" She placed her hands on her hips. "I've been her caseworker for the past six weeks and never once met you."

He growled and stepped forward, his lips curling in a feral smile as he came within inches of her face. "Don't you *ever* insinuate that I'm not there for my daughter. You don't know shit. You're just one of many the county has assigned in the past four years. It doesn't mean a damn thing to me."

"Apparently it doesn't since you never bothered to get in contact with me even though I left my card at your daughter's house many times."

His eyes grew darker at her show of defiance, and fury etched across his face. "You wanna know where I was? At the clubhouse, like the fucking county has dictated. *You* determined I wasn't a good bet for my daughter because of my lifestyle. Fuck that. If she were with me, she wouldn't be lying here on the brink of death." His voice broke just slightly on the last word, and Breanna, pissed as she was, felt her heart melt a bit for him. No parent should see their child fighting for her life.

"I know you're angry right now, Mr. McVickers, but this is hardly the place to discuss the what-ifs of the situation."

"Fuck off, lady." He turned back to Chenoa and slipped his hand inside his cut. He withdrew something and touched his daughter's forehead, nose, eyelids, chin, and ears with it, then placed it under her hand.

"What's that?" Breanna asked as she inched closer to the bed.

"A Navajo talisman. We use it for healing. It's a bear claw and a turquoise stone."

She stared at Chenoa's serene face. "I'm sorry this happened, Mr. McVickers. I'd been so hopeful that your daughter would've reached the milestone in her recovery. I had no idea she was using heroin. Did you?"

His face hardened. "No."

"She's a tough young lady. She'll pull through, and when she does, I know of an excellent rehab center that I think she'll thrive in. We can talk about it later, but I think—"

"I don't give a damn what you think. I'm gonna be honest with you—I don't like or trust you. I don't trust any government worker. You don't give a damn about my daughter. She's just another fucking case number to you. As long as you draw a paycheck, you'll go through the motions. You don't fool me at all, so stop with your fake-as-hell sympathy. Once Chenoa pulls through this, I'm in charge, and I don't give a fuck whether you or the county likes it. I have nothing more to say to you."

He turned away and Breanna just stared at the words "Night Rebels MC" on the back of his leather vest. She didn't know what to say. Part of her chalked up his contempt of her to his obvious upset over his daughter, but a larger part knew that this was who the man was. Hard, fierce, and proud. She was just ready to respond when Chenoa's mother walked in, her face tight with worry.

"Breanna, what happened?"

Before Breanna could answer, Chenoa's mother glanced at Steel and then made her way over to him, reaching out her arms. He pulled her into a tight embrace. "Mika," he whispered. Her arms were around his narrow waist and she buried her head in the crook of his neck. "She's gonna be okay. Fuck, she *has* to be okay."

Mika answered back in whimpers.

She then pulled away, grabbed a tissue out of the box sitting on the hospital tray, and went over to Chenoa, stroking her forehead. She leaned down and whispered something in her daughter's ear, then turned to Breanna and smiled faintly. "Thanks for being here. I don't know what happened. She was doing so well," Mika said softly.

Steel stood next to Mika. "So you know her?" He jerked his head in Breanna's direction, his eyes riveted on his daughter's placid face.

"Of course. She's Chenoa's social worker. She's been helping her out."

"Why the fuck doesn't anyone tell me anything?" His jaw jutted out.

"Because you're always consumed with the Night Rebels. I haven't seen you in over a month." Mika grabbed their daughter's hand. "She's gonna make it, isn't she?"

"Yeah. There's no way I'm letting my baby girl leave this world."

"She'll pull through. The doctor said I got to her in time. Besides, she's a strong girl," Breanna said. Steel scowled at her. She licked her lips and shoved her hands back into her hoodie's pockets. "I'm going to find the nurse. I have to talk to her." She turned around and walked toward the door.

As she left the room, she heard Mika's voice. "Really, Steel? You're checking out the social worker's ass while our daughter's lying in a hospital bed? You never change, do you?"

His deep voice washed over her. "I wasn't doing shit. Did you know Chenoa—" At that point he was out of earshot as Breanna walked over to the nurse's station.

I can't believe he was checking out my butt. A strange tickle in her stomach pissed her off. *Why am I flattered by it? He's an angry, rude biker. He probably checks out every woman's ass. He's despicable.* The head nurse came over and helped her with some of the information she'd need to finish her report. As she sat there writing her notes, she sensed *him.*

Glancing sideways, she saw him lean against the counter.

"I want to talk to the doctor. Now," he commanded, his voice like a whip.

The middle-aged nurse picked up the phone. "I'm paging him, sir."

That's when Breanna saw him look in her direction. She shifted her eyes back to the report she was writing, accidentally knocking over a cup of coffee the nurse had given her. "Damnit," she muttered under her breath as she pushed her chair back from the small desk. She grabbed several tissues and sopped up the brown liquid leaking onto her report.

"Here." His voice was gruff and rumbled from deep inside him.

She took the wad of paper towels he handed her. "Thanks," she murmured as she wiped up the mess. Breanna tossed the wet towels in the trash and glanced up at him. His steady gaze on her unnerved her. Gathering her papers and shoving them into a manila folder, she rose to her feet, expecting him to move back a little, but he didn't. Her body brushed against his and a strong jolt zinged through her. "Can you please step back? I'm trying to get out."

"I'm not stopping you." She pressed her lips together and rearranged the papers in her folder. "Am I making you nervous, lady?"

When she looked up, she knew he'd be wearing a smirk on his full lips. Anger replaced nervousness. "Not at all." She stood up again and pushed him back. She must have caught him off guard, because he stumbled back slightly. For a brief second, rage flashed in his gaze, but then admiration replaced it.

"I'll be back tomorrow to see Chenoa." She tossed her hair over her shoulder and walked to the elevator. *I bet he's checking out my ass again.* Tempted to turn around, she resisted. She stepped into the elevator, breathing a sigh of relief when the metal doors shut, staring at her reflection in the shiny gold-toned doors. Her face was flushed.

What the hell's the matter with me? And why did I tell him I was going to be back tomorrow? He's such a jerk. She forced all thoughts of him out of her mind as she walked across the parking lot. When she settled in her car, she cranked up the radio and sang along until she arrived at her house on the other side of town.

The first thing she did when she entered the kitchen was go to the freezer; she hadn't eaten since earlier that morning and she was starving. The minute she took out a frozen pizza, her front doorbell rang. Knowing only her brother would come to her house at eleven at night, she grimaced and shoved her dinner back in the freezer. She padded over to the door, looked out of the peephole to make sure, and then opened it. Her brother, tall and skinny, smiled at her as he wiped his runny nose with a tissue. "Hey. Did I wake you?"

Breanna took in his haggard appearance and flushed skin and sighed inwardly. "No, I just got back from the hospital. A client of mine ODed on heroin." She looked fixedly at him. He fidgeted and scratched an open sore on his neck. *Is he injecting* there *now?* She moved aside. "Come on in."

He slinked past her and plopped down on a large cushy chair by the fireplace. "You got any pop?"

"Diet Coke. Is that good?" He nodded and she headed to the kitch- en. Seeing her younger brother strung out on drugs broke her heart. Nicholas was the youngest of the four of them. He was twenty-one to her twenty-nine, and she always felt very protective of him, especially since their mother had basically stopped caring about them when Nicholas had only been four years old.

"Can you hurry with that pop?"

She grabbed a cold one out of the refrigerator and went back into the living room. After she handed him the can, she settled on the couch. "Why are you here?"

He took a large gulp. "Can't your brother come by and say hi?"

She shook her head. "Not this late and when he's obviously using. Did you come by for money?"

His body stiffened and he acted indignant, but she saw the panic lacing his eyes. It was the panic of a user who was scared to death he wouldn't get his next fix. It angered and broke her heart at the same time. "You always think I want money." He finished his drink, crushed the can, and threw it on her glass-topped coffee table.

"You do," she said softly. "When you're on the stuff, I never hear from you unless you need money. Shelby and Jeremy tell me the same thing."

He snorted. "Shelby shouldn't be talking. She's nothing but a whore moving from one guy to the next that she meets online. Do you know she's shacking up with a married man? The dude's doing that shit in front of his wife, and Shelby brags all the time how he gives her everything and nothing to his wife. And Jeremy is in and outta jail all the time, so why the fuck is he saying anything about me?" His nostrils flared.

Nicholas was right. She and her siblings were the quintessential fucked-up family. "That may be true, but you're putting up smokescreens. Do you need money?"

He averted her gaze. "I always need money. Who the fuck doesn't?"

She rubbed her temples. *I can't keep doing this, but I can't stand the thought of him alone on the streets.* "How much do you need?"

He smiled. "Just a few hundred. My rent's due and I'm a little short." He averted his eyes.

She knew he was lying, and he knew she knew; it was a game they played each and every time. "Spend the night here. I was just ready to heat up a frozen pizza. It has pepperoni on it." When he looked everywhere but at her, she knew he'd walk out the door and head straight to his dealer. When he was young, the promise of pepperoni made him settle down, his big blue eyes widening as he watched her set a bubbling slice of pizza on his plate.

If only life were that simple again.

"Can I take a raincheck? I'm beat and I gotta get up early for work tomorrow."

She stared fixedly at him. "Don't lie to me, Nicholas. You quit your job at the grocery store three weeks ago."

Without missing a beat, he flashed her a too-wide smile. "I got another job. Working at the car wash. The tips are pretty decent." He scratched at the sore on his neck again. "So, you got the money?"

She went over to her purse and counted out three hundred dollars before handing them to him. "You should put a bandage over that." She pointed to his bleeding sore. "You're going to get an infection."

He leaned in and kissed her on the cheek, then squeezed her to him. "You've always been the one to worry about me. You've always cared. I appreciate it." He pulled away and ambled to the door. "I'll call you over the weekend. Maybe we can grab a bite to eat or something."

She nodded and watched him disappear into the misty night, the long shadows enveloping him. *I'm losing him. I don't know how to stop it.* Breanna closed the door, her heart heavy. First Chenoa, then her brother. Two young people caught up in a macabre dance of death.

She went back to the kitchen, opened the freezer, and stared at the pizza. Hunger had left her, so she closed the door and sat on the kitchen chair, numb from exhaustion and sadness. Then Steel's face—angry and proud—flashed in her mind. *Whoa. Where did that come from?* Chenoa's father intrigued her, but she knew he was an outlaw biker and that meant bad news all around. She found him to be rude, cocky, and an overall jerk.

She'd go over the following day to see if Chenoa was better. She hoped the biker wouldn't be there. *Then why did you tell him you were going to be there?* She was tired. She didn't know what she was saying, and the way he stared at her made her nervous as hell. It was like he was seeing into her, becoming a part of her.

She didn't have time to think about him.

Breanna swung around and opened her laptop. If she was going to keep helping Nicholas, she'd have to get a part-time job on the weekends; a county employee's salary was barely enough for her to live on. And with Jeremy getting out of jail soon, she knew he'd need some money until he could find employment. She pulled her hair into a high ponytail and crossed her legs on the chair. Instead of typing "bartending" and "waitressing jobs" in the search engine, she typed "Night Rebels MC."

I'm just curious, that's all.

But she knew that wasn't all by a long shot. She couldn't get the rugged biker out of her mind. *I seriously need to get laid. It's been like five months since I broke up with Mark.* She shook her head and closed the computer, knowing the biker's penetrating green eyes would stab at her dreams that night.

I can't let him get to me. I hope I never see him again. As she thought the words she knew they were a lie. She was very much looking forward to their next encounter.

Damnit.

Chapter Two

STEEL LOOKED UP as Dr. Sanchez entered the room. He came over and introduced himself to both him and Mika, then glanced down at Chenoa. Her eyes had fluttered open twenty minutes before the doctor had come in, and Mika was feeding her spoons of chipped ice.

Dr. Sanchez smiled at the young girl, then looked down at his chart. "Your daughter is doing well. I've given her naloxone. It's an opioid receptor antagonist, which means the substance quickly attaches to the same areas of the brain that heroin seeks out. The good news is that Ms. Quine had your daughter brought in just in time, so the drug will reduce and most probably reverse all the symptoms of the overdose." He turned to Chenoa. "You gave us quite a scare, young lady. You're lucky you're still alive. Heroin overdose is very serious business, and many addicts don't live through it." He wrote down something on the chart, then addressed Steel and Mika. "I want to keep her in the hospital for a few more days for observation, make sure there isn't any lasting damage from the overdose. I'll arrange a time when we can meet to go over some options after release."

"What does that mean?" Chenoa asked in a soft voice.

Dr. Sanchez smiled. "We rarely send an addict home before we have some safeguards in place. Rehab is what we recommend. I'll talk to your parents about it."

The dark-haired girl pushed herself up a little more. "I don't need rehab. It was a mistake. I was stupid. It was the first time I tried it." Her eyes darted to each parent.

Mika put down the glass of ice and hugged her daughter. "I believe you, sweetie. I'm here for you, you know that."

Steel narrowed his eyes. "You can bullshit your mom, but you're not doing it to me. You're a fucking addict. I can see your lines from here." Dr. Sanchez cleared his throat. Steel glanced at him. "I'm just telling it like it is, Doc. Too much denial's been going around here. Chenoa, your ass is in rehab, and you and I are gonna have a serious talk. I don't give a shit what you or your mother wants. I'm fucking in charge now."

Chenoa hung her head and the doctor squeezed her hand. "I'll be back tomorrow morning to check on you. It was nice meeting you."

Steel jerked his head at the doctor and watched him walk out of the room.

"Can you keep your temper in check for once?" Mika said as she sat down in a chair near the hospital bed.

"Not when it's about our daughter putting shit in her body. What the fuck were you thinking, Chenoa? Where'd you get the stuff?"

"Dad, I'm tired. I'm not ready for the third degree right now. Can it wait?"

Steel wanted to grab her by the shoulders and shake some sense in her. *"Can it wait?" Fuck no!* He opened his mouth but then shut it when he saw his daughter's eyes close. She looked so fragile lying on the bed, her black hair a stark contrast to the white sheets covering her. Her skin was pale, and her usual pinkish lips were drained of color. He decided to talk to her later; for the moment, he'd let her rest. As long as she was in the hospital, she was safe and he wouldn't have to worry about her.

"I'm taking off," he said to Mika. He went over and kissed his daughter on the forehead.

"I'm going to stay the rest of the night with her. We're so lucky Breanna got to her when she did. We could've lost our baby." Mika's voice broke and Steel saw a couple of tears escape.

"Yeah, we gotta figure this shit out. I need to know who she's hanging with. Do you know her friends?"

"Some of them."

"*Some*? Fuck, Mika, you need to know *all* of them. She's hanging with the wrong crowd."

"I can't monitor every minute of her life."

"Why the fuck not? If she wasn't into this shit, I'd agree with you, but she is. She's given up any right to privacy. I want to know everyone she knows. I need to find out who she got the stuff from. And how the hell is she paying for it? Are you giving her extra money?"

"No. I hardly have enough some months to pay all the bills. Thank God I have Roy helping out."

"That's another thing. I don't like that fucker you've been going out with."

Mika's eyes widened. "Since when do you have the right to tell me who to go out with? I don't tell you about the many women you screw, do I?"

"No, but I'm not exposing Chenoa to them either. I don't give a shit who you date. I just don't like him living with you while Chenoa's in the house. There's no reason for you to be living with him. She's only seventeen years old. Anyway, she told me that Roy gives her the creeps."

"She's never liked any man I went out with. She keeps holding out hope that we'll get back together. Roy's always been nice and treated her well. I won't have you or her dictate who I can or can't go out with."

"As I said, going out with him is fine. Shacking up is a different story."

"I'm too tired for this. Believe me, Roy isn't the problem. You not seeing Chenoa as much as you should is the bigger problem. You didn't even know she had a new caseworker."

"How the fuck would I know about Miss Uppity Bitch if no one told me? I don't get shit from the Department of Human Services. And you keep badmouthing the club to Chenoa every chance you get. You have her terrified to step one foot into it."

"Your family and your life is the club. You don't fool me."

Steel ground his teeth. "I'm not rehashing this shit again. You always take the focus off yourself. I'm outta here." He swung around and marched out the door, his breathing heavy. He was pissed at Mika and at himself for not seeing the signs of Chenoa's drug use. As he thought back, he should've wondered why she'd started wearing long sleeves all the time.

Maybe Mika has a point. Maybe I was too consumed with the club that I let Chenoa stand by the sidelines. I'm gonna fucking fix that.

The chill of the night air felt good as he made his way across the parking lot to his Harley. He swung his leg and settled on the leather seat, starting the ignition and letting the iron horse roar to life. Whenever shit got to be too much, he'd jump on his bike and ride, loving the way the wind wrapped around him, the way his body moved with his motorcycle like they were one fusing with the road.

He sped past the closed businesses on Main Street. Alina was a small town of only eight thousand people, nestled in the southwestern part of Colorado and surrounded by the high and rugged San Juan and La Plata mountain ranges. The town rested on that imaginary border between mountain and desert: close enough for high elevation views, low enough for the arid environment of the high desert. Alina was about forty miles away from the Four Corners, where the borders of Colorado, Utah, Arizona, and New Mexico meet. He grew up in the area with his three siblings. His mother was Navajo and his father—the bastard—was Irish. He grew up in poverty on the Navajo reservation that was about thirty miles from Alina. Except for him, his whole family still lived on the reservation.

His Harley blasted around curves as he rode farther away from town. He ached to feel the wind around him, to banish all thoughts and to be one with Mother Earth. He made his way to Mount Hesperus, one of the Navajo people's sacred mountains. He'd been going there since he was a kid. His mother had explained how her people believed that the sacred mountains were integral to their worldview. They respected them and believed that they had spiritual power. Steel often went to Mount Hesperus, where he would open himself up and let the spiritual power that surrounded the peaks interact with him.

Steel believed that everything in life was a balance; if there was a communion of order and disorder, the universe would be good. At that moment, his life was out of balance. His daughter had ODed on heroin, and he knew she was fucking lucky to be alive. *What about the next time? She doesn't even think she's an addict. Fuck! How did things get so out of hand?*

A maelstrom of emotions came over him. He had to bring the chaos under control.

He stopped his bike and hiked up a steep path until he made it to the top. Without the obstruction of streetlights, the stars filled the inky sky, shining like a million fireflies. They seemed so close that Steel felt like he could reach out and touch their blazing heat. He breathed in deeply, the chilled air icing his lungs. Quiet surrounded him, and he welcomed it. Calmness began to seep through him, abating the turmoil within him. He turned his head skyward and whispered to the wind, "Give me wisdom to help my little girl." Wet streaks ran down his face. It was there, on that sacred mountain, that he could let the tears no one ever saw flow freely. After a moment, he wiped his face. "Mother Earth, watch over Chenoa. Hold your hand before her in protection."

After several more minutes of quietude, he made his way to his bike and headed back.

He pulled into the lot of the Night Rebels' clubhouse. It was about fifteen miles from Alina, and it sat so far back from the road that, unless someone knew it was there, it would never be spotted. The club was a two-story stucco building that had been used as a warehouse back in the day. The brothers who lived at the club had rooms in the basement or second floor. The first floor was reserved for communal living: kitchen; large room where the brothers drank, argued, played pool, and fucked; meeting room; smaller rooms for visiting brothers. There were seventeen members, seven club girls, two prospects, and a whole lot of hang-arounds during parties.

About half of the brothers lived at the club. A couple of them, Rooster and Tattoo Mike, had old ladies and lived with their families in town. The rest of the members preferred the freedom of easy sex and booze every night of the week. Steel was no exception. He liked having women at his disposal twenty-four seven, and for the past three months, Alma—one of the club girls—had been his favorite. Steel had no intention of settling down with any woman, but Alma was a good listener and he loved the way she sucked him. When he wasn't with her, she played with the other brothers and it didn't bother him in the least. In time, he'd tire of her and go back to the variety pack. They were all one happy family.

The moment Steel entered the large room, several of his brothers came up to him, drawing him into a bear hug.

"How's Chenoa?" Paco asked. Vice president of the club, Paco was a six-foot-tall, well-muscled heartbreaker.

"Good for now."

"We're here for you if you need us," Goldie said. The blond road captain turned to his brothers. "Am I right?"

They all voiced their agreement as they raised their fists in the air.

Warmth filled Steel as he surveyed the wave of raised arms. *This is my family. Mika just doesn't fucking get it.* Since he'd started the Night Rebels twelve years ago, he knew he could always count on his brothers to be there 100 percent. They were a group of men who stayed together out of loyalty and love for each other and the club. They were more family to him than his blood siblings who couldn't give a damn about him. "Thanks. I got some bad shit going on with my little girl, but I'm gonna take care of it."

Paco gripped his shoulder. "Like Goldie said, we're with you, brother."

Steel nodded. "We gotta find who the fuck's supplying the shit in our county. That's for tomorrow's church. Go ahead with the party." He pulled away and threw back a few shots of tequila that his brothers had brought to him. The sharp taste burned all the way down. *Fuck, that's good.*

"Wanna get in on a game of pool?" Shotgun asked. "We can pair against Skull and Sangre. We'll beat their sorry asses."

Steel laughed for the first time since his mother had called him about

Chenoa. "It's tempting, but I'm pretty worn out. Another time." He went over to the long bar that filled one corner of the room. Across from the bar, a couple of pool tables and a poker table were in use. A large-screened television filled the back wall opposite the bar, several south-west-patterned couches and chairs in front of it. Instead of watching the images on the screen, the brothers and the club girls were curled around, pleasuring each other.

The prospect tending the bar nodded at Steel. "Another shot?" Patches asked.

"The whole fucking bottle." Patches placed a bottle of Patrón in front of him. Gripping it, Steel ambled out and climbed the stairs to his large corner room on the second floor. Inside, he placed the bottle on his dresser and then kicked off his boots, shrugged off his cut, and sank down into an overstuffed chair, placing his feet on the small table in front of him. He opened the bottle and drank deeply from it, his goal to get good and drunk. As he took another swig, he heard a faint knock on his door. "Come in."

The door slowly opened and a petite woman with long brown hair and a plunging neckline showing off her ample cleavage came in. "Hey. How are you? I heard about your daughter. Is she okay?" She draped her arms around his shoulders. The faint scent of patchouli wafted around him.

"Hey, Alma. Yeah, she's good. Thanks for asking."

She leaned down and kissed his jawline, her fingernails scratching his bare chest. A shiver ran through him for a few seconds but then died away. He gently moved her hands away. "Sorry, but I'm not feeling it tonight. I'm beat."

Her face fell. "Do you want someone else?"

"Nah. You know right now, you're my favorite. I just wanna finish drinking and crash. Go back down to the party. Sangre's had a boner for you for the last several nights."

"But I was busy with you." She grinned.

"Yeah." He raised his eyebrows, which made her laugh. "Why don't you give him a good surprise?"

"Okay. You sure you don't need me to soothe your worries?"

"I'm sure. Have some fun." He smiled as she pranced out of the room, then pulled himself up and locked the door. Taking out his phone, he noticed his mother had called him a few times. It must have been when he was at Mount Hesperus. He dialed her number.

"*Shimá*." He and his siblings had always used the Navajo word for mother.

"How's Chenoa? I've been worried all night," she said.

"Yeah, sorry about that. I should've called you. She pulled through. She was damn lucky she got to the hospital when she did."

"It was her caseworker. Where was Mika? The lady said that she couldn't get a hold of her. When I think what would've happened had she not been there…." Her voice broke.

"Yeah. We were lucky. I'm beat, *Shimá*. After I see Chenoa tomorrow, I'll come by your place."

"Okay. Do you have the caseworker's phone number? I want to call and thank her."

"I don't. Mika has it. Call her in the morning and get it from her. Go on to sleep now. It's late." He hung up the phone, switched off the lights, and positioned his chair toward the window, staring out into the blackness as he brought the bottle to his lips.

The social worker's face jumped into his mind. He smiled when he remembered how defiant she looked when she challenged him. He had to give her credit for not backing down. *She had a nice ass and a decent rack.* He shook his head and took another sip of tequila. *She was actually damn pretty. What the fuck was her name? Brenda?*

When he'd first entered the room, he was shocked to see her with his daughter. And the first time he saw her electric blue eyes, he was taken aback. He'd never seen such a beautiful shade of blue before, and coupled with her long golden hair, her sexy curves, and her full lips, he would've taken a taste of her if the circumstances had been different.

Then she told him she was a government worker, and his lust blazed into anger. There was no way he'd want anything to do with her; she was the establishment, and that didn't sit well with him. He swallowed another drink. *But she sure is pretty. Fucking sexy.* And the way she looked at him when he'd come into the room made his dick go hard. Her face gave her away, and he knew if he wanted it, he could have her in his bed in a couple of days. He'd give her the best fucking she'd ever had. But he had no intention of doing it. He didn't need *her*, and even if she begged him—which he was damned sure she would end up doing—he wouldn't have anything to do with her. She was the worst kind of citizen—a government employee. *She* was the reason Chenoa couldn't come to the clubhouse and visit him.

Anger rode up his spine and he pushed the bottle away. He should fuck the know-it-all county worker and then never touch her again. *It would serve her right.*

Shit, I've had too damn much to drink. He stumbled over to his bed and flopped down. Closing his eyes, strands of hair as gold as sunshine danced in front of him until he passed out.

Chapter Three

THE SUN FLOODED his room through the uncovered window. Steel groaned as the light seeped through his cracked eyelids. He covered his eyes with his arm, pressing down hard in a vain attempt to stop the throbbing in his temples. His mouth tasted like he drank a bottle of sand, and he grudgingly grasped the end of his nightstand and pulled himself up. Sitting upright, his head pounded relentlessly. He pulled open the nightstand drawer and took out a bottle of aspirin, shaking out three pills and popping them in his mouth before swaying to the bathroom to get a glass of water. As he gulped them down and looked at himself in the mirror, puffy eyes greeted him. He splashed cold water on his face to cool down his hangover. Glancing at the clock on the shelf over the toilet, he realized that he'd overslept. He hurriedly jumped in the shower, having wanted to be at the hospital an hour before.

After drying off and throwing on some clothes, Steel walked into the clubhouse's kitchen and poured a cup of coffee. He loved it black and strong, so Lena, the woman who worked in the kitchen, always made sure she had a pot waiting for him just the way he liked it. "Want a breakfast burrito?" she asked as he sat at the island sipping his coffee. He shook his head. "You sure? Not good to start the day on an empty stomach."

"I started plenty of days without food when I was a kid. It didn't hurt me." He knew if he didn't nip the conversation in the bud, Lena would talk his ear off, and that was the last thing he wanted in the shape he was in.

Lena had started working in the kitchen three years before after her old man—Cross Bones, one of the brothers—left her for a woman half her age. In her early forties, Lena had been devastated. What made the betrayal even worse was that the other woman was the old lady of Chains, another club member. The club kicked Cross Bones out and brought Lena in to supervise and work the kitchen. She'd been lost when her old man dumped her, missing the club she'd become a part of through him. In the past three years, the Night Rebels had enjoyed some damn tasty dishes. The club girls helped out, but the understanding was that what Lena said went, and none of the brothers would ever contradict her. For the most part she and the club girls got along, and the men were well fed.

After he finished his coffee, Steel jerked his head at Lena and went out to his Harley, jumping on and riding to the hospital. When he entered Chenoa's room, she was sitting up in bed, a breakfast tray in front of her, her dark eyes glued to the television.

"Hey, sunshine. How're you feeling?" He came over and kissed her head while running his fingers over her cheek.

"Dad...." She grimaced when he said her nickname.

He laughed. Ever since she was a baby, she was always smiling and grinning at everything, and her eyes would light up just like the sun. He'd started calling her his little sunshine from then on. Now that she was seventeen years old, he still called her "sunshine." She pretended not to like it, but the way her eyes lit up, he knew she still loved the term of endearment. "They feeding you pretty good in here?"

She lifted the silver dome over a bowl of lumpy oatmeal. "What do you think?"

He ruffled her hair. "Fucking nasty. I'll smuggle you in a cheeseburger with fries and a strawberry shake."

Her eyes danced. He loved it when they did that. Looking at her wide grin and glittering eyes, he wished he could freeze the moment forever. He never wanted her eyes to turn flat or her face to grow placid. She'd always be his little girl—his sunshine—and he wanted to protect her from the world.

"Can you go now and get it? I'm starving."

"Large fries and shake?"

"You know it." He walked toward the door. "Dad?" He turned around. "Thanks. I love you."

He nodded. "I love you too, sunshine."

AFTER SHE'D EATEN, Steel pushed the tray away and sat down next to her, taking her hands in his. "You scared the shit out of your mother and me, you know?"

She bowed her head. "I'm sorry."

"I'm not saying this shit to make you feel bad, just telling you like it is. You got a problem, little girl." He held up his hand as she began to respond. "I don't want to hear your bullshit denials. You're an addict and you gotta fix yourself or you'll be lost forever. I know your mom and I don't want that, and I'm pretty sure you don't either."

"I want to go home." She looked up at him.

"I know you do, but you're not ready to be on your own. You gotta stay in here for the next three weeks to detox your system." She groaned and covered her ears, but he gently pulled away her hands. "I know you don't want to hear or face this shit, but you got yourself in a mess and you gotta get out of it. I'll come by every day to visit you. Your mom will be here. You've got our support. You just have to get better, and stay away from drugs. It's shit and you know it." He stared pointedly at her.

"Can't I do it through an outpatient program?"

"No. ODing tells me you're in deep. After you get out, I'm in charge. I want to know all your friends' first and last names. You can write out the list today and I'll take it with me when I come back to see you."

"Dad, you're going to kill my social life. I know you won't just hang onto the list. You'll browbeat and bully all my friends so that by the time I get out of here, I won't have any left."

"Your real friends will be left."

She shook her head, her dark eyes narrowing. "Mom's cool with my friends."

"Your mom doesn't know half the shit you do. Anyway, this is between you and me. And you gotta get your ass back to school. Your mom told me you dropped out a couple of months ago."

"Breanna is setting me up with taking classes to get my GED. You should be happy about that since it'll keep me busy." She stared at the television.

When he heard the caseworker's name, he paused. "Has she already come by to see you?"

"Yeah. She was here for about an hour. She left a few minutes before you came."

"Is she coming back?"

Chenoa shrugged. "I don't think so. Why?"

"No reason. Just wondered." *Why the fuck am I asking my kid about her snobby social worker? What the hell's up with that?*

Just then he heard footsteps and looked at the door, his pulse quickening a bit. When he saw Mika walk to the bed, a twinge of disappointment ran through him. He turned his head toward Chenoa.

"Hi, baby. It's great seeing you up. You must be feeling better." Mika put her purse down on the tray, then turned to Steel. "You brought her lunch?"

"Breakfast, actually." She smiled at him. He rose to his feet. "Sit down. I'll sit over there." He headed to a chair in the corner of the room and sank down, watching the two of them talk. He noticed how Mika's long black hair fell to her waist. Back when he'd met her in high school, her long hair had charged every teen hormone he'd had in his body. Back then, he'd been constantly hard for her, and when they'd started dating, he'd fantasized twenty times a day about being with her.

When he'd hit thirteen years old, his sonofabitch father, in one of his many alcoholic rages, had told him to make sure that he never made a bitch pregnant because it would tie him to her for life. The example he'd always give was how he'd knocked up Steel's mom and had to marry her. He'd then tell Steel that he was the bastard who forced him to marry. As he'd grown older, he'd listened to his father less.

One night when Mika had been fifteen years old, she'd sat on top of his dad's beat-up pickup and looked up at the stars glittering in the summer sky. She'd grabbed his hand and told him she was carrying his baby. At first he'd just stared at her as thoughts spun through his mind like a spinning top. When he hadn't said anything, she'd begun to cry. He'd wanted to say something, but he'd lost his ability to speak. He hadn't been able to comprehend that he was going to be a father at sixteen years old. He'd figured he'd knocked her up the night he had taken her out to Dolores River Canyon, spread a blanket on the ground, and popped her cherry.

Seven months after Mika had told him he was going to be a father, his baby daughter was born. They'd named her Chenoa, meaning "dove" in Navajo. Steel had loved his daughter right from the start when he'd seen her strip of black hair and her tiny fisted hands jerking all around. From that day on, Mika had taken more than a possessive interest in their daughter. He'd always felt that Mika had wanted to keep Chenoa closer to her than to him.

And she was still doing it. Mika constantly accused him of not doing enough, but he was always there whenever their daughter needed anything. He jutted out his chin. *Mika and the damn county are the ones who're keeping Chenoa from coming to the club. If she were able to come, I'd see her all the time.*

He stood up. "I gotta go. I'm going to see your *Análi*." He went over and kissed her.

"Tell *Análi* I said hi. Maybe she can visit me?" Chenoa picked up the remote and changed the channel.

"If she's up to it, I can bring her by tomorrow. I'll see you later tonight." He left the room. On the way out, he snickered when he saw several of the nurses checking him out. He took the elevator down to the lobby, then headed to the parking lot, hopped on his bike, and drove to his mother's.

She lived in the same house he'd grown up in on the reservation. He pulled into the driveway next to an unfamiliar blue Ford Focus. Swinging open the screen door, he walked into the living room, expecting to see his mother in her favorite recliner, but it was empty. As he glanced around, he heard her softly talking in the kitchen. He shook his head; he'd often come over unannounced and find her in a conversation with herself. He strode into the kitchen, then stopped dead in his tracks. His mother sat at the kitchen table, her hands clasped together on top of it, and the back of a woman faced him as she stood in front of the refrigerator. The woman had long blonde hair tumbling down her back, touching the top of her ass. *That ass. I know it. I fucking thought about it last night far too much.*

"Steel, how are you?" his mother asked.

Breanna whirled around, and he laughed inwardly at the shocked expression on her face. In her hands, she held a carton of eggs that were ready to hit the floor. He jumped over and grabbed it, his hand grazing her soft breast. Static electricity shocked his system.

Whoa! What the hell?

He placed the carton on the stove and took a step back in order to get a better view. His gaze ran over her, lingering on her to-die-for hips and full breasts. *I didn't notice how stacked she was last night. What's wrong with me? I'm acting like a fool. I've seen stacked babes before. I've fucked enough of them. And what's up with her scent?* It wasn't in-your-face; rather a fresh, clean smell, like rain on a spring day. It was enticing and was playing havoc with his dick.

Focus, man.

He crossed his arms. "What the hell are you doing here?"

"You don't go in for pleasantries, do you, Mr. McVickers?"

"Steel, watch your manners," his mother admonished. "Ms. Quine is here about my food stamps."

Steel pulled his gaze from Breanna to his mom. "Why the fuck are you on food stamps? I keep asking if you need money and you keep telling me no. I don't want you taking anything from the goddamn government."

His mother looked down and unclasped her hands.

"We have food stamps to make sure everyone eats," Breanna said.

Steel glared at her. "The government wants to make everyone dependent on them. They'd love to cripple us all."

She smiled. "You're a bit paranoid, aren't you?" She picked up the carton of eggs and went over to the stove. Looking over her shoulder, she said, "Your antigovernment attitude is becoming annoying."

Steel narrowed his eyes. "Your fucking meddling in my family's life is pissing me off in a way that's gonna get you hurt." When she stiffened and stayed silent, he rocked back on his heels. With a dismissive nod, he turned to his mother. "You're getting off the goddamn program, and I'm giving you money for groceries."

"You always react before you know what's going on," his mother said softly as she brushed stray hairs from her face. "I've got a lot of mouths to feed. The grandkids live with me and they're all eligible for the program. I called the department to report the loss of my card. Ms. Quine is who they sent. She's trying to help me."

He snorted, pulling out the kitchen chair with his foot and sitting down. "Just great. How are you trying to help, Ms. Quine?"

"You don't have to patronize me. You mother has lost her EBT card."

"What the fuck is that?"

"Steel, please." His mother placed her hand on his.

Breanna turned to face him. "It's short for Electronic Benefit Transfer. It means that instead of having paper currency for the benefits, they're put on a card. It's sort of like a debit card."

Her face had wisps of red streaking across it, and he liked that he was making her nervous. He had no idea why he liked it, but he did. "How fucking efficient and clever. And the *government* just happened to send *you*?"

She scrubbed the side of her neck with her fist. "I'm one of three social workers assigned to the reservation. Since your daughter is one of my clients, your mother was naturally assigned to me. We like to keep family cases together. It makes sense to do it that way. Do you have any more questions?"

"Yeah. Why the fuck are you here?"

"Steel!" His mother smacked his forearm lightly.

"No worries, Mrs. McVickers. Your son is not the first rude person I've met. So many people take out their issues and frustrations on others. I just ignore it. It goes with the territory of being a social worker."

Steel shook his head. "You still haven't answered my question."

"I don't have to, since you're not my client, but I will to show you how an adult acts in this type of situation. Your mother has misplaced her card again. I need to ask her some questions because this is the sixth time in the past eight months that she's reported a lost card. When I came over, she told me she was faint. She also told me she hadn't eaten in a couple of days. That's why I'm at the stove with a skillet and some eggs. Would you like me to make you an omelet, Mr. McVickers?"

He was torn between chewing her ass out for her snarky attitude and shaking some sense into his mother. He turned to her. "What the fuck's going on with you? Why haven't you eaten anything, *Shimá*?" He pounded his fist on the table and both Breanna and his mother jumped. "How can I help you when I don't know what the hell is going on? Fuck! First Chenoa and now you?" He kicked back from the table and ran his hand through his long hair.

"Yelling at your mom isn't going to solve—"

Baring his teeth, he pointed his finger at Breanna. "I've heard enough outta you. Stay the fuck outta this."

She blinked several times, then turned back to the stove.

"*Shimá*?"

His mother sighed. "I don't like worrying you. You have so much on your mind with your club and Chenoa. Sometimes the money's tight with all the grandkids." She wrung her hands and quickly added, "But I love having a full house. And I didn't eat because I didn't have an appetite. Don't be mad."

He cleared his throat as the fire in him burned down. "I'm not mad.

I want to help you. Did you see Pa?" She shrugged. Out of the corner of his eye, he spotted Breanna watching their exchange. "I know you did. You get like this whenever you run into him and he makes you feel like shit. *Shimá*, the asshole's been gone for many years now. You need to let it go."

He reached out and gently stroked her cheek with the backs of his fingers. Her skin was smooth and soft, even at her age. He loved touching it. It was like velvet… just the way he remembered it when he was a little boy and his mother would squeeze him tight, her face pressed against his.

"I know," she said softly. She wiped away imaginary crumbs from the multicolored oilcloth. "I still love him."

White-hot anger ran through him. *How the fuck can you still love a man who treated you like shit for years?* He sucked in a deep breath. "I know, but you have to let go. He sure as fuck has." The last few words came out much harsher than he'd intended. If he could swing it, he'd make sure his mom never saw his bastard father again.

She nodded.

A woman coughing grounded him, bringing him back to the here and now. He'd forgotten the nosy social worker was still there. "You still hanging around? Can't get enough of me?" He winked.

"Don't flatter yourself. I'm here for her." She leaned down and put a plate with a large omelet on it in front of his mother.

The glimpse down her blouse was his bonus for having to endure her insufferable cockiness. "I didn't imagine you checking me out at the hospital. By the way, I never thanked you for making sure Chenoa got to the hospital in time."

She raised her brows. "You're actually saying something nice to me?"

"I'm trying to tell you I appreciate what you did, and you have to act like a smartass. Damn, woman."

She cocked her head to the side. "You know, I don't like being called 'woman,' 'lady,' or 'babe.' My name is Breanna, but for you it's Ms. Quine. And you can stop puffing out your chest. You don't intimidate me. I come from the other side of the tracks, so I don't bully easily."

He stared at her, his lips curling up slightly. *She's got a fire in her, that's for fucking sure. I like her spirit.* "I'm not trying to intimidate you. All I wanted to say is thanks for helping my little girl. You've got a major chip on your shoulder, *Ms. Quine.*"

She gazed intently in his eyes. "You're welcome. I was just relieved that I arrived in time to help your daughter. I don't know who called me, but I'm presuming it was someone she was shooting with. I know she always has my card with her. I'm happy Chenoa's doing great. I stopped by and saw her earlier this morning."

After a few seconds, he said, "Yeah, she told me. You and I both know that she's gonna have a helluva night as she starts going through withdrawals. You don't believe this was a one-time deal, do you?"

She pursed her lips and shook her head.

"The omelet is so delicious, Breanna. Thank you."

She smiled. "You're welcome, Mrs. McVickers."

Steel kept looking at his mom's food, his stomach rumbling. He watched Breanna turn back to the stove, and in a few minutes she placed a steaming plate in front of him.

He looked up at her. *She's beautiful.* "I didn't ask you to make this for me." He picked up a fork.

"I know." She moved away and went over to the sink, filling it with soapy water.

As he ate, he watched her clean the dishes and wipe the stove. Something tender stirred inside him for this woman, but he didn't want any part of it. He shoved it down and finished off the last bite of his omelet.

Breanna dried her hands and smiled at his mother. "Mrs. McVickers, I have to go. I'll make sure you receive a replacement card as soon as possible."

"You don't need to worry about that. I'll buy her groceries." Steel pushed his plate away.

"It's not that easy. She and her grandkids are entitled to the benefits. Unless she fills out a form for herself requesting her benefits to stop, she'll still receive them. Your sister is the only one who can take the grandkids off the benefits. But I think it's very nice that you're going to buy groceries for your mom. Her fridge is desperately in need of some food."

He scowled at her.

"What? I'm agreeing with you. What's your problem?" She grabbed her purse and slung it over her shoulder.

"*You're* my problem."

"Whatever. I'll see you, Mrs. McVickers." She picked up her folder and walked out of the house.

He watched her go, a part of him wishing she'd stayed. He felt a twitch in his dick when he thought of her. *My cock's talking only 'cause she's pretty and hot. I don't need this shit.*

"Why did you act like that with her?" his mother asked.

"I don't like the way she's meddling in my family's business. We don't need her or her help." He rose to his feet and went over to the sink to wash his plate.

"I've never seen you act like this before with a woman. You're even nicer to Mika, and you know how badly she treated you."

He put the plate away. "I don't trust her or the government. Anyway, why're you sticking up for a woman you barely know?" He leaned against the kitchen counter.

"She's a nice girl." He shrugged. "I saw the way you looked at each other. You got something between the two of you."

"You're seeing more than there is, *Shimá*. Leave it alone, okay?"

"Remember that dream I've had for many years about you and a woman building a life together? Forging through many things only to come out stronger?" Sighing, he nodded; he'd only heard the story a thousand times over the years. "Well, each time I have it, the woman has yellow hair. When I saw the way you looked at her when you came in, I knew she was the woman in my dreams."

He shook his head. "If *she's* the one you've seen me with, it sounds more like you've been having nightmares. Go on and get your sweater so we can get going. I have a bunch of stuff I gotta do before I go back to the hospital."

"Are you making fun of the visions? You know we believe in them."

The hurt in her voice made him feel bad. "I was just joking. Look, *Shimá*, there're a lot of blondes running around Alina, so I doubt she's the one you've been dreaming about. Anyway, you know I like dark-haired women. Now go get ready."

His mother stood up and went to her bedroom. While he waited, he thought about what she'd said. Dreams and visions were important to the Navajo; they were believed to be prophecies for what was to come. Did he believe in them? To a certain extent. Did he think his mother's dreams meant that he would hook up with the pain-in-the-ass social worker? *No fucking way!*

"I'm ready." As they walked out of the house, his mother handed him her car keys. He backed out his motorcycle so he could get her car out, and then they drove to the nearest grocery store, Roy's Market. It was owned by the dirtbag Mika was dating. He'd have preferred to have gone into Alina to buy groceries, but his mother had insisted on going to Roy's. There was something about the guy Steel didn't like. He couldn't put his finger on it, but Roy rubbed him the wrong way.

While his mother went down the aisles throwing things in her cart, he spotted a woman with long blonde hair in the distance. His heart picked up a few beats as he walked toward her. When she turned around, he realized it wasn't Breanna. He also realized he'd wished it had been.

All this talk of dreams and a hot blonde has turned my brain to mush.

He sauntered away. As he looked for his mother, he wondered if the cute caseworker had a boyfriend. Pissed that she was on his mind, he tried to push her away, but he wasn't having any luck. He wanted to know more about her. He knew she was attracted to him, but he also knew that she wanted nothing to do with him. That suited him just fine because he didn't want anything to do with her either.

Then why am I wondering what she's doing right now? I have to stop

whatever shit is going on with me.
I don't want her.
I don't have time for her.
I don't want to get to know her.
Yeah… right.

Chapter Four

BREANNA STEPPED DOWN the concrete stairs from her client's house, the third one in the last few weeks to have lost her EBT card. Once again, the client's lost card was the fifth replacement in the past six months. Breanna had a niggling feeling that the lost cards were somehow related.

As she opened her car door, she spotted Steel driving a green Toyota Camry with his mother in the passenger seat. She ducked inside her car and scrunched down, not wanting him to see her. He drove by, glancing at her car and then back at the road. She pushed up a little and watched the car until it disappeared.

Mad at herself for hiding like a criminal from the biker, she threw her purse on the floor. There was no doubt about it—Steel disturbed her. He made her feel things she had no business feeling. The absolute last thing she ever wanted was a biker.

Her father's ruddy complexion flashed in her mind. He was a big man: six foot four and over two hundred and fifty pounds. He'd been an absent father, even though her parents were together until she was in her teens. Her dad had belonged to the now-defunct Desert Lizards MC. Even though he had a wife and four kids, his heart, soul, and body belonged to the club. He'd missed all the important events in their lives, like birthdays, holidays, and football games. When he hadn't been in jail, he'd been hanging out with his brothers, riding his Harley, and carousing with club girls. And when he'd decided to come home, he'd always reeked of cheap perfume, whiskey, and cigarettes. Then he'd disappear for weeks on end on road trips, or would crash at the clubhouse. She'd grown to hate leather and denim, the sound of cams, and the shine of chrome.

Her mom had taken her sham of a marriage badly. Instead of showing a backbone and booting the louse out, she'd given up and let Breanna take over the household. Her mom had taken to the couch and her bed when Breanna was twelve years old. She'd become a mother to her younger siblings: cooking the meals, making sure they did their homework, washing their clothes, and taking care of them when they were sick. Her mom had done nothing but cry and stare vacantly out the picture window in their living room. The only thing her dad had done was give them a monthly stipend. He hadn't seemed to care that his wife was in a severe state of depression or that his oldest daughter's childhood was gone. All he'd cared about was his MC. Breanna had to raise herself and her siblings, and she resented her dad like hell. Once the club dismantled, he'd taken off with one of the club girls. He didn't even say goodbye to her or her siblings. He just left, never to be heard from again.

Her mom had ended up in a nursing home at the age of forty. Breanna was the only one of her siblings who went to see their mother. She'd smile and talk a bit, but most of the time she'd cry about how much she missed her husband. Breanna had sores in her mouth from biting the insides of her cheeks so she wouldn't say what she really thought. Her mother never asked how she was doing or anything about Jeremy, Nicholas, or Shelby. All she talked about was her husband.

A pickup truck sped past Breanna honking its horn, the noise bringing her back to the present. She swallowed the lump in her throat, the images from her past overwhelming her. *After enduring my dad, I can't even believe I'm spending any amount of time thinking about Steel.* But she was attracted to him even though she didn't want to be. Her brain wanted one thing and her body craved him. *He's an arrogant sonofabitch who'd break any woman's heart. I'd bet everything I own that he's a player.* But he was so gorgeous, even with that wicked scar on his face. She shivered as she imagined how he got it.

Shaking her head, she turned on the ignition and drove to the satellite office located by the entrance to the reservation, the cool air from the air conditioner enveloping her when she entered. Goose bumps pricked her skin and she wished she'd brought her cardigan with her.

"Hey, Breanna. How'd it go?" her coworker, Joel, asked.

"Okay. Don't you think it's cold in here?" She rubbed her arms vigorously with her hands.

"Not really. We got a couple of investigators sharing our space. The one guy keeps sweating. He's the one who keeps turning up the air."

"Investigators? Why're they here?"

Joel shrugged. "The feds sent them. Something must be going down."

"Maybe it's the rash of lost EBT cards. I can't believe how many replacement cards our office is issuing. How many times can someone be that spaced out? Something doesn't ring right. Have you noticed it with your clients?"

"Not really. I don't really pay that much attention. I just do what I have to and wait for five o'clock to hit. I'm the stereotypical county worker." He laughed and leaned back in his chair, running his eyes up and down her hourglass figure. "You're looking real good, Breanna."

Self-conscious, she pulled down her knit top. "Thanks," she muttered. She and Joel had been working together in the satellite office for the past few months. Each time she came in, he was generous with the compliments. He'd hinted about them going out for a drink one night after work, but she'd played it dumb. Every time he brought it up, she'd change the subject. She wasn't sure why she kept him at a distance. He was nice-looking, intelligent, and educated. Most women in the office were dying to have him ask them out, but there was something about him that put her off. She didn't know what it was, but she was wary of him. He seemed too cheerful, too solicitous, too much of everything.

"You up for grabbing a bite to eat after work?" His eyes scanned her face.

"Can't. I already made plans." *With a movie and a frozen Mexican dinner.*

"Bummer." He kept his gaze on her.

She shrugged and slid behind her desk, opening her laptop. For the next hour, she inputted all the information from the clients she'd seen the day before and earlier that day. She glanced out the window every so often, and when she saw a green Toyota Camry, her stomach fluttered. She squinted her eyes and smiled when she saw Steel behind the wheel, his sunglasses shimmering in the sunlight. From her position, she could see his arm resting on the open window, his biceps tight and muscular. For some unknown reason, she wanted to curl her fingers around them and feel their hard muscles against her skin.

What's wrong with you? Stop it. Now. She forced herself to look back down at her open files. *Maybe I should ask Joel to take on Chenoa and her grandmother. That way I won't have any contact with* him. But that wouldn't be fair to Chenoa. Breanna had built a rapport with her, and the young lady trusted her. She couldn't very well break the links just because the girl's father made her body misbehave.

I definitely need to get out more.

She picked up her phone and called one of her best friends, Lacey.

"Hiya. I'm itching to go out drinking and who knows what else." She laughed. "Do you want to go out for dinner and check out a couple of bars tomorrow night?"

"That's too funny. I was going to call you to see if you wanted to do something on Saturday night, but Thursdays are good bar nights too." Lacey's laughter sounded like bells tinkling.

"Great minds think alike. I'm not sure if I'll be available on Saturday." Breanna lowered her voice. "I have an interview for a waitressing job, so if I get it, I may have to start on the weekend."

"You're getting a part-time job? Doesn't the county pay well?" Lacey asked softly.

"Not if I'm helping family as well."

"Nicholas?"

"Of course. Spare me the lecture. Whatever you want to say I've already said it to myself. I just can't pretend he doesn't exist. I have to help him out."

Lacey sighed. "I wasn't gonna ask you why you're doing it. Nicholas is a sweetheart. He's your brother, and of course you want to help him. It sounds like you definitely need to unwind. This'll be fun."

"What time do you want to get started?"

"Seven thirty works for me."

"Me too. I'll come by and pick you up. I better get back to work. See you tomorrow night." Breanna put her phone down, a sense of relief washing over her.

That's been my problem all along. I need to get laid.

No matter what it took, she had to keep the green-eyed man out of her head.

Chapter Five

AFTER CHURCH, THE brothers shuffled to the main room where they had shots of whiskey and tequila waiting for them on the bar. They spoke in low voices, the mood somber. Even the club girls knew to keep their distance; a few of them even rose up from the couches and padded down the stairs to their rooms.

The cause for the consternation among the brothers was that heroin was in their county, and it'd affected their president in the worst way. It had slipped into the area like a thief in the night, robbing sense and self-respect from the ones who gave in to its false promises.

"We gotta find out if the Satan's Pistons are bringing the shit into our territory," Crow said as he threw back his shot of whiskey. Crow had been a patched member for a little over a year, but his computer skills made him an asset to the club. He used to live in Arizona and was well acquainted with the Satan's Pistons MC. He'd had a couple of run-ins with them when he was a teen, and the long, angry scar that went from his rib cage past his belly button was his badge of honor. He'd been attacked by three Pistons one hot summer night when he was out in the desert with his girl. The bikers had stolen his car and wallet, raped his girl, and sliced his side, leaving him for dead. But he didn't die; he grew bitter, and hatred consumed him. He crossed the Arizona border and ended up in Alina, Colorado, where he met a couple of cool bikers on Harleys. He followed them to the Night Rebels clubhouse and three years later he was a patched member.

"I wouldn't put it past the fuckin' Skull Crushers to be in on this. When we and the Insurgents kicked their asses a couple of summers ago, they calmed the hell down, but I bet they're getting antsy. They need money. I wish the prez would give us the go-ahead so we could throw their motherfuckin' asses outta our territory once and for all." Muerto kicked over a stool and several members looked over, then turned back to their conversation. They were used to the club secretary's short temper. At six feet, black hair past his collar, ebony eyes, and furious tats of demons, skulls, and bloody knives adorning his chest and arms, he exuded danger. One of his favorite things to do was fight. Steel, Paco, and the other brothers saved his ass several times when his temper boiled over. His dark features mixed in with his angry rebelliousness, drew women to him.

"The asshole Crushers aren't in on this. They don't have the brains or guts for it." Paco dunked his chip in a bowl of salsa on the bar.

"I dunno. They're stupid enough to get mixed up in it." Muerto signaled the prospect for another beer.

"I'm with Paco on this one. If an MC is involved, I'd go with the fuckin' Pistons. This is right up their alley." Crow's hazel eyes brimmed with hate.

"What do you think, Steel?" Paco crunched on his chip.

"I'm not sure an MC is involved in this. The Skulls would be signing their death warrant if they are, and the Pistons know if we traced this to them it'd be war." Steel leaned against the bar and looked at his brothers. They wore the faces of concern, loyalty, and determination. He knew they'd take to their weapons and engage in battle with the Pistons if they were involved in this mess.

"The damn badges are lookin' to us to solve the problem. Lazy asses." Crow hopped up on one of the barstools.

Steel nodded. "They always do. Fuck, we should be getting a cut of their pay."

Paco, Muerto, and Crow laughed.

The Night Rebels and the sheriff's department had an understanding: as long as the brotherhood kept hard drugs out of Alina, the sheriff would turn a blind eye to their illegal gun running. It'd worked for the past decade, until now. And it ate up the brothers that the junk had slithered into their territory.

Ruby, Alma, and Angel came into the room and walked over to them. Steel tilted his chin at them. Ruby cozied up to Crow. "You guys gonna just stand around and talk all afternoon?" She rubbed against him like a cat in heat.

Crow grinned and slinked his arm around her small waist. "You got something better in mind?"

She put her finger in her mouth, then traced Crow's lips with it. "Uh-huh." He sucked her digit into his mouth as he cupped her ass cheek. "Let's go have some fun, baby," she rasped.

He nodded at the brothers and walked away with her.

Angel looked pleadingly at Muerto, who laughed, scooped her up in his arms, and walked toward the basement stairs.

Alma ran her fingers up and down Steel's arm. "You wanna have some fun too? It's been a while for us." She stood on her tiptoes and planted a kiss on his chin.

Steel looked at her big brown eyes and silky dark hair. *I should take Alma to my room and fuck her good and hard. She's dying for it.* Alma had the looks he loved: dark hair and eyes with an olive complexion. *Not blonde and pasty like the mouthy social worker.*

"What do you say, dude? Poor Alma's practically begging you for it," Paco said.

Steel pushed her away gently. "Sorry, *chica*, but I got work to do." He turned to Paco. "You interested?"

The vice president's gaze lingered on Alma's well-endowed chest. "Fuck yeah." He looped his arm around her and drew her close to him.

Steel saw the look of regret in her eyes. "Then it's all good." He strode out of the room and went to his office. Instead of sitting behind his desk to attack the mountain of paperwork he had to go over from the various businesses the club owned, he went to the window and looked out at the Harleys that were parked in the lot adjacent to the clubhouse. The chrome sparkled under the afternoon sun, and he had the urge to take a long, hard ride to clear his head. The last thing he wanted was a war with Satan's Pistons.

He ran his fingers through his long hair, exhaling loudly. A knock on the door broke his concentration. "Come in."

Paco came into the office, darting his eyes from the desk to Steel and then back to the desk. "Need some help with the paperwork?"

Irritated by the intrusion, Steel looked back outside. "Nope. I thought you were with Alma."

"I will be. She's doing something."

"What?"

"Some girl shit." Silence descended on the room. Paco cleared his throat. "You okay?"

Steel looked over his shoulder. "Yeah. Just worried about Chenoa, and all the shit that's going down."

"You usually fuck a club whore when you're stressed. Alma's wondering why you haven't had her in your bed."

Steel shrugged. "You know me. I get bored."

"Just like that? You coulda fooled me. A couple of days ago you didn't seem bored with her."

The president whirled around. "What the fuck? You don't want her? Fine, tell her to find another brother. There're plenty of them who like her lips wrapped around their cocks."

"I didn't say I didn't want her. I'm just wondering why you don't. Pussy always makes you relax."

"This isn't your fucking business. Back the hell off." He frowned. *I wish Paco would shut the hell up and get out.* "Go fuck Alma." He turned his attention back to the parked Harleys.

"Something's under your skin, dude."

He inhaled a long breath then blew it out slowly. "I got a meddling social worker who's in my business. She pisses me way the hell off. I need to set her straight, but I do think she's trying to help Chenoa. And she was at my mom's house yesterday. I was so fucking pissed when I saw her. Then she made this damn good omelet. But she's got a mouth on her. Has some burr up her ass about bikers, I think. I don't know.

She's just a pain in the ass." He swiveled around, heat rising inside him when he saw Paco's grinning face. "What the fuck you smiling about?"

"Is she hot?"

Steel bristled. "What the hell does that have to do with what I'm saying?"

Paco laughed. "So I'll take that as a yes. Bro, I've never seen you so bothered by a woman. Now I get why you've been pushing Alma away. This woman's got a hold of your cock. She must be fuckin' sexy."

Steel clenched his teeth. "I'm not *bothered* by her or any other chick. And no one's got a hold of my dick. As a matter of fact, I don't like her. She's a know-it-all, sassy, and uptight as fuck. I just don't need her around interfering with me and my family."

Paco nodded, a sparkle in his eyes. "Sure. Gotcha."

Steel crossed his arms. "I got work to do. I'm sure Alma's waiting for you."

"Right. I can't wait to meet her when you bring her to the club." He chuckled and ambled out.

Steel slammed his fist against his thigh and swung around, looking outside again. In the distance, the San Juan Mountains loomed. *Bring her to the club, my ass. Paco was way the fuck outta line.* He kept his gaze on the mountains, letting their calming effect wash over him. *My life is outta balance. Chenoa is safe for now, but what about the next time?* And he knew if she didn't give up the drug, there would definitely be a next time. He had to bring that chaos under control.

Then there was the caseworker who'd been invading his thoughts too much. He didn't trust her. He didn't need someone from the outside coming into his life, especially her. Why did she bug him so much? He'd admit that she was a hot piece of ass, but he could go in town and find several women who were hotter and prettier. He shifted his stance. *She does something to me. I don't know what the fuck it is, but it's something real and deep.* And he was madder than hell that he felt a pull toward her. When they'd touched in his mom's house, he felt a jolt rip through him like lightning.

Fuck, I'm getting soft. Staring out the window and thinking of her like a goddamn pussy.

He pushed away from the window and kicked a chair across the room. He was done thinking about her. He had a ton of work to do. Invoices from the ink shop, the strip bar, the repair shop, the pool hall, and the marijuana grow store lay before him. The businesses did well, but having the grow and recreation license killed it for the club. Banger, the president of the Insurgents MC, was instrumental in securing the grow license for Steel and his brotherhood a few years back, getting the Insurgents' lawyer to pull some strings. The one store made more money than the last two gun sales they'd done. He no longer had to juggle a full-time job and the responsibilities of running the MC.

The other club businesses also brought in a steady income. The tattoo shop, Get Inked, was the most popular one in Alina. Some of the residents from the neighboring towns came to it for their high-quality tats. Tattoo Mike was the ink artist and he ran the shop. Lust, the club's strip bar, was jam-packed most weekends and had a steady flow of customers during the weeknights. It was known for beautiful dancers, utmost discretion, and strong drinks. And both the pool hall, Balls and Holes, and the auto and bike repair shop, Skid Marks, made a good income most of the year.

He took out the club's checkbook and began writing checks. Breanna's face popped in his head, and he wondered when he'd see her again.

He shook his head.

Yep. I'm acting just like a fucking pussy.

Chapter Six

BREANNA PULLED OVER and stared at the map. "I know the bar's around here. Why the hell can't I find it?" She glanced at the clock on the dashboard, realizing that if she didn't find the place soon, she'd be late for her interview with the owner of the bar. She closed her eyes and leaned her head back. *I know that all I'm doing is enabling Nicholas, but I can't turn him away.* She'd always had a soft spot for him, and she knew he used that to hit her up for money or crash at her place when he found himself evicted. She sighed, opened her eyes, stared at the map for the last time, and then pulled away from the curb.

By the time she found Cuervos, she was ten minutes late. She reapplied her burnt sienna lip gloss, ran her fingers through her hair, and hurried to the front door of the establishment. On a corner lot, the outside of the bar was a nondescript tan stucco building with a bright green awning over the windows. Neon signs advertising different brands of beer lit up the windows and the thick glass door. She pulled open the door and stepped in, momentarily blinded by the dim lights. Looking around, she saw several men and a couple of women sitting at a beautifully crafted wood bar drinking. On the wall behind the bar were shelves of bottles, as well as a large moving picture of the mountains and a clear lake that seemed to mesmerize the patrons. Booths lined the walls on three sides, wooden tables and chairs filling in the middle. Classic rock tunes played out of a brightly colored jukebox, and she noticed a couple of pool tables and a dartboard. The place had a good feel to it. It wasn't a dive, just a neighborhood bar where people could come in for a drink and a bit of food.

The tangy scent of buffalo wing sauce curled around the place. She walked up to the bar and coughed in hopes of garnering the bartender's attention. He turned around, a man in his early thirties with dark eyes, looking her over. "What can I do for you?" he asked as he swiped his rag over the top of the bar.

"I'm looking for Jorge Mendez. I have an interview with him."

"That's me. Are you Breanna Quine?" She nodded. "You're ten minutes late." He put his rag away.

"I know. Not a great start to an interview, is it? I left in plenty of time, but I got hopelessly lost. I didn't see the small street where I was supposed to turn. I can't believe I couldn't find it."

"It can be tricky. The bar's on one of those quirky streets that's only a few blocks long. Let's go in the back." He called over a guy who was opening boxes and stocking the shelves to take over at the bar. Breanna followed him down a long hallway and into a room. "Have a seat," he said. "You said you've tended bar and waitressed before, right?"

"Yes, I've done both on and off for a little over six years. I'm applying for the part-time position—weekends only. I work during the week, so I can only do Friday and Saturday nights, and Sunday during the day if needed."

For the next twenty minutes, he asked her several questions about her bartending and waitressing skills. He questioned her on the ingredients for a slew of drinks, and she got them right each time. He told her the bar had fifteen beer taps, and it served basic food like buffalo wings, nachos, sandwiches, and pizza. Jorge pushed his chair back. "You got the waitressing job if you want it. Sometime you may have to bartend if Cory is a no show. Friday and Saturday nights the place is packed. I tend bar, but one bartender isn't enough. Cory has some drama with a girlfriend, so he's not always reliable."

"That's cool. I can handle being behind the bar."

"There's a good mix of people that come here. We get guys just off work from the bank next door stopping in for a few beers drinking next to rough guys covered in tattoos. Everyone gets along, for the most part." He paused and ran his gaze over her again. "Don't take this the wrong way, but you're a very pretty woman, and you're gonna have men leering at you, saying things, and flirting with you. You're gonna have to know how to handle it."

She cocked her head and caught his gaze. "I'm okay with a few smart comments and stares, but if someone touches me, I'll deck them." She smiled sweetly.

He laughed. "You won't have to do that. I'll beat you to the punch. I had a gal in here who was a nervous wreck any time a guy winked at her. She was in tears after her shifts. Obviously, it didn't work out. Good to hear you've got some gumption."

"Do the people tip well, for the most part?"

"To be honest, if you show some cleavage and flirt just a bit, you'll do real well. You've got a pretty face and shape. You shouldn't have any problem. Tips are where the money's at." He stood up. "If you want the job, you can start this Friday."

She rose to her feet and extended her hand. "I'll see you on Friday, Mr. Mendez."

He shook her hand. "Call me Jorge."

"Is there anything special I should wear?"

"Black mini skirt, heels are good, and a sexy shirt, but nothing over-the-top."

She nodded. "I'll be here at seven o'clock on Friday."

As she drove home, she kept trying to figure out a way that she could live on what she made, but she couldn't. *It won't be so bad. I'll do it until I can pay off or make a dent in my debt.* She had just finished paying off her student loan, but two of her credit cards were maxed from when she paid for Nicholas's rehab the previous year, and when the county cut everyone's hours for nine months.

She pulled into the garage and went inside. In her bedroom, she slid open her closet doors and pushed through the hangers, pulling out a spandex mini skirt she sometimes wore when she went out clubbing with her friends.

When she'd spotted a red halter corset with a front of overlay black lace in a catalog, she'd ordered it, but when it arrived and she'd tried it on, it was too revealing. It wasn't really her style, and she'd planned on returning it but never got around to it. She held it up against her and looked in the mirror. The low-cut neckline would definitely help bring in the bigger tips.

She threw it on the bed, then went back to her closet and scrounged around for her three-and-a-half-inch black heels. Just looking at the way the shoe curved made her feet hurt. *I have no clue how I'm supposed to stand and walk in these for eight hours. It'll be torture.*

She dropped the shoes and padded over to her small desk, sat down, and opened her laptop. Checking her bank account, she saw she was nearing the overdrawn mark. She sighed and glanced at the top strewn on her bed. *It's only going to be for a short time. I can do this.* She stood and hung up her outfit. *At least I won't be as stressed about paying the bills as I am now, and I can save to pay for Nicholas to get into rehab.*

She glanced at her clock radio and realized that she'd promised Chenoa she'd pop by and visit her. Scooping up her keys from her dresser, she headed out of her house.

"WHEN AM I getting outta here? I'm fuckin' climbing the walls," Chenoa said as Breanna filled the girl's water pitcher.

"Detox is always a bitch. In a while, you'll feel so much better." She placed the pitcher on the table near the bed and looked into Chenoa's dark eyes. "Remember how shitty you're feeling. Don't forget it. Memorize it. Own it. It's important because you don't want to go through this again. When you get out and you feel the pull of the drug, remember this moment."

Chenoa rubbed her arms, then twisted and untwisted her hair while she paced around the small room. "What the hell do you know about it? You told me you never used." She scowled at Breanna.

"I've been going through detoxes most of my life. It started with my mother, and I'm still doing it with my brother," she answered softly.

"Addiction affects *everyone*, not just the user." She patted the chair's cushion. "Why don't you sit down?"

She shook her head. "I gotta keep moving. It feels like a million insects are crawling all over my skin. I'm done with feeling like I have the flu. Now it's just this restlessness."

"That's the addiction, the psychological part. And you have to take it day by day."

"I need something to make me feel happy again. I'm so depressed." She hung her head as she kept circling the room.

Breanna caught her and pressed her close, her arms curling around the petite girl. "It's going to be okay," she soothed as she stroked her hair.

Chenoa's breath hitched, and then her small shoulders began moving. Wetness dampened Breanna's neck as she held the sobbing girl, running her hands up and down her back. For several minutes they stood in the middle of the room, Breanna giving comfort and Chenoa desperate for it. The teenager was in the dark abyss of addiction, and it would be a lifelong challenge to climb out of it and never go back.

Pulling away slightly, Chenoa wiped her nose with her hand. "Thanks. Sorry for the meltdown." She grabbed a tissue and blew her nose.

"You don't ever have to thank me for helping you out. Believe me, I know how hard this is for you. I want to help you. You can't do this alone."

"Yeah, well… I wanted to tell you thanks for everything." She looked down at the floor and shifted from one foot to another.

"Your mom tells me that when you get out of here, she's taking you on a major shopping spree. I know how you love clothes and makeup. I took your advice and invested a bit of money, bought a beautiful mauve lipstick from Lancôme. It was expensive, but what a difference."

The mention of makeup made Chenoa smile and she happily engaged in conversation, telling Breanna about the different cosmetic lines. Breanna exhaled slowly, content that she had momentarily distracted

Chenoa from the pull of heroin. Chenoa sank down in the chair and Breanna sat down in the one facing her, her back to the door.

As they chatted, the scent of the desert and the wind wisped around her, and she knew *he'd* come in. She held her breath; she'd been wanting to see him since their last encounter at his mother's house.

"I seem to run into you a lot. You must really like my family." His deep voice caressed her like black velvet as he walked past her and went over to Chenoa, leaning down and kissing the top of her head. He ruffled her hair. "How's my sunshine doing?"

She shrugged. "Okay. I just can't wait to go home. Breanna and I were talking about makeup. She said Mom was gonna take me on a huge shopping trip when I get home. I bet we're gonna go to Colorado Springs, or even Denver."

"Is that right?" He glanced at Breanna. She caught his gaze, her insides jumping when she saw desire lacing them. "Sounds like you gotta hurry and get better." His eyes still held Breanna's as his lips twitched into a half smile.

She couldn't turn away; she felt magnetically drawn toward him. He mesmerized her, pulling her in even though she wanted to break away and leave. She needed to get far away from him. He made her think of ecstasy-filled nights with his full lips exploring every inch of her body while his fingers trailed to the aching place between her legs, parting them open and teasingly sliding—

"You okay, Breanna? Your face is really flushed." Chenoa's voice broke in on her musings.

"I… uh…." She stopped as his eyes slowly traveled up her body. She sat immobile, biting the inside of her cheek when his gaze landed on her chest. His stare was hotter than the summer sun.

"I think Ms. Quine may be having a hot flash." He raised his brows as a smirk played across his lips.

She pushed up from the chair. "I'm fine, Chenoa." She purposely avoided looking at him, but out of the corner of her eye, she saw him watching her. His green eyes burned with desire and danger. The pulse between her legs made her clench them together, and he chuckled. Angry at her body for reacting to him so strongly, she threw her shoulders back and raised her chin. "I should let you and your dad have some time together. I have to get going. I'll try and come by over the weekend. You have my number if you need anything." She grasped the strap on her shoulder bag and walked toward the door. "Bye, Chenoa."

"You're not gonna say goodbye to me? Where are your manners, *Ms. Quine?*" His tone mocked her, and she wanted to slap him hard against his face.

"Goodbye, Mr. McVickers."

"It's always a treat to see how nervous I can make you."

She whirled around, anger burning her gut. "You don't make me nervous. I rarely let myself get flustered. Maybe you like *thinking* that your badass demeanor scares people. I don't know. I'm a social worker, not a psychologist."

He laughed and leaned against the wall, his finely toned body apparent beneath his tight black jeans, white muscle shirt that molded over his torso, and his drool-worthy biceps. "I don't think shit, lady. I *know.* Men avoid me and women clamor to me. They like the danger element. It makes them check me out and get all flushed. Kind of like you just were."

"Dad!" Chenoa reached out and grabbed his wrist.

If Breanna could look in a mirror, she knew her face would resemble a tomato. Steel winked at her, then turned to his daughter. "I'm just teasing your caseworker, sunshine. She knows it. We're just having a little fun, aren't we, Ms. Quine?"

Breanna looked at Chenoa's puzzled face and smiled. "Yes. You take care of yourself. I'll see you soon." She spun around and walked out the door, the intensity of Steel's stare boring into her.

When she went outside, she gulped in the warm air like she was starving. *I have to get a grip. I acted like a schoolgirl back there. He makes me so fucking mad! He's despicable. And so damn sexy.* She groaned. She'd have to figure out a way to limit her contact with him. Next time she saw his mother she'd find out his schedule and plan her drop-ins to Chenoa and his mother when he was at work.

He's so damn cocky. Thinks every woman's waiting for him. Yeah, right. She'd show him she wasn't *every* woman. Now if only her body behaved, she'd be as good as gold.

She slid into the driver's seat and switched on the ignition. As she drove out of the parking lot, she spotted a wicked-looking Harley, the fading rays of the sun bouncing off the chrome, and she just knew it was his. An image of her arms wrapped around his hard, tapered waist, her breasts pressed against his back as he rode fast and furious, made her tingle. *I wonder if he screws as hard as he rides.* Her legs clenched again; it seemed like that was becoming their response when she saw or thought of him. There was no way her body was going to behave around him. The best course of action was to avoid him altogether.

She drove out of the parking lot, cranked up the music, and ignored the way her body quivered.

Chapter Seven

CUERVOS BAR WAS packed and Breanna's feet were already screaming at her after just a few hours. As long as the men were focused on the sporting events on the big-screen TVs, they were cool, but if they weren't interested in the sport, they were focused on her cleavage and her butt. She and another girl, Jill, who was busty and skinny, were the only waitresses on duty. She didn't have time to think about anything but getting drinks to the customers.

"You doing okay?" Jorge asked as she placed the beers and mixed drinks on her tray.

"I think so. I didn't expect it to be this busy." She grabbed a handful of coasters.

"Not a lot of things to do in Alina on the weekend. Also, Fridays are usually payday for most of the people. They like to come and spend it here. I'm good with that." Jorge smiled broadly.

She laughed. "I'm beginning to like payday Friday too. I've done well so far with my tips. I better get these drinks to the customers." She lifted the heavy tray and made her way through the maze of people. Black Sabbath's "Crazy Train" blared from the jukebox, and she sang along with it as she placed down the drink orders at various tables.

When she went back to the bar for more drinks, Jill leaned against it, messing with her phone. "Hey," she said as she lifted her head.

"Hey. Where's Jorge?" Breanna looked around the bar but didn't spot him.

Jill shrugged. "I've been waiting here for about five minutes. If he doesn't get here soon, people are gonna take it out on me and not give me good tips." Breanna set down her tray and went behind the bar.

"What the fuck are you doing? Jorge's gonna be pissed."

"He hired me for waitressing and to be a relief bartender. No one's tending the bar, so tell me your order." She filled Jill's order, a couple of others from patrons seated at the bar, and then she started on hers. She bent over and opened a cabinet filled with liquor bottles, pulling them out while trying to find the Bloody Mary mix. As she was scrounging around, she felt two hands on her hips, thumbs pressing into her behind.

"Nice ass," a deep voice said.

Outraged, she jumped up. "Get your hands off me!" She whirled around and crashed into six feet one inch of pure concrete. Steel, to be exact. As in Chenoa's father, outlaw biker, and gorgeous man.

What the fuck?

The smile on his face disappeared. "What the hell are you doing behind my bar?"

"*Your* bar? I thought Jorge owned it." She brushed away several tendrils that had fallen across her face.

He shook his head. "Fuck. You're the new waitress Jorge hired. He told me he hired a hot-looking chick, but I never thought it was you. I thought butting your nose into people's lives was your thing." He leaned back on his heels and boldly assessed her. Self-conscious, she pulled her skirt down and tried to raise her top. "I don't think that's gonna work. You've got some dangerous curves, Ms. Quine. Now you look like my kind of woman."

She felt heat spreading over her neck and cheeks, and she swallowed hard. "Instead of checking me out, make yourself useful and tend bar. Jorge's disappeared and I have a bunch of people waiting for their drinks."

"You like being bossy, don't you? I like it, to a certain degree."

"I couldn't care less what you like, Mr. McVickers. If you want your customers happy, you'll cut the small talk and start filling my and Jill's drink orders." She stepped forward, but instead of moving out of the way, he stepped to the side slightly, making her slide past him, her breasts brushing against him. Jolts of desire shot through her, and from the heated glaze in his eyes, she knew he was feeling something too. She hurriedly pushed herself into the crowd to get away from his penetrating stare. He exuded danger and raw sex, and it both thrilled and scared her. She couldn't get involved with him. If she did, she knew she'd be setting herself up for a major heartbreak. Bikers were like her dad: selfish, unfaithful, and cocky assholes.

For the rest of the night he stared at her, and it made her so nervous that she spilled several drinks, which resulted in either no tips or small ones. *Jorge didn't tell me he had a partner. I can't believe* he's *my boss. I can't believe he's seen me dressed like a slut.* The way he kept looking at her legs and cleavage made her mind scream in anger. It also made her body tingle, and she was beyond pissed about that.

"Can you grab me some cocktail napkins at the bar?" Breanna asked Jill as she passed by. The less time she spent at the bar, the better. She had no choice when she had orders, though, and each time she went up, his gaze locked with hers, pulling her in. It seemed like he'd tattooed a smirk on his face because he wore one every time she glanced at him.

He's so infuriating!

"They're all out. I was gonna grab some in the back, but I got two large parties. Can you get them?"

"Sure. Are they in the last room on the left?"

"Yep."

Breanna put the drinks down on the table and ambled to the storage room. As she rummaged through the shelves looking for the napkins, she heard the door close behind her. She stiffened as the scent of leather floated in the air. *It's him.* She placed her hand on her stomach, hoping it would stop the fluttering.

"Need some help?" His voice slayed her every time she heard it.

"I'm good." *If I don't turn around, maybe he'll leave.*

"You're really not. The cocktail napkins are on the other side of the room."

"I'm not looking for them." *He's so cocky.*

"Jill told me you were. Why can't you admit you're wrong? Do you need therapy to help you do that?" He chuckled.

She gritted her teeth and turned around. "Look, I don't like you and you don't like me. We have to work together for your daughter's sake, and I need a second job to make ends meet. If you want me to go, just say it. I can find another job."

His green eyes pierced the distance between them. She held her breath, her heart beating so fast she was sure it'd break through her rib cage. A deep fire blazed in his gaze, but it was one of desire, not anger. She stood immobile as he came over and grabbed hold of her shoulders, drawing her to him. She titled her head back and he crushed his lips on hers—fiery, passionate, and demanding. She wanted to pull away, but she couldn't; she was losing herself in the kiss.

"Breanna," he whispered, and she savored the way he said her name, her heart pounding at his voice. He pressed his tongue to the seam of her lips and she parted them, allowing him in. Their tongues tangled as their breath mingled, and she ran her fingers down his back, tugging him closer until there was no space between them, until she could feel the beating of his heart against her chest.

When his hands started to slide under her miniskirt, she broke away and pushed back. He cupped her chin and tilted her head back. "We both want this." He gently brushed his lips across hers. She wanted to throw caution aside and press into him, fusing her body with his as they had wild sex, but her brain kept niggling at her. He was her client's father, a biker, and off-limits. She had stepped on the line, but if she went any further, she'd definitely be crossing it. She couldn't do that.

"I lost my head for a moment," she mumbled as she pushed away from him.

"I have that effect on women." He chuckled as he held her gaze.

She pressed her lips together as she finger-combed her messed-up hair. "Is this the way you initiate all the waitresses on their first night?"

"Pretty much." He smiled but his tone was harsh, like he was pissed at her.

She grabbed a large pack of cocktail napkins. "Does your club own part of the bar?"

"Just me. Jorge and I go back a long time. We've been buds since we were ten years old. His dad owned this bar, and when his old man got sick, Jorge asked if I wanted to be part owner. I had some money saved, so I bought into it. I'm rarely around. I have enough to do with the club's businesses. I had no idea Jorge hired you. Fucking small world, right?"

"You said it. I better get back out there. I'm sure Jill's cussing me out for taking so long." She grasped the doorknob and turned it. Looking over her shoulder, she smiled weakly. "About what happened... it'd be best if we forgot about it."

He took a small box from one of the shelves. "No worries, Ms. Quine. It's forgotten."

Her shoulders slumped as a heaviness spread throughout her body. "That's good," she said softly, then walked out of the room. For the rest of her shift, she snuck peeks at him, but he was either serving drinks, laughing with several bikers in the bar, or flirting with the women. She didn't catch his eye once.

That's what I wanted, so why am I feeling like shit because he's not paying any attention to me? Maybe he's right. Maybe I do need therapy.

Once her shift was over, she grabbed her purse and left the bar. She couldn't wait to get home and soak her feet in a tub of warm water and Epsom salts.

Steel hadn't been at the bar when she left. She wasn't sure where he was. She'd spotted him cozying up to a woman who was practically spilling out of her ill-fitting top an hour before her shift ended. *He's probably banging her in the same room he kissed me. These bikers are all alike.*

She slid into the driver's seat and put her car in gear, gripping the steering wheel firmly, perturbed that she cared about him flirting with a woman. It was crazy. He was a free agent, as was she. They didn't even *like* each other, so why did she feel pissed, irritated, and disappointed at the same time? *I have to quit. I won't be able to work around him. I'm sure*

I can find another waitressing job fast. Thoughts of what would have happened if she had let him go further swirled in her mind as she made her way home.

Once inside her abode, she kicked off her heels and moaned as she rubbed the balls of her feet. She took out a teal plastic tub and turned on the water, laying down a thick bath towel on the floor before placing the tub on top of it. She stirred in half a cup of Epsom salts and dragged one of her straight-backed chairs over, then lowered her aching feet into the warm, soothing water. It felt divine, like a slice of heaven.

She glanced at her phone and noticed four missed calls. Her stomach tightened as she scrolled through the numbers, praying that they weren't from Nicholas. Relief flooded over her when she heard Nicholas's landlady's voice. She'd left four messages, the anger in her voice palpable by the last one. She emphasized that Nicholas was one month behind on his rent and if it wasn't brought current, she'd have no choice but to evict him.

Breanna sighed. She'd just given him three hundred dollars to help pay his rent, which obviously went into his bloodstream instead of to his landlady. Tears stung her eyes. She took her feet out of the water and dried them, then went over to her purse, pulling out the wad of bills she'd received as tips that night. She counted the money and was shocked by the amount; she'd be able to cover Nicholas's rent and then some.

She put the money back into her purse. *I have to keep this job. The money's too good. I'll just keep my distance from him. It shouldn't be hard since Steel seems to have a short attention span when it comes to women. All I have to remember is to not be alone with him or do something I'll regret.*

She switched off the lights and ambled to her bedroom. Undressing, she slipped between the covers. With her body aching and exhausted, she fell fast asleep.

Chapter Eight

"**D**AMN, YOU'VE GOT a hot waitress working for you. I'd like a piece of her. Who is she?" Sangre asked as he threw back a shot of Jack that Steel placed in front of him.

Steel stiffened and instinctively looked around for Breanna, but he couldn't spot her. "Keep away from her." He took out his razor blade, cut open a box, and started putting bottles of whiskey on the bar shelves.

Sangre motioned for a refill as he leaned back against the barstool. "You aiming to fuck her? I thought you didn't mix business with pleasure, but from the way she's built, I'd make an exception too if I were in your place."

Steel poured the amber liquid into the shot glass. "I'm just telling you to stay away from her. I don't need to give you any fucking reason why."

Sangre raised his hands in surrender. "No worries, Prez. I should've figured you'd have already staked a claim on her fine ass." He chuckled and then brought the whiskey to his lips.

Steel scowled, then tore down the box and threw it in the recycle bin. He glanced around again for Breanna but didn't see her. "You going back to the club?" he asked Sangre as he washed the glasses.

Sangre nodded. "I thought I'd find someone to curl around me. I need something soft and curvy tonight." With his finger, he slid his glass toward Steel. "You lost interest in Alma? I noticed she and Paco have been getting it on for the past few days."

Steel shrugged. "This thing with Chenoa is eating me up inside. I can't really focus on pussy right now." He bent down low to pick up another box. *I'm only half bullshitting. The only pussy my dick seems to want is Breanna's, and that pisses the hell outta me.*

"I'm gonna take off. You gonna be here tomorrow night?" Jill asked as she pulled on her sweater.

"Most likely." He ignored Sangre's gaze. "Have you seen the new waitress?" He pretended to be engrossed in checking out each liquor bottle he took out of the box.

"Breanna? She left about a half hour ago. Jorge told her to take off a little early. I think he felt sorry for her feet. She was walking as though she was on glass." Jill laughed softly. "In a week or so, her feet will be used to the torture." She opened her purse, took out a cigarette pack, and tapped it against her finger to slide out a cigarette, putting it between her lips. "See ya."

As she stepped out, Steel saw a flame flicker from her lighter. A billow of smoke rose up around her before the door closed.

"I'm gonna get going. See you at the club." Sangre pushed his six-foot frame off the stool and sauntered to the door.

In a few minutes, Steel heard the roar of Sangre's cams as his Harley pulled out of the parking lot. He glanced out the window and saw Sangre turn left at the corner before disappearing. Steel drew in slow, steady breaths and massaged his temples. *I can't believe I fucking kissed her. What the hell was I thinking?*

Heat flushed through his body as he cracked his knuckles. He picked up the bar rag and wiped the counter vigorously. Ms. Quine was a distraction he couldn't afford. He had an MC to run, the threat of a rival club war, and his daughter's addiction to deal with. The last thing he needed was a woman—*this* woman—messing with his head. He didn't need or want that sort of complication in his life. He was just fine with the club girls. He didn't want a citizen—a damn *government* worker—stealing into his life.

"You're gonna rub the varnish off if you keep wiping the same spot." The cash register rang as Jorge opened it, taking out the bills.

Steel's nostrils flared. "I know what the fuck I'm doing."

"Chill, dude. I was only joking. What's up with you? You've been tense most of the night."

"I got shit on my mind, that's all."

Jorge paused, then gripped Steel's arm. "I know. It's gotta be tough." Steel grumbled something inaudible. "What do you think of our new waitress? She's hot, isn't she? She killed it in tips and this was her first night."

Steel threw the rag into a laundry bag. "She's okay."

"Okay? She's stacked just like you like them. You must've noticed that. I thought you'd be making passes at her all night, but you actually acted like a gentleman."

"She's not my type. I like dark-haired women."

"But she's got a good rack, right?"

"Yeah, I'll give her that." He picked up the laundry bag. "I'm gonna take this to the back." He walked away, knowing Jorge was probably confused by his reaction to Breanna. He didn't want to hear about her anymore. Didn't want to remember how soft her lips were against his, how silky her hair was, or how her body came alive beneath his touch. *I gotta rein it in. I can't let a pretty woman with a body that's made to be fucked rule my cock.* He had to get laid, then her amazing blue eyes and soft lips would flee from his head. Going without pussy made a man think and act like a goddamn fool.

He grabbed his leather jacket and ambled out of the back room. Jorge was counting the money when Steel entered the bar area. "Need some help with that?" he asked as he shrugged on his jacket. Jorge shook his head as he continued counting. "Okay. I'm gonna take off." Jorge nodded and Steel took out his keys, heading out the door and locking it behind him.

The ride to the clubhouse was fast and just the thing he needed to clear his mind of the blonde vixen. He pulled into his spot and made his way inside, the sweet scent of weed hitting him like a tidal wave when he entered the main room. The room looked like it was invaded by fog, and the red lights that had replaced the normal lighting accentuated the fast beats of "Ace of Spades" by Mötorhead. Steel smiled when he saw some of his brothers, the club girls, and a few hang-arounds dancing to the music. Under the lights, their skin glistened, and he had the urge to join them. He'd love to have had Breanna grinding her ass against him, helping him forget all his cares as the music carried them away.

He made his way through the labyrinth of people, a double shot of tequila greeting him when he got to the bar. He jerked his head at the prospect who was busy filling glasses, opening beer bottles, and wiping down the counter. The fiery sting of the booze warmed him, and he motioned for another. There wasn't anything like a shot of grade-A tequila to make him relax. He'd always preferred tequila to whiskey, although he never turned away a shot of Jack. Some bikers saw this as an affront to the brotherhood, but he thought they were assholes, so it didn't bother him any.

As the liquor warmed his blood, he began to relax. From a distance he saw Diablo marching toward him. He still marveled at the sheer size of the club's sergeant-at-arms. At six feet four inches, Diablo was built like a tank. He was covered in tattoos from his neck downward. A scowl was his usual expression, and Steel found him to be a dark and brooding man of little words. He'd done a stint for manslaughter in the state pen a few years back. Since he never talked about it, Steel didn't know too many of the details, but he knew the nasty scar he had on his arm was a reminder of the night he'd killed a man.

"I'm surprised you aren't shaking it. I know Mötorhead's one of your favorite bands." Diablo shrugged. "What're you drinking?"

"Jack. Double."

Steel pointed to the prospect, who immediately grabbed a bottle of Jack and poured it in a glass. When he placed it on the counter, Steel picked it up and handed it to Diablo. The brawny man downed it in one gulp. "You want me to start securing more arms in case we go to war?" he asked as he shook his head to the prospect's offer of another drink.

Steele nodded, and before Diablo moved away, Skull and Brutus came over. With Skull's blond hair and Brutus's dark, they were a strong contrast to each other. Both were muscular and had their fair share of tats, although Skull's were basic mayhem while Brutus's were mystical. "How's it going?" Skull asked Steel and Diablo.

"Good," said Steele. Diablo just scowled.

"You got your sights on one of the hang-arounds, Diablo?" Brutus pointed to an attractive woman whose arms and legs were covered in tattoos. "She's hot. Why don't you try her out? She's new. She's giving you the eye, dude." He brought his beer bottle to his lips. Diablo stared straight ahead.

"Fuck, bro. You're not even gonna check her out. The chick has it bad for you." Skull elbowed his arm. Diablo visibly stiffened.

"She's a sure thing. That's fuckin' gold." Brutus laughed, and then Skull joined in. Steel smiled as he watched the two members rib Diablo, who didn't look like he was going to take much more of it.

"What the fuck are you saving it for, dude?" Skull asked as he grabbed another drink. The prospects were required to know what each member drank and to have the drinks given to them before they had to ask.

When Steel saw the vein at Diablo's temple pulse, he intervened. "Leave the brother alone. He doesn't have a hard-on each time he looks at a chick like you two losers do." He chuckled. Skull and Brutus busted up laughing, but Diablo never once cracked a smile.

He leaned into Steel. "You want me for anything?" Steel shook his head. "Then I'll go." He stalked off as Skull and Brutus stared after him.

"What the fuck's up with him?" Skull asked. "It's like he's allergic to pussy. I've never seen him with a chick. Damn, his dick must be withered up or something. Have you ever seen him with a chick?"

Steel shook his head. "Nope. He's a great sergeant-at-arms, but he's fucking strange. Maybe he gets it in town."

"With a citizen? No fuckin' way," Brutus said as he grabbed a handful of popcorn the prospect put in front of him. "And there's no way he's paying for it. That'd be just fucked in the head."

"Well it's his business. If he doesn't want pussy, then he doesn't. Sometimes I think life would be much easier if pussy weren't around."

Breanna's face flitted through his mind. "A whole lot easier."

"Hey." Paco came up to the trio and knocked fists together with them. "I got some news from the network. Word on the streets is that a shitload of smack is here and they're looking for buyers."

The jovial mood of the couple of minutes before left the group in a matter of seconds. Steel narrowed his eyes and jutted out his jaw. "We need to set up a buy. I gotta find out who the supplier is. Motherfuckers."

"I was thinking the same. The only one who can pass for a legitimate buyer is Jigger." Paco picked up his beer bottle.

Steel searched the room for the brother. At five foot seven with a baby face, Jigger looked more like he was sixteen rather than twenty-six. He had a sprinkling of angry tats on the side of his neck and down his arms. "Is he here?"

"I see him on one of the couches. His dick is shoved in some chick's mouth. She's got a cute ass from what I can see." Skull craned his neck further.

"Go get him. He can finish up later." Steel leaned back against the bar.

A couple of minutes later, Skull returned with a confused Jigger, his erection poking against his jeans. Steel chuckled under his breath. "We need you to do a smack buy. I know you're planning to go for a week to visit your kid in Durango, but postpone it by a week. I want to do this buy real soon. You gotta hang out where the teens are to find out how to arrange the buy. Inspiration Point is probably a good place to start."

"That's still a favorite make-out place? I remember taking a lot of girls up there when I was in high school, hoping to score. Seven times outta ten I did. Good times." Skull placed both elbows on the bar.

"Yeah, it's still popular. You'll also need to hang out at Jake's Bowl and Arcade. It's packed. Chenoa and her friends go there a lot. We can set up the particulars tomorrow," Steel said.

Without flinching, Jigger nodded. "Sure. No problem."

Pride welled up inside Steel. The brotherhood never questioned his decisions or complained when their plans went awry. It was the brothers' ironclad loyalty and sense of family that got to Steel each and every time it was challenged. He clasped Jigger's shoulder without saying a word. He didn't have to; the look in the member's eyes told Steel that he was feeling the bond just as strongly as Steel. "You can go and finish up with your pick of the night."

"Looks like you gotta find yourself a substitute, dude." Paco pointed at the woman Jigger had been with. She was now riding Sangre's cock as he sucked her tits.

"Fuck," Jigger said, and then Steel saw his eyes go bright. He turned in the direction of the brother's gaze and saw Alma approaching them. Jigger glanced at Steel.

"Go for it. I'm not gonna have her tonight." Steel laughed inwardly when he saw Jigger's excited face; it was like he'd handed the man a million dollars. He figured he owed it to him for dragging his ass over right before he came with the sweet chick who was blowing him.

"You're cool with it, right?" Jigger looked anxiously at Steel. Brutus, Skull, and Paco laughed.

"I said I was, didn't I? Go for it before I change my mind."

Jigger scrambled away and stopped Alma before she came over to Steel. He whispered something in her ear and she looked at Steel, disappointment lacing her eyes, before she looped her arm around Jigger's. The two of them disappeared into the crowd.

"You passing Alma off again?" Paco asked.

"Yeah. I've got too much on my mind," Steel answered.

"Is there something you wanna talk about?"

"Nope." Steel crossed his arms.

Before the vice president could answer, Angel padded over and wrapped her arm around him. He pulled her close and took a handful of her soft ass cheek in his hand, squeezing it.

She laughed. "You're being a naughty boy." She ran her purple-painted fingernail over his face.

"Yeah? And what are you gonna do about it?" he said huskily. She giggled and leaned into him, her hand dropping to rub his crotch. Steel snorted while Paco kissed her. He pulled away and looked at Steel. "We done here?"

Steel nodded and watched Paco and Angel grope each other as they walked away. Glancing around, he saw many of his brothers and the women engaging in various acts of sex, and he felt a pull on his dick. *I should grab one of these chicks and drain myself in her.* Plenty of women had been giving him the eye ever since he'd entered the clubhouse, but he knew he wouldn't do it. He'd finish his drink and then head up to his room, wanting to go early the next day to see Chenoa. He also didn't want any woman except the blonde pain in the ass who'd been on his mind far too much, and who'd become a major burr in his side.

He threw back his last drink, pushed away from the bar, and climbed the stairs, all the while cursing the hot social worker for stirring shit up inside him.

Chapter Nine

THE FOLLOWING MORNING, after visiting with Chenoa, Steel sat on his Harley in the hospital's parking lot, plugging in his sister's phone number.

"Hi, Steel. To what do I owe the honor of a phone call from you?"

"I wanna know why you're dumping your kids with *Shimá*. You know she's not well, or doesn't that matter to you, Chitsa?"

He heard her sigh loudly.

"How is this your fuckin' business? *Shimá* likes having my kids with her. The older ones help her around the house, and the younger ones make her feel useful. Why do you think you know everything?"

"'Cause I do. Your older kids aren't doing shit around the house. Last time I was there, the fridge was bare, the bedrooms were a mess, and *Shimá* looked pale, tired, and weak. She hadn't even eaten. Don't try to bullshit me that you give a damn about our mother."

"I do. It's just that I've been very busy and feeling stressed. I thought it would help if I was away from the kids for a while."

"Translation: you're shacking up with some asshole who doesn't want your kids around. Fuck, Chitsa. How can you dump your children at *Shimá's* whenever a jerk you're into tells you to? How do you think that makes your kids feel?"

"I don't need you lecturing me. My children are just fine. Anyway, they like hanging out at *Shimá's*."

"Why wasn't there any food in her fridge? She told me she's getting food stamps for the four children and herself. Are you buying the food and keeping it for you and whichever asshole you're fucking now?"

"Times are tough. I sometimes don't have any food. *Shimá* told me that I could use some of the money for me, but she's been losing the cards too much. I'm going to have to take charge of them."

"No, you're gonna get a fucking job, take your kids back, and act like a mother. *Shimá* could use some help with the grocery shopping. We can take turns. I've gotten you two jobs you blew off. You can work at one of our businesses. We need a receptionist at the tattoo shop."

"I can't work right now. I'm having too many allergies this summer. Maybe in the fall when the weather turns cooler."

"Does your loser work?"

"He's not a loser. He's between jobs."

"So no one's working, and you have *Shimá* taking care of your kids. That stops right now. Visiting their grandmother is one thing, but living with her and you taking advantage of her is another."

"If *Shimá* had a problem with it, she'd tell me. She hasn't, so butt the fuck out of my life."

"You know damn good and well *Shimá* would never tell you the grandkids are too much. She's always trying to do everything for all of us. You're taking terrible advantage of her. It stops now, Chitsa. You don't want to make me madder than I am."

There was a long pause.

"I gotta go."

"You take care of this or I will."

"Okay. It's better when I don't hear from you."

"It's better when you're not a selfish bitch."

"Nice talking to you. Not." The phone went dead.

Steel took in deep breaths, slowing exhaling them to calm his ire. His sister had always been so selfish. Even when she was young, she never wanted to share with him, their brother, or their cousins, and she never helped their mother even when she was sick. Steel remembered that he and his brother, Wayne, helped their mother by cleaning the dishes, dusting the house, and peeling the potatoes, even though their father made fun of them and called them pussies. But Chitsa just sat around like a princess, not lifting a finger. Their mother never once called her on it.

He pulled his hair back and secured it with a tie, then switched on the ignition. His younger sister drove him crazy. She'd had four children by four different men, and she acted like they were such an inconvenience in her life. He felt sorry for his three nephews and niece.

What a fucking mess life is right now.

He pulled out of the parking lot and sped toward the reservation, wanting to see his mother. He may even run into Breanna. The thought of seeing her in her professional clothes, her golden hair tumbling down her back, made his dick twitch.

On second thought, it'd be best if I don't see her.

The road to the reservation was two lanes that cut right through the desert. The sprinkling of sagebrush and yucca plants on the red, rocky sand stretched for miles while the majestic San Juan Mountains loomed in the background, some of the higher peaks dusted in white powder. The contrast between the desert and the high mountains was one of the reasons Steel never wanted to leave the area. He loved the desolation of the parched desert and the richness of the mountains.

The reservation was smack-dab in the middle of the desert off the main road, marked by a wooden sign with black letters reading "Navajo Tribe—Ancestral Reservation Area." Located on the reservation, or "rez" as the residents referred to it, was a gas station and a small convenience store. The lack of businesses and economic development were some of the major factors in creating the extreme poverty that was rampant on the reservation.

Parcels of green grass dotted the desolate landscape. As Steel rode deeper into the reservation, some of the run-down houses and junked-up cars made him remember why he couldn't wait to move away from the crushing poverty. As he turned down one of the streets, he spotted his dad with his young wife who was bursting with a child. His stomach turned and he darted his gaze away from his dad, not acknowledging him as the older man whistled and waved.

His father had cheated on his mother since about the time their sister was born. It could've been sooner, but that was the earliest memory Steel had of seeing his father kissing and touching other women. His mother had simply accepted that her husband could not be monogamous, even though he could tell it killed her each time his father spruced himself up and went out to meet one of his ladies.

For Steel, it was bad enough that the philandering made his mother unhappy, but it was the humiliation his father subjected her to that made Steel hate him. He'd openly parade his women in front of her, even having them spend the night while his mother would share the bed with her children. Sometimes the sound of his father fucking one of his sluts would keep Steel awake, but most of the times his mother's quiet crying kept him from sleeping, anger and sadness battling inside him as he listened to her whimpers.

When Steel had reached fifteen years old, he finally confronted his father and told him that he could fuck whichever whore he wanted, but not in front of his mother. His father, older and worn down by years of heavy drinking, balked and then threatened to beat the shit out of him. Steel, at nearly six feet, had towered over his father. The glint of hatred shining in his eyes must have caused his father concern because he'd just cussed him out and stormed out of the house. But he never brought another woman into the house again.

Three years later, his father moved out of the house and took up residence with another woman he'd been banging on and off for two years. His mother had been devastated that her husband had left her, and she'd never gotten over it. Since he'd left, his father had lived with several women over the years until he'd married the year before. His marriage had been a double whammy for Steel's mother, since it closed any hope she'd held out for a reconciliation with her husband. To top it off, the woman he'd married was the daughter of *Shimá's* best friend.

Steel couldn't see what the young woman saw in his dad. It wasn't his money, since his lazy-ass father hadn't worked a proper job since Steel was born. His father, Irish on both sides of his family, came from Chicago and graduated from Northwestern with a degree in accounting.

He'd gotten a job in Durango, a city about an hour away from Alina, and that's where he'd met Steel's mother. She'd been working at one of the restaurants he'd frequented. They dated and his mother got pregnant, so his father had married her. He never let her or Steel forget that he'd married her only because she'd been pregnant and he was a gentleman.

His father had worked twice a year, selling cards for Easter and Christmas. The fucker would raise himself from his chair, don a suit, cap his scotch bottle, and for two weeks he'd go to neighboring towns selling cards to various stores and residents. Then he'd come back exhausted, all his money practically spent on women and booze, giving the last few dollars to his wife. The rest of the year he'd spent sitting on an over-stuffed chair, philosophizing about life in between gulps of scotch, fucking any woman who'd have him, and beating his children.

Steel's mom worked as a certified nursing assistant in one of the nursing homes in town, and if money was real tight, she'd pick up a second job at Leroy's Diner on Main Street. When Steel turned twelve, he started working at a horse ranch, keeping the job until he left Alina to go to Pinewood Springs. His brother also worked. The only two who didn't work were his sister and father.

And his dad had the goddamn audacity to whistle and wave to him? *Fuck him. Probably wants to show off that he can still knock up a woman. If I were him, I'd wonder if it's mine.*

Steel parked in front of a neatly kept white brick house. He'd grown up in that house, but his mother was fastidious, so it looked like it was brand new. Steel paid for people to mow and water the lawn, replace the roof, and maintain both the exterior and interior of the home.

He took the steps two at a time, knocking lightly on the front door before he entered. His mom was in her recliner, head back and eyes closed. His gaze swept over her, taking in her slackened, weary features and her thinning gray hair. His heart clenched at the sight. The strong woman with long black hair and bright dark eyes had been replaced by a weathered woman whose eyes no longer sparkled. Work, worry, disappointment, and heartbreak had taken their toll on her. His father had done that to her.

"Oh, *Shimá*, I'll never understand how you can still love the worthless sack of shit. You should've thrown his ass out years ago. Look what loving him has done to you."

His mom stirred and her eyes fluttered open. She blinked rapidly as if trying to focus her gaze on him, then smiled. "*Shiyáázh*. What a pleasant surprise. I must've dozed off. How is Chenoa?"

Steel padded over to her and leaned down, kissing her cheek. "She's doing fine. I'm worried about how she'll do when she gets out. I still don't understand how this happened."

His mother stroked his arm. "And you never will. You have to accept that it has and work with her to make sure she doesn't fall down again."

He breathed out. "Yeah. Easier said than done. Drugs are fucking hard to kick. I hope she has the strength for it." He creased his brow. "How've you been?" He sat down on the couch.

"Good. Chitsa called." She chuckled. "You really made her mad. She was screaming and calling you a lot of bad words."

"I'm glad I pissed her off. Is she taking the kids back?"

His mother smiled, then grabbed his hand and kissed it. "Thank you," she said softly. "Sometimes I'm not good at saying no, especially to any of you."

"I know. Chitsa should've known better. You let me know if she starts her bullshit again." She nodded. "Promise?"

She kissed his hand again and whispered, "I promise. You're a good son. You always worried about me. You're my firstborn, and we've always shared a strong connection. I love Chitsa and Wayne too, but you have always been my protector." He grunted and she laughed. "I know you don't like talking about the touchy-feely stuff. Just know I love you very much and I appreciate what you do for me, *Shiyáázh*."

"Yeah. So how're you feeling? You eating?"

"I'm feeling tired, but I'm an old woman so that's to be expected. I've been eating. I wish you'd come over for dinner sometimes. I hate eating alone."

"I'll try and come by more often at dinnertime. I meant to ask you about the food stamp cards. How do you keep losing them?"

She shook her head. "I don't know. I think that I have them in my purse or in the top drawer of my dresser, but then when I go to use them, the cards are gone. I could swear I had them. Maybe my memory is slipping."

Steel pursed his lips. "You're not losing it. Someone's taking them from you. Besides Chitsa's kids, who else has been in and out of here?"

Her eyes widened. "No one except for Chenoa and Wayne sometimes. I usually meet up with my friends at the community center to play cards and kibitz."

A knot formed in his stomach as his brow wrinkled. "Chenoa comes over here a lot, doesn't she?"

"Yes. She's such a good girl. She helps me cook and clean the house. In the past few months, I haven't seen her that often. She'd only come for a few minutes and then leave. I shoulda known something was going on with her."

"Don't even go there. You're not responsible for this. Hell, I didn't pick up on the fact that she was wearing long sleeves all the time, or that she acted suspicious about shit a lot. I guess I just didn't fathom that my kid would be caught up in drugs." She patted his hand and he pulled it away. "Anyway, did the most recent cards go missing after Chenoa was here the last time?"

"What are you saying? Are you accusing your daughter of stealing them?"

"Just answer me truthfully, *Shimá*."

She nodded. "I was planning to go to the store right after she left. Chitsa was coming by to take me. She needed some things too, but when I went to get them, they were gone. Chitsa wasn't too happy. Neither of us had enough money to buy a lot of groceries."

Adrenaline rushed through him. *Chenoa's selling the food stamps for cash. Fuck.* "Next time you need money, you call me. I'm sick of this shit. I can help you. Did you tell Chitsa about Chenoa being there and that the cards were missing after that?" She shook her head. "Don't tell her any of this, okay?"

"I won't. I didn't want to believe it, so I convinced myself I'd misplaced them. I can't believe she'd do that to me."

"Drugs make you do stuff like that. It's all about the fix. Nothing else matters." He felt a heaviness descend on him. He wished he could hold his daughter in his arms for the rest of her life. He wanted to keep her safe, wanted her to have the best life possible. He wanted her off drugs forever. His stomach hardened. "I gotta go over and talk to Mika. Are you good?"

"I'm fine. I'm going to relax and watch TV. Wayne's coming over and we're going to have dinner together. Stop worrying about me." She smiled.

"Tell Wayne I said hi." He stood up and walked over to her, kissing her forehead before rifling through his jeans pocket. He stuffed two hundred-dollar bills in her hand. "This is for you. Not Chitsa, not the grandkids, just you. Buy yourself a new housecoat." He shuffled to the door before she could give him the money back. "I'll stop by in a day or so," he said over his shoulder, then closed the door and went to his bike.

When he pulled into Mika's driveway, she stepped out on her front porch and began walking toward him. He got off his bike and leaned against it, waiting for her to reach him.

"Is everything okay with Chenoa?" she asked, her brow creasing.

"Yeah. She's doing great. I just stopped in to see my mom. I wanted to ask you a quick question before I take off. Have you ever misplaced your food stamp card?"

"My EBT card?" Her puzzled look made him chuckle. "Yeah. Why're you asking?"

"I just wondered. When's the most recent replacement you've received?"

"About a month ago. I couldn't find my card anywhere. Come to think of it, I've had about eight cards go missing in the last six months.

It's weird. Why're you interested in my EBT cards?"

He shrugged. "My mom mentioned she's getting government help. I want her off it."

"What're you two talking about?" Roy stepped onto the porch. He ran his hand over his shaved head, his beady eyes fixed on Steel. Pricks of anger stabbed at Steel's nerves.

"Nothing, honey. Steel's just updating me about Chenoa."

Roy walked over and stood by Mika, his arm snaking around her shoulders. Steel's six-foot-one frame loomed over Roy's five-seven one, and the man thrust his shoulders as though to make himself appear taller than he was. "How is she?"

Steel's scalp tightened and he clenched and unclenched his fists to calm the burn that was threatening to explode inside him. "She's fine. I'm talking to Mika. Why don't you come back in five?"

Roy narrowed his eyes. "Why? Are you saying something you don't want me to know about?"

Mika turned to him and kissed him lightly on the cheek. "No, sweetie, it's just that—"

"I'm fucking outta here. I'll catch you later, Mika." His body temperature was rising. He turned away and swung his leg over his motorcycle.

"Wait. You don't have to go," she said, pulling away from Roy.

"I fucking know I don't have to. Later." He revved his engine and reversed his bike down the driveway. Mika's face wore the mask of regret, while Roy's was full of loathing. Steel's lips curled into a wide grin, and then he laughed when he saw Roy grab Mika and hold her close, like he was telling Steel that she was *his* property. *Like I give a fuck. He's asking for a beat-down in the worst way.* The only thing that held him back was Chenoa. He didn't want the fucker taking out his frustrations on his daughter—or Mika for that matter. *I don't know what in the hell Mika sees in him.*

Once Chenoa got out of rehab, he'd have to make sure that Roy got his ass out of Mika's house. There was no way in fuck he was letting her stay in the house with him there. It never ceased to amaze him that both his dad and Roy had permission by the tribal council to live on the reservation. Very few non-natives lived on the reservation, and the ones who did had to obtain permission from the tribe to do so. He wondered how much it cost his dad and the fucker to get the council's permission.

He shook his head in disgust as he rode toward the entrance to the reservation. The Department of Social Services was keeping his daughter away from him and it was pure bullshit. They were trying to protect Chenoa from the influences of his bad lifestyle, and she ended up on heroin.

But I'm the problem. What a goddamn joke. This fucking shit's gonna stop now.

He swung his bike in the direction of the satellite office and pulled into the small parking lot adjacent to it. A blast of cold air slammed into him as he entered the small building. An unmanned reception desk was the first thing he saw. He marched down a short hallway and came into a room that had several partitions and desks set up.

A young man in a short-sleeved button-down shirt and tie sat behind a large desk, staring at a monitor. He jerked his head up when Steel cleared his throat. "Can I help you?"

Steel saw the apprehension in his eyes and laughed inwardly.

"I need to speak with Ms. Quine. Now."

"Really? I mean, she's not here right now. She's out doing some field work."

"When's she coming back?"

The man wiped the sweat glistening on his forehead despite the below-freezing temperature in the office. He shrugged. "Not sure. Was she expecting you?"

Steel whirled around and stormed out, slamming the front door. He pulled out his phone and called Jorge to get her home address. He'd pay a personal visit to Ms. Smart-Mouth.

This shit with the department is gonna end tonight.

He sped out of the reservation and onto the open road.

Chapter Ten

GOOSE BUMPS PEBBLED Breanna's arm when she came into the office. *Why the fuck is it always a deep freeze in here?* She placed the stack of files she held in her arms down on her desk and walked over to the thermostat, shaking her head in disbelief when the digital number fifty-eight appeared on the reader. *That's insane!* She punched in seventy, then returned to her desk. The cold blowing air abruptly stopped and a satisfied smile spread over her face.

As she reviewed her cases from that day, Joel walked in with a can of Pepsi. She held her head down, pretending to be absorbed in her work, hoping it'd do the trick in keeping him from approaching her.

No such luck.

"Hey, you're back. How'd it go?" he asked as he brought the can to his lips.

"Okay. I got a lot more done than I thought. It seems like the majority of people have a knack for misplacing their EBT cards. It's wild." She turned toward her keyboard. "I want to input the information while it's still fresh in my mind." Joel took a few loud gulps, then crushed his can and threw it in her wastepaper basket. The clash of metal on metal jarred her and she jumped slightly. "I'm kinda busy here. Sorry I can't chat."

"A tough-looking Native came in to see you. He was so fuckin' pissed."

Breanna's fingers stiffened and she couldn't tap another letter. "Did he give his name?"

"No. He was real mad that you weren't here. He didn't give me a chance to get any information. When I said you were out and I wasn't sure when you'd be back, he just stormed out of here."

She sucked in deeply. "Was he tall and built, with a scar on his face?" She knew it was Steel before Joel confirmed it.

"Yeah. So who is he? Does he live on the rez?"

Knowing he came to the office looking for her made her insides quiver, like she was ready to fall off the edge of a cliff into a soothing pool of crystal clear water—exciting and welcoming at the same time.

Before she could answer, Janet, another coworker, came into Breanna's cubicle. "Special Agent Powers told me to tell you guys that we're all meeting in the conference room."

The "conference room" was a round table with six chairs in the breakroom. Breanna turned off her monitor and followed Joel and Janet. Two men sat at the table: Special Agents Richard Raley and Jim Powers. They were investigators with the FBI, and all three of the caseworkers had filled several afternoons surmising why the men were sent to their satellite office. Raley was in his mid-forties, with blue eyes and brown hair that was graying at his temples, whereas Powers was a good ten years younger with dark brown hair and darker brown eyes. Each man was in good shape, but Special Agent Powers looked like his after-work obsession was pumping iron at the gym. They rarely spoke to the social workers, preferring to keep to themselves behind their closed office doors.

Breanna opened the compact fridge, took out a bottle of water, and then sat down, unscrewing the top and taking a deep drink. She stared at the two men as they shuffled papers around, heads bent, eyes fixed downward. After several minutes, the men looked up, and Investigator Raley cleared his throat.

"I wanted to call this meeting to introduce ourselves to you and to let you know why we're here. I'd like for us to work together, and if you ever have any questions, problems, or information, please find either me or Jim"—he tilted his head in the direction of the younger man to his right—"and let us know."

The three caseworkers nodded. Breanna sat back in the hard plastic chair and listened as the FBI agent told them they were sent to investigate food stamp fraud. The missing EBT cards immediately entered her mind. *Was Steel's mother committing food stamp fraud?* She couldn't believe the soft-spoken, kind woman would be capable of something like that, but looks could be deceiving.

"Why the hell do people want EBT cards?" Joel asked.

Powers spread his hands out on the table. "The ones selling them need the cash, and the ones buying them are normally unscrupulous retailers. The cards are bought for thirty or fifty cents on the dollar. So if someone has an EBT card for three hundred dollars, then the buyer will give either one hundred fifty or as low as ninety dollars cash for the card. If the buyer is a retailer, he'll use the three hundred dollars to buy cheap food wholesale, then mark it up three or four times in his store and make a killing. Food stamp fraud costs the taxpayers millions of dollars every year."

"And the seller gets cash to buy stuff he can't with the card, like alcohol and tobacco. A lot of times the cash is used to buy guns or drugs. Sometimes drug dealers will take EBT cards instead of cash, giving the junkie twenty-five cents on the dollar. Then the dealer will resell it to a retailer," Raley said.

Breanna took another sip of her water. "What do you want from us?"

"Information. We need to know who's reporting an inordinate amount of lost or stolen cards. One time can be excused, but if someone has reported more than two cards missing in a six-month cycle, then fraud is highly likely." Jim locked his hands together and placed them behind his head.

"Breanna's been asked by the department to check out clients who've had too many cards reported as lost," Joel said.

"Is that so?" Jim turned to her, and she nodded. "What have you found out?"

"I'm still gathering the information. I should have a report finished by the end of next week." For reasons she couldn't comprehend, she didn't want to tell these FBI agents about Steel's mother or Mika. Both of the women reported several cards missing, and the common denominator seemed to be Chenoa. She wanted to talk to Steel about it first—Chenoa had enough problems going on in her life—although Breanna knew she was teetering on a thin wire between doing her job and covering up a possible fraud.

"I want to see the report as soon as you complete it, okay?" She nodded. "This is a county-wide problem, but it appears as though it's happening in higher frequency at the reservation." Jim turned to Richard. "Anything else you want to add?" He shook his head. "Okay then. Get us that report, Breanna, and let's all work together in stamping out the fraud. Remember to keep your ears open, but don't be foolish and try to play amateur sleuth. The investigating part is our job. Don't forget that."

Breanna pushed her chair back and stood up. She had a ton of work to input before she got off work, so she settled at her desk and opened the first file on top of the stack.

"That's a load of shit they just fed us," Joel said as he lounged against the makeshift wall.

She looked up, surprised at the angry scowl on his face. "I don't think so. It seems like there's an excessive number of lost cards being reported at the rez. I'm sure the feds wouldn't waste their agents for the hell of it."

"What's the fucking big deal anyway if someone wants some extra cash to buy a bottle of beer or a pack of cigs? They're so damn poor around here, why not let them have some fun?"

Breanna turned toward him. "I think the problem is that they're being ripped off by getting half or less for the amount of their EBT card. Also, the money is used for drugs, and most probably is being taken from their children's mouths. It's not a victimless crime by any means."

"I think it is, and I'm not gonna be part of this fucked-up investigation. Don't the feds have bigger crimes to solve?" Joel ran his hand through his mop of hair.

"I'm with Breanna on this one. I feel sorry for the children whose parents are selling their cards on the black market for drugs. Also, the retailers who are crooking the clients are giving them a double whammy by making them pay four times the prices for pop, meat, and other things in their stores," Janet said. Breanna and Joel stared at her. She blushed. "What? Okay, I was eavesdropping. I couldn't help it. We don't really have walls."

Breanna laughed, but Joel continued to scowl. "No one's forcing anyone to go to the high-priced markets."

"Yeah, maybe not in bigger cities like Durango or Pueblo, but in Alina and the neighboring towns, there aren't a lot of choices. Roy's Market is the closest one near the rez and it's damned overpriced. Just saying." Janet crossed her arms.

"I agree with Janet. Sorry to break up the discussion, but I really have a lot of work to finish. I don't want to be here until seven or eight tonight." Breanna turned back to her monitor.

"Whatever," Joel grumbled as he sulked away.

"What the hell is his problem?" Janet whispered when he'd turned into his cubicle.

"Beats me. I think he wishes he was the big rugged agent instead of the social worker." Breanna smiled and Janet chortled. "Gotta get to work." Janet nodded and scampered away.

At five thirty, Breanna rubbed her aching eyes and turned off her monitor, then raised her arms high above her head and stretched. She was tired and stiff, and she couldn't wait to soak in a nice hot bath when she got home. Janet and Joel had already gone home, and when she went into the parking lot, her car was the only one there. Apparently the agents had also left.

On the way home she tried calling Nicholas for the fifth time. As before, there was no answer. She punched in her sister's number and asked if she'd heard from Nicholas. Shelby told her that she hadn't seen the fucker and didn't care if "he rots in hell." Breanna decided she'd pass on calling Jeremy to see if he'd heard from Nicholas. Since he'd been released from jail, he'd been laying real low, and he and Nicholas hadn't gotten along since puberty anyway.

She pulled into her garage and slipped into the kitchen, checking her answering machine just in case Nicholas had called her landline. Ever since he'd started using drugs, she set up a landline in case her cell phone didn't work and he—or worse yet, the police—ever had to get a hold of her. She went to her bathroom, turned on the bath faucets, and stripped out of her clothes. She couldn't wait to shut out the world.

An hour later she shuffled into the kitchen, her pastel yellow bath-robe snug around her. She opened the refrigerator and pulled out a berry-flavored wine cooler. She grabbed a can of mixed nuts from the cupboard, went into the living room, plopped on her couch, and switched on the TV. As she finished her wine cooler, someone knocked on the door. Wrapping her robe around her tightly, she walked over and looked through the peephole. Shock jolted through her when Steel filled her field of vision. She swallowed hard, then opened the door a crack.

"What do you want?" she asked.

"I need to talk to you about Chenoa." His voice was gruff and his eyes bored into her.

"Did something happen?" She opened the door a little wider.

"Nah. She's good. I just wanna talk to you about her situation when she gets out."

Her heart raced and her mouth was as dry as the desert. "I'm exhausted right now. I don't get paid for overtime. Come to my office tomorrow and we can talk. I'll be there all day."

His green eyes flashed. "Open the damn door or I'll kick it in. I went by your fucking office today and you weren't there."

"Maybe next time you can do something unusual, like make an appointment. I told you I'll be there tomorrow, so come by then." She started to close the door when his deep voice stopped her cold.

"You've got one last chance to open the fucking door or I'm coming in *my* way."

She gasped. "You wouldn't dare."

He grabbed the screen door in his large hands. She heard it groan as he pulled it from its hinges before he busted through her front door, pushing her backward. She fell on the ground, her robe opening and revealing her nakedness. His eyes slowly traveled up her body. Crimson stained her cheeks when his gaze landed on her chest. His stare was hotter than the embers of a glowing fire.

Regaining her composure, she tugged at her robe and covered herself, then struggled to get on her feet. He extended his hand and she smacked it away as she pulled herself up, brushing her tousled hair from her face. "I hope you're proud of your Neanderthal actions. What the fuck is the matter with you?" She tightened the tie around her robe. "You're going to pay for a new screen door, a front door, and to fix the door frame." He laughed, which just pissed her off more. "You actually think this is funny? You asshole!"

"You're real cute when you're pissed. Fuck, you got a fire in you. I'd love to see how it spills out in other ways." He pulled her to him. She struggled and squirmed, trying to get out of his arms. She had to; being that close to him was making her body heat up, and she couldn't have *that* happen. "Settle down, will you?"

She gathered all her strength, placed her hands on his chest, and shoved him away. "I don't want to settle down. I want you out of here. Now." She placed her hand on her hip.

"Just wanna let you know that you're beginning to cross a line with me. I don't take orders from anyone."

"Not even when you're trespassing?"

"Especially when I'm doing illegal shit." He smiled and cocked his head. "Sorry 'bout your door. It was a shitty one. Not safe at all. I'll make sure I reinforce it before I leave."

The way he looked at her, with his head to the side and a boyish grin on his face, melted her panties. *Tread carefully, Breanna. Don't do anything stupid.* She rolled her eyes and waved her arm toward the couch. "Have a seat. Do you want a beer?"

"Sure. You got any munchies?"

His audacity never ceased to amaze her. "Pretzels and nuts."

"That'll work." He hopped onto her couch, took the remote control, and channel surfed. She groaned loudly and went into the kitchen to grab the items.

She watched as he guzzled the beer, his sensuous lips wrapped around the mouth of the bottle. She remembered how pliable and full his lips were on hers when they'd kissed at Cuervos. How strong his arms were around her, how heated his touch was as they pressed their lips together passionately. The memory of it sent a pulse of desire between her legs. "You want another one?" she rasped.

He pinned her with his gaze. "Yeah," he said huskily.

She forced herself to get up rather than throw herself against his hard chest, heading to the kitchen and grabbing another beer. "What did you want to talk to me about?" she asked as she handed him the bottle. His fingers touched and lingered on hers before she slipped them away, her skin tingling from the small encounter.

"I fucking hate the asshole Mika's living with. I don't trust him. There's something about him that isn't right. Anyway, there's no way in fuck I'm letting Chenoa move in with him. I told Mika I want the sonofabitch gone, but I'm not sure she's strong enough to throw his ass out."

"What do you want me to do about it? I can't tell Mika who to live with."

"You sure as fuck are doing it with me." His soft features had grown hard and his eyes blazed.

"That's not fair. The orders were in place way before I came on board. I had nothing to do with them. I can see if the issue can be opened again. I can't promise you anything."

"I didn't come here to ask your permission or your fucking department's permission. I came here to tell you Chenoa isn't going back to her mother's as long as that fucker's living in the house. I don't ask permission for anything. Remember that." He fixed his gaze on her lips.

Desperate to change the subject, she grabbed her wine cooler and laughed. "Do you like berry-flavored wine coolers? I love them. I know they've got shit for alcohol, but they're very refreshing."

"I never had one. How does it taste?"

"Yummy. If I drink a six-pack, I'll get a slight buzz. You should taste one." His penetrating stare was making her nervous. She laughed and then took a big gulp, a few drops of the liquor clinging to her lips.

She went to wipe her mouth with her finger but he stopped her, his face a couple of inches from hers. "Let me do that." With the tip of his tongue, he lapped up the drops on her lips. "Very tasty," he said in a low voice. Her chest rose and fell rapidly as their gazes locked on one another's, their breaths ragged and uneven. "I have a problem, Ms. Quine. Maybe you can help me with it."

Is he fucking crazy? Talking about his problem when my body is on fire? He smells so good. "What is it?" She tried to focus on what he was saying instead of how each part of her body tingled with desire.

"I can't get you out of my mind."

"What?"

"I need to kiss you." He placed a small gentle kiss on her lips. Then her chin. Then her neck. She held her breath. "I need to touch you." He clasped his hand over her breast, his fingers expertly slipping inside her robe, scorching her skin. "I need to fuck you. Good and hard. Just the way I know you like it."

She let out her breath with a long moan, and he captured her lips and swallowed it.

Then they were thrusting their tongues in each other's mouths as her fingers wrapped around his long hair while his grabbed fistfuls of hers. Her body was buzzing like an electric wire ready to short-circuit.

"You're so fucking sexy, woman."

She pressed closer to him and helped him untie her robe. He cupped her breast and then pulled his mouth away from hers, running his tongue and lips over her jawline. "There are so many nasty things I want to do to you," he breathed against her neck as his finger lightly grazed her nipple. She threw her head back and let her body feel the wicked deliciousness of his digits tweaking and twisting her hardened bud. Each pull went straight to her pussy, which was growing wetter by the second.

"That feels real good," she murmured as he trailed kisses down her neck. He tugged at her robe, revealing her creamy shoulder. She yelped when he sank his teeth into her soft flesh, causing pain and pleasure as he bit and licked her simultaneously. When his mouth made its way to her hard beads, she cried out in pleasure when he sucked them into his mouth, his tongue swirling around them between nips with his teeth.

"I bet you're real wet, aren't you, baby?" he said against her skin as his fingers feathered over her skin, descending toward the throbbing between her legs.

Then her phone rang and all desire was swept away. *It's probably Nicholas.* She squirmed away from Steel and jumped up, clasping the tie around her robe as she dashed to her phone.

"Are you fucking serious?" he growled.

"I've gotta get this. It may be my brother. I've been trying to get a hold of him all day."

He slammed his back against the couch and kicked the two beer bottles on the table out of the way before he placed his feet on it.

She picked up the phone and her heart sank when she saw the call was from Lacey. Tears pricked at the corners of her eyes. *Why don't you call me, Nicholas? Damnit. I hate going through this.* Deciding she'd call Lacey back later that night, she let the call go to her voicemail. She placed the phone in her robe's pocket and sat down on one of the table chairs.

Steel craned his neck. "What the fuck are you doing over there?"

She wrung her hands in her lap. "It wasn't my brother. I'm worried about him, that's all."

"Come on over here and I'll make you forget about him." He winked at her as he patted the space next to him on the couch.

She shook her head. "We're attracted to each other. We lost our heads."

Steel stood up and walked to her. "I didn't lose shit. I knew exactly what I was doing, and you were fucking loving it. What's this high school bullshit?"

"You're my client's father. I also have your mother on my caseload. You being here is crossing the line, but what we were doing on the couch was way beyond that. I could get fired for this."

"I'm not gonna fucking tell. And what we were doing on the couch is totally natural. Which asshole screwed you up about men?"

"What do you mean? I'm not screwed up about men."

"So you think being a tease is normal? I know you want me, but you fucking turn me on, and then you bust my balls. Hell, woman. What's your goddamn deal?"

"I admit I'm attracted to you, but I already explained how I could lose my job. We need to act like adults and move on. Anyway, I don't want to get involved with anyone right now."

"Are you for fucking real? What the hell were we just doing before your damn phone rang? Baby, you're more than involved."

"I'm sorry. I know you're disappointed, but I just can't. I'm sorry I led you on."

He laughed wryly. "You don't have to be sorry. I'm not gonna beg you. I don't have to. I got plenty of pussy, more than I want. I just feel sorry for you. You're so fucked up that you don't even see it." He stormed over to the door. "No worries, Ms. Quine. I won't touch you again." He stepped out, but then turned around. "I'll send a prospect over to fix your door. Right now I can't fucking stand the sight of you." With that, he walked away.

Breanna ran over to the door ready to call him back, but she stopped and stared at his retreating back.

He roared his cams and sped off, leaving a trail of noise without a backward glance.

Heaviness engulfed her as she watched him disappear. He was right; she'd acted like a scared little fool. *Why do I lose all reason and decorum around him? Am I a cock tease?* She didn't think so. She was a scared little girl who didn't want to get her heart broken by a biker like her mother had. She wasn't her mother and he wasn't her father, she knew that, but the crack he made about having a bunch of women to screw reinforced her fear that all bikers wanted was easy sex.

Sighing, she closed her door the best she could, hoping the prospect would come fix it before it got dark. She went into the kitchen and took out another wine cooler. From the freezer she pulled out a box of macaroni and cheese and put it in the microwave. Ten minutes later she took her dinner and drink to the living room, switched to one of her favorite TV shows, and tried to ignore the creeping regret that wound its way around her body.

I should ask for a transfer from the rez to the Alina office.

But she knew she wouldn't. She couldn't. Steel was already in her blood, and she didn't have any idea what to do about it.

She wanted him, yet she didn't.

He's right. I'm fucked in the head.

She blew on her forkful of mac and cheese and stared at the TV.

Another night in paradise.

Chapter Eleven

NICHOLAS QUINE WAITED in the shadows by Centennial Park, his entire body tingling in anticipation of meeting with his dealer. He needed a fix so bad that he could almost feel it coursing through his veins, bringing him that high that he craved. He looked at his phone for the umpteenth time in the last fifteen minutes. The dealer was now thirty minutes late. A cold sweat broke out over him as the notion of not getting his fix pricked at the edges of his mind. He pushed it away; he didn't—couldn't—go there.

He looked at his missed calls and a sliver of guilt broke through his desperation. Sixteen missed calls from Breanna. He blew out a ragged breath. *Why can't she let me be?* He knew she meant well, and he appreciated that she was the only one in his fucked-up family who gave a damn about him, but this was *his* life, *his* choices. Even though she may not agree with those choices, he had the right to live his life the way he wanted to.

"Where the fuck is he?" he muttered under his breath. He knew he should at least text Breanna to let her know he was okay, but he couldn't even focus enough to do that. All he could think about was getting the drug. The craving was so strong that it was like life itself was dependent on getting and consuming heroin.

Then he heard the soft crunch of footsteps on gravel. His heart pounded, his eyes brightened, and his mouth went dry. He stepped from the shadows, a wide grin spreading over his face. "I didn't think you were going to show, bro." His insides exploded with joy; he'd get his fix. All was very good.

"You got the money?"

"Yeah… well, I don't have cash. I heard you're good with food stamps."

"How much do you have on your card?"

"A hundred bucks. That can buy me a couple of ounces, right?" Nicholas picked at the dry skin on his lips.

"With EBT cards, you get thirty cents on the dollar. So that'd be thirty bucks. That gets you a half gram for Mexican Mud."

"Fuck, I wanted an ounce. How much is that?"

"Forty bucks. If you can cough up ten bucks cash, you'll get your ounce." The man kept looking around as he spoke. "You got the extra cash? I don't have time to fuck around."

Nicholas shoved his hand in his jeans pocket and pulled out two five-dollar bills along with his EBT card. The dealer snatched them from him, switched on a penlight and examined the bills and the card, and then handed Nicholas a baggie. "Enjoy." He turned around and walked away, disappearing among the black maple trees.

Shoving the baggie in his pocket, Nicholas sprinted to his car parked in the alley and sped away to the abandoned warehouse on the outskirts of town. His synapses jumped like lightning strikes against the sky. When he arrived at the warehouse, he slipped in through a space in the boarded-up door. The random lighters looked like glowing eyes in the darkness. Trash was strewn on the concrete floors, and the walls were scrawled with graffiti. Nicholas made his way to a corner at the far end of a large room, leaned back against the crumbling wall, and took out his baggie.

As he prepared his drug, his phone rang and Breanna's name flashed on his screen. He turned off his phone, a tinge of guilt weaving through him. But the drug was too big a pull for him; it trumped everyone and everything. In a few seconds he'd be soaring and nothing would matter.

Nothing at all.

Life was good.

Chapter Twelve

THE FOLLOWING MORNING, Breanna kept looking out the window, expecting to see Steel and his Harley come by, but it was quiet. Several times she went to call him, but she pulled back. It was better that they didn't have any contact with each other. She'd secured his number from his mother in case she had to get a hold of him in regard to her or Chenoa, but she also liked having it. As crazy as that was, it made her feel connected to him.

The landline on her desk rang and she picked up. It was her supervisor returning her call. She'd phoned her late the night before and left a message saying that she thought it would be in the best interests of Chenoa if she could spend more time with her father, possibly live with him. She didn't expect that the department would go along with it, and was pleasantly surprised when her boss agreed that it may benefit Chenoa to have more access to her father.

"You'll have to interview him and find out where he's staying. The department doesn't want her living or spending extended periods of time at her father's motorcycle clubhouse," the supervisor said.

"I'm sure Mr. McVickers would move away from the clubhouse if he had to. He definitely wants his daughter with him. He'll do anything it takes."

"Let's start with the interview. Then you can put your report together and present it to the panel. We'll reevaluate the situation at that point."

The minute Breanna hung up the phone, she took out her cell and, with trembling fingers, dialed his number. Her pulse quickened with each subsequent ring.

"Yeah?" His deep voice made her skin tingle.

"Mr. McVickers?" she said in a firm voice. She was proud that she could hide the way her body responded to him. Even his voice had her shaking all over.

"It's you. I told you my name is Steel. Use it."

She gulped. *He's such a jerk. I have to keep remembering that.* "Whatever. I've decided to write a reevaluation report to the department recommending that Chenoa be allowed to have more interaction with you. I called my supervisor about it, and she's amenable to the reevaluation." A long pause ensued. "Did you hear me?"

"I heard you. What do you want, a medal?"

Her nervousness dissipated and a slow burn started deep within her. *What an asshole!* "Hardly. I need to ask you some questions and come see your clubhouse before I send in my report. It's a requirement."

"You wanna hang with me? I can go for that, baby. I'll just have to remember not to touch you, but after last night, that won't be too hard."

She gripped the phone tightly. "I'm doing this for Chenoa because I think it'll be good for her. I'm not doing this to 'hang with you.' Does later this afternoon at around four o'clock work for you?"

"Four it is. I'll text you the directions."

"I'll see you then. Thank you." She hung up before he could respond. He pissed her off so much. Just when she thought he was a decent guy, his true jerk came out. Her phone pinged and she opened the text to read the directions. She'd only been inside a biker clubhouse once, when she'd gone to look for her dad when she'd been sixteen years old. Her mother had passed out on the bed from taking too many pain pills and she'd called 911. Since she'd been a minor, she hadn't had any authority to make decisions for her mother's medical care.

When she'd entered the clubhouse, the stench of body odor, beer, stale smoke, and sex had washed over her. It'd been so dark inside that she hadn't been able to see much until her eyes had grown accustomed to the dim lighting. Several men checked her out, hunger brimming in their gazes. Barely clothed women were performing various sex acts with several men. She'd been ready to turn around and hightail it out of there when she'd spotted her father sitting on a chair. His pants were down and a woman knelt in front of him, sucking his dick. Her face must have been a mask of horror because a few of the men had guffawed, which made her dad turn toward her. He'd seemed pissed to see her, even when she'd told him that he had to come to the hospital. That moment had marked the beginning of her hatred for him.

And in less than two hours, I'll be entering another biker clubhouse, but this time I'm prepared. I know what goes on behind the darkened windows. She was pretty sure Steel would act like a jerk and try to embarrass or shock her. *No chance in hell. Dad already broke me into the biker lifestyle.*

She pulled out some files and began updating them, wanting to catch up on her backload as much as she could before she met with him.

Later that afternoon, as she turned down the barely visible road, she wondered if this was a good idea. She knew the department would ask if she'd been to the clubhouse to assess it, so she did have to go, but the flutter in her stomach told her she *wanted* to go. As crazy as it sounded, she wanted to see him again. She'd even spent twenty minutes before she'd left fixing her makeup and hair.

Don't get caught up in his masculinity. Stay focused. You've got a job to do.

The clubhouse, a white stucco two-story building, loomed in front of her. She stopped at the metal barricade, and a man of barely twenty years old motioned for her to roll down her window.

"Why're you here?" the tattooed man asked.

"I'm here to see Steel. My name is Breanna Quine."

He looked at his clipboard. "Hang on." He picked up his phone and dialed. "Yo, a Breanna Quine is here to see you…. Okay, sir." He pushed a button and the gate slowly opened. "Go on in."

"Thank you," she said to his retreating back.

Breanna parked her car and walked to the front door, taking a breath before she opened it and walked in. A few men sat at the bar, some played pool, and a few were on the couch watching car racing on a big-screen TV. Several of them glanced her way, their eyes roving up and down her body. Before she felt any real discomfort Steel came into the room, his gaze locking on hers. His lips twitched into a small smile. She waved and walked toward him.

When they met in the middle of the room, his gaze boldly traveled up her body, but instead of feeling indignant, she was flattered that he found her attractive and desirable. She threw her shoulders back, making her breasts strain against her sleeveless knit top. Jerking his head back slightly, he snorted. "Follow me." He turned around and strode out of the room.

She trailed behind him until he stopped in front of a door. Opening it, he looked over his shoulder. "We can talk in my office." He stood aside and she brushed past him, preparing to sit in one of the chairs in front of the desk. "Over here," he said.

She whirled around and saw him seated on a couch. "I'd prefer to sit here," she replied, holding the back of the chair.

"I wouldn't. Get over here." His tone left no room for argument. Grudgingly she went over to the couch, sitting on the far end. "That's a good girl." He gave her a cocky grin, and she bit the inside of her cheek. "Now what can I do for you?"

She began by asking him basic questions, like how often he was at the clubhouse and the workings of the club. Of course he was evasive about the club's business, but she'd known that would be the case.

"If the department wanted you to have a home away from the club, would you get one?" she asked as she jotted down some notes.

"If it meant I could have Chenoa with me, fuck yeah."

"Do you have a girlfriend?" *Whoa. Where the hell did that come from?*

He stretched his long legs out. "Does the county wanna know, or do you?"

Crimson colored her cheeks. "The county," she lied.

"I got a lot of women, but no one special… at least not yet."

"How long have you and Mika been divorced?" *The department doesn't give a shit about that either. I'm so out of line.*

"We were never married. Did she tell you we were?"

"She led me to believe you'd been."

"Nah. I was sixteen when she got knocked up. I dropped outta school to work on a ranch full time to provide for her and Chenoa. We were planning to get married when she turned eighteen. I got my GED and the rancher promoted me to supervisor. I thought I had the bull by the horns."

"And you didn't?"

"I've learned when you have that feeling it means something's gonna go to shit. I went over to her house one day and found her and my best friend fucking up a storm. I beat the shit out of him and walked away from her, but never from Chenoa."

"That must've been awful." She uncrossed her legs.

He shrugged. "It was a long time ago."

"How did you end up in the Night Rebels?"

"I started the club about twelve years ago. I left Alina and went to Pinewood Springs, where I joined up with the Insurgents MC. I'd still be there if my mom hadn't gotten sick. I left to take care of her, but I missed the brotherhood a lot. I called up Banger—he's the president of the Insurgents—and told him that I'd like to start an MC in Alina. And here we are. We're affiliates with the Insurgents."

"And no doubt you've given yourself to the *brotherhood* wholeheart-edly." Her words came out harsher than she'd intended.

He stared fixedly at her. "Did a biker fuck you over?"

"What?"

"You've had an attitude toward me since we met at the hospital that first night. Lady, you don't like bikers. Did you date one and he preferred his Harley over you?"

Her face reddened as she crossed her arms over her chest. "First off, my name is Breanna not 'lady.' And no, I didn't date a biker. My father was one and he chose the MC, his Harley, booze, and women over his wife and four kids." Satisfaction spread through her when she saw his face fall slightly.

He whistled softy. "Fuck…. It must've been tough growing up like that."

"You think? Anyway, it's in the past, but I do have a bad taste in my mouth when it comes to bikers."

"I get it, but not all bikers are jerks like your dad. I'm a biker and I'm dying to have my daughter in my life full-time. There're a lot of lousy dads and they're not all bikers. I know. Don't squeeze all of us out because of your old man."

"We're way off topic here. I've said too much. This interview isn't about me."

"You scared to talk about yourself? Why the fuck do you keep hiding behind your cool exterior? The way you kissed and responded to me last night told me what I already knew—you've got a raging fire inside you, babe."

"That's inappropriate." She ignored him when he sneered and shook his head, glancing down at her clipboard instead. "Chenoa's doing well so far. I hope she can stay clean. I know how hard this has been on you and Mika."

"You're just Chenoa's caseworker. You don't know shit, *Breanna*. You have no clue how we feel about our daughter's addiction, so don't play the fake empathy card with me. It's really beneath you."

Her nostrils flared as a poker of white-hot fire prodded her insides. "I know *exactly* how it feels to have someone you adore hooked on drugs. I know how it feels to have your heart shatter every time your loved one walks out your door, wondering whether or not you'll get that dreaded call that he ODed. What the fuck do you know about me? My brother is an addict. I raised him, but I was a poor substitute for a mother or father. While my parents were having their selfish crisis, we were all falling apart. So don't you fucking tell me I don't know what it feels like." Her voice cracked and she turned away quickly. She didn't want him to see the tears in her eyes.

Get a grip. Take deep breaths. Slowly. Again.

Then she felt his strong arms around her and she jerked her head up.

His face was inches away from hers, his hot breath washing over her. His stare pierced right through her like a sword. Before she could pull away, his lips crushed against hers, moving, tasting, kissing her with such passion that she almost burst into tears.

"I'm sorry you have a brother who makes you worry. Let's stop fighting each other," he whispered against her lips.

Being in his arms made her feel so safe and protected, like nothing bad could happen to her. She threw her arms around his neck and kissed him hard, messy, and passionately. He drew her closer, his kisses searing her lips, the heat of his body pressing against her. His fingers caressed her curves and landed on her rounded ass. "Fuck," he said against her lips.

The reality of the situation hit her and she pulled back. "How do we always get into this position?" she said as she smoothed down her hair.

"Because we're attracted to each other, but you keep fighting it."

"I know I do. It's just that I can't get involved. I'm so fucking confused. I don't really know you, and it seems like you want us to start from the end and work backward. Then there's the whole ethical dilemma about me being your daughter's caseworker. And your mother is thrown into the mix, and then—"

He tugged her to him and stopped her from talking by pressing his lips on hers again. She moaned. He pulled away. "Just stop, okay? You want to do this right? Let's go out to dinner tomorrow night. I'll pick you up at seven."

"You're asking me out on a date?" All her consternations stopped, she was that surprised.

"Yeah. What? Haven't you ever been asked out before?"

She nodded. "Yes, of course. It's just that I didn't think bikers dated."

"What the fuck does that mean?"

"I thought all you guys do is screw and move on. Do you date often?"

He crossed his arms and leaned back. "Do you want to go? And to answer your question, no, I don't *date* often, but I want to date you. Is this something you're gonna talk my ear off about?"

She laughed and cupped her chin with her fingers. "I'd love to go out to dinner with you tomorrow night. It's just that I was taken aback by your question, that's all."

His hard features softened, his scowl melting away. "Good. I'll pick you up on my Harley at seven. I'm gonna start looking for a place to rent. You're a persuasive woman, so I'm pretty confident you can get the department to see your side of things."

"You know I'm doing this for Chenoa because I truly believe she would benefit greatly by spending a lot more time with you. Even though I like you, my focus will always be on what's best for her."

"As it should be." He placed his finger on her lips then trailed it down to the base of her throat. "So you like me now?"

She swallowed and met his gaze. "Yes. I do."

"That works out fine, Ms. Quine, because I like you too. A lot." Silence filled the space between them until a knock on the door broke through it. "Come in," he said, his gaze still locked on hers.

The door opened and a baritone voice said, "You busy? I got something I need to tell you."

He broke away from her. "We just finished. Hang for a few while I walk Ms. Quine out."

She rose to her feet and placed her pen in her purse. "No worries. I'm good. Go ahead and speak with your friend." She spun around and stared into the dark eyes of a tall, well-built man. *This club has some of the best-looking bikers I've ever seen.* She noticed the "Vice President" patch on his cut and his name—"Paco"—underneath it. She turned to Steel. "Thanks for answering my questions. I'll send over the report in the morning. Bye." She felt her cheeks warm as she passed by Paco's watchful gaze.

"I'll be seeing you," Steel said as she closed the door behind her.

In the parking lot, she glanced at his office window and saw him standing there, watching her. Warmth spread through her before she waved and slid into the car, her emotions still reeling from what had just happened. She couldn't believe he'd asked her on a date. *Like a normal man.* At that point, she realized that her view of bikers was screwed up because of her dad.

As she turned onto the main highway, she vowed that she'd give Steel a chance, pushing aside her prejudices. She was still a bit squeamish about him being her client's father, but she knew he was dedicated to Chenoa, and they were both working toward the best thing for her.

She turned on the radio and cranked it up when Bon Jovi's "Living on a Prayer" came on. Giddiness bubbled through her like champagne at a celebration. For the first time in a long time, she was happy and excited. And it was wonderful.

Chapter Thirteen

STEEL LEANED AGAINST the wall, his arms crossed over his chest as he watched his brothers shuffle into the meeting room. The club normally had church once a week, but if something pressing came up, he'd call an emergency one to flesh out the problem and try to come up with a solution. The topic for the day's church was the buy that Jigger had set up.

"My fuckin' 1200 Custom could outride your Roadster any damn day," Eagle said as he pulled out one of the chairs from the large table.

"Put your money where your fuckin' mouth is," Crow answered. "Let's test it out this Saturday on Old Trail Road."

"I've got five hundred bucks on Eagle's Custom," Cueball said as he tipped his chair against the wall.

"Three hundred on the Roadster," Sangre said, throwing three hundred-dollar bills on the table.

Soon all the brothers were in on the betting, and the two piles of bills were growing larger as the minutes lapsed. Steel looked on in amusement. He secretly thought Eagle's 1200 Custom could beat Crow's bike, but since he was the president, he decided not to join in the betting. The jovial ribbing turned into snide remarks, followed by shouting, and then the inevitable fistfights.

After a few brothers punched each other, Steel stepped in. "Take your fucking seats! We got shit to discuss. You wanna fight? Do it after church." He slammed the gavel on the wooden table. Some of the brothers grunted, wiped their noses, and stared daggers at one another, but they sat down, joining the other members. Steel nodded, then looked at Jigger who was nursing a bloody nose. "You got shit to report?"

He tipped his head back, pulling another tissue from his pocket and stuffing some of it up his right nostril. "Yeah. The first thing I wanna say is I'm fuckin' stoked that I'm not a teen anymore." The membership roared, clapped, and whistled. "And I'm never gonna throw another fuckin' bowling ball again." Again, laughs and retorts from the brothers.

"So you've proven you can do stand-up comedy if your ass gets thrown outta the club, which I'm aiming to do if you don't get to the goddamn point." Steel pushed the chair in front of him with his steel-toed boot. Paco snickered, along with a few other brothers.

Jigger stood up. "Sorry, Prez. I got the info for a couple of dudes selling smack in the area. I've set up the buy for next Thursday night. I figured it'd be better 'cause this cow town dies at about eight on weeknights."

"Did you find out the motherfucker's name?" Steel asked.

"Goes by something real original—Candyman."

The members busted up again, and Steel banged his gavel down a few times. "Figures. Do you have his phone number?"

Jigger nodded. "I set up the buy by using the number some fifteen-year-old gave me. Candyman uses a burner phone 'cause I called the number the next day and it was no longer in commission."

"This Candyman isn't the main source, but we'll bring him back here and 'persuade' him that, if he likes living, he best cooperate with us. Any volunteers?" All hands in the room shot up as the members yelled out and cursed the drug dealer. "You fucking animals," Steel joked as he picked Crow, Sangre, Diablo, Cueball, Skull, and Brutus to be part of the welcoming committee for the following Thursday night.

The rest of church was filled with reports from Sangre about the money coming into the club from its various businesses. Some discussion was had on securing contractors to repair the roof of the clubhouse, as well as other administrative issues. When Steel slammed the gavel down, announcing church was done, the men jumped up and made their way to the main room to have a drink.

Sangre leaned over and scooped up the bet money. "I better oversee this one," he said to Steel and Paco as he counted the bills and secured them with rubber bands. After he was done, he left to join the other brothers.

"How about a game of pool? I got three hundred bucks to lay down tonight," Paco said as he pushed in the chairs.

"Not tonight. Maybe tomorrow. I got somewhere I gotta be."

"You gonna see Chenoa again? I thought you spent most of the day with her."

Steel narrowed his eyes. "How the fuck is it any of your business where I'm going?"

Paco stopped sliding a chair and looked up. "What the hell's up with you? Since when are you so damn testy?"

"I just gotta get going." As he walked out the door, he turned sideways and pointed at a chair. "You pushed that one in a little crooked. Better fix it."

"Fuck you," Paco said as he went over to straighten the chair. Steel laughed and left the room.

An hour later he came into the main room and went up to the bar. The prospect set a shot of tequila in front of him. "Thanks, Rugger," Steel said as he brought the drink to his lips. Out of the corner of his eye he saw Paco racking up the balls on the pool table. He threw back the shot and jerked his chin at the prospect.

Outside, pomegranate pink emblazoned the sky as the sun started its descent over the craggy mountain peaks. The eastern sky was already darkening to obsidian as a few scattered stars poked through, shimmering brightly. Steel stretched his leather gloves over his hands and swung his leg over his Harley. He was just ready to switch on the engine when he heard footsteps approaching him. He looked over and saw Paco and Skull coming toward him.

Fuck!

"Hey, don't mean to keep you, but Skull and I have an ongoing argument we need you to settle," Paco said.

"What is it?"

"What year was the belt drive given to all Sportster models? I say it was 1992 and Skull—"

"You're fuckin' wrong, dude. It was 1991. I'd bet my Fat Boy on it." Skull scrubbed his face with his fist.

Steel adjusted himself on the seat of his bike. "Don't. It was 1993." He held up his hand as the two brothers started to argue. "I don't have time for this. Google it and see that I'm right. I gotta go."

Paco came up close to him and sniffed. "Fuck, you smell good." He wiggled his brows and Skull guffawed. "You seeing the pretty blonde who was cozy on your couch yesterday?"

Steel scowled. "Fuck off."

"He's seeing her," Skull said. "Question is, are you gonna fuck her?" He slapped his hand against Paco's arm and the two men laughed.

Steel's nostrils flared as he bared his teeth. The urge to jump off his bike and pummel Skull into a bloody pulp seized him. Their laughter died as they stared at him. "I was only joking, dude. I just thought she was some chick. Sorry," Skull muttered.

Breathing heavily, Steel willed his rage to simmer as he sat immobile on his Harley. Paco tugged at Skull's shirt. "Steel's gotta get going. Come on." He pulled his friend away, then stopped. "I've never seen you like this about a chick, so I didn't know. I just thought it was business as usual."

Steel shook his head. "She's just a chick, but I don't want anyone talking shit about her."

"Yeah. No worries. Have a good time." Paco walked back to the clubhouse with Skull on his heels. They looked back at him before they went inside.

Steel slammed his hand on the handlebars. *Fuck those assholes!* He switched on the ignition and sped away from the clubhouse. He didn't have a clue as to why he wanted to annihilate Skull for joking around about a chick. He would've done the same thing if the roles had been reversed, but he hated hearing Skull talk like Breanna was just a piece of ass. She was different from any woman he'd ever met. She intrigued and fascinated him, but she also exasperated and pissed the hell out of him, and she was always in his head.

He slowed down when he entered the town and made his way to her small house, parking his motorcycle on the street and striding up to the porch. He rang the bell and the door flew open. Breanna smiled broadly at him and opened the screen door, moving aside as he entered her home.

"I see the prospect did a good job of fixing your door," he said as he sat on the back of the couch.

She swatted his forearm lightly. "You're damn lucky he did."

He raised an eyebrow. "Oh yeah? And what were you gonna do if he didn't?"

"Make you come over and do it."

"Coming over here wouldn't be a chore for me, baby." He ran his gaze over her body, loving the way her tight jeans showed off her rounded curves and toned legs. Her crop top revealed enough skin to throw his dick in overdrive. A small sparkle from the top of her belly button hinted at hidden treasures further below. He sucked in his breath as he imagined what she would look like when he ripped her clothes from her tempting body.

"My face is up here," she said, breaking his pornographic reverie.

He slid his gaze upward and captured hers. "And it's a beautiful one. Your hair makes you look angelic, but I bet you got more devil in you than anything else."

She tilted her head back, her laughter sparkling like diamonds under a bright light. He gripped her arm and drew her to him, then planted a kiss on her throat. He loved the way it vibrated against his lips. He cupped her ass cheeks and squeezed them but she twisted away, her golden hair swaying with her. "You promised to behave."

He cocked his head to the side, a half smile tugging at his lips. "I didn't promise shit. Besides, there's no fucking way I could promise you that. You're too tempting." He licked his lips and chuckled when crimson painted her cheeks.

"Aren't we supposed to go out to dinner?" She turned away and picked up a small purse. "I'm starving, and before you turn that into something sexual, I mean for food—like enchiladas and burritos."

He laughed as he straightened up. "I did promise to feed you. Let's go." He walked outside and waited for her to lock the door, then grabbed her hand and walked down the sidewalk to his bike. "Your dad take you on Harley rides when you were a kid?"

"Yeah. I haven't been on one for a long time. I'd say it's been about fifteen years or so."

"It'll come back to you. Just make sure you hold me real tight and press yourself close."

A puzzled look crossed her face. "Is that to keep my balance better?"

He swung his leg over and sat on the leather seat. "Nah. It's for me to feel your tits against my back." He winked at her. "Get on." She climbed on, putting her feet on the footrest and then placing her hands lightly on his hips. "You're gonna have to hold on tighter. My custom is one helluva powerful machine. If you're not holding on, you're gonna find yourself on your cute ass." She rolled her eyes but didn't reposition her hands. "All right. You've been warned." He turned on the ignition and the iron horse roared to life.

When he pulled away from the curb, he heard Breanna yelp, then felt her arms wrap tightly around his waist. He could've told her that he warned her, but he let it go because he was enjoying how incredible she felt pressed into him. She was the only woman who'd ever been on his bike aside from Chenoa. He never thought he'd ask a woman to ride with him, but there was something about Breanna that made her the exception to his rules. The novelty both excited and angered him, but for that night, he'd decided to just go with it.

Jalisco's was located in the middle of the block on Main Street. With a brightly painted yellow exterior and large terracotta planters overflowing with pink, red, purple, and blue flowers by the entrance, the restaurant was a landmark in Alina. The interior was just as colorful, each wall painted a different shade of green and yellow. Acrylic paintings depicting village and landscape scenes from Jalisco, Mexico, adorned the walls. In the back, a patio with about fifteen wrought iron tables and chairs welcomed guests during the summer and autumn months. Strands of red, green, yellow, and orange chili pepper lights strung around the perimeter of the patio made the area festive.

Steel watched how her lips curved around the rim of her margarita glass, wishing like hell they were around his dick. The tip of her pink tongue licked the granules of salt off her bottom lip and he shifted in his chair.

"It's such a beautiful night," she said as she picked up a chip and dipped it in the salsa that sat in the middle of the table. "I'm glad it's not too hot. We lucked out." She smiled and her whole face lit up like a star on the darkest night. Without thinking, he reached out and rubbed his thumb under her lip. She pulled back slightly, her smile dissipating.

"Don't stop. I love the way you smile. It lights up your whole face, like a beam of sunshine."

She licked her lips and he followed her movement. "You're a very unique man. I can't quite figure you out."

"How's that?"

"You're president of an outlaw club. You're definitely a hothead." She put her hand up near his face as if to stop any comments by him. "You are and you know it. You wear a smirk on your handsome face most of the time, yet you say things that are so beautiful. Even romantic." She shook her head. "I just can't figure you out."

"You think I'm handsome?"

She burst out laughing. "You *know* you are. And it figures that's all you got out of what I said."

He leaned back and smirked on purpose. "I appreciate a pretty woman with a nice smile. I tend to relate things to nature due to my heritage. The Navajos have a deep relationship with nature—they respect and fear it at the same time. There's nothing I like doing more than taking off on my bike and getting lost in the solitude of a mountain peak or valley. It cleanses the soul."

She placed her hand on his and squeezed it. "You're an anomaly among bikers, and I mean that in a good way."

"And you're different from government workers I've dealt with in the past." He slipped his hand on top of hers, brought it to his mouth, and kissed it. "And that's fucking awesome."

A comfortable silence fell between them, broken only when the waitress came up with two steaming plates. "Tamale platter?" Her eyes darted between them. Steel jerked his chin at her and she set his dinner in front of him. She placed a smothered burrito in front of Breanna, checked if they wanted anything else, and rushed away.

"Are you going to share with me how you got the scar on your face?" Breanna asked as she cut into her burrito.

"Sure. I got in a knife fight about ten years ago. Sonofabitch was asking for it from the moment he walked into the bar. I was in Pueblo hanging with some buddies I used to go to high school with, and a couple of assholes started shit up with me. I was wearing my cut, and they kept asking me if I was a badass biker." He shrugged and took a drink of beer. "I showed them I was. Believe me, their scars look worse than mine."

"Did you get arrested?"

"Nah. The owner of the bar was a good friend of one of my buddies. He waited to see how things played out before he called the badges. By the time they got there, I was gone. When I got back here, I crashed at the rez and the medicine man fixed me up."

"What happened to the two guys?"

"I heard they ended up in the hospital."

"So you got in a fight because they challenged you?" She put her fork down.

He shook his head. "No, I cut them when they touched my colors. They're just lucky I didn't kill 'em. I would have, but my buddies stopped me." He scooped up the green chili with a chip, then plopped it in his mouth.

"Your colors? Refresh my memory. They're your logo, right?"

"They're more than a club's logo. They're the club's identity. It's the patch that full members wear, and it isn't earned easily. Someone disrespects your patch, they disrespect you and the whole brotherhood. In my world, respect will be given, or it will be taken. I know brothers who are serving time for killing someone who disrespected their patch. It's everything." He clenched his jaw. Just thinking about the fucking assholes who disregarded his colors made his blood boil. *Fucking morons!*

"I didn't mean to upset you. I guess I shouldn't have been so nosy." She placed her fork down and when he raised his eyes they met hers.

"I'm not upset. My world is pretty simple. We see things as black or white. A person gives respect, he gets it back, but if he doesn't he becomes just another victim." He pushed his empty plate away and leaned back, his gaze scanning her tight face. "Easy."

The corner of her mouth went up slightly, and then she began arranging the sugar in the ceramic holder. After she finished, she started organizing the various hot sauces by size.

Steel looked on in amusement. "They're just gonna get all mixed up again."

She glanced at him, her cheeks reddened as she pulled her hands toward her and then clasped them together. "I'm a compulsive organizer," she scoffed.

"You told me your old man was a biker. You shouldn't be surprised about what I just told you. It's our world."

"I know. I guess I didn't know all the particulars of it. I mean, I guessed about a lot of stuff, but I wasn't privy to the ins and outs of it. My dad was rarely home, and when he was, he was consumed with my mom. He basically ignored us. The only attention we got was either his threats or his leather belt against the back of our thighs. Nice man, huh?"

"Sounds like my old man. Fuck them. We survived in spite of them. You want another drink? You look like you could use one."

Her smile warmed him. He didn't want their night out to be clouded by fear, hate, and loathing.

"Are you trying to get me drunk so you can take advantage of me?"

The coy expression on her face made him go tight in his jeans. *What the fuck's wrong with me?* She had such an effect on him, more than any woman ever had. When he'd been with Mika, she'd been his first love—and he was sixteen with raging hormones. But in all the years since then, no woman touched him past his lust for that moment. The social worker sitting in front of him did crazy shit to him. He didn't know how she was doing it, but deep stirrings that he'd kept buried for years began to surface. What had been a delicious distraction was fast becoming an obsession.

"Well, are you?" Her voice brought him back.

"Am I what?"

"Trying to get me drunk?"

He chuckled. "I don't want you drunk, baby. I want you stone-cold sober when I run my hands over your curves and give you what we've both wanted for a while."

She picked up her margarita. "And that is?"

"A good hard fucking. One like you've never had."

"You're pretty confident about your sexual abilities, aren't you?"

"The only complaint I get is that the woman is too sore the next day from our fucking. Or sometimes their voices are gone from screaming so much."

She poked at his hand, giggling. "You're so full of yourself."

"I'm not bragging. I'm just telling it like it is. You need to find out for yourself."

"Maybe I will." She winked at him and his dick twitched. He wanted nothing more than to grab her, kiss her deeply, lay her down on top of the tiled table, throw her legs on his shoulders, and fuck her deep and hard.

Her phone rang and she leapt in her seat, then slipped her hand in her purse and took it out.

He saw her expression go from hopeful to disappointed in a matter of seconds. "Are you expecting someone to call you?" His tone was edgier than he meant for it to be, but he couldn't help but wonder if she was seeing someone.

"I am. My brother, actually. I haven't heard from him in a few days. I worry about him."

"He's the one using?" She nodded. He blew out a long breath. "That's fucking tough."

She wiped the corner of her eyes with her napkin. "It is."

The busser cleared their plates, and Steel ordered a *sopapilla* à la mode with two spoons. As they ate, they laughed and talked about everything from the biggest gossips in town to the economic state in the county.

When she slipped her arms around his waist on the ride back, it felt natural to Steel. It was like she belonged on the back of his Harley. He helped her off his bike when they got to her house, then walked her to the front porch, bent down, and gave her a soft kiss on the lips. Every nerve in his body burned; he had to hold himself back from slamming her to him and plunging his tongue deep down her throat while he rubbed his hard dick against her. He knew if he pushed it, she'd be pissed, so he forced himself to act like a gentleman even though all his instincts were in overdrive.

Breanna unlocked her door and then paused. He caught her blue orbs when she looked over her shoulder. "Do you want to come in for a beer?"

Fuck yeah! I'm in. "Sure. That'd be cool." He sauntered in, laying his jacket on one of chairs in the living room before he went over to the couch and sank down.

"This is just for a beer, you know that."

"Yep."

"Okay. I don't want you getting any wrong ideas." She headed out of the room.

"Don't have any." *I'll play the game, babe.* For some reason, women felt it was important to let him know that they weren't really thinking about fucking when that's exactly what they were doing. Besides the club girls who knew they were at the club to fuck whichever brother needed their womanly attentions, women were always telling him that they'd never done something like this before if it was a one-night stand, or that they just wanted to talk. Then twenty minutes into their "conversation," he had his tongue down their throats and his fingers in their wet pussies. He sniggered, thinking he'd give Breanna maybe twenty-five minutes before they were all nice and cozy.

"Here you go," she said as she handed him a beer.

He took a deep drink. "You've got a nice place here. I like what you've done to it. Do you own it?"

"No. I wish I did, but on my paltry salary, I'll be lucky if I can ever buy a place."

"Is that why you're moonlighting at Cuervos? Do you wanna save up for a house?"

"Not exactly. I need to pay off some debt, and I help out my family, especially my brother Nicholas."

"He doesn't have a job?"

She shrugged. "He told me he does. Who knows?" She turned toward him and tucked her feet under her. "If you get your own place, I'm pretty sure Chenoa will be able to stay with you. I haven't heard anything yet, but my supervisor seemed pretty hopeful. You really should lock that up. I can add an addendum to my report."

"I was gonna look for a place this weekend. I want Chenoa with me." She nodded. He patted the empty spot beside him. "Why the fuck are you so far from me? Come over here."

"Are you going to behave?" The way she looked at him from under half-lidded eyes drove him wild.

"Of course." He grinned. She moved closer to him and he put his arm around her. "That's better." Under his touch, he felt her relax and press into him. He twirled a couple strands of her soft hair around his finger, the delicate scent of apricot and powder curling around him. *I want her so fucking bad.*

She craned her neck and looked up at him; desire heated her gaze. He bent down and gently kissed the lips that had been tempting him all evening. She looped her arm around his neck, a soft moan escaping her. The sound of it flared his lust and he yanked her closer to him, then took her mouth in a deep, wet, claiming kiss.

He slid his hand over her shoulders and under her crop top, the feel of her soft skin playing havoc with his cock. As he stroked his hands over her tits, he pushed his hard dick against her thighs. She sank deeper into his hold and he kept kissing her, breathing in each of her tiny moans and whimpers. "You make my blood boil. I can't fucking get enough of you," he rasped between kisses.

"I feel the same. It's crazy but in a good way," she said softly, and just the sound of her voice, the vibration of her lips against his, brought out the brute in him. He pulled her onto his lap, positioning her cute ass on his raging hard-on, and tugged at the hem of her shirt. Her straining nipples had been enticing him long enough; he had to suck the hard beads. Now.

Then her landline rang and she stiffened under his hands before pulling away. "Sorry, but I have to get this." She sprinted to the phone in the other room.

What the fuck is up with her goddamn phone? I swear I'm gonna smash it.

He waited for several minutes for her to come back, but she didn't. He strained his ears, but he didn't hear her talking. Then he heard it— muted sobs that pierced his heart. He jumped from the couch and followed the sounds to a bedroom in the back of the house. The door was slightly ajar, and he slowly pushed it open. The room was dark, but he could see her sitting on the edge of the bed, slumped over.

"Breanna?" he whispered as he went over to her. "What's wrong? Did you get some bad news about your brother?" He sat next to her, the bed creaking under his weight. She shook her head. "Then what's going on?" He placed his arm around her and drew her to him. She laid her head against his chest as he gently held her. Her small shoulders rose and fell, and occasionally she wiped her cheeks and sniffled. He cupped her chin and tilted her head back, staring into her glistening eyes as he tenderly brushed the hair back from her face. "Do you want to tell me why're you so upset?" She shrugged and placed her head back on his chest. "Please?"

She cleared her throat and, in a nasally voice, said, "I'm terrified something's happened to my brother. He's never gone this long without calling me. I thought it was him on the phone because he's the only one who really calls me on the landline. But it wasn't. It wasn't...." She circled her arm around his waist and held him tightly.

He rubbed her back in a circular motion. "Shh… it's okay. If something bad happened to him, you would've heard by now. Alina's a small town. I can see if I can find anything out. I'll put some feelers out and see what they bring in."

She looked up, her gaze wide with hope. "Will you? I'd be so grateful if you could do that. I'm just beside myself."

He swept his lips against hers. "I'll see what I can do."

"Steel?"

"Yeah?"

"Can you stay the night with me? I don't mean like banging each other. I just want you to hold me. I don't want to be alone. I know that isn't what you want, and you may think I'm weird for asking, but can you stay with me?" She stretched out her arm and reached for the box of tissues on the nightstand. Steel picked up the box and handed it to her. She took a tissue and blew her nose.

He watched her as she dried her tears with several tissues. *Stay the night and not fuck?* He'd never done that before with a woman. All the women he'd been with always wanted to screw; if they didn't, they weren't in his bed. He'd found when he was angry, sad, or worried, fucking helped give him some relief. Could he spend the night with Breanna and not touch her except for his arms around her? Would his dick make it through the night?

Breanna rose to her feet. "I'm sorry. I shouldn't have asked you. We don't have that kind of relationship. Actually, we don't have a relation-ship. I just lost my head."

He grabbed her hand and gently tugged her back down on the bed. "I'll stay with you. It's cool." *I fucking hope so. Why the hell did I commit to this?* Maybe it was because he couldn't stand to see a woman cry. He never could. He figured it had to do with his mother, who'd weep over her disappointing life when she thought her children couldn't hear. Maybe it was because Breanna was wiggling her way into his heart—a thought that terrified and warmed him at the same time.

If the brothers find out about this, they'll never believe it. They'll also never let me live it down.

Later that night, he watched as she slipped into bed wearing a night-shirt. He'd taken everything but his jeans off; he didn't trust himself.

She rolled over to him. "Thank you," she whispered in the dark. Then she gave him a light kiss and curled up next to him. He wrapped his arm around her, tugging her close to him. She smacked her lips and put her arm around him, her breasts pillowed against his chest. Her breathing grew deeper and he knew she'd fallen asleep.

His dick hadn't settled down since she'd come into bed. *How the fuck am I gonna get through the whole night without touching her?* She smelled so good, and her soft body nestled next to his was more than any man could take.

He took deep breaths and focused on the vast expanse of the San Juan Valley. He had to calm his body down.

It's gonna be a long fucking night.

Chapter Fourteen

SLIVERS OF LIGHT peeped through the drawn blinds, casting thin golden stripes across the Berber carpet. Breanna sat up at the edge of the bed and reached for her phone, yawning while her sleep-bleary eyes struggled to focus. She glanced at her screen and saw she had a text. She hurriedly opened it, her heart pounding.

Nicholas: *Just touching base. Been super busy. I'm good. Call u tomorrow.*

She reread the text at least four times before sending her "K" reply. She padded over to the window, lifted one of the blind slats, and looked out. In the distance, the mountains were silhouettes against a mango sky. There was no drone of cars or machinery, only the chirping of birds as they scattered between the trees. A cool, delicate air kissed her skin as it floated in through the cracked window. The town had the subdued quiet of dawn.

She went to the bathroom and splashed cold water on her face, relief coursing through her. *At least he's alive.* She groaned softly when she saw her blotchy skin and swollen eyelids. She cleaned up a bit, brushed her tangled hair, and switched off the light.

As she approached the bed, she heard Steel's soft breathing. He looked peaceful as he slept, only his angry tattoos and the jagged scar hinting at a darker side to his life. She couldn't believe he'd stayed the night, holding her close until she'd fallen asleep. She'd expected to have awoken to an empty bed, figuring he'd slip away in the night once she'd conked out. But he didn't, and she cherished him for it.

Breanna quietly inched toward him, admiring the way the golden pink hues of dawn lit up his finely sculpted chest and arms. Without thinking, she traced her finger lightly over his biceps and then his torso as her stomach fluttered and a low throb began between her legs. *He's so good-looking.* She admired his thick, ebony hair as it fanned out around him, brushing his shoulders. Taking a strand between her fingers, she brought it to her nose, inhaling his earthy scent. She loved the way the wind, sunshine, and rain mingled with his leather scent. She leaned over him, her blonde tresses skimming his chest, and kissed his full lips gently. He didn't stir. Stroking his face, she kissed him again, and then lay down, covering herself with the sheet.

She closed her eyes and was drifting to sleep when the mattress bounced slightly. Right when she opened her blue orbs, Steel's face came into focus. Without saying a word, he pulled up and hovered over her, his hand on either side of her head. As he lowered his head, her lips parted in anticipation of the impending kiss. When his mouth covered hers, she dipped her tongue inside, the low rumble from his throat telling her he liked it.

They kissed deep and slow. The more their lips pressed together, the more her body quivered and shook until her insides turned to mush.

His mouth moved from hers and trailed to her neck and behind her ears. She moaned when he lavished a mixture of nips, licks, and kisses on one of her erogenous spots. While he ravished her ear, neck, and shoulder, his hand glided under her nightshirt, stroking the curve of her hips and the soft skin of her belly. She squirmed under his searing touch, and she ran her fingers over his tapered waist and down the corded muscles of his arms.

"You're so soft and beautiful," he murmured against her skin. His voice sent tiny tingles through her; it usually did. She didn't know what it was, but his deep, rough voice turned her way the hell on. His chest hovered scant inches from her and she arched her back more, trying desperately to press her tits against him, the desire to feel his heat against her skin overpowering. His wandering fingers found her breasts and cupped the underside of them while he nipped at the soft skin on her shoulder.

As she lost herself in the scent of him, the feel of him, an electric jolt zapped through her, landing on her pulsing, damp pussy. He'd found another one of her most erogenous zones—her nipples. It was like there was a circuit from her buds to her mound, and his index finger and thumb were pinching, tweaking, and flicking her nipples to hardened, needy beads. It was exquisite, and a throaty moan fell from her lips.

"The sounds you make get to me," he whispered in her ear, tracing the tip of his tongue across the nape of her neck as his hand molded over the soft curve of her tits.

"What you're doing feels so good. It's driving me fucking crazy, but it feels amazing."

He chuckled and tugged her nightshirt over her head, then trailed his mouth to her reddened nipples. When he sucked one of the stiff buds in his mouth, the coil in her stomach wound tighter. She glided her hand down toward the ache between her legs, but he grabbed her hand and brought it up. "Not yet, baby. Just relax and enjoy the sensations."

"But I need to come. I don't think I can take it." The truth was it'd been a while since she'd been with a man, or had an orgasm. She was usually too damn tired when she came home from work, and if she wasn't tired, she was worrying about Nicholas.

"I'll let you come in time. Trust me. It'll be more powerful if you wait. You're gonna love it. Besides, your pretty pussy is for me alone."

She pushed up, arching her back, trying desperately to get some relief. If she could grind against his leg, she'd be good, but he moved away slightly, frustrating her efforts. He resumed his attention on her tits and she ran her fingers down his toned abs to the waistband of his jeans. She tried to open them but didn't have any luck. "Take your jeans off," she said in a low voice. "I want to feel your dick against me."

He unzipped and shoved down his jeans, kicking them off, his rock-hard cock poking at her. She reached down and curled her fingers over it, surprised at how thick and long it was. Her mouth watered as she imagined licking and sucking on it. "Do you want me to suck you?" she asked as her fingers slipped to his balls, stroking and cupping them gently.

He inhaled roughly through his teeth. "That feels good, woman. Fuck, you got a good touch. I'd love to have your lips wrapped around my cock, but if you do that, I'm gonna blow, so let's save that for another time. I want inside your pussy real bad." As he rolled her nipple between his fingers, her arousal escalated steadily. Then he glided his hand down her body. "Fuck, you're wet… right through your panties," he said as he stroked her clit through the cotton fabric.

She whimpered and rolled her hips, trying to hump his hand to get some relief. He laughed and slowly trailed his tongue down to where his hand was. With his teeth, he pulled down her panties, and then he circled his tongue around the soft flesh of her inner thighs as he spread her legs wider. Then when she thought she couldn't stand it anymore, he gave her aching pussy a long, slow lick, and her body exploded. He hadn't even gotten to her sweet spot, hadn't even put his fingers inside her wetness; he'd just given her one lick and that sent her over the edge. Her body bucked as she squeezed her eyes shut, moaning with each burst of pleasure. A small part of her was embarrassed that she'd come so fast, but most of her was riding the wave of rapture, wishing it would never stop. From the distance—it seemed like she was so far removed—she heard something tear open.

Her eyes flew open when her legs moved up, Steel's heated gaze pulling her in. He rested her ankles on his shoulders, then held his long, stiff cock in his hands and rubbed it over her clit. She noticed he'd put a condom on. "I loved watching you come. It was sexy as fuck," he said as he leaned over her and then kissed her deeply. "You ready for a hard, fast ride?"

She licked her lips and nodded. Her throat was so dry from all her moans and cries that she didn't think she could say an intelligible word aloud.

He ran his fingers between her wet folds, flicking her sweet spot gently. The unwrapped coil in the depths of her stomach began to slowly wind. He kept rubbing her as he slowly pushed his dick inside her. Her walls immediately molded themselves around him. "You're so damn tight, baby. It feels fucking amazing."

Each time he leaned in further, she bent over even more until his thrusts were deep and powerful. He plunged into her hard and fast, and she watched him lose himself in his need, in her warm, wet pussy. Their gazes locked and he leaned down and brought his mouth to hers as he continued to push into her; his kisses melted her heart while his fucking melted her heated sex.

He pulled up and bent her further back, slamming into her as she yanked his hair, both of them losing themselves in passion. His cock found a spot inside her that felt awesome. As he hit it over and over, a rush of warmth and tingle spread through. The pressure intensified, along with a deep pleasurable sensation. A shivery bliss coated her; whatever he was doing felt intensely delicious. Then as he penetrated deeper, the pressure burst and all-out rapture flooded her as she relinquished all control to her body. She writhed her hips and cried out as her orgasm took her over the edge and beyond.

As her pussy contracted rhythmically around Steel's cock, he leaned down and kissed her tits. "I'm fucking coming!" Then a low growl came from deep in his throat as he plunged into her one last time before stiffening and lying still on top of her, his face buried in the crook of her neck.

She raked her fingers through his hair while her body slowly came down from one of the most intense orgasms she'd ever experienced in her life. She was completely depleted, doubting if she could get up and walk at that moment. It was the best sex she'd ever had.

"That was amazing," she said in a weak voice.

Steel raised his head and smiled at her, then kissed the side of her face. "You're amazing." He winked at her and rolled on his back, pulling her close to him, her back against his taut stomach. He placed his arm around her and she put her hands on top of it. Sated and spent, they fell asleep while daylight covered the town.

BREANNA PLACED A BLT sandwich in front of him and scurried back to the refrigerator to take out a beer. She handed it to him and sat in the chair opposite him.

"You're not eating?" he asked before he took a big bite.

"No. I'm more of a night eater." She sipped a tall glass of water with lime.

He washed down his sandwich with his beer. "Did you ever hear from your brother?"

She smiled. "Yeah. He texted me early this morning. Says he's okay. Thanks for asking." She placed her hand on his, a small frown forming when he slipped it away and stood up.

"I gotta check in at the clubhouse, then go see Chenoa. Thanks for the sandwich and the good time." He put on his leather jacket and pulled his hair back in a ponytail. She sat watching him, a hard knot forming in her stomach. "So I'll see you." He came over and pecked her on the cheek, then walked out of the kitchen.

She stood and followed him until he left her house, looking through the screen door, watching him climb on his Harley. The bike sprang to life and he jerked his chin at her before he took off, leaving a trail of noise. She stood at the screen long after he disappeared from her sight. Numbness filled her. Did they have the most incredible sex ever, or did she dream it?

He just walked out and left. Just like that. What a fucking asshole! I knew *I shouldn't have slept with him.*

Pissed at herself for weakening because he showed her some compassion the previous night, she stomped back to her bedroom and retrieved her briefcase. She had an appointment with one of her clients in less than thirty minutes.

On her way, she fumed about how stupid she'd been letting his gentlemanly act manipulate her. *He knew exactly what he was doing.* When he left he didn't tell her that he'd call, nor did he make any plans to see her again. *It was like I thought all along—just a good time and then on to the next woman. A typical biker.* She could've asked him if they'd get together again, but she'd rather eat glass than do that.

As she turned onto Santa Nella Road, she vowed to keep her interactions with Steel 100 percent professional, both with his daughter and mother and at Cuervos Bar. The one thing she refused to become was a sometimes fuck-toy. And she'd make sure she stuck to her guns no matter how badly her body wanted him. Having mind-blowing sex didn't help, but she was hardly ready to lose herself completely with a man who'd end up being like her dad.

No way. Mr. Thinks He's the Best Lover can just go fuck himself.

Grabbing her file from the briefcase in the passenger's seat, she opened the door and slammed it behind her, walking up the sidewalk to her client's porch. The bright sunlight stung her eyes and a low throb ached at the base of her neck. She felt a headache coming on. She rubbed the back of her neck, wishing she could go home and crawl back into bed. The day was already proving to be a long, annoying one.

As far as Breanna was concerned, five o'clock couldn't come soon enough. She packed up her files and walked out of her office. Most of her day was spent dropping in on clients, paperwork, and thinking about Steel. She couldn't help but whip her head in the direction of a motorcycle each time she heard one at the reservation. Her heart would race and she'd hold her breath in anticipation of seeing his corded legs hugging his black and chrome Harley. But none of the bikes proved to be his. She'd bet he hadn't thought of her once that day.

She'd planned on stopping by the rehab center after work, but she was so drained and out of sorts that she decided to call for an update on Chenoa's progress instead. She'd go see the teen the following day when she was more like herself.

When she arrived at home, she opened the kitchen door and walked in, immediately feeling like something was amiss in her home. She wasn't sure what it was, but the feeling washed over her and prodded her to check it out. When she went into the living room, she gasped as she saw the ransacked area. Chairs were overturned, papers strewn about, a few items knocked off her bookcases. She darted her eyes all around and a sinking feeling filled her. *Nicholas did this.* At first she was mortified that he'd be the first one to come to her mind, but as she noticed her iPad, TV, and various other electronic devices were gone, anger slinked up her spine. Over the years, she'd worked with so many drug addicts that she knew the drug superseded everything and everyone.

She sighed and slumped on one of the straight-backed chairs. Deciding not to call the police, she plugged in the number of a locksmith she'd used before, making arrangements for him to come by later that night. Rekeying all the locks would cost most of her tip money she'd made the weekend before. She thought she was finally making some strides in her debt, but she could never really get ahead in this life.

She put her phone down, propped her elbows on the table, buried her face in her hands, and sobbed.

Chapter Fifteen

"**Y**OU GONNA BE at Lust tomorrow night?" Sangre asked.

Steel looked up from the invoice Sangre had brought in from the ink shop. "No. I'm gonna be at Cuervos."

"Again? Are you down some people, or does that blonde waitress got you by the balls?" Steel scowled and pinned Sangre with a hard look. "I'm just fuckin' around. You gotta admit you've gone over there more in the past few weeks than you have all year."

"Jorge needs help manning the bar. His relief is a fuckup." He glanced back down to the invoice.

"Maybe Goldie, Muerto, Crow, and I will come by later to have a few beers and see what other chicks are out there. It gets kinda boring having the same club girls and hang-arounds week after week."

"Sure, come on by. I'll buy you guys a beer." He swiveled his chair to face his computer screen. All the brothers knew that was his way of telling them the conversation was over, so Sangre walked out of the room. Steel stared at the screen, thinking he should call Breanna. He blew out a breath and leaned far back in his office chair. He'd acted like a jerk when he left her house the previous morning. He'd spent one of the best nights with a woman, and he had to act like an asshole. And the worst part was that he didn't have a clue why he'd behaved that way.

Steel rose to his feet and went over to the window, pulling up the blinds to stare out at the San Juan Mountains. Breanna stirred up emotions in him that he didn't want to acknowledge. He'd been hard with lust for her for a while, and he figured he'd screw her a few times to get her out of his system, then move on. When they were at the Mexican restaurant, he'd enjoyed spending time with her, conversing with her, being with her, so much so that it'd surprised the hell out of him. The women he hooked up with were there for some sexual fun and nothing more, but Breanna was different. When she'd invited him into her home for a beer, he'd figured he was going to get lucky, and he would have if she hadn't been so upset about her brother. But what blew his mind was that he willingly spent the night just holding her. When he felt her kiss him early that morning, his dick responded right away.

He scrubbed his face. The sex between them was incredible, but the connection he'd felt with her was what blew his mind. He'd never felt connected to a woman beyond sex in the way he did with Breanna. Even his time with Mika was more about raging hormones than anything else. *What the fuck am I gonna do?* He really couldn't take on Breanna. He wasn't ready to give his life to a woman, let alone his heart. He'd have to keep his distance. *Then why the fuck am I going to Cuervos tomorrow night?*

She'd surprised him by not calling or pretending to bump into him at the rehab center. So many women played that game with him to try and get him to go out with them again. It never worked, but he knew if Breanna had done it, it would've. She had a pull on him.

"You busy?" a deep voice said behind him.

Steel turned around and jerked his chin at Diablo. "No, just thinking 'bout shit. What's up?"

"I got everything arranged for tonight with Jigger and the dealer. Things are gonna go down at nine o'clock."

"Yeah, that's what Jigger told me and Paco. When we find out who the source for the drugs is, I'm gonna kill the sonofabitch."

Diablo's chuckle was low and deep. "Let's see what the dude knows. Lots of times the ones peddling on the streets are just pawns and don't get shit from the big ones on the top. My little brother was doing that shit in Salt Lake City. He was so desperate to keep his habit going, he'd do anything. The big guys knew it and they used the fuck out of him until he got so lost in his addiction, they left him to rot on the streets." His face darkened and his fists clenched.

"I didn't know, dude. Sorry for your loss. That fucking sucks." Steel suppressed his surprise at Diablo's sudden revelation. He was glad for it, since it meant that he was becoming more comfortable with the brotherhood. Diablo was a man of few words, and Steel didn't even know he had any family members.

Diablo nodded. "I just came in here to let you know we'll be ready to go."

"Appreciate it." Steel walked back to his desk and sat down. He watched Diablo leave, shutting the door behind him.

Pulling out a ledger, Steel took out a stack of bills. He had a shitload of paperwork to do before they headed over to the drug buy that night. He'd wasted enough time staring out the window and thinking about *her* like a damn pussy. He fired up his computer and began going through the invoices as the time ticked slowly by.

THE FAINT EVENING glow dwindled as darkness consumed the town. A dim light oozed from a malfunctioning streetlight into the alley. In the half light, Jigger appeared smaller than he was as he leaned against a graffitied brick wall smoking a cigarette. Steel, Diablo, Crow, Goldie, and Muerto distanced themselves in the shadows of the alley. The pungent smell of trash wafted on a light breeze as the din of metal garbage lids echoed down the alley while raccoons and possums foraged for food.

Steel heard the crunch of footsteps approaching. From the way Jigger tossed down his cigarette and stubbed it with his boot, he knew he'd heard it as well. Jigger shoved his hand in his oversized jeans pockets and walked toward the footsteps. A tall shadow appeared and Jigger stopped. From his position, Steel could see the man hold out his hand and clench it when Jigger placed the money in it. He moved over to the sputtering streetlight and counted it. Out from the shadows, Steel was surprised to see how young the dealer was; he looked to be about Chenoa's age. A sick feeling soured his stomach; he didn't like torturing teens to get the information he needed. He would, of course, but it didn't mean he'd like it.

"Uh... you're short," the young dealer said as he looked around nervously.

"You told me forty bucks. I gave it to you. What kind of shit are you trying to pull?" Jigger asked as he took a step forward.

Easy, brother. Go with it. Don't blow this. Steel's body stiffened as he listened to the exchange between the dealer and his brother.

"It's not me, dude. The price has gone up by ten dollars. You got it?"

"That's fucked. I don't have it."

The dealer shoved the forty dollars he had in his hands into his pants. "You got a food stamp card?"

Steel's ears pricked up. *Food stamp card? What the fuck?*

"I don't have food stamps," Jigger said tightly.

"Stay cool, dude. Do you know anyone who has the card? I can pay you thirty cents on the dollar so you'd be able to get some cash."

"I guess I could steal one." Jigger looked around. From the perplexed expression on his face, Steel knew that he didn't know what to do with this turn of events.

"You know, I'll give this to you for the amount I told you. But so you know, the EBT cards are gold."

"EBT?" Jigger crossed his arms.

"Food stamp benefits. Anyway, you got the cards, you can get cash, drugs, alcohol, even a pretty good-looking hooker." The tall man sniggered.

"Okay. I'll remember that. Where's my stuff?"

The lanky teen pulled out a cellophane packet. "Mexican Mud. The best shit you'll get in the county." He handed it to Jigger. "It was good doing business with you. Call me if you need me." As the dealer turned around, the waiting brothers stepped out from the shadows. Panic spread across the young man's face. He looked at Jigger. "What the fuck is this? You a cop?"

"You're gonna wish we were," Muerto said as he seized the guy's arm. The dealer struggled and pulled in a vain attempt to break free. "You keep fighting me, it's gonna get worse."

"Gag the fucker and bring him to the cell." Steel turned away and held his hand out to Jigger. "Give me the shit. I wanna see what's got a fucking hold on my daughter." He stared at the cellophane packet holding the small black rock that looked like a piece of coal. This shit was what seduced Chenoa and almost killed her. He shook his head and shoved it in his pocket. "Let's get the fuck outta here."

The cell was a place in the clubhouse to bring people who needed to be persuaded to tell the Night Rebels information, or needed to be taught respect, or simply needed to be eliminated. It was in the far left corner of the basement and had a reinforced steel door, soundproof walls, no windows, and various tools for implementing the club's desired effects. Knives of various sizes lined the back wall; metal bats, pliers, and wrenches hung from hooks on the side wall; and gallon jugs of chemicals, cleaning products, and disinfectants were neatly lined up on a large steel table. Steel beams suspended from the ceiling had pulleys and hooks in them. Metal folding chairs were stacked against the front wall. A curled-up hose and concrete floors made for an easy cleanup.

By the time the Night Rebels arrived back at the clubhouse, they had bound and gagged the sniveling dealer. Dragging him down the stairs by his shirt, the young man groaned and grunted until he was thrown on the cold floor in the cell. As Steel stared at him, the man's eyes grew wild with fear. Steel gestured for Diablo to sit the dealer on a chair. Diablo unfolded the metal chair, pulled the man up by his shirt, and slammed him down. The young guy bowed his head.

"Ungag him," Steel said, and Diablo complied.

"I didn't do anything. Please. I swear. It's just a crappy fuckin' job. I don't even get paid that much."

Steel went over to him as he was babbling and backhanded him across the face. Blood spurted from the man's nose. "Shut the fuck up! You fucking sold smack in our territory, and you're trying to tell us you didn't do anything? You're a piece of shit."

The man's eyes widened as blood dripped down his chin onto his white T-shirt. "I didn't know it was your territory. They didn't tell me. I'm sorry. I don't even know who you are. I'll go to another area and sell. You can have your territory back."

"I thought I told you to shut the fuck up," Steel said. "The whole county is our territory, and we don't allow that shit you're selling on our turf." The young man looked confused. "Who gives you the shit to sell?"

"I get it from a distributor. He goes by the name 'Candyman.' I've never met him. It's usually mailed to me, or I pick it up at different locations. I have to pay the money first. I pay it through the Internet using bitcoins. Can I have a tissue?"

Diablo went close to the man and yelled, "No you fuckin' can't!" He boxed his ears and the dealer cried out.

"Where does Candyman get the Mexican Mud?" Steel leaned against the metal table.

"I don't know. I'm just a small-time hood. I deal to support my own habit." He hung his head down.

"Why the fuck did you want the food stamp cards?"

"Candyman said they bring good money 'cause we buy them cheap and resell them at a marked-up price. I preferred cash, but sometimes people don't have it, especially the ones who live on the reservation."

Crimson filled the space between Steel and the young man. He kicked over the chair, throwing the man on the ground. The dealer moaned and looked up at Steel's blazing eyes. *This fucking dirtbag probably sold smack to Chenoa. I wanna kill him.* The young man started to open his mouth but then closed it and kept his gaze locked with Steel's. "You deal at the rez?" Steel asked through gritted teeth.

"Sometimes," the man answered tentatively. "Mostly just on the streets."

"How old are you?"

"Just turned eighteen last week."

"Happy fucking belated birthday," Muerto said as he kicked him in the stomach. The man groaned and curled over.

Steel watched the young man who was bleeding, bruised, and squirming in pain. *This fucker isn't the ringleader. He's a goddamn addict who's supporting his fucking habit, but he knows more than he's saying.* "What's your name?"

"Jason," he said as he winced. "I think my ribs are broken."

"Why the fuck do you think we care about that?" Muerto said as he gave the man another kick. Diablo, Goldie, Crow, and Steel laughed. Muerto spun around. "This fucker's been too pampered. We need to toughen him up a bit."

Steel pushed away from the table and knelt down beside the whimpering man. "I'm not buying your story, Jason. And when I think someone's lying to me, it pisses me and my brothers off to no end. So we can play this a couple of ways. You can either tell it to us straight and live, or keep bullshitting us and after a painful couple of days, we'll spread your ashes over the dump. The choice is yours. We got a lot of time. Think about it. I'll be back, and then you can give me your decision." Steel stood up. "Get his ass back on the chair. See if you can give him a taste of what's gonna happen if he chooses noncooperation." As Steel opened the heavy door, he heard Jason cry out in pain when Muerto and Goldie sat him down.

Outside, the moon hung full beneath an eclipse of blazing stars in the black sky above him. He breathed in the fresh air, then slipped his hand inside his cut and took out a joint from a small pocket. Cupping the flame with his hand, he lit the joint and inhaled deeply. Looking up, the brilliant specks carpeting the velvety blackness winked at him.

He wished the lanky kid would give up everything he knew. Steel had no problem killing someone who hurt or threatened the brotherhood, who disrespected his patch, or who betrayed him or his brothers, but he wasn't enjoying offing an eighteen-year-old addict.

Fuck! I gotta find out who's supplying the shit. I gotta stop this. Now.

"He's ready to talk, Prez."

He hadn't even heard Goldie come out. Without saying a word, he stubbed out his joint and walked back into the clubhouse, descending the back stairs to see what Jason had to say. When he entered the cell, Jason sat slumped over, his hair matted in blood, his T-shirt soaked in dark red, and his arms covered in angry, red marks. Steel went over to him and pulled his head back. "Have you chosen to live or die?"

"Live," he said in a low voice.

"Good choice. Now let's do this again from the top."

Over the next thirty minutes, Jason revealed that he got the drugs from a couple of guys who worked for Candyman. The two guys had spiked blond hair, wore blue jeans, and usually wore leather jackets or vests, but he didn't know their names. He said that his pay was fifteen percent of the sale. Most of the money he earned went up his arm. Jason also revealed that he thought a biker gang was the supplier, but he wasn't sure. He'd heard some talk among the other dealers about that. He'd sworn that was all he knew.

Steel believed him. Jason was a low-rung dealer who wouldn't be privy to the internal workings of the network. "I'll tell you what, Jason. We're gonna put you on our payroll. And we pay better than fucking fifteen percent."

Jason's eyes widened. "You want me to work for you? What do you want me to do?"

Diablo kicked his chair. "First off, have some respect. You don't fuckin' talk to the prez until he asks you a goddamn question. You're not a fuckin' brother."

Steel chuckled. "You're gonna be the club's snitch. We need to find out who's dealing on our turf, and you're gonna help us do it." A flash of hope crossed Jason's eyes. "Yeah. You're gonna live, but it may only be for a short time if you double-cross us. Betrayal is not something we like, and the punishment is the betrayer pleading for death. You get my drift?" Jason bobbed his head up and down. "Good. You got anything you wanna say now?"

"Yeah. I don't know if you'll believe me or not, but I was planning to stop dealing 'cause it was getting harder to make enough money, and the food stamp card thing was starting to freak me out. I didn't want the feds breathing down my neck. I'll help you out."

"Doesn't seem like you got a choice," Crow said.

"He has a choice. It may not be a good one, but we always have a choice. Isn't that right, Jason?" Steel narrowed his eyes. The young man nodded. "Then we understand each other. Perfect." He turned to Crow and pointed. "See this guy? He's in charge of you. Don't fuck this up. You don't want to get on his bad side."

"No, you fuckin' don't," Crow said as he put his face a mere inch from Jason's.

"We're gonna untie you and you can wash up. It's best if you spend the night here. You got a problem with that?"

He rubbed his wrists as Crow cut the rope from his ankles. "I need a fix bad. I'll go through a shitty night if I don't get something."

"Life's fucking tough. You're going to have to man up to it. We'll make sure you have a bathroom at your disposal for tonight." Steel walked toward the door.

"Man, please. I can't handle the withdrawal. I need something. Anything." Jason's voice hitched.

"One more thing. The dudes with the spiked blond hair, did you notice any patches on the front or back of their leather jackets and vests?"

Jason paused, his eyes rolling up. "Uh... yeah, I remember. They had a real cool patch on the back of them. It was a big ass skull with a hammer crushing it. I was gonna ask them about it 'cause I wanted to get one, but they weren't the friendly type." He wiped the sweat rolling down his face. "I need something bad."

"Give him some joints to calm him."

Steel walked out the door, went up to the bar, and hit his fist against Paco's and Skull's. "We got a fucking snitch on the payroll."

"Yeah?" Paco asked.

Steel nodded. "I hope he doesn't fuck up. He's an addict, so there's a big chance he will." He threw back his tequila shot. "The motherfucking Skull Crushers are in on this. The kid described their patch. The kid picks up the drugs from them. He also thinks it's a biker club supplying the smack. I gotta call Hawk in the morning to see if he's heard anything. The Insurgents have access to more information than we do. The kid's barely eighteen. Fuck." He threw back another shot, intending to get good and drunk.

"The way I look at it, the Skull Crushers just signed their goddamn death warrant." Paco slammed his fist on the bar. Skull followed suit.

"Yep. That's the way I look at it too. We'll call an emergency church for tomorrow early afternoon. The way these fuckers are drinking tonight, I need their asses sober and their full attention. I'm gonna head upstairs. I'm beat." He clasped Paco's and Skull's shoulders, grabbed a bottle of tequila from the bar, and headed upstairs.

In the quiet of his room, he kicked off his boots and hung up his cut, then switched on the small lamp on his nightstand and killed the overhead lights. Turning on one of his favorite bands, Five Finger Death Punch, he settled into the chair, took a deep drink of tequila, and listened to "Bad Company."

He closed his eyes, Breanna's bright blue ones sparkling in his mind. A longing so intense filled him, and his chest cavity ached. He shook his head as if to dislodge her image from his mind.

And he did. Chenoa's dark eyes came into focus, but they weren't bright. They were dull, almost lifeless, and an icy fear wound around his spine. "Don't leave me, sunshine."

A thickness in his throat formed and he squeezed his eyes tighter, trying to make his mind go blank, to absorb the music, to not think.

He took another long drink and swallowed the lump in his throat, but his mind ricocheted between the sparkling blue orbs and the dark, dying ones.

He drank until he saw nothing but blackness.

Chapter Sixteen

BREANNA SLIPPED THROUGH the back door at Cuervos. The parking lot was already full for a Friday night. She'd made it a point to drive around the lot and the front and back of the bar before she parked and went inside. She'd been looking for Steel's motorcycle, telling herself that she hoped he wasn't there, and then dealing with the disappointment when she realized he wasn't. That's the way the past few days had gone with her, a back and forth of *I hope I never see him again* and *I wish he'd call.* Whenever she called the rehab center to get an update on Chenoa's progress, her heart always melted when the staff told her how much time Steel spent with his daughter. Dr. Turner, who ran the rehab facility through the hospital, told her it'd been a long time since he'd seen a father as devoted and determined to help his daughter.

A man who loves his daughter as much as he does can't be all bad, can he? And he's great with his mother. So why the fuck is he acting like a jerk with me?

She stuffed her tote into her locker and slammed it shut. Glancing in the mirror, she touched up her lip gloss and tried to pull down her skirt. She did it each time she wore the short spandex skirt, and each time it stayed exactly the same length.

I better get some good tips tonight to make this shit worth it.

"Hey, Breanna, how're you doing?" Jorge asked as he handed two patrons their drinks at the bar. "We're gonna be slammed all night. I hired another waitress the other day. Her name's Mindy. That should help you and Jill out."

"That'll be a big help." She smiled and walked into the crowd.

A couple of hours into her shift, Breanna had already made a little over a hundred dollars in tips. She knew the attention she gave the guys helped her get more than the standard 10 percent, so she flirted with them and made them feel special. She never crossed the line, and for the most part, the men were tame and respectful. If she had to bend down a little lower than normal when she set down or picked up the drinks from the table, then so be it. She needed the money, and standing on high heels for eight hours was sheer torture.

She approached a table of three businessmen dressed in jackets and ties. She hadn't seen them in the bar before, so she figured they weren't locals, probably staying at the small hotel down the street. Setting three coasters down, she smiled. "What can I get for you gentlemen?"

One of the men, who wore a navy jacket and khaki pants, grinned at her. "You're a pretty one. Do you have any specials?" The other two men gazed at her cleavage.

"We have killer nachos for four ninety-nine, wings in original and chipotle sauce, all mixed drinks are half price until ten, and we have ten beers on tap."

"What do you recommend?"

"The nachos are awesome, but I'm not a wing girl, and all the tap beers are excellent. The bar's known for it."

"What kind of girl are you?" the man sitting across the table asked. He looked to be in his thirties and sported a beard and stylish haircut.

"A hardworking one." She took their orders and squeezed through the crowd to hand them to Jorge.

He glanced at it and smiled. "The nachos are a big hit tonight."

"I keep pushing them." She laughed and placed the drinks Jorge had made for one of her other tables onto the round tray. When she picked up the heavy tray, both Jill and Jorge yelled out. She stopped in her tracks. "What's wrong?"

"Your wrist looks like it's ready to break," Jill said, her eyes filled with shock.

"The damn tray's too heavy," Jorge said as he leaned over and quickly took off some of the drinks. "Come back and get these. It's not worth hurting yourself."

"What? It's not that heavy."

"Doesn't your wrist hurt?" Jill asked as she absentmindedly rubbed hers.

Breanna looked at them and then started to laugh. "No, it's fine. I'm double-jointed in my wrists and hands. I've been like that since I was a kid, so I forget how weird it looks to other people. Don't worry about it. It's just the way I'm built." She grabbed the drinks Jorge took off and placed them back on the tray.

"You sure that's normal?" he asked.

"It is for me. Really, it's fine," she said to Jorge's and Jill's doubtful faces. "I'm good. See?" She lifted the tray and walked away laughing.

The businessmen consumed two orders of nachos, baskets of wings, and taquitos along with numerous glasses of beer. She figured she'd receive a big tip from their table. She'd learned that they were comptrollers from Kansas and they were in town overseeing the accounting operations of the Alina National Bank.

By the time she placed another round of beers in front of them, they were inebriated. As she turned to leave, one of the men grabbed her arm and pulled her toward him. "How about a little kiss from our favorite waitress?"

She smiled and tried to pull out of his grasp. "If I do that, I'll have to do it to all the guys."

"You can treat us special since we're out-of-towners."

"That wouldn't be fair, would it?" she said.

"It isn't fair that you've been teasing us all night, honey," the man in the navy jacket said.

"I haven't been. You nice gentlemen are just so easy to talk to." She pretended to go along with them as she tried to pull away, glancing at the man who still held her arm. "Why don't you let go of my arm. I have other customers I have to serve. I promise I'll be back." *If he doesn't let go of me, I'm going to slap him hard.*

"I will if you give me a kiss. Just a small one." He pointed to his cheek. "Right here."

Before she could answer, a low, feral voice said, "Get your fucking hand off her."

A slow shiver rode down her spine as butterflies exploded in her stomach.

The man's eyes grew wide as he dropped his hand down to his lap.

"Don't fucking touch her or any of the waitresses again, or I'll not so nicely throw your ass outta here."

She glanced at Steel, surprised at the fierceness in his eyes. He clasped her hand in his and pulled her away from the table, dragging her past the bar and down the hallway to one of the closed doors. He pushed it open and shoved her inside.

The room was smaller than the storage room, resembling an office. There was a large mahogany desk, a black leather couch, several chairs and lamps, and a small refrigerator. He shut the door behind him. "Sit down," he said.

"I have customers to wait on."

"I already told Jill and Mindy to handle them."

Her face flushed with anger, she placed her hands on her hips and glowered at him. "Do you think I'm doing this job because I'm bored? I need the money. If I don't take care of customers, I don't get the tips. It's pretty basic."

He trailed his gaze over her slowly, making no attempt to hide the fact that he was checking her out. "I would think you'd be thanking me for getting that fucker to take his hand off you. Or maybe you liked it."

Her nostrils flared and she narrowed her eyes. "How dare you say that to me. And I didn't ask for your help. I was handling it just fine until you came in with your badass act."

"Bullshit. I saw you struggling to break away from him. The fucker had no intention of letting you go. You weren't handling it."

"It's none of your business what I do."

"And the way you wear your top, you're practically handing your tits to the guys. You're giving off the wrong impression."

"I haven't asked for your opinion. And did you get a look at Mindy's blouse or Jill's crop top?"

"I don't give a fuck what they wear. They aren't you."

"You're exasperating. I don't have time to stand here and argue with you. I've got to get back to work." She marched to the door, but as she placed her hand on the knob, a strong arm snagged around her waist. She screamed and clawed at it with her nails. "Let me go, damnit!"

He pulled her roughly, almost violently, to him, and then he took her mouth with a savage intensity. Twisting in his arms and arching her body, she sought to get free. "Calm the fuck down!"

Being in his arms both aroused and infuriated her. "You can't just kiss me whenever you fucking want to. You act like you just came out of a goddamn cave," she gritted. "I didn't give you permission to touch or kiss me."

He let go of her, his expression clouded in anger. "Permission? Baby, I think we're beyond that, don't you?"

"Are we? I hardly think so. And here's a newsflash. Just because we had sex doesn't mean you can boss me around or grope me whenever you want. It was fun, but that's all it was."

All of a sudden, he stiffened at her words and stepped away from her. "I never planned on it being anything more. What I did out there was help out a waitress. I would've done the same thing if it were Jill or Mindy, so don't let it go to your head. Go on and serve your tables. We're done here." His voice dripped ice, each shard stabbing her heart.

She tossed her head and walked out, acting like his words hadn't just pained her. *I'd rather die than let him see how he's hurt me.* He was the worst kind of man, pretending he cared when all along he just wanted to fuck her.

For the rest of her shift she avoided Steel, which was surprisingly easy to do since he avoided her as well. His cool, aloof manner irked the hell out of her, but she pretended that it didn't. Out of the corner of her eye, she'd see women approaching him, flirting, laughing too loudly, and touching his arm, hair, or face, and a burning sensation filled her body from the core. Each time he drew his ear a little closer to a woman's lips or smiled too warmly, anger and hurt would pull at her. And when she thought about the memory of their night together, a dull ache pulsed between her legs. *Damnit! Why can't I just forget about him?* She had to conquer her involuntary reactions to his build, his smile, his laugh… to his everything.

"You need some help with that?" Jill's voice broke through her thoughts.

Breanna had a tray full of drinks on one hand and a pack of cocktail napkins under her arm. "I think I got it. Thanks, though." She scrambled away, happy to get lost in the crowd.

As the night began to wind down, she noticed a few nice-looking bikers wearing the same logos on their cuts as Steel. They were hanging by the bar, chatting with him, and drinking. A couple of them looked in her direction, and she noticed Steel stole a few glances at her. She thought she recognized one of the men as coming into the bar in the past, but she wasn't sure.

But she *was* sure that they were talking about her. He was probably bragging how he fucked her. She knew how bikers were. She remembered the times when her dad had some of his brothers over for a night of boozing, and they'd compete with stories of their conquests, even though her mother had been in the next room and could hear everything they said.

Steel's such a sonofabitch. I have to look for a new job. I can't do this anymore. This is too awkward.

Glancing at the time, her heart soared when she saw it was two o'clock. Jorge had announced it was last call for drinks a bit earlier, but she'd become absorbed in clearing off tables and wiping them down. She placed her tray on the bar and went to the back to her locker. When she took off her heels, she moaned aloud and sat down. Rubbing her aching soles felt like heaven. She heard footsteps clumping down the hall and something told her it was Steel. She slipped her flats on, slung her tote over her shoulder, closed her locker, and rushed out of the room.

When she opened the back door, she heard his deep voice behind her. "Breanna." She acted like she hadn't heard it and rushed to her car.

"Breanna, I know you can hear me. I wanna talk to you," he said.

She slid into her car, started the ignition, and drove out of the parking lot. Glancing in the rearview mirror, his stare pierced her. She looked straight ahead and breathed a sigh of relief as she drove farther away from the bar, and from him.

Chapter Seventeen

S TEEL SAT ON the edge of his bed the following morning. His head
was still reeling from the previous day's church. The membership
had voted to take out the Skull Crushers. The rival MC had been a pain
in the Night Rebels' side since the Crushers had loosely started their club
a few years before. They weren't a proper club in the true biker sense;
rather, they were a bunch of punks who hung out to do illegal activities.
They knew nothing about respect, the brotherhood, and the outlaw
world.

Steel had known the showdown would someday come between the
two. The beat-down that his club and the Insurgents had given the Skull
Crushers a couple of summers ago had quieted the rival club down for a
while, but they seemed to have forgotten that the Night Rebels meant
business.

At church, they'd decided to wait until they found out which MC
was supplying heroin to their county. Paco had pointed out that if the
Skull Crushers existed no more, the supplying MC would probably go
underground for a while. Steel mentioned that he wanted to talk to
Banger and Hawk from the Insurgents to get their take on the situation.

Steel grabbed a bottle of water he had placed on his nightstand before he crashed the night before. He guzzled it all down, crushed the
bottle, and threw it in the trash can across the room, then blew out a
steady breath.

He wanted to see Breanna again. He didn't buy the indifferent attitude she'd given him after they left the back room. He'd caught her
sneaking glances at him, and she didn't seem all that happy when
women came up to him. *Fuck. I don't want to care for this woman.* But he

did. He couldn't explain it, but she did something to him. There was something wonderfully irresistible about her and the unexpected attraction they shared.

He picked up his phone and tapped in her number. She answered on the fourth ring.

"What do you want?" she asked.

"I'm picking you up for dinner at seven. Be ready." A gasp from her made him smile.

"You have a lot of gall," she said.

"We've already established that a long time ago. So seven. I gotta go."

"Wait! I can't go. I have to work tonight."

"No worries. I'm the boss, remember?"

"I need the money," she said softly.

"You can take your comp day."

"I have comp days for part-time employment?"

"You do now, and it includes tips. Seven o'clock. See you." He hung up, a weight that had been heavy on his chest lifting. He jumped to his feet and went to the bathroom to take a shower.

He was actually going out on his second date with Breanna. That blew him away since he hadn't taken a woman out on a second date since high school. What surprised him even more was that he was looking forward to it. Deciding not to analyze what had come over him, he made up his mind to just go with it, unwrapping a bar of soap and stepping into the shower.

AT SEVEN O'CLOCK he knocked on her door, a small tinge of anger curling in his stomach when she didn't answer. He lifted his leg and set his foot on the planter on her porch. It had never occurred to him that she'd stand him up.

Did I misread her? What the fuck's wrong with me? He'd always been spot-on when it came to gauging women and their wants. After Mika had cheated on him and he'd left her, he made a point of reading women's body language, their facial expressions, the hidden meaning between their words. Even though they sparred a lot, there was an electric spark that sizzled between them, and he'd been positive Breanna had felt it.

He pressed his lips together and stood upright. *If she doesn't want it, then fuck her. I don't have time for this shit anyway.* He jumped down the stairs and was walking to his Harley when he heard her yell, "Steel!" He paused for a few seconds, then turned around slowly.

At that time of day, the sun had dipped lower to the west. Breanna stood on the porch, her white eyelet sundress bathed in honeyed tones from the sun's lessening rays. He sucked in his breath as he took her in: cascading golden hair, rose-colored lips, mesmerizing bright eyes. She clung to the stone pillar on her porch, her gaze locked on his. A warm, infectious smile spread over her face.

"You coming or what?" he said in a gruff voice, but his senses were alert and his jeans were tight as hell.

"Hang on a minute, will you? I got home late from work and I've been scrambling. Let me grab my sweater." She bounced back into the house, and all Steel could think about was peeling her sundress off her later that night. Coming back in sight, she slammed her door shut and then headed down the sidewalk.

All he wanted to do was run up to her, gather her into his arms, and kiss her deeply, but he stood still. When she got to him, he turned around and swung his leg over the bike. "Get on."

She snuggled in behind him. "I should've worn pants. I forgot how disastrous it is to wear a dress on a bike." She laughed, and the melodic sound of her voice squeezed his hardening dick.

He started his bike and screeched away from the curb, extremely aware of her body behind him. The way she circled her arms around him, her tits pressing against him, and her feminine aroma of vanilla and apricots ribboning around him just about sent him over the edge. He'd never tire of the feel and scent of her.

They rode past the businesses on Main Street, the neatly manicured lawns on Linda Vista Road, and the worn-down and crumbling homes in the seedier part of town. On either side of the road lay red-tinted sand, sagebrush, and the jagged peaks of the mountains in the distance. They turned down a small road, following it for a few more minutes until Steel stopped in front of a brightly colored pink house. The shutters on each side of the windows were a neon lime green, and the awning over the large porch was turquoise. Pots of cacti and wildflowers dotted the yard around the home, and copper symbols and animals covered in a green patina dangled from the eaves around the house. Two large German shepherds barked and ran toward the motorcycle.

Steel killed the ignition and got off the bike, then held his hand out and helped Breanna off. When the dogs came closer, she grabbed his arm and pressed closer to him. He chuckled. "No need to be afraid. These two are major softies." He bent down and petted each of them. "They're cool." Breanna reached out and did the same. "Come on." He rose to his feet, holding her hand as they walked to the front door.

"What is this place?" she asked.

"It's a Navajo restaurant." He laughed when he saw her jerk her head back. "Yeah, I know. It looks like a house. It actually is, but the owners live in the back. The front part is the restaurant. It only seats about twenty people, but the food is fucking good. I thought you'd like to try it since you work on the rez."

"I love it. This is a great idea." Her eyes sparkled and he leaned over and kissed her cheek.

"You're so beautiful," he whispered against her ear. Then he pulled back and opened the door for her.

Inside, a few tables were set up in the dining area. A woman in her fifties smiled widely when she saw Steel. White threads weaved through her black hair that was pulled back in a single braid hanging down her back. She wore a bright orange peasant blouse and a long yellow skirt. A chunky turquoise and silver necklace around her neck glimmered under the lights.

"Steel. *Yá'át'ééh*." She came over and hugged him.

"*Aoo' yá'át'ééh*," he replied. He reached behind him and grasped Breanna's hand, tugging her in front of him. "I want you to meet Breanna."

The woman looked her up and down before extending her hand. "Welcome. I'm Haseya." Steel noticed her gaze lingered on Breanna's hair.

Breanna shook her hand. "It's so nice to meet you."

Haseya nodded. "How's your mother?" she asked Steel.

"Better. How's business?"

"Very good. I'm so glad you and your... friend came in. Please, sit anywhere you like."

Steel put his hand on the small of Breanna's back and led her to a small table by the window. They sat down and Haseya brought over a beer, setting it in front of Steel. "What would you like?" she asked Breanna. She ordered an iced tea and the woman scurried off.

"This is so charming," Breanna said as she looked around. "Were you speaking Navajo with her when you came in?"

"Yeah. My mom taught it to us, and Mika and I have taught it to Chenoa. It's important to keep your heritage and traditions."

"I agree. I'm not sure what I'm comprised of. My parents didn't tell us too much about our background. I've heard Navajo spoken on the rez. It sounds like it'd be a hard language to learn. What did you say to each other?"

"Just 'hello' and 'how are you.' I guess Navajo would be hard to learn. A lot of the older people speak it, but the young ones, not so much. The food is really good. They usually have two dishes on the menu. The lamb stew is the staple dish, and it's fucking amazing. Lamb and mutton are a staple for Navajo food, along with corn and squash."

"I've only had fry bread, and I loved it."

"That's 'cause it's fucking good." He smiled and brought his beer bottle to his lips. He wanted to share his heritage with her. He was pleased that she liked where he'd chosen for dinner.

As they dined on lamb stew and fry bread, he told her about life on the reservation when he was a kid, and how being in the Night Rebels changed his life for the better. She shared how she wished her siblings would stop fucking up and own up to their lives, and how rewarding and heartbreaking it was being a social worker.

After their meal, Heseya put a plate of orange and pineapple slices in front of them. "I remember how much you like these," she said as set down two small plates. "Enjoy."

"*Ahéhee',*" he said as he speared a slice of pineapple and placed it on Breanna's plate. She bit into it, the juices running down her chin. He leaned over and wiped them away and then put his finger in his mouth and licked it. Her lips curled up into a small smile before she took another bite.

Leaning back in his chair, he crossed his arms as he watched her eat. He cleared his throat. "I've wanted to tell you that I didn't mean to hurt you when I left that morning. It had nothing to do with you. It's just that I didn't know what the fuck to make of it." He uncrossed his arms and ran his hand through his hair. "You're different from any other woman I've ever known."

Taking her napkin, she wiped her mouth then pushed her dish away. "After you left that morning, I was confused, and I suppose hurt too. I figured you were a typical asshole biker. It brought up memories of my dad, and they weren't the good ones." Pausing, she stared out the window then looked back at him. "Sometimes it seems like you're a real jerk, but then I see you with Chenoa and it blows me away. The fact that you brought it up is huge." She reached over and placed her hand on top of his.

Moving his hand slightly, he clasped hers in his and squeezed it while his gaze captured hers. He wanted to tell her that she twisted him up inside, and he didn't want to care for her like he did. But he didn't say anything. He wasn't a man used to talking about his feelings, so he just held her gaze for a long time, relishing in how comfortable he felt with her.

After they were finished, they said goodbye to Heseya and left the restaurant. As they walked to his motorcycle, she grabbed his hand and squeezed it. "Thank you."

He stopped and looked at her. "For what?"

"For tonight. For sharing a part of your heritage and life with me."

He smiled. "Being Navajo is my heritage, but my life is the Night Rebels. The brotherhood will always be the first blood that runs through my veins."

"Then share that with me tonight."

"What do you mean?"

"I want to go to your clubhouse now. I know you've got a party going on tonight, so I want to see how you live. I could use a shot or two of whiskey."

He shook his head. "I don't think so. It gets pretty rough and raunchy. Let's go to town and listen to some music."

She crossed her arms. "Do you think I'm a shrinking violet? Nothing surprises me. I want to go. I don't want to stay all night, maybe just or an hour or two. Are you going to take me there?" She pressed closer to him.

He paused for several seconds, then finally nodded. "We'll go just for a bit. You gotta stay close to me, and don't wander off alone. Looking the way you do, the brothers would be all over you in a second."

"Don't worry, I know the score."

"All right. Let's go."

WHEN THEY PULLED into the clubhouse, the music could be heard in the parking lot, the heavy bass making the walls shake. He escorted her into the club, and the heat of too many people hit him like a wave. He tucked her under his arm and walked over to the bar. Several members stared at her, then averted their eyes when he glared at them. He picked her up and plopped her on top of the barstool, then leaned against the bar. "You want a Jack?" he said in her ear. She nodded. He motioned the prospect for a Jack, who set Steel's shot of tequila in front of him and a shot of whiskey next to it. Steel gave it to her.

From the side, he saw Paco and Sangre coming over to him. He knew they wanted to check out Breanna and that they'd make up some fucking lame reason for coming over. He couldn't blame them; she was pretty and had a body biker's loved: nice rack, small waist, curvy hips, and a rounded ass. He motioned for the prospect for another Jack for Breanna.

"I'll be right back. I'm gonna talk to some brothers. Stay put, okay?" He stroked her cheek as she nodded. He went over and met them.

"Hey, bro." Sangre hit his fist against Steel's. "Were you at Cuervos or Lust tonight?"

"Neither."

Sangre slid his eyes over to Breanna. "Isn't that the waitress from your bar?"

"She's with me."

"I figured that by the way you're guarding her. I thought she wasn't your type." He snickered.

"A hot woman like that not his type? What the fuck are you smoking?" Paco asked.

"I didn't say it, Steel did."

"Who the fuck cares, bro. She's with me now and that's all that matters." Steel threw his shot down his throat. From the distance, he saw Alma sneaking glances his way as Crow sucked on her tits. Her eyes were wide, yet her brows were furrowed. Steel gave her a weak smile, feeling bad for her. Even though he never promised her anything, he had been spending a lot of his nights with her curled around him. He never had her exclusively, but most of the other brothers stayed away from her while she shared his bed for the past few months. She was a club girl, plain and simple. Steel turned away.

For the next couple of hours, he shot the shit with the brothers who kept coming up to him and sneaking peeks at Breanna. He should've been pissed, but he wasn't. He knew they were shocked he'd brought a citizen to the club.

"You holding up okay?" he said in her ear. Being so close to her was driving him crazy. He could feel the heat coming from her body, and he longed to hold her tight to him.

"Yeah. I think I'm a little tipsy, though. I used to be able to drink anyone under the table when I was in college, but I've become a lightweight." She giggled.

He nuzzled her neck. "You're cute when you're tipsy." He brushed his lips against her skin. "You're soft too."

She placed her arms around his neck and tugged his hair. "You're cute too."

"Watch it, baby. You're playing with fire," he growled.

"Maybe I like playing with hot things." She licked her lips and he dipped his head down, his tongue tracing the soft fullness of her lips. She brought her finger to her mouth. "I liked that."

"I like you."

"Really?"

"Yeah. Really."

All of a sudden she grimaced. "I don't feel so good. Where's the bathroom?"

He quickly got up and took her to the restroom. She slammed the door shut. A few minutes later she emerged, wiping her face with a paper towel. "False alarm. I think it's too hot in here, and I had too much whiskey."

"Do you want me to take you home?" he asked.

She ran the paper towel down her throat. "Do you mind?"

"Not at all. Let's go." He flung his arm around her shoulder and walked out of the club with her. Outside, the cool night breeze felt good as it fanned over his face. "It was too fucking hot in there. You feeling better?"

Breanna had her head back, and he could see the rise and fall of her chest as she inhaled deeply. "I'm feeling a whole lot better. It was a sauna in there."

"We shoulda gone to the backyard. In the summers, we always have a makeshift bar during parties. I don't know why I didn't think of it."

"That would've been better. How can so few women take care of so many men? It was like an orgy in there. Doesn't anyone believe in privacy?"

Steel shrugged. "Everyone's used to it. The club girls get off on being watched, and some of the brothers do too. Not all the guys are into it."

"Are you?"

"No. I like my privacy. But I'm down if another brother wants to fuck his brains out with a chick while we all watch. It's harmless as long as both people are cool with it."

"I guess. It just seems like all you guys do is drink and screw. I'm amazed anything ever gets done at all."

He chuckled. "We're a fucking amazing club. You ready to go?"

He waited for her to climb behind him, and then he took off. He pulled into her driveway and walked her to the front porch. "I had a really good time."

She smiled. "Don't sound so surprised. I had a good time too. Are you headed back to the clubhouse?"

"Yeah. I'll have a few more shots, and then I'll call it a night." He stared into her eyes that appeared darker under the inky sky.

"Do you want to come in for a nightcap?" she asked softly.

His gaze locked with hers. "Are you sure? 'Cause if I come in, baby, I'm not leaving until morning."

"I'm sure," she said in a low voice.

"Let's go inside." He followed her into the house. When she closed the door, he crushed her to him and kissed her deeply as she flung her arms around him and kissed him back.

"I'll get your beer and meet you in my bedroom. You remember where it is?"

"Yeah," he breathed as he peppered her neck with nips and light kisses. She pulled away and went into the kitchen. He watched her as she took out two beers and two bottles of water. Shuffling to the bedroom, he kicked off his boots and stripped to his boxers, then sat on the bed and waited for her to come in.

She handed him a beer and sat down next to him. He placed the beer on the nightstand and drew her into his arms, kissing her deeply. "You got some sexy shit under your dress?"

"Maybe. You like lingerie?"

"On you, fuck yeah. I wanna peel it off." He slid his hand down to the hem of her dress and shoved it up past her hips. Looking down, he sucked in his breath when her sheer gold panties revealed her smooth lips. He whistled softly. "Fucking beautiful." He slid his hand over the top of the translucent fabric, running his fingers up and down. "Does that feel good?" he asked between kisses.

"Hmm.... Let me take my dress off," she whispered as she tried to straighten up.

"I'll do it." He tugged her dress over her head and it rustled to the floor. A sheer gold bra encased her full breasts, the creamy skin tempting him for a taste. He lowered his head and lightly bit the tops of her tits, then dipped his tongue in the cleavage. Her skin was like velvet, and tasted salty-sweet. The heady scent of vanilla and apricot wound around him, making his dick pulse. With his teeth he lowered each bra strap, loving the way she gasped and arched her back, pressing her tits closer to his mouth. He slowly unclasped her bra and it fell in his lap.

With tenderness, he cupped her breasts, loving the way they were heavy yet soft. His fingers grazed across her nipple and when she sucked in her breath, the sound went straight to his cock. "You have beautiful tits, baby." He flicked her nipples with his tongue, loving the way they turned into hard needy beads. As he played with her breasts, his hand skimmed down her taut stomach, landing on the small patch of fabric between her legs. He slipped his hand inside her panties, his fingers parting her swollen lips. "Damn, you're wet. I like that." Leaving her tits, he kissed her passionately before he trailed his mouth down her throat, nipping at her delicate skin.

"I like that," she croaked. She had her hands buried in his hair, her nails scratching his scalp.

He continued to kiss a path down over her tits, around her rib cage, and over her belly, her whimpers and shivers as he touched her fueling his fire. When he nipped at the soft, sensitive flesh of her inner thighs, she pulled his hair so hard his scalp ached. "You loving this?"

"Uh... huh. You're doing some good stuff to me."

He slowly slid her panties down, throwing them on the floor, and then licked his way up from her calves back to her inner thighs. She tried to clench her legs, but he held them open with his shoulders as he traced circles with his tongue on her skin, inching his way to her sopping pussy. When he finally got there, he sucked her softly and then licked her dripping lips slowly, alternating with plunging his tongue inside her. She bucked underneath him, and her whimpers drove him wild. He started sucking and licking harder and faster, and then he slid up her body, forging a wet trail until he covered her mouth.

"Taste yourself, baby," he said against her lips as she slipped her tongue into his mouth. "You're delicious. So fucking sexy. I want to eat all of you." They kissed deeply, a tangle of teeth, tongues, and lips. Then he pulled away and let his tongue wander over her body until it made its way back to her pink, juicy pussy.

Once again, his tongue dove between her swollen folds, and her whole body jerked. "You're loving this, aren't you, baby?" She writhed beneath him, gasping. He slid his finger into her tight hole, and he felt her quiver. As his finger slid in and out, his palm rubbed against her clit, and her pussy walls clamped around him.

"Fuck," she rasped. "That's so good."

He looked up at her and saw her thrash about on the pillow. "Open your eyes. I want you to look at me as you come." She locked her gaze on his, and the glimmers of heat, rapture, and abandonment fueled his lust. He shrugged off his boxers, pulled out a condom from his jeans pocket, and slipped it on.

Her breathing was returning to normal, and he hovered over her and kissed her deeply. "Turn around, baby. I wanna fuck that tight pussy good and hard." She rolled over and pushed up on all fours. He squeezed her rounded ass cheeks, then moved his hands around in a circular motion, loving the feel of her soft skin against his calloused palms. Bending over, he kissed and then bit firmly into each cheek.

"Ow!" she cried. "What the fuck?"

"Sorry, baby. Your ass is so tempting, I got carried away." He kissed and licked where he bit her, noticing a reddening of the skin. He kneaded her ass some more, then lowered his head and kissed her lower back. "You okay if I swat your ass? I'll be gentle."

"Okay, but not hard like you just did."

He kissed and nipped her, then lifted his hand and smacked her beautiful globes. Her skin turned pinkish. "You want it harder?" he whispered against her skin. She nodded and mumbled her answer into the pillow. He swatted her butt harder and then slipped his finger into her folds, smiling when it came out covered in her wetness. "It's fucking turning you on, isn't it?"

Three spanks in a row; she moaned and wiggled her sweet ass.

Steel's cock was ready to burst, so he spread her legs wider and pushed on the small of her back so she was lower down and her ass was up higher. "Perfect," he said as he rubbed his hand over her ass cheeks. He swatted her a few more times, and then he plunged into her. For each thrust, he would pull all the way out before burying it to the hilt, his fingers digging into her hips. Soon he found his rhythm and her walls tightened around him, telling him she was reaching a climax.

The sound of her wetness mixed with the slapping of his balls with every deep thrust. "It feels so damn good. I love watching you as I fuck you," he growled.

She cried out and her pussy spasms clamped tightly around his thrusting cock. His legs stiffened and a pulsing pressure built inside his dick until it burst. Streams of pleasure filled his condom, his cock pulsing as her walls held him tightly.

"Fuck," he groaned. He lay atop her for a moment until his breathing slowed, his heart still pounding in his chest.

That was fucking awesome! I've never come like that before.

As he eased out of her he stroked her damp back.

Flopping on his back, exhausted, he pulled her to him, kissing her face, neck, and lips. "Incredible, baby." He nestled her in the crook of his arm.

"It was fantastic. Wow. I've never had such powerful orgasms." She kissed his chest.

Neither had he, but he had to digest it before he'd admit it. He had to see what the fuck was going on with him and this woman. It was like she cast a spell on him. *Maybe she's seen one of the seers on the reservation.* He shook his head. *That's stupid.* Then his mother's dream came to him, and he fought it back. *That's even dumber.*

She threw her arm around him. "Good night."

"Night." He didn't know what it was, but he'd just had the fucking best sex in his life with a woman who he really liked. He didn't give a shit if it was a spell or his mother's prophetic dream. All he knew was that he wanted to spend more time with her and get to know her a whole lot better.

As the clouds passed over the moon, they slept soundly wrapped in each other's arms.

Chapter Eighteen

THE FOLLOWING MORNING, Breanna woke with a start. At first she was disoriented, and when she glanced at the digital clock on her nightstand, panic set in. *I overslept. I'm going to be so late for work.* Her heart raced, but then she remembered the previous night and she smiled. It wasn't a work day; it was Sunday, so she could sleep in and cuddle with Steel. *How delicious.* The way he touched and brought her body to ecstasy was seared on her mind and skin.

Licking her lips, she rolled over to cuddle next to him, but his space was empty and cold. With a dazed look, she stared at the empty spot. A sudden chill hit at her core, replacing the warm, cozy feeling she'd experienced a few minutes earlier. Silence engulfed her.

She sat up and turned to the bathroom; the door was wide open and the light switched off. *That bastard took off on me!* Her face flushed. *What an idiot I was, giving myself to him again. He must really think I'm a fool.* She clutched at her stomach and squeezed her eyes tightly, willing herself not to cry. *That's the last time he makes an ass out of me. I'll never have anything to do with him.* She picked up her phone and called Jorge.

"Hi, Breanna. Are you calling to see if I need you tonight?"

"No. I hate to do this to you, but I've got to quit. It's not working out."

She heard him blow out a long breath.

"Is it because of Steel? I picked up on your feelings for him."

"I don't have any feelings for him. It's not about Steel. I'm too busy at work right now and I can't handle the part-time job anymore. I guess I bit off more than I could chew."

"You didn't mention anything about it on Friday."

"I'm sorry, Jorge. It's just not working anymore. I gotta go." She hung up and dragged herself to the bathroom. She cursed herself for being pulled in by Steel's charms. The previous night she'd let her guard down because he was acting like she was special, but in the end, she'd ended up being just another woman he fucked. *Asshole.*

When she came out of the bathroom, her hair damp from her shower, the aroma of cardamom and coffee tantalized her. *What the fuck? Is Nicholas here?* Then she wondered if the house was on fire. She threw on a white T-shirt over her jean shorts and dashed out of the room, running to the kitchen. She stopped short when she saw Steel at the stove, cracking eggs into a frying pan. On the side of the stove, tortillas bubbled on a grill she'd forgotten she had. In another skillet, chorizo sizzled.

"What the hell's going on?" she said.

Steel turned around and winked at her, a sweet smile curling his lips. "I'm making you breakfast. Grab a cup of coffee and have a seat. I had to go to the grocery store because you didn't have shit in your fridge. What the hell do you eat, woman?"

"Mostly frozen stuff. I thought you'd gone."

He scrunched his face and waved the spatula he had in his hand. "Why the fuck would you think I'd leave without telling you?" She shrugged and looked down. He laughed and came over, kissing her lips gently. "You look beautiful." He walked back to the stove. "I'm making the eggs over easy. I hope you eat them that way."

She sat down and watched him in amazement. "I do. I'm kinda speechless right now. No one's ever made me breakfast before. My mom stopped cooking for us when I was like eight years old." Her stomach grumbled and he chuckled. "I'm glad my pans are finally being put to use. I've never used the griddle. I don't really cook."

His eyes widened. "You don't know how to cook? I wouldn't have guessed that by all the shit you have in your kitchen."

She smiled. "I like the *idea* of me being a cook, but I never was very good at it. Boxed meals, spaghetti, beans, and rice were pretty much our staples when I was growing up. My mom rarely cooked, and when she did it was always processed stuff."

"I gotta get you on a different path, woman." He opened her cupboard.

She leapt up. "Let me set the table." She went over to him and ducked under his arms.

He wrapped his arms around her midriff and nuzzled her neck. "You smell good, baby."

His unshaved face scratched against her skin and she giggled. "Thanks for doing all this. I appreciate you."

His hands cupped her breasts and he massaged them. "You can show me how much after we eat." He drew her closer to him and rubbed against her, his hardness jutting out. "Feel what you do to me, woman?"

She leaned her head back against his chest and craned her neck. He lowered his head and pressed his mouth against hers. His tongue pushed through the seams of her lips and plunged in, and they kissed deeply until she moved her face away. "I should get the plates down." He chuckled and then moved away while she took out two colorful stoneware plates and matching mugs. He poured her a cup of coffee.

She sipped it. "I love the addition of the cardamom. I never would've thought of it."

"I had it like this at an Indian restaurant I went to when I was in Denver one time with Hawk and Throttle. I flipped for it. I don't drink it like that very often, but I wanted to see if you liked it. You strike me as someone who likes the exotic." He winked.

After a scrumptious breakfast, Breanna started to clean up. "I could get used to this," she joked as she placed the dishes in the dishwasher. "How did you get back in the house after you went to the grocery store? I didn't give you a key."

"I don't need a key. Let's just leave it at that."

"You know, I'm enjoying riding on your Harley. It's been a long time since I've been on a motorcycle. I forgot how much I love the feel of the wind whipping around me. How freeing it is. I love how it makes me feel like I'm flying." She looked up from the sink and met his intense gaze. "What? Why're you looking like that at me?"

He came over and tugged her to him. "You make me so fucking turned on, woman. I'd love to take you for a ride on my Harley, then pull over and fuck you long and slow on it. You loving the ride is fucking hot." His mouth covered hers hungrily and she pressed closer to him, her body aching for his touch. "Breanna," he rasped as his hand slid down to her ass.

In one fluid movement, he lifted her up, walked over to the kitchen table, and set her on top of it. He shoved up her T-shirt, exposing her full breasts, and eagerly sucked and feasted on them as she moaned and writhed beneath him. As they touched and tasted each other, their arousal rose higher until Steel turned her around on her knees and spread them open wide. He slid under her, and when she felt his tongue lapping up her sweet juices, she nearly lost it. As he licked her, one hand played with her tit and nipple, while his other kneaded her ass cheek. His wandering fingers went from her ass to her heated slit, pressing against it as his wicked tongue steadily lapped her clit.

When he pushed two fingers inside her, wiggling them, she cried out, "I want you inside me. Fuck me."

He chuckled against her folds, and the vibration from his lips made her crazed with desire. "You taste so good, baby. Like honeyed salt. Fucking good." He lapped harder as his fingers thrust in and out of her. "You like that?"

"Mmm… I love how you make me lose control," she breathed. He pushed out from under her and she heard him rip open a packet before he unzipped his jeans, his stiff cock jutting against her ass. A quiver surged through her veins as her insides jangled with excitement. She looked over her shoulder and met his heated gaze as he took his cock in his hands, slowly teasing her clit with its throbbing head. "That feels so damn good," she croaked.

"I'm gonna make you feel even better," he said as his dick left her clit and slid into her, just the tip. "You like that, baby?" He leaned over and kissed her back, then slid his cock fully inside her. "Fuck," he said in a low voice. Then he pulled out, her body trembling in anticipation for the next thrust. He didn't disappoint, slamming into her once more, burying his hardness deep inside. He grabbed her by the waist and thrust forward. His pace was quick and hard, and she let out whimpers of delight as the tingling warmth gathered between her legs. Her head snapped back as he grabbed a fistful of her hair and yanked, her back arching while he buried himself deeper inside her. He reached around and stroked the side of her sweet spot with a single finger while he rode her hard and fast.

Pressure began to build between her legs, and then a tidal wave of pleasure overtook her as her orgasm echoed through her body. She felt him bucking into her and heard him grunt as he found his release. Her breathing slowed and she collapsed on the table, his dick throbbing inside her. It was the best feeling in the world. *I could get addicted to this.* She sighed contentedly. "That was awesome," she said, wiping the drool from her mouth.

He blew out a warm breath that tickled her back. "Fuck, woman. You're in my blood." He feathered short kisses over her shoulders, then pulled out and lay beside her, drawing her close to him so her back fit against his stomach as he stroked her hair. "You wanna go for a ride today? I got a special spot I'd like to share with you."

He wants to spend the whole day with me. I was so wrong about him. Fuck, I quit my job! I gotta call Jorge and tell him I want it back. "I'd love to." She brought his hands up to her face and kissed them.

They finally sat up and Steel helped her off the table, clasping her body tightly to his. "We should get ready to go," he whispered in her hair.

"I know. Why don't you go first, and I'll clean the table." She tilted her head back and gave him a devilish grin.

He lowered his head and kissed her. "Okay." He smacked her ass and then let her go. "I love the way your ass feels against my hand." He winked and swaggered to the bedroom.

Breanna gathered her clothes from the floor and slipped on her T-shirt and shorts, then took out the cleanser from under the sink and began to clean the table. She heard Steel's voice flitting from the bedroom and strained to hear what he was saying, but she couldn't make anything out except the occasional "fuck" that peppered his conversation. A couple of minutes later, he came back into the kitchen, his face serious and tight.

"We're gonna have to go on our ride another time, baby. I gotta go."

"Has something happened to Chenoa?" A knot formed in her stomach.

"No. I got club business. I'll call you later."

Disappointment wove through her. She remembered her dad had always used "club business" as an excuse for disappearing for days on end. She hated those words.

"Hey." He came up to her and cupped her chin in his hand. "Don't sweat it. We got some shit going on that has to be taken care of. That doesn't mean we can't go for a ride during the week."

"I know," she mumbled as she ran her hands over his T-shirt.

"I'm just gonna take a quick shower. Then I have to go." He kissed the tip of her nose and padded back to the bedroom.

She sank down on the couch, turned on the TV, and stared blankly at the screen. She hit Mute on the remote and called Jorge.

"It's me," she said.

"Changed your mind?"

"Yeah. I was just having a moment. Sorry."

"I figured as much. Steel and I go back a long time. He's a decent guy. He gets a bad rap because he's president of an outlaw biker club, but he's really an upstanding guy. Don't let him know I told you that." He chuckled. "So, I'll see you Friday night?"

"Yes. Thanks, Jorge. No more drama from me, okay. God, I hate it when women create drama, and I pulled that crap on you."

"It happens. No worries. Friday, then."

She hung up and wrapped her arms around her knees. A few

minutes later Steel came out, his black hair damp. She jumped up and opened the door for him. "Thanks again for last night and breakfast."

He kissed her passionately. "You're welcome. I'll call you." Putting on his sunglasses, he walked into the brightness of the day. He smiled at her before he pulled away from her house, and then he was gone.

An empty ache filled her, and she chided herself for being such a whiny wimp. She turned off the TV and went to her bedroom, deciding she'd take another shower and then settle down and read a good book. It'd been a long time since she had a chance to read for pleasure and she decided she'd take advantage of it.

She knew she was hooked. He'd told her she was in his blood, but he was in her heart, and she didn't even know how the hell it had happened.

I've done exactly what I said I wasn't going to do. I've fallen for a biker. My brothers and sister are going to shit bricks. They aren't going to believe it. Hell, I don't believe it.

She laughed aloud, then covered her mouth with her hand.

And it feels wickedly wonderful.

Chapter Nineteen

W HEN STEEL WALKED into the meeting room, the brothers were already assembled and Paco sat with his chair leaning against the wall. The clamor of voices stopped when Steel walked to the head of the table. He jerked his chin at Paco who returned the gesture before Steel picked up the gavel and pounded it on a wooden block on the table. "Church is now starting. Paco called me and said that there's some angry shit going around here about the decision I made about the fucking Skull Crushers. I don't go for saying shit behind my back instead of to my face. Even though I'm president, I wanna hear if you got something burning up your ass. So, let's have it." He scanned the room of bikers.

Eagle cleared his voice. "Some of us are wondering why the pieces of shit are still breathing when they're dealing smack in our county. What the fuck's up with that?"

"Yeah. We decided a few days back at church that we'd take care of them. What the hell happened? We've been waiting for the word." Brutus crossed his arms across his massive chest. Army and Rooster slammed their fists on the table in agreement.

Steel glanced at Diablo, who stood in the back surveying the situation. As sergeant-at-arms for the club, his job was to make sure no harm came to the brotherhood or to the members, especially the president. Steel could see his muscles tighten as his stiff body stood in a pounce stance.

The president looked back at his brothers. "Is that about it? Anyone else want to say something?" Silence was the response. "Okay. I get why some of you are fucking pissed and want to rush over and decimate the fucking punks, but I also know that it's not the right timing." A few grunts and angry noises bounced around the room. Steel slammed the gavel down. "I gave you time to voice your shit. Now it's mine. Shut the fuck up. First off, the Skull Crushers aren't the supplier in this mess we have going in our county. Skull has some shit to report that has bearing on this."

Skull stood up and placed his palms on the table. "We heard from our snitch and he said that another shipment came in. This time the Skull Crushers weren't the ones distributing the smack. He said it was a skinny guy with light brown hair and blue eyes. He'd never seen him before. Our snitch asked the guy where the fucking Crushers were, and the dude didn't know what he was talking about."

"Is this skinny asshole the main distributor?" Crow asked.

"Nah. It seems like he works for whoever is the biggie in the county. The snitch doesn't know why the Skull Crushers weren't involved with this shipment, but the skinny fucker said there's been a change in personnel."

"Fuck that," Eagle muttered. "We gotta find out who's distributing the smack to these peons. Our snitch, the skinny fucker, and a few other assholes on the street are just users who need money, so they're doing the dirty shit while some fat fucker is getting all the money. When we find who that is, we'll find the supplier. I say we pick up this skinny dude and persuade him to give us some names."

"He may not know anything more than our informant," Skull said. The membership grumbled in agreement.

Steel put his foot up on the chair and leaned forward. "We gotta find this local distributor, that's for sure, but he's just the middleman. We need the supplier. When we find how the pieces fit together, the distributor, the Skull Crushers, and the supplier will all be eliminated."

"What're we gonna do about the ones selling the shit on the streets?" Eagle asked.

Steel shook his head. "They're just addicts. They'll move on to another street corner in another county."

"I still say it's the Satan's Pistons," Crow said. "This sounds like shit they'd do."

"Maybe, but the thing that doesn't convince me is that they don't have a connection with the Skull Crushers. It doesn't make any fucking sense," Steel said. At that moment, his phone rang and he pulled it out of his cut. "It's Hawk. Let's see if the Insurgents have any ideas about this."

He put the phone up to his ear. "Yo, brother," Steel said.

"Hey. I wanna say I'm fuckin' sorry about your daughter. Fuck. That must be rough. How's she doing?"

"Thanks, dude. She's doing better. We're in church now trying to figure out where the fuck the drug is coming from. Our snitch told us it was from an MC. We already know the Skull Crushers are involved, but they're definitely not the heavy." In the distance, Steel heard the rough voices of Banger and Throttle.

"I'm gonna put you on speakerphone so Banger and Throttle can get in on this talk. Hang on," Hawk said.

Steel switched his phone to speaker and placed it down on the table. "Can you guys hear me okay?"

"Yep," Banger said as Throttle and Hawk grunted.

"Good. Have you heard anything from the network about a biker club involved in transporting smack into southwestern Colorado?"

"No, but I'll do some digging," Hawk said.

"If I had to make a guess, I'd say those assholes Dustin and Shack are behind this. Probably talked the Demon Riders into it," Banger replied. Dustin and Shack were two renegade Insurgents who joined the Demon Riders MC when Banger ordered a group of his brothers to go to Nebraska and shut down the charter club there. Dustin was the president and Shack the vice president of that club. They'd been warned numerous times to clean up their act. They were prostituting underage girls, selling and using hardcore drugs, using minors at their strip club, and treating the national club without respect. They'd been a pain in the Insurgents' and their affiliates' asses since the Nebraska charter was dismantled.

"I'm with Banger. They were hit bad financially when we fucked up their guns deal with the Gypsy Fiends in Louisiana," said Throttle.

"The Demon Riders. Fuck. I never thought of them." Steel picked up the beer Crow had placed down in front of him. "Makes sense." Murmurings circulated through the room as the brothers discussed the possibility of going to Iowa to kick some Demon Riders ass.

"And they got a connection to the Skull Crushers. Remember that fuckin' sonofabitch Viper? The Skull assholes had been helping him. I'm with Banger too. I'll dig deeper, but I'm pretty fuckin' sure we'll find Dustin and Shack in the middle of all this."

"If we find out they're the ones, it'll be war. There's no damn way I'm gonna be satisfied with them just stopping. I want their goddamn hides." Steel slammed his beer bottle on the table and the brothers raised their arms in the air, their fists clenched.

"Night Rebels forever, forever Night Rebels," they chanted. Steel smiled; he fucking loved the brotherhood.

"If the Demon Riders are in on this, you can count us by your side. I've been itching to take Dustin and Shack out for too long," Banger said.

For a couple of seconds, Steel was overcome with admiration. His brothers were still chanting, and his Insurgent brothers were willing to lay their lives on the line to help him and the Night Rebels out. *This is what brotherhood is all about.* "Thanks. I'll take you up on the offer of support. We're gonna find out who the local distributor is and take care of him."

"I'll get back to you with the info," Hawk said. "Glad Chenoa's back on track."

"Thanks." Steel stared ahead as a bittersweet feeling filled him. Is *she back on track? For how long? Fuck.* Steel hung up and the members discussed the particulars for another thirty minutes before he adjourned the meeting.

As he was walking out of the meeting room, Paco came beside him. "Do you have any idea who this local fucker is?"

"I'm not sure. Since the food stamp angle came up, I'm wondering if that asshole Roy's involved."

"Roy?"

"Mika's asshole that she's shacking up with. He owns that overpriced grocery store by the rez. He'd make a huge profit by buying the cards for pennies on the dollar. Then he can turn them around to get cheap groceries for his store and charge out the ass for them."

"Oh yeah."

"Mika's had several of her food stamp cards go missing in the last eight months. I don't know, there's something about him that rubs me the wrong way." He pulled out a couple of joints and handed one to Paco. "I'll tell you one thing. If I find out he's the one who's distributing smack in Alina, I'm gonna make sure he dies a slow, agonizing death. If he did that to Chenoa, I'll be damned if I show any mercy."

Paco grasped his upper arm. "I hear you, and I'll be right behind you."

When they entered the main room, it was already packed with brothers, club women, and several hang-arounds. Music blared from the overhead speakers. "What're you drinking?" Paco asked as they walked across the room.

"I'm not staying. I want to visit Chenoa and have dinner with her." Steel pulled out his leather gloves. "I'll see you later." He and Paco bumped fists, and then he left the clubhouse.

As he raced down the road, he almost called Breanna to see if she wanted to tag along with him at the rehab center, but he decided he needed the time alone with Chenoa. He hoped Mika wouldn't be there; he wasn't in the mood to talk to her. She continued to insist that she and Roy live together. A few nights before, they'd had a big fight over it, and he wasn't in the mood to rehash it.

He pulled into the rehab center's parking lot and parked his bike, relieved not to see Mika's car. Striding into the lobby, he went to the elevators and pushed the third floor. Chenoa's door was slightly ajar when he got to it, so he knocked softly and then went in. Chenoa wasn't there. He opened her closet door and saw her clothes hanging on plastic hangers. He went back in the hallway and spotted Dr. Turner. The doctor waved at him.

"Where's Chenoa?" he asked.

"She's in group therapy." The doctor lifted his arm and looked at the watch on his wrist. "She should be out in about fifteen minutes. She'll be glad to see you."

"How's she doing? The fucking truth."

A small smile twitched on Dr. Turner's lips. "She's doing great here. The first couple of weeks were intense, but the drug's out of her system. The worst thing with addiction, especially with opiates, is the psychological pull of the drug. As long as she's in a controlled environment, she'll do really well, but the true test will be when she leaves rehab."

"I fucking know that. Is she strong enough to fight it?"

"I honestly don't know, Mr. McVickers. Each case is unique to the individual. I wish I could give you more assurance, but with any addiction, the urge is always there. I hope Chenoa is strong and can resist it, but only time will tell."

"Not the fucking answer I was looking for." Steel clenched his fists.

"But the only one I could truthfully give you."

Steel nodded. "That's fair."

"Dad!"

Steel whirled around and saw Chenoa dashing toward him. She flung her arms around his neck and he lifted her off the ground, hugging her tightly to him, her legs dangling and kicking against his thighs. *She's so light. I wonder if she's eating enough. I'm getting her a double cheeseburger for dinner.* "How's my sunshine?" He kissed her forehead, then put her down.

Chenoa giggled. "I'm fine, especially now that you're here. Let's go to my room."

When they entered, she sat on the small couch and gestured for him to sit next to her. The couch faced the window, and he could see the bluish tint of the San Juan Mountains filling the horizon in the distance as he sank down.

"Do you remember how I used to take you on long rides around the mountains?"

"Yeah. It was so awesome. When I get out I wanna go again. I can't even remember why we stopped doing it."

"Because you told me you outgrew it." He grasped her hand. "I'm so proud of you, sunshine. I know this has been fucking hard for you, goddamn grueling, but you're seeing it through. You got spirit, and if you ever feel like you're gonna fall, tell me. I'll always be there to catch you no matter what, but you gotta fucking let me know."

"I know that, Dad. I just did something real stupid, but I'm not gonna do it anymore. It's finished."

He scanned her face. Her eyes glimmered and he leaned over and kissed the lid of each one. "I hope so. I don't wanna lose you," he said against her skin.

"You won't. All this is in the past. I'm ready to begin the present and look forward to the future."

"Is that what they're teaching you in rehab?" She nodded. "Just remember that I'm always here for you. I was thinking I'd go get us some double cheeseburgers, french fries, maybe some wings, and two thick milkshakes. You down for that?"

"Is salad a choice in your grease-fest menu?" She laughed.

"Sure, but only if it's in addition to what I named."

"Deal." She placed her arms around him. They held each other tightly for a long while, and then she pulled away. "I'm starving. Can you go now?"

He laughed and rose to his feet. "I'll be back in a few."

"Ranch dressing for my salad," she called out as he walked out of the room.

HE STAYED WITH Chenoa until she fell asleep a few hours after they'd eaten. She'd told him that they made everyone get up at seven in the morning. She had so many therapy sessions, classes, and chores that by the time ninethirty hit, she was exhausted.

He bent down and kissed her head, tucked the covers under her chin, and headed out. When he got to his Harley, he decided he'd swing by Breanna's and spend some time with her. He wanted to tell her about Chenoa and share his fear of her relapsing. *What the fuck?* He never shared anything with anyone, let alone a woman, and fear wasn't part of his vocabulary. But this thing with Chenoa scared the shit out of him, and he wanted to talk to Breanna about it.

He wasn't too sure what he wanted from Breanna. She definitely stirred him in a way no woman ever had, but he was ready to start a war with the Skull Crushers, and most probably the Demon Riders if Banger's prediction of the club being the smack supplier were true.

Then he had Chenoa to worry about. She'd be out of rehab in less than two weeks; he couldn't have a relationship with Breanna complicating everything.

He'd told her earlier that day that she was in his blood, and it was true. He knew he didn't just want a fling with her. She meant something to him. He wanted her, but he didn't want the permanence of a relationship. Anyway, he fucking stunk at relationships. He couldn't commit 100 percent because he had the brotherhood, and he didn't want a woman asking him to choose. Besides, Breanna's dad fucked her up about the brotherhood; she had baggage, and he didn't know if he could deal with it on top of everything else that was going on in his life.

He did know that he wanted to see her and talk with her. He wanted that very much, and the thought of having another session of awesome fucking made him ride that much faster to her house.

When he rounded the corner, he spotted Breanna on the front porch, the light from the overhead fixture basking her in a golden glow. A tall, skinny man stood close to her, his arms wrapped around her and hers around him. Anger roped around Steel as he watched them standing in silence, holding each other while the sounds of summer encircled them. Hardness replaced any tender feelings he may have been suppressing. His impulse was to jump off his bike and beat the shit out of the man who had his arms around his woman. *Whoa.* My *woman?* The truth was she wasn't his woman; he hadn't claimed her. But he thought they had something.

Fuck it! If she wants to fuck around fine, but I'm done.

With his jaw jutted out, he swung his Harley around and sped off, his back stiff and his insides churning. He took the road out of town, riding like a bat out of hell; he needed to ride hard and fast to burn off the anger that was threatening to spill over. He didn't want to think of anything—not Breanna fucking another man, not the Demon Riders, not the lure of heroin for Chenoa. He just wanted to connect with the wind, the night, and the mountains.

He just wanted to be.

Chapter Twenty

BREANNA STOOD ON the porch hugging Nicholas, her heart exploding with joy. After several nail-biting days of no contact with him, he'd finally graced her doorway. When she'd first heard the doorbell, she'd hoped it was Steel. She hadn't heard from him all day, and she wanted to see or at least talk to him.

When she opened the door, Nicholas's lean face smiled at her. He looked so much better than the last time she'd seen him. She flung the door open, stepped outside, and drew him into a bear hug. "I'm so glad you're okay. I was so worried." Her voice cracked and she buried her face in his shoulder.

"Come on. Don't cry. I just got super busy. Sorry I didn't call." He stroked her back as he held her tight.

She lifted her head and saw something flash in the night. Squinting, she saw a flash of chrome at the same time loud cams filled her ears. *Steel!* Her heart beat quickly in anticipation of seeing him, but then confusion set in when she saw him hang a U-turn and ride away from her.

That's odd. Maybe he forgot something. I'm sure he'll be back.

"I hate those jerks who ride these big Harleys and think they're so badass. They tear up the streets with all their noise. Such fuckin' posers."

Breanna drew out of Nicholas's embrace as she laughed. "I know that guy and his Harley, and believe me when I tell you he's definitely no poser. Just the opposite." Warmth spread through her as she thought about their time together the day before, and earlier that day.

"Are you hooked on that jerk?" Nicholas frowned.

"No. I just know him from work. Let's go in. The mosquitoes are biting." She stepped inside and he followed her.

"Bullshit. That look on your face means you've fallen for some dude. A biker? Don't you remember how great Dad was?" He snorted.

"Dad was a selfish person, and I'm pretty sure he would've been one whether he was or wasn't a biker. Anyway, enough about all that. Tell me what you've been doing." *Besides shooting up.* "You look healthier."

"I feel better. I have a new job and I'm making some decent money for once." He wiped his runny nose. "Do you have a Kleenex?" She reached behind her and took the box from the small table in the foyer. He took a couple. "Thanks."

A runny nose was one of the signs that someone was using smack. She swallowed the lump that began forming in her throat. "That's great. Where're you working?"

"I'm selling a product to people. The more I sell and the more I get interested in this product, the more I make. It's been going great."

She sat down on the couch and he followed suit. "What're you selling?"

He blinked rapidly. "It's something to make people feel better."

"Like a health elixir?"

He grinned broadly. "Yeah."

"Are you hungry? I have a frozen pepperoni pizza I can pop in the oven, or a meatloaf dinner."

"Let's order a pizza. I'm paying."

"Are you sure you have enough?"

"I told you I'm working now. You call it in. I want extra cheese and extra pepperoni."

"Okay." She dialed the number, but suspicion crept through her. Something was off-kilter. *Where did he get his money?* She hated that she didn't believe him. Maybe he was off the stuff and *had* fallen into a good job. He could be very persuasive; she and her debt were proof of that. She should be happy for him instead of suspicious, but she couldn't stop the niggling feeling that something was more wrong with him than ever.

When their pizza came, Nicholas ate like he hadn't eaten in several days. She nibbled on one piece, wondering why Steel hadn't phoned her yet. She was positive that it was him who'd been across the street earlier. *Why did he take off in such a hurry? I hope Chenoa's all right.*

It was probably something related to the club. She remembered her father getting phone calls during dinner and he'd hang up, put on his black gloves, and leave without anything more than a "club business" grumble. It had driven her mother crazy and had made Breanna scared to death.

I hope he calls me.

While they watched a movie on TV, she felt her eyelids grow heavy. Before she could get up and drag her butt to her bedroom, she fell fast asleep.

BREANNA WOKE UP to a chorus of birds in the maple tree right next to her living room window. Rays of brightness cast squares onto the floral couch and the dull hardwood floor. She blinked a few times, trying to adjust her eyes to the golden illumination. She was on the couch, wearing her clothes from the previous night, an empty pizza box and several cans of pop littering the coffee table.

She bolted up. "Nicholas?" she called out.

No answer.

Had he left while she slept, or was he curled in her second bedroom, sleeping like a baby? She rose to her feet and shuffled to the guest bedroom. It was empty. She went to her bedroom, but it was empty as well. She groaned and rubbed her neck, working out a kink that had sprung up from sleeping at an angle all night.

She went back to the living room and cleared off the coffee table; she hated the smell of left-out food. When she went into the kitchen to toss everything in the trash, she noticed a piece of paper on the table. "Had to run. You looked so comfortable on the couch that I didn't want to wake you. I had a nice time with you. It was like the old days. Thanks. I'll call you. Nicholas." She smiled and folded the note, shoving it in her pocket.

After cleaning up the mess, she went over to her laptop and checked her e-mails, hurriedly opening the one from her supervisor. She read it and yelled out, "Yesss!" Her supervisor told her that she and the others were impressed by her report and they'd decided to allow Chenoa to live with her father on the condition that he live away from his club. Joy surged through her.

I have to tell Steel. He's going to be thrilled. Oh, but he has to get a house ASAP.

She checked her phone, a thread of disappointment weaving through her when she didn't see any text messages or phone calls from him. Deciding not to get bent out of shape, she decided she'd go to the clubhouse and personally deliver the message. *Don't kid yourself, Breanna. You know it's because you want to see him.* She dashed to the bathroom to shower and get ready for her day.

When she arrived at the clubhouse, the member manning the gate recognized her and motioned for her to go through. She pulled into a space near the front door and walked into the main room. It wasn't very crowded, and she supposed the early hour was probably the reason; partying all night didn't go hand in hand with early-morning rising.

She went over to the bar and waited for someone to notice her. A member came over. "Hang-arounds aren't allowed in the club until tonight. Who the fuck let you in?" a tall man with a dark beard and darker eyes asked.

"I need to talk to Steel."

The man ran his gaze over her. "I told you, hang-arounds aren't allowed in here right now."

"I'm not a hang-around. I'm a social worker. I have some news about Chenoa. I've got to speak with him."

A slow smile replaced the man's scowl. "Oh, you're the blondie he's been hanging with. Stay put. Lemme go find him." He disappeared down a long hallway.

She lifted herself onto a barstool and grabbed one of the napkins, which she proceeded to tear apart in tiny pieces. A couple of men stared at her, but they kept their distance. A redheaded woman came over to her, wearing a tight T-shirt and jean shorts. She stood in front of Breanna and pointed to the front door. "What the fuck do you think you're doing in here, skank? Get your ass outta here before I kick it out."

"I'm waiting for Steel."

"I'm sure you are, but the only women who get him at this time of day are the club girls, not hang-arounds. Get your ass out!"

Another woman with long black hair came up and stood by the redhead. "Aren't you the bitch who was with him on Saturday night?"

Breanna stiffened. "Don't fucking call me a bitch."

"Okay. Weren't you with him on Saturday?" The black-haired lady crossed her arms.

"Yeah. What of it?"

"Nothing." She and the redhead exchanged looks. "Well, I hope you got some time because Steel's busy with Alma right now. You can wait if you want."

"Alma? Who's that?"

The redheaded woman took one step closer to Breanna. "She's been Steel's main girl. Has been for the past several months."

Breanna's stomach dropped, and it felt like she'd been sucker punched. "I gotta go. I just remembered there's something I have to do." She slid off the stool.

"You see, Steel has his women right here at the clubhouse. He doesn't need anyone else." The black-haired woman looked at the redheaded one. "Am I right?" The woman nodded.

"Leave her the fuck alone, Fina. Why don't you and Lucy go help Lena in the kitchen if you're bored." A tall buffed man with brown hair and eyes came toward her. "Steel'll be here in a minute. Want something to drink?" Speechless, she just nodded. "You want a beer or a shot?"

"Orange juice, please."

"You want a couple of shots of vodka in it?"

"No, thanks."

He pulled out a carton of orange juice and poured her a glass.

"Thank you." She brought it to her lips.

"I'm Paco. You're Breanna, right?" She nodded as she swallowed. "Good to finally meet the woman who's fuckin' with our prez's head." He came out from the bar and stood in front of her, his dark gaze checking her out. "I can see what he sees in you."

"Back the fuck off, Paco." Steel's hard voice made her jump.

He laughed. "I saw you coming, brother. I knew that'd get you."

The bearded man who'd approached her first laughed loudly.

"Why don't you two fucking hyenas move it," Steel said.

"Let's go play some pool, Army. I'm in the mood to make some money," Paco said as he strode away.

"Then you're playing with the fucking wrong person. I'm gonna—"

Breanna couldn't hear his voice anymore. She turned to leave.

"What the fuck? Where're you going? Army said you had some news about Chenoa."

She spun around. "The department has decided that Chenoa can live with you if you have a house. They don't want her near the clubhouse," she said in a flat voice. Turning away, she stormed out the door. Her eyes were stinging; she pulled out a tissue and dabbed the corners.

"Breanna. Wait up. What the fuck?"

Footsteps pounded behind her as she ran to her car and jumped in, slamming the door just as he reached her. He tried to open the door but she'd locked it. He pounded on the window. "Open up. What the fuck's the matter with you?"

She turned on the ignition. A huge bang on her window made her jump. She turned and ice curled around her nerves; his face was a mask of rage, his eyes burning and his lips pulled back. "Roll down the fucking window or I'll break it!"

She took several deep breaths and released them, trying to calm her nerves and push away the hurt and tears. She pressed the button and the window rolled down halfway. "What do you want? I've got to go to work. I don't have time for this shit."

"Why the hell did you take off?"

"I told you, I've gotta go to work."

"You're fucking lying to me. Why'd you come all the way out here to tell me the good news and then run away all pissed off? Tell me what's going on."

"Aren't you busy?" she asked coolly.

He raised his eyebrows. "Busy with what?"

"Alma."

His brows furrowed and his eyes widened. "Alma? What the fuck?"

She tapped her fingers against the steering wheel. "I'm kinda in a hurry here. We don't have any claim on each other. We had some fun. You're free to do whatever you want with whoever you want."

He narrowed his eyes. "And so are you. I saw you taking advantage of that last night."

"Last night? What're you talking about?"

"I came by and saw you on the porch. You looked pretty cozy with that dude."

She scrunched up her face, trying to remember what she was doing on the porch. *Nicholas. That's right.* "Is that why you took off?"

He shrugged. "Like you said, baby, you and I are free agents."

Sniffing, she shook her head. "That guy was my brother, Nicholas."

"Your brother?"

"Yeah. You should've stopped over. I've wanted you to meet him. He's the one who's been using."

He ran his fingers through his long hair. "Fuck," he said under his breath. He looked at her and smiled sheepishly. "I misunderstood the situation, just like you're doing with Alma."

"So she's not your main squeeze?"

"The club girls have vicious tongues sometimes. They're very protective of each other. I wasn't with Alma. I haven't been with her since I met you."

"You mean since we slept together?"

He caught her gaze and held it, then reached out and lightly stroked her jawline with his thumb. "No. Since I met you."

Tingles of desire teased her as warmth spread through her. "Oh."

"Yeah, 'oh.' You wanna come back inside so we can talk? It's fucking hot out here."

She smiled and unlocked the door. "Sure." She followed him back into the clubhouse and avoided the brothers' gazes. A few more members were in the main room, and she noticed Lucy and Fina were sitting at a table, shooting daggers at her. "I really should get going. I've got a bunch of work waiting for me at the office."

"Let's have a quick drink. I wanna tell you I'm fucking stoked about Chenoa being able to live with me. You ran out so damn fast I didn't have a chance to tell you that. I know you're the reason the department changed their minds." He picked her up and set her on the stool, then settled himself between her legs. He stroked her cheek. "You went to bat for me. You had my back. When I first met you, I figured you were just like all the others who fucked me over with Chenoa. I was wrong." He put his hand on the back of her neck and tugged her to him, then kissed her tenderly.

The gentleness of his kiss fueled by his unassuming words sent the pit of her stomach into a wild swirl. She opened her eyes and peered over his shoulder, suddenly becoming self-conscious at all the gazes fixed on her and Steel. Pulling away a bit, she cleared her throat. "You're going to have to move out of the clubhouse."

"Why'd you pull away from me, baby?" He drew her close to him again. "Don't bother with being shy. The brothers don't give a fuck, they're just bored, and the club girls will back off now that they see you're my woman." His mouth captured hers and his tongue slid in, sending shivers of desire racing through her.

"Am I your woman?" she mumbled between kisses.

"All the way. You good with that?" His mouth brushed against hers as he spoke.

"I'm more than good with that." She looped her arms around him and kissed him deeply, glad she was sitting as a lightness spread through her body, mingling with a heat that radiated through her chest. *I'm Steel's woman.* She cracked open her eyelids and noticed that the men had gone back to talking among themselves and the club girls had left. "I really do have to go. I can't blow off work, even though I want to in the worst way."

"We gotta go up to my room so I can claim you the way a man should," he said, his hot breath fanning over her face.

She grimaced and kissed his chin. "You're so bad, tempting me like that, but I *do* have to go. I have a meeting I can't miss. When're you going to find a rental?"

"Today. I'll come to your place tonight. Does seven work?" She nodded. "I can't wait to claim you, baby." He helped her off the barstool and gave her ass a swat. "A preview for tonight," he said when she opened her mouth to protest. He gave her a quick peck on the lips and then walked her to her car. He opened the door for her and, as she slipped in, said, "Being my woman means we're only with each other."

She smiled. "I know. I'll see you later tonight." She drove away and kept glancing in her rearview mirror. He stood in the same spot watching her. She turned down the small road and he disappeared from her sight.

I'm Steel's woman and he's my man. Her body buzzed as she said the words over and over again in her head. The enormity of it covered her like a warm blanket.

Best day ever!

Chapter Twenty-One

JOEL COUGHED AND sneezed as he reached for his fifth tissue from her Kleenex box on her desk. "This is bullshit," he muttered as he blew his nose.

"I keep telling you it's freezing cold in here, but Janet and I are the only ones who think so."

"It's not the cold. It's the fucking desert heat. It kills me."

"It does take some time to get used to it. I'm from here so it doesn't bother me, but you're from Kansas where it's a lot more humid. I remember going to Dodge City to a biker rally with my mom and dad. It was the only trip we ever took as a family. Anyway, it was in the summer and was so humid that I could hardly breathe. I guess it's just what you're used to."

"Your story doesn't help with my fucking stuffy head. Anyway, I've put in for a transfer. I'm sick of feeling miserable all summer long."

"I didn't know."

"I also applied for some federal positions. I just need a change." Joel grabbed another tissue. "We got that inane meeting. We better get going."

Janet came by Breanna's cubicle. "You guys headed over to the meeting?"

"Yeah. Poor Joel's miserable with allergies." Breanna pushed her chair from her desk.

"And the fucking dryness this state is famous for." Joel walked in front of them.

"Everyone I know is sick with that head and respiratory stuff. It's crazy. Seems like you and I are the only ones clearheaded." Janet laughed.

"I keep saying it's all this AC. I turn it off at night. If I don't, then I get a sore throat."

"So you just sweat all night?" Joel opened the door to the meeting room.

"I have an attic fan. The nights are cool for the most part, so it works nicely."

"I want to get one of those," Janet said.

"You're both pathetic," Joel growled as he took his seat at the table. Breanna and Janet followed suit.

During the meeting with Special Agents Raley and Powers, Breanna kept replaying Steel's words "You're my woman" over and over in her mind. His growly voice, his heated eyes, and his sensuous lips when he told her that would forever be seared in her memory. Each time she thought about it, her stomach fluttered and her nerves tingled. She couldn't believe that she was his and he was hers.

"Do you have anything to add?" Raley's voice broke in on her day-dreaming.

"What? Uh… no, not really," she replied, as she felt her face and neck redden.

"Do you even know what we're talking about?" Raley asked.

She glanced around the room. Joel rolled his eyes, Powers leafed through a code book, and Janet looked at her with an "oh shit" expression on her face. Breanna swallowed. "The EBT cards?"

"Good guess. Did the agents being in the room tip you off?" Joel said as picked up a bottled water.

She frowned at him. *What the fuck is his problem? Is he trying to get me in trouble?* Ignoring him, she turned to Raley. "I'm sorry, I did zone out for a few minutes. I have this bad headache and it's just throbbing."

Raley smiled. "It's okay. I know it's damn hot in here, but a freezer in your offices. Not sure what's going on with the AC. I called the repair guy, but he hasn't shown up."

"No worries," Agent Powers said. "We were just asking if any one of you have any names you could give us of suspicious persons. You know the reservation a lot better than we do."

"Have you looked closely at Roy's Market? It's a small grocery store a couple of miles from the rez, but the prices are unusually high. A lot of the Natives go there because they don't have cars and the store is close. Those types of markets tend to be more expensive, but that one is unduly high. It's way higher than the small convenience store that's attached to the gas station on the rez."

"Who runs the store?" Raley asked as he popped open his can of Dr. Pepper.

"A guy named Roy Eldridge. He lives on the reservation," she replied.

Powers raised his brows. "Really? I didn't know he lived here."

"You know him?" she asked.

"Not really. I've stopped at the market to pick up some stuff before coming to work. Nothing big. Just pop and sandwiches. I did think the prices were high, but it seemed typical for those types of markets."

"Is he Navajo?" Raley asked.

"No, but he has permission from the tribe to live on the rez. He's living with a woman who's Navajo," she answered.

"He sort of gives me the creeps," Janet said in a tentative voice. All eyes turned to her. "Maybe I'm wrong. I don't know."

Breanna smiled when she saw the woman's face turn beet red. Her coworker lacked confidence, and people generally made her nervous. Breanna was surprised she was a social worker, a totally people-oriented field. "He gives me the creeps too." Janet smiled at her.

"Maybe he's a lech with women," Joel added after yawning loudly.

"We'll check him out. Thanks, Breanna," said Agent Raley. "Anyone else?" When no one answered, he cleared his throat. "That'll do it. Keep sending us the reports on lost or stolen cards."

Breanna walked to the office and Janet came up beside her. "Thanks for backing me up," she said.

"No prob. Roy does give me the creeps." She lowered her voice to a whisper. "And I wouldn't be surprised if he was involved in all this. I mean, two dollars for a twelve-ounce can of Diet Coke? Something's not right."

"I know," Janet said. "It's good you spoke up. At least the agents will look into it."

"You women really give a shit about all this, don't you?" Joel came over to them and leaned against the doorframe.

"I'm not up for another discussion about whether or not EBT fraud is a victimless crime. I've got a ton of work to do before five o'clock." Breanna went behind her desk.

"Me too. That's why that meeting was just bullshit and a waste of time. When they start paying me overtime, then I won't give a damn about how the department wants to waste my time. But until then, I'm going to resent like hell these fuckin' meetings." He walked away.

"Do you think he has an opinion on food stamp fraud?" Janet asked. She busted out laughing and Breanna joined her.

At five o'clock, Breanna turned off her computer and rubbed her eyes. She hated sitting all day at the screen, as it killed her eyes, neck, and shoulders. She wished she could afford to get a massage; it would be divine to have someone rub out all the kinks of a desk job.

When she got home, she quickly cleaned up her place, took a shower, and slipped on a pink jean skirt and an ivory crop top. She made sure to put on her new white sheer bra and thong. A few spritzes of her favorite perfume and she was ready for Steel.

Standing in front of the open freezer, she surveyed the selection of frozen dinners. *Something tells me he isn't a frozen dinner type of guy.* She groaned audibly and slammed the freezer door shut. For the past several years she'd wanted to take cooking classes, but the nearest community college was an hour away, and she didn't have the time to make the commute. She watched cooking shows all the time, but living alone hardly gave her any incentive to try and prepare elaborate dishes.

She went over to one of the drawers near the stove and took out six take-out menus, but nothing grabbed her. She sighed and decided pizza was the easiest, so she pulled out the flyer and set it on the kitchen table.

A few minutes before seven, she heard the roar of his cams as he burst onto her street. Her stomach did flip-flops. It was crazy, but she was so damn nervous to see him. *What if he tells me he changed his mind? What if he was just trying to teach those club girls who's boss?*

The ring of her doorbell made her jump. *I act like I'm fourteen and this is my first date with the boy I've been crushing on. Totally pathetic.*

She smoothed her hair down and opened the door. Her gaze traveled over him, taking in his tight jeans, his snug crotch, the dancing ink on magnificently sculpted arms, the muscle shirt molded to his firm chest, his beautiful hair, his silver and turquoise feather earrings, and his rugged face. She swung open the screen door and fell into his arms, kissing him passionately.

"Nice way to greet your man, woman." He nuzzled his face in the crook of her neck and inhaled deeply. "Your scent is intoxicating." He scooped her up and stepped inside, kicking the door closed.

She buried her face in his chest as he marched her to the bedroom and laid her on the bed. "And what do you think you're doing?" she asked as she watched him kick off his boots and strip off his clothes. His erection was obvious.

He got on the bed and hovered over her. "Claiming you the right way." He crushed his mouth over hers, plunging his tongue deep inside. As they kissed, his hands roamed over her curves and under her skirt, searing her flesh. Each touch inflamed her arousal even more; by the time he'd taken off her clothes except for the thong, she was burning with need and desire.

"Are you on birth control?" he said against her inner thighs.

"Yes. Are you clean? Have you been tested?"

"I'm good, baby. I want to take you raw and feel every inch of you around my cock."

She pulled his hair and squirmed. The way he was touching, licking, and biting her thighs and belly was driving her crazy. Each time he came near her throbbing clit he'd back away, biting and licking everything around it. He was teasing her to a frenzy. "I can't wait to feel all of you too."

For the next two hours, her life was suspended in rapture as Steel claimed every part of her, marking her as his woman. The love bites over her breasts and belly would be doozies by the following day, and she was pretty sure her ass would be red from his erotically charged spanks and bites. She'd never experienced such intense lovemaking as she did with him, and she couldn't get enough of it. She was addicted to him, and she didn't want it any other way.

As she lay in his arms, bubbles of joy fizzed through her, and she realized for the first time in her life she was truly happy. Her happiness took her by surprise; it was light as a feather, bright as a beam of sunlight. It was a foreign feeling to her, and this rough biker had made it happen. She looked up at him and kissed his Adam's apple. He lowered his head and pulled her up to him, kissing her gently. "I love you. You're the only woman who has conquered my heart, soul, and body."

She clutched his waist. "And I love you. I've never trusted a man enough to let love into my life until you. I felt a pull toward you from the first time I saw you."

"I felt the same pull even though I fought it, but all along you've been the woman who was destined for me."

They held each other in a comfortable silence as the lingering light was obliterated by the rapidly falling night. A tangy, earthy scent filled the room from their arousal, and they lay sated, their legs tangled together as she watched the shimmering stars emerge from the passing clouds. Aside from the occasional hoot of a hidden owl, a loud grumble was the only sound to permeate the silence.

A low chuckle made his skin vibrate against her cheek. "Are you hungry?"

She pushed against her stomach, trying to stop the noises. "I thought we could order a pizza and watch a movie. Does that sound good?"

He twirled her tendrils around his finger. "Whatever you want. I'm happy eating you."

She giggled. "Should I order it now?"

He rolled her on top of him. "We'll order it in an hour."

She bent her head down and they kissed hungrily as a cool breeze sifted in through the window.

Chapter Twenty-Two

T HE MAN STUBBED out his cigarette in the overflowing ashtray, then tilted the chair back and crossed his hands over his stomach. "Pretty fucking stupid to sell to the president of an outlaw MC. What the hell were you thinking?"

"How the fuck did I know the asshole had a daughter living on the reservation? I didn't even know he was Injun."

"Now you do. What a mess."

The young man with white-blond hair shook his head. "I told Dustin about it. He said the fuckin' Insurgents are snooping around, trying to find out where the shit's coming from. He wants to cool it for a while until things die down."

The man scowled at him. "And how the fuck am I supposed to make money? I paid a lot of money for a product that I can't sell. That won't do."

The short, blond-haired guy wiped his mouth with his hand. He'd been drooling and it repulsed the distributor. He was beyond angry at the inept MC who'd been privy to the smack operation. He'd told Dustin to just leave it to him, but he'd insisted on bringing in the group of punks—something about owing them or some shit like that. All he knew was his operation was in jeopardy, and he wasn't ready to call it quits by a long shot.

"Maybe you could set up shop in another county. One that's not controlled by the Night Rebels."

The man's fingers itched to be around the young idiot's throat. He wanted him out of his sight; he was irritating the fuck out of him, and the urge to strangle him was intensifying. "Maybe you could shut the fuck up."

"Just trying to help." The young man glowered. "You need to treat me with respect. My brothers don't fuckin' like the way you've been treating us."

"Do I look like I give a fuck? Your *brothers* are a bunch of morons. You live in this godforsaken county. Why in the hell didn't you let me know an outlaw MC controlled the area? They have a fucking deal with the sheriff's department to keep hard stuff out of the county." He spat into a tissue; his phlegm was yellow. *On top of all of this, I probably have a goddamn sinus infection. I hate this fucking dry heat.* "How long does Dustin want to cool it?"

The blond shrugged. "I dunno. He didn't say."

"And what do we do with our customers? Just tell them we've closed shop?"

"Nah. They'll go to another county or something. Quit asking me so many fucking questions." The young man paced.

"We're done. You and your club of dumbasses lay low. I'll talk to Dustin. I'll figure it out." The only positive thing in this disorganized mess was that the Skull Crushers—he *hated* the name—would be out of the picture, and he could have all the control. He preferred working alone. He had no intention of "laying low" until Dustin gave the word. As far as he was concerned, all these outlaw biker clubs were morons, including the Night Rebels. He just didn't like that he had to worry about a crazed president trying to play vigilante. He'd sell off the smack and then set up shop in another state, but he sure as hell wasn't losing a hundred and fifty thousand dollars because Dustin fucked this up. He also had a drawer full of EBT cards he had to sell.

He fixed his stare on the club member whose blotchy red face made him sick. "Why the fuck are you still here?"

"I said watch it." The distributor gazed at him placidly. "I'm going because *I* want to, not because you said so."

The man didn't say a word.

The Skull Crusher shoved his hands in his leather jacket and slinked out.

The brown-haired man picked up the phone, dreading the call to Dustin. He was sick to death of working with incompetent criminals. He couldn't wait until he could move on to another location. *Just a couple more years of this, and I'll be on easy street.*

Paradise was not so far away.

Chapter Twenty-Three

STEEL SMILED AS Breanna walked around the house, opening cupboard and closet doors. He couldn't believe how much she meant to him. He'd fought it, not wanting her to complicate his life, but not having her was what was making his life difficult. She complemented him, and he couldn't imagine why he'd fought it so long. He hadn't told his mother yet; he knew she'd be thrilled and smug since she'd had the visions. He planned to tell her when he went to the reservation later that afternoon.

"I think this will be wonderful for you and Chenoa. I love the stream that runs through the backyard. And you'll have privacy since the next neighbor's house is several blocks away." She wound her arms inside his jacket and around his back. "I'm sure Chenoa will love it."

"I hope so." He lowered his head and kissed her gently on the lips. "I gotta admit it's gonna be fucking strange not being at the clubhouse. I've lived there since I started the Night Rebels. It's so damn quiet here."

"It'll take you some time to get used to it, but your brothers can come and hang with you here, and having Chenoa will help."

"Yeah. I can't wait for her to live with me. When I went looking for a place, I'd hoped you'd be moving in with me as well."

She rested her forehead against him. "I know, but we already talked about that. I'd love to be here with you, but you need this time alone with Chenoa. It has to be about her. Besides, I'm still keeping a low profile about our relationship. I don't want people at work finding out, especially my supervisor. I don't want to risk causing you and Chenoa any problems. I don't think the department would be too happy about me loving a high-risk client's father. It would throw suspect on my report."

"When are you gonna come out of hiding? We can't fucking pretend we're not together. I don't wanna wait too long for you to move in with me and Chenoa."

"Give it some time with Chenoa. Once everything settles, then I'll move in. She's going to need a lot of support and attention."

Steel nestled his face in her hair, the scent of gardenias filling his nostrils. He loved it. "I know. I just hope she's fucking honest with me. I don't want her sneaking and doing shit behind my back."

"You need to be supportive and patient."

"To a degree. The hardest part of all is where the toughest and most unselfish love is. I'm not sure she'll get that. I just hope she still has the will to fight and the hope to dream." He rocked back and forth slightly with Breanna in his arms. All of a sudden his heart was heavy, and he wished he could speed up time and have all this behind him and Chenoa. He was ready for the task, but so much depended on her. If only he could take her burden upon him. If only he could fight it all for her. But he couldn't.

A knock at the door made Breanna pull away from his embrace. He walked over and opened the door, a man in his late forties with graying temples smiling back at him. "Sorry I'm late." He walked in. "Did you have a chance to inspect the house?"

"Yeah," Steel said. Breanna came over and stood next to Steel, her arm pressed against his.

"This your girlfriend?" The man took out several papers from a manila folder he had in his hand.

"Yeah, she's my woman."

She extended her hand. "I'm Breanna."

The man shook it. "I'm Les. I own the house. Do you like it?" She nodded. "Good. Are you moving in with Steel and his daughter?"

"No," she said.

"Well, if you do move in, I'll just need to know. When's your daughter moving in again?"

"In a week. Is that the lease agreement?"

Les nodded as he handed it to him. "Review it and let me know if you have any questions. If it's all good, go ahead and sign it. I brought a couple of copies."

Steel took the papers from Les and read them. "Looks good." He signed the lease and gave it back.

After the landlord left, Steel picked up the set of keys Les had given him and turned to Breanna. "I gotta talk to Mika. I'm going to the rez."

"I have a client I need to see, but I'll be at the rez later. We should celebrate your new house tonight. Dinner? My treat."

He draped his arm over her shoulders. "Dinner sounds great, and it's my treat." He placed his finger on her mouth. "And don't fucking argue with me about it 'cause I'm not gonna change my mind."

She brushed his finger aside. "I wish you'd let me do something for you. You're always paying and helping me out."

"You can give me a killer blowjob after dinner." He winked and smacked her ass. "I gotta go."

She giggled. "You're so bad."

"Is that a yes?"

"You know it." She swung her arm around his neck and drew his face close, then kissed him deeply. "Just a preview," she whispered.

His dick jerked. "You're making me hard, baby. If we don't get outta here, I'm gonna throw you against the wall and fuck you hard."

She laughed and grabbed his hand, and they walked out together. As he sat on his Harley, waiting for her to drive away, his phone rang, Chenoa's name flashing on the screen.

"Hey, sunshine. What's up?"

"Hi, Dad. Nothing. I just wanted to say hi. What're you doing?"

"I just signed a lease on our new place. I hope you like it."

"Do I get my own bathroom?"

"Yeah. This place has three bathrooms and three bedrooms. The basement is finished, so you and your friends can hang out there without your old man around."

She laughed. "Sounds perfect."

He smiled and his heart swelled; her voice was bright, like sunlight dancing on a crystal clear lake. "I can't wait to spend time with you. It's been something I've always wanted to do."

"Me too. I'm so glad Ms. Quine pushed for this. She's the best social worker I've had. She acts like she really gives a shit."

"She does."

"Did you talk to Mom yet?" she asked in a low voice.

"I'm heading over there now. Don't stress over this. I'll take care of it."

"I don't want her to think I don't wanna be with her or see her. I love her and all, but I just want some time with you."

"I know, sunshine, and your mom will get that. Leave it up to me."

"Thanks, Dad. I can't wait to get the hell out of this place."

"Tired of the fucking accommodations?" She sniggered. "I'll stop by later and see you. I gotta get to the rez."

"Say hi to *Análí* for me."

He hung up, the heaviness he'd felt earlier beginning to dissipate. As he rode to the reservation, the sun beat down from a blue sky where not even a wisp of cloud was apparent. Heat licked at his tanned face and bounced off the road, sending up a wavering haze. On each side of the two-lane highway, the scorched sand shimmered beneath the intense white rays of the sun. Sweat trickled down the back of his neck as he veered to the left and entered the reservation.

He decided to stop in and see his mother first before heading over to Mika's place. A few houses down from his mother's, he spotted Mika and her dirtbag boyfriend walking her dog. Mika looked up and waved.

He pulled over and killed the engine. "Hey," he said as he got off his motorcycle.

Mika held her hand up in front of her face as if to block the sun from it. "Hi. How's your mom?"

"Okay. I'm headed over to see her, but I wanted to talk to you." He glanced at Roy who stood behind Mika, a frown creasing his forehead. "I just signed the lease on a place in the Pleasant View neighborhood."

Mika put her hand down and covered her open mouth. "I never thought you'd move from the clubhouse. What made you do it?"

Steel stood in front of her to block the sun. He took off his sunglasses and placed them inside his cut. "Chenoa. She told me she wants to live with me for a while."

"What the fuck? No. My daughter is staying with me."

"She's my daughter too, and you've had her for seventeen years, Mika." He took off his cut and placed it carefully on the bike's seat. A sheen of sweat glistened on his bare back and chest.

"You're trying to take her away from me." Mika's voice hitched.

"I'd never do that. She'll always be close to you and love you. It's just that she and I want some time together. I also need to make sure she stays clean. She needs to be in a new environment. You know, away from the rez. The lure of heroin is powerful, and I wanna give her a fighting chance. She also needs to be in school."

"I just can't believe you're taking her from me." She wiped the tears rolling down her cheeks.

"Mika, how can you think that? I'd never take Chenoa from her mother. She'll always be in your life. It's just that our goal as parents should be to do whatever's best for her so she doesn't get pulled back into the arena. We're working together here, not against each other." He knew she was hurting, but it was natural for Chenoa to want to live with him and get to know him better.

Roy stepped from behind Mika. The stench of stale sweat rolled off him. "This is fucked. Chenoa's used to our house. She needs her mother. Too much change is gonna set her back."

Steel's face flashed into a menacing sneer. "Stay the fuck outta this."

"I think I have a say in this since I've been supporting your daughter for a while now."

"What you think doesn't mean shit. And you haven't given a fucking penny to her."

"I've supported her emotionally."

"Why the fuck are you still talking?" Steel's fists clenched and his muscles tightened.

Mika wiped her cheeks with both hands. "Come on, you two. Roy, take Buttons and I'll meet you at home. Steel and I have some things we have to talk about."

"I have a right to be here," Roy protested.

"That's where you're fucking wrong." Without warning, Steel's balled fist collided with Roy's jaw, knocking his head back like a willow caught in the wind.

He stumbled backward and brought his hand to his jaw. "What the fuck?" he yelled as he regained his balance. "I think you broke it, you goddamn asshole." He lunged forward, and soon the two men were sweating, grunting, and punching.

Mika rushed over and grabbed Steel's arm, but he yanked it away. "Fucking back away. Now!" His voice was raw and brutal. She did as he ordered, and soon several people came out of their houses to see what the ruckus was all about. From the corner of his eye, Steel saw a group gathering. With his steel-toed boot, he kicked Roy hard in the shin. Roy went down on his knees, crying out in pain. Steel pushed him to the ground with his foot and then sat on his chest, pummeling Roy as he held up his hands to ward off the blows.

"Steel, you're going to kill him!" Mika screamed.

His unleashed anger propelled him to beat Roy harder, ignoring Mika and the growing crowd. All he wanted was to annihilate the piece of shit. All the building rage from the previous months came through him as all reason escaped and hatred rooted within him. "You fucking sonofabitch!" he raged.

Then a familiar voice yelling "Stop!" echoed in the distance, pushing through the fog of fury, and he paused and turned. He saw Breanna jumping out of a car and rushing toward him. He looked down at Roy's face, which was beginning to swell, and shoved off him. He stood up and Mika ran over to her boyfriend, cradling his head and whispering something in his ear.

"What's going on here?" a toned man with short brown hair asked.

"Stay the fuck outta this," Steel growled as he wiped blood from his nose.

"Steel, this is Special Agent Raley. Special Agent Powers is behind him. They're FBI agents," Breanna said in tight voice.

Steel glanced at them, then turned his head and spat blood on the grass.

Raley and Powers went over to Roy and helped him up. "You fuckin' asshole. You better stay the fuck away 'cause I'm coming for you." Roy took the tissue from Mika and sopped up the blood on his lip.

Steel lunged for Roy. "Come for me now, you sonofabitch. I didn't see your pussy ass beating mine."

Powers pushed Steel back. "Will you calm the hell down? You wanna end up in the back of our car?"

Steel glowered. "You can't do shit about this." Just then, an SUV with the bronze words "Navajo Tribal Police" emblazoned on the sides pulled up. Raley and Powers threw warning looks at Roy and Steel, then walked over to talk to the officers.

Breanna took a bottle of water and a few tissues out of her tote. She opened the water, soaked the tissues with it, and wiped his face. That simple gesture touched his soul. He smiled at her and swept his fingers down her arm.

"Unbelievable. Figures you're fuckin' the social worker," Roy said loudly as he shook his head.

Steel looked up and caught Mika's piercing stare. "Tell your asshole to shut the fuck up or I'm gonna finish what I started," he said through gritted teeth.

The two FBI men whipped around, their gazes on Breanna, who was turning various shades of red.

Contempt burned in his throat as he jumped forward and sank his fist into Roy's stomach. "That's for insulting my woman, motherfucker."

Roy bowled over and groaned.

"What's going on here?" one of the tribal policemen asked.

Steel spun around, his face breaking out into a wide smile. "Sam. How the fuck are you?"

"Dude." Sam bumped his fist against Steel's. "It's been too damn long. How's your ma?"

"Okay. Yours?"

"Getting old. Fuck, we're all getting old." He laughed as his partner came up beside him. "I don't know if you remember Sani. He was a few grades behind us in high school."

Steel shook his head. "Nah, I don't remember. Sorry, bro."

Sani smiled. "No sweat. I was just a freshman when you were a senior. I've heard a lot of stories about you. Not sure how many of them were true."

"If it deals with chicks, they're all true. I can attest to that. This guy was a woman magnet back when we were in school." Samuel punched Steel lightly in the arm. Steel glanced quickly at Breanna; she was talking with the two FBI men.

"So what happened here?" Sani asked.

Samuel turned to Mika. "Hey, Mika. Is this dude with you?" He pointed to Roy. She nodded. He looked at Steel. "Why don't you tell me what happened."

Steel crossed his arms. "He's trying to cause disruption between Chenoa and me. I told him to fucking butt out. He didn't."

Samuel nodded, then asked Roy, "Do you agree with that?"

"No. I've been living with Mika and Chenoa, and I have a right to be involved in what happens in her life. The bastard is a hothead. He's always hanging around here, flirting with Mika. He threw the first punch."

"Did you adopt Chenoa?" Samuel asked as Sani wrote in his notebook.

"No."

"Are you her stepfather?"

"I'm like one."

"But are you legally her stepdad?"

"No."

Samuel wiped the sweat off his face. "Did you see who threw the first punch, Mika?"

She nodded. "Steel." He stared impassively at her.

"Did you throw the first punch, bro?" Samuel asked Steel.

"Fuck, I don't remember. I just know he pissed the shit outta me. He was getting in my face, and then we were going at it." Several people in the crowd agreed with him, stating that they'd seen the whole thing and Roy threw the first punch.

"They're fuckin' lying! They're protecting *him* because he's one of them. I'm the outsider." Roy broke away from Mika's grip and came closer to Samuel. "I didn't throw the first punch. He did. I was just protecting myself."

In the end, Roy was issued a summons for court, charging him with simple battery—a misdemeanor. They didn't charge Steel for anything.

"You're fuckin' crooked. I'm being railroaded here!" Mika pulled Roy back and stroked his arm.

"What a pussy," Steel said. Mika threw him a scalding look. He laughed.

"Mika, take him back home because I'm ready to run him in." Samuel took a step toward the couple.

Mika said something to Roy in a low voice, and then they walked away.

Samuel cupped Steel's shoulder. "You take care. Don't be a fucking stranger. Next time you come by to see your ma, look me up. We can catch up."

"I'll do that. Say hi to your mom." He glanced at Sani. "Good seeing you, dude."

The two tribal police officers went to their SUV. As they spoke briefly with the two agents, Steel motioned for Breanna to come over. When she came up to him, he whispered, "Don't tell the fucking badges shit about me." She nodded and pressed her lips together. He wanted to kiss those lips and hold her close. "I'll see you later tonight. I love you, baby."

"Me too. Are you okay? Your face is really starting to swell." She looked over her shoulder when the two agents called out her name. "I have to go." She backed away.

"Seven tonight," he said in a barely audible voice.

"Okay," she mouthed, and then she whirled around and walked quickly to the waiting car.

He watched as the car faded away into the distance, then went over to his bike, slipped on his cut, and made his way to his mother's house for a visit.

Chapter Twenty-Four

STEEL WATCHED AS Chenoa spread cream cheese over her bagel. They were sitting on the back patio listening to the gurgling stream while flashing green and blue dragonflies flitted about. A breeze wafted the sweet smell of freshly mown grass toward them.

He loved these easy early afternoons they shared. She'd been living with him for the past two weeks, and she seemed to be thriving.

"I think it's awesome that you're dating Breanna. I knew there was something between you guys. I saw it every time she came into the room at the rehab center when you were there."

"I wish you would've told me." He winked at her when she gave him that "oh Dad" face. "You nervous about starting school next week?"

She took a large bite out of her bagel and chewed for a few seconds. "Kinda. I wish I could've just studied for my GED. Breanna had it all arranged."

"Just give it a try. If you hate Jefferson High, then we can talk. I think it's important for you to be involved in high school activities and not have so much free time. High school can be cool, but I don't want you to stress it. If it's bad, you tell me. Okay?"

"Okay." She stared off into the distance. "It shouldn't be too bad. Michela and Josie are gonna be there. They said it's not a bad school. So we'll see." She turned and smiled at him.

When she smiled, it lit up her whole face. He never grew tired of seeing it. "Remember, if it's not working, let me know, sunshine. I'm in this with you. You don't have to go it alone, ever." He reached out and grabbed her hand, brought it to his lips, and kissed it.

"You know what I wanna do? I wanna go to the clubhouse and play a game of pool with Uncle Paco. I never took him up on the bet he made me a few months ago before I… well… you know."

"Yeah." He stroked her hand. "Why the hell not? Get your shoes on and we'll ride over there. The brothers will be happy to see you."

Fuck the department.

She gobbled down her bagel and jumped from the chair. "I'll only be a few seconds." She dashed into the house.

WHEN THEY ARRIVED at the clubhouse, Chenoa practically jumped from his Harley before he shut the motor off. He caught the helmet she threw at him and laughed as he watched her run through the opened doors, her long black hair swaying. When he entered, he saw Chenoa already sitting at the bar with a group of the brothers around her hugging and talking with her. Her dark eyes sparkled.

"It's fuckin' great to see Chenoa," Paco said.

"She wanted to see everyone, especially you. I think she's gonna challenge you to a pool game." Steel took the tequila shot the prospect put in front of him. "Play a fair game, and let her win or lose on her own."

The vice president nodded. "How's it going with your social work-er," he asked in a low voice.

A broad smile broke over Steel's face. "Fucking good. And her name's Breanna. What do you got going?"

"Nothing, just the way I like it. Club girls and an occasional hang-around satisfy me. I don't need the fuckin' drama of a citizen. I never thought you'd end up with one, let alone an employee with the goddamn government." He took a long pull on his beer. "The brothers are all surprised."

"I'm fucking surprised. She grabbed hold of my balls and there was nothing I could do."

"You guys talking chicks?" Sangre asked as he approached the bar. "Chenoa's looking real good, bro." Steel glared at him and he threw his hands up. "No, I didn't mean it like that. Fuck, she's a kid and your daughter. Do you think I'm fuckin' nuts?"

"Yeah," Goldie said as he sidled up next to the trio.

Sangre gave him the middle finger. "What I meant is that she looks healthy and happy. It's a good thing to see. Damn, you guys got dirty minds." He chuckled.

Steel laughed. "If anyone's got a dirty mind, it's you. All you ever do is think about fucking. You're the damn opposite of Diablo." The brothers laughed, then changed the conversation to Harleys when Chenoa came over.

"Dad, can I go for a ride with Uncle Rooster? He told me he got a brand-new Harley and he said I had to ask you."

"Sure. Just make sure you wear a helmet." He caught Rooster's eye and winked at him.

Rooster nodded and rose to his feet. "You ready to get going, little lady?"

Steel loved the way Chenoa's eyes brightened when she was excited. She scurried over to Rooster and they walked out. Steel trusted Rooster with his life. He and Tattoo Mike were the oldest members of the club. At thirty-six, Rooster had an old lady and a couple of kids, but he gave the brotherhood 100 percent.

His old lady, Shannon, was a hard drinking, tell-it-like-it-is kind of woman, but she had a heart of gold. She and Tattoo Mike's old lady, Sam, were best friends. Sam was a tough lady who didn't take any shit from anyone. Steel liked her because she called it like it was, but she knew her place among the brothers. She showed respect to her man, and she didn't disrespect any of the brothers. Even if a brother called her Samantha—her given name—to tease her, she'd hold her tongue, but her eyes shot daggers. If a non-brother called her Samantha, she'd rip their head off.

Shannon and Sam had no use for the club girls, and sometimes Steel had to call them on it. He felt that all the women should get along. He understood the chasm between the club girls and old ladies, but he didn't tolerate name-calling, rudeness, or deliberate cruelty being leveled at the club women. The old ladies respected that, but there was always tension crackling in the air whenever the two groups bumped into each other at the clubhouse.

"Things going good with Chenoa?" Crow asked as he sat down at one of the tables near the bar.

"Yeah. We'll see how it goes when she starts school next week. One day at a time, you know?" Steel motioned for Ruby to come over.

She sauntered over and wrapped her hands around his bicep. "You're feeling good," she said in a soft voice.

Steel smiled and moved his arm. "Can you have Lena fix me a roast beef sandwich with tomatoes?"

Her toothy smile filled her face. "Sure. You want any sugar with that?" She leaned in close and pressed her impressive chest against him.

He laughed. "Nah, just the sandwich. Too much sugar will get me in trouble."

"I'll take the sugar you're offering him," Sangre said as he grabbed another beer.

"I know you will. I can count on that." Ruby tossed her head and sashayed toward the kitchen, all eyes on her curvy hips as they swayed seductively from side to side.

Paco whistled softly. "You gotta admire a woman who can move like that. Fuck, she's got a great walk."

"Yep. Pure art. Who needs to go to a fuckin' art museum when you got living art in the clubhouse?" Goldie shook his head. "I was so into her swaying ass that I forgot to tell her to get me a sandwich too." He rose from his barstool. "I'll be back."

"Where're you going?" Crow asked.

"The kitchen. I'm gonna tell Lena to make me a sandwich." As he turned to walk away, several members yelled out their orders. "I'm not a fuckin' waiter," he said grudgingly as he grabbed a piece of paper and a pen.

Steel saw Skull walk in and he called him over. "What's going on with our informant? Any new leads on who the distributor is?"

Skull shook his head slowly. "Nope. It looks like things are going quiet for now. It's like everyone's paranoid or something."

"It's probably because some dumb fuck figured out they sold smack to an outlaw's daughter," Paco said, moving over to Steel and Skull.

Steel nodded. "You're probably right."

"I wish we could pay the fuckin' Skull Crushers a visit and persuade them to tell us." Paco smiled at Ruby when she placed roast beef sandwiches in front of him and Steel. As she turned to leave, he gripped her arm. "I'll be looking for you in about an hour, sweetie."

"I'll be waiting." She blew him a kiss and walked out.

Steel sniggered, then picked up his sandwich and took a bite. "I'd love to persuade the fucking punks, but not at the risk of closing down the whole operation before we know who's responsible." The brothers nodded. "We gotta send Jigger in with a wad of cash to make a buy. Greed is a powerful motivator."

"Whoa. We're just talking 'bout you, dude," Sangre said as Jigger walked into the clubhouse.

He dragged a chair over to their table. "Oh yeah? What about?"

"You gotta set up a buy. I want you to hang at the arcades and bowling alley again to see if you can get in touch with a dealer."

"Fuck," he said as he exhaled. "I always get these types of assignments."

"That's 'cause you got a pretty boy's face," Crow teased. Some of the brothers guffawed and others sniggered.

"Can you even grow a fuckin' beard?" Skull asked as his brothers howled.

"Fuck that!" Jigger pushed his chair back.

"Good thing you got your patch. Otherwise, you wouldn't get any prime pussy." Sangre sat back and crossed his leg over his thigh.

Jigger's eyes shot flames, and his neck and face were covered in red splotches. Steel held up his hand. "That's enough. We got some business to discuss. Jigger, you look like a goddamn high schooler. It fucking sucks, but that's the way it is. Hang out this week at the arcades and see what gives. School starts next week, so it's gonna be busy."

"Will do." Jigger picked up his beer.

"Who knows, you may find a girlfriend." Crow wiggled his eyebrows, then busted out laughing when Jigger gave him the finger.

Steel's phone pinged, and he looked at the text.

Breanna: *Thinking bout U.*

He smiled.

Steel: *I like that.*

Breanna: *What're U & Chenoa doing?*

Steel: *At the club.*

Breanna: *WTF?*

Steel: *???*

Breanna: *She's not supposed to B @ club.*

Steel gritted his teeth.

Steel: *What's ur fucking point?*

Breanna: *Ur mad @ me.*

Steel: *Busy. Gotta go.*

Breanna: *Don't shut down on me.*

Steel: *I'm not.*

Breanna: *It's just I'm worried bout Dept & Chenoa.*

His lips pressed into a white slash; she was pissing him the hell off.

Steel: *Don't B. She's not ur kid.*

When he hit "Send" he knew she'd be hurt, but he didn't want her questioning his decisions. When it came to Chenoa, he was very protective.

As he waited for a response from her that never came, he knew he'd crossed the line. The truth was that he was thrilled Breanna cared about Chenoa; she genuinely liked her. He ran his fingers through his hair. *Shimá's right—I'm a hothead.*

He wasn't used to apologizing, especially to women. For him, it was a sign of weakness or an attestation that he'd failed at something.

He started to type an apology to her when Chenoa burst through the door, her hair tousled, her eyes bright, and her voice shrill with excitement. "It was the best, Dad. Uncle Rooster's Harley is so badass." She went over to him and plopped down. "What're you eating? It looks good."

"Roast beef. I'll get you one. Is Rooster's bike better than your old man's?"

She smiled slyly. "No. Nothing's better than yours."

"Right answer." He ruffled her hair.

"I'm gonna fix up. I'll just go into the kitchen and fix my own sandwich." She rose to her feet.

"Ask Lena to do it. She likes doing that shit." He watched as she bounced away, and then he turned to Rooster. "Thanks, man."

"You don't have to tell me that." He clasped Steel's shoulder.

The rest of the afternoon he and Chenoa hung out with the brothers. She lost two games of pool to Paco, but she beat his ass at darts. It was the perfect day.

When six o'clock rolled around, Chenoa came up to Steel and leaned against him. He put his arm around her shoulders and kissed the top of her head.

"Dad, why don't you call Breanna and we can go out to eat. I'm craving Mexican food real bad."

"Sure. I'll see if she can come." *I forgot to send her an apology. Fuck.* "I'll go outside and give her a call. It's quieter." He went behind the clubhouse, plugged in her number, and waited for her to answer. She didn't. A frown crossed his forehead, making his fine lines deepen. He decided he'd send her a text in case she was in a meeting. It seemed that she was always in a meeting with either the special agents, the department, her coworkers, or clients. He'd jump out of his skin if he had her job.

Steel: *Hey. Chenoa & I r going for Mexican. Want to join us? 7 or 7:30?*

No answer. *She's pissed.* But a part of him was too. The truth was she wasn't Chenoa's mother, and he didn't feel like she had a right to tell him what he could or couldn't do with her. *She was only thinking of you.*

The damn department doesn't want Chenoa around the club. She was only scared they'd find out. That was fair. Maybe he was being unreasonable.

Steel: *I don't want u to think I don't care what u think. I may have said some shit I didn't mean.*

Again, no answer.

He jutted out his jaw. *If that's the way you wanna play it, baby, that's fine with me.* He walked back to the clubhouse and went over to Chenoa. "Looks like Breanna can't make it, so it's just gonna be the two of us."

"That's cool. Maybe we can go earlier. I'm starving."

He laughed. "We can go now." She leapt up and went over to the brothers to say her goodbyes. When they went outside, he looked at her. "Jalisco's Restaurant?" She nodded enthusiastically and they left the clubhouse, his arm around her shoulders, tightly tucking her to him.

During dinner he kept glancing at his phone, expecting a text from Breanna, but he didn't hear anything from her. After paying the check, he and Chenoa headed for his Harley. Before he turned on the ignition, he looked over his shoulder. "I wanna stop by Breanna's. You down for that?"

"Yeah. That's fine. I wanted to show her the new lip gloss I got."

When they arrived at her house, he saw her car in the driveway. His muscles tightened as they went up the walk. He had to remember to not blow his stack and make the situation worse, no matter what happened. He rang the doorbell.

After a few minutes, she opened the door. Her hair fell around her like a halo, and she looked killer in her T-shirt and shorts. She raised her brows and opened the screen door. "Hi, Chenoa. How are you?"

Steel ground his teeth.

"Hi. Dad and I just finished dinner. We went to Jalisco's and it was so good. I want to show you this real cool lip gloss I ordered online."

Breanna smiled. "Come on in." She turned and he and Chenoa entered her house. "Do you want something to drink?" She looked at Chenoa only.

"I'll have a Coke, if you have it." Chenoa glanced at Steel. "Do you want anything, Dad?"

He shook his head as he clenched his fists, struggling for control. *No one fucking ignores me.* He stood near the front door with his arms crossed over his chest as Breanna placed a can of Coke in front of Chenoa and then sat down next to her, gushing about how beautiful the color of her new lip gloss was.

This is fucking bullshit.

"Remember you promised to show me your new kit of eyeshadows for the smoky eye look?" Chenoa asked as she picked up her drink.

"I forgot. I'll go get them." Breanna rose from the couch and went to her bedroom.

Steel followed her with narrowed eyes. "Chill for a few, okay, sunshine?"

Chenoa nodded and picked up the remote control from the coffee table.

He went into Breanna's room and closed the door.

She gasped when she came out of the bathroom holding a red oblong box. "You startled me," she muttered as she brushed past him.

He gripped her arm and yanked her to him. "What the fuck?" he gritted.

"Let go of me." She tried to pull away, but he only held on tighter.

"You don't fucking treat me like you did, woman. That's bullshit. If you're pissed at me, you fucking talk to me. You *never* disrespect me. Ever." His voice was deep, gravelly.

"You're hurting me," she said. He let go of her arm. "So you want me to respect you, but it's okay if you don't do the same to me? Sounds like the typical biker double standard my dad was famous for." She lifted her chin in defiance.

"I'm not your fucking father, so don't always compare me to him when things seem fucked up to you. And my version of respect isn't a double standard. I treat you with respect. I said something about

Chenoa not being your kid and you got all fucking bent out of shape. Why the hell didn't you answer my text?"

"I just figured you didn't want me around Chenoa since she wasn't my daughter."

He snorted. "Bullshit. It's more like you were pouting and trying to punish me for saying something you didn't like. I don't go in for games, baby. If I don't like something, I'm gonna tell you. If I like something, I'm gonna tell you. You're acting childish as fuck."

Her mouth twisted into a grimace. "I was only concerned because I don't want the department to revoke Chenoa living with you. It's a very real thing that can happen. Then you tell me not to worry since she's not mine. Since when do people have to be related in order to care about them? I *do* care about Chenoa, and I did even before I met you. So your remark was fucking stupid."

The scalding anger which had been coursing through his veins earlier began to seep out, a radiating warmth slowly replacing it. He swung her into his arms and held her tightly while she twisted to get free.

"Let me go," she huffed, her face red.

"No," he said softly. Her upper lip curled in disdain. "Don't give me that look, baby. I'm admitting that I may have said something to piss you off, but you need to talk to me about it instead of ignoring me."

"Can't you just say you're sorry? Is it that hard?"

"I sent you a text," he said curtly.

"You mean the lame one that said you *may* have said something you didn't mean." She laughed dryly. "Didn't do it for me."

Why the fuck do I want this woman? She irritates the hell outta me. "I told you I don't play games."

"I'm not playing games. This is about owning something you did that hurt me. If you can't do that, then we have a real problem."

"What the fuck do you want from me?" he asked in a low voice taut with anger.

"An apology." Her gaze held his.

"Fuck, woman." Apologizing wasn't his style. He'd make up for shit he was sorry he said or did through actions, not words. Maybe it was because when he was growing up, his father used to make him apologize for being a bastard every time he whipped him with a belt or tree branch. "I owned it. You fucking know that. Saying a few words doesn't mean shit." He inhaled sharply. "When I was growing up, my dad always made a shitload of promises to all of us and never fucking delivered. Not once." He remembered how his dad would tell his mom how much he loved her, but he treated her like shit most of the time. Steel lived in a world of action and few words. Actions were the reflection of a person's heart and soul; words were cheap knockoffs.

Breanna stroked his cheek. It was as if she felt the pain from his childhood, and she understood. "I know," she whispered. She clasped her hand behind his neck and pulled his face to hers, kissing him with such tenderness that it took him aback.

"Oh, baby." He tugged her closer and held her snugly as he kissed her passionately. "Never doubt that I love you. You're very important to me and Chenoa."

"Thanks for that. And you're right, I acted silly. I should've told you how I felt."

"It's in the past. I want you to come back to my place. I need you, baby." He cupped her ass and squeezed her rounded cheeks. He could squeeze her fine butt all day long. He'd never been so crazy in love with any woman the way he was with her.

"What about Chenoa?" she whispered between kisses.

"She's cool. She likes that we're together. I want you to spend the night. I'm tired of waking up without you next to me."

"Me too. I've missed you so much." She pillowed her head against his shoulder. "I'll go over tonight, but first I have to show her my new eyeshadows. She's been waiting."

They went out and Chenoa craned her neck. "Did you guys make up?"

Breanna sank down on the couch and handed her the makeup box. "Why're you asking that?"

"Because it was obvious you had a fight. I mean, this is the first time I've ever seen my dad so glum and anxious over a woman. He must've checked his phone like a million times during dinner to see if you'd contacted him."

"You're exaggerating a bit, aren't you?" He laughed and ruffled her hair. "Let's head out."

ONCE THEY WERE home, Chenoa made a big bowl of popcorn that they all shared as he sat through one of the corniest love stories he'd ever had to endure. He knew that Chenoa and Breanna would unite forces against him and he'd end up watching some crappy-ass movie. He didn't mind if it meant spending the night with his two favorite girls.

After the movie, Chenoa went up to bed and he and Breanna made out for a little bit on the couch. When they moved it to his bedroom, she was nervous about making too much noise when they made love, but as he heightened her arousal, she let herself go. Steel loved watching how she gave in to her passion the more he teased and played with her. And when he hovered over her and shoved his hard cock inside her, he covered her mouth with his and swallowed her moans of pleasure as he fucked her long and good. Her nails digging into his flesh heightened his sexual delight, making him crave her again before they'd even finished.

As he plunged into her over and over, her face contorted and he knew she was close. He rubbed his index finger against her hard, slick spot and sucked her nipples as the tide of ecstasy ripped through her. Watching her come while trying to keep her moans and whimpers low turned him way the fuck on. When she opened her eyes, they were misted with love and satisfaction. He stiffened and held her gaze as he rasped, "Breanna," and then he filled her. His cock kept twitching in her as her pussy walls clamped around him, milking his dick dry. She kissed his head and caressed him as he panted before collapsing on top of her, his chest heaving.

After a long while, he rolled off her and tugged her close to him. They fell asleep from total exhaustion, locked in each other's arms.

Chapter Twenty-Five

CHENOA SAT IN Jefferson High's cafeteria picking at her lukewarm burrito. She'd been in school for almost a month, and she hated it more each day. She'd been so bummed when she'd found out Michela and Josie weren't in any of her classes. Because she'd skipped so much school, and her mom hadn't followed through with the homeschooling the way she should have, she was in a bunch of remedial classes.

She glanced at the wall clock. *Josie and Michela should be here soon.* Hanging with them during lunch and after school were the only highlights of her school days. She felt like a fish out of water; she was the only person from the reservation at the school. She'd met Josie and Michela when her mom had joined a mom's group when she'd been like five years old. They'd gone to grade school together for a few years, but after her mom had a falling out with their mothers, she'd been pulled out of the town's elementary school and enrolled in the reservation's. When she reconnected with Josie and Michela on social media, they'd become fast friends.

Chenoa opened her Spanish book and went over the vocabulary for the quiz later that afternoon, jerking her head up when something hit the table she was sitting at. Her stomach twisted in a knot when she saw Hannah, Abigail, Morgan, and Hailey standing in front of her. They were the popular girls in the school, especially the junior class. They were the cheerleaders who spurred on the mediocre football team with their inane cheers, and they walked around bullying anyone who didn't fit into their definition of beautiful. For the past week, they'd latched onto her. Chenoa wished she were invisible again like when she'd first started the school year.

She stared blankly at them.

"You're at our table," Hannah chirped. She was the ringleader who wore too much lipstick and gloss, and way too many hair extensions.

"I didn't know you could reserve tables," Chenoa replied.

"I don't think you heard Hannah," Morgan said as she placed her hands on the table and leaned forward. "You're at our fucking table." The other girls sniggered.

Chenoa looked around and noticed several empty tables. "I was here first." She swung her hand in a semicircle. "There are plenty of empty ones." She spotted Michela and Josie and waved them over.

"What's going on?" Josie asked under her breath, her eyes wide as she took in the perky quartet.

"They're saying—"

Hannah interrupted Chenoa. "She's sitting at our table."

"Oh," said Josie. She and Michela immediately jumped up. "Let's go over there." Josie pointed to a table on the other side of the room.

"Fuck no. I'm not going anywhere. You don't own this table." Her dark eyes flashed.

"Leave it alone, Chenoa," Michela whispered. "They get any table they want. It's easier to move than to make a big issue out of it."

"I don't give a damn." She jutted her chin out in defiance and stared at Hannah. "You're not getting this table 'cause I'm not fucking moving. If you wanna do something about it, just say the word."

Hannah's face twisted and the other girls with her gasped. It seemed like she was weighing her options, but Chenoa's blazing eyes and clenched teeth stayed steady. "I shouldn't expect too much from reservation trash," she said. Abigail, Morgan, and Hailey laughed. "Let's go, girls." They walked away and Hannah said over her shoulder, "Watch yourself, squaw. You've made an enemy." They went out through the doors leading to the courtyard.

"Why the hell didn't you just move?" Josie asked as she set her backpack on the floor. "Hannah and her clique can make your life at Jefferson miserable."

Michela nodded. "Josie's right. That was a bad move. Nobody challenges Hannah and her sisters."

"I'm not letting that bitch tell me what to do. I don't give a shit about what she says or does. I can hold my own. She doesn't bother me." But the racial slurs Hannah had said pierced through Chenoa, even though she'd never admit it to her friends. *Why the fuck is Dad making me do this shit?* Licks of fire burned through her as she pushed away her burrito.

When she got home from school that day, her dad was in the garage messing with his Harley. His big smile melted her heart.

"How was school?"

"Fine."

"Everything going okay? Anything you wanna talk about?"

"Everything's fine and there's nothing I wanna talk about. I got a lot of homework, so I'm gonna go to my room and get started on it."

Steel wiped the grease from his face with a rag. "I'm grilling steaks tonight. Some of the guys are gonna come by for some chow. You wanna invite any friends?"

"Nope," she said over her shoulder as she walked inside the house. She closed her bedroom door, threw her backpack across the room, and then flung herself on her bed. Chenoa loved her mom and dad so much, and her dad was trying so hard to be there for her. She saw the fear in the fringes of his eyes and it made her feel bad and guilty. She knew she'd put it there. As long as she could remember, she never saw fear in her dad, and now she saw it every day. *I'm scared too, Dad.* She'd been out of rehab for almost two months, and still the memory of the heroin rush clung to her. She wanted to feel it again. At times she felt as though she was being deprived of air, the want of it that prevalent.

She hated how overpowering smack's lure was; it felt like someone was constantly pulling on her sleeve, relentlessly attempting to guide her in the opposite direction she was trying to go. *I can't go back to using. I can't. I don't want to disappoint Mom or Dad. And Dad's trying so hard. Fuck! Why can't I get the memory of it out of my mind?* She hit her head repeatedly with her fists, hoping the pain would mask the thought of the drug.

I just have to make it. I just do. I'll be okay. I'm okay.

Her shoulders slumped and she stared at the Navajo-patterned comforter on her bed that her mother had given her. Her mind was a clouded gray, and her briny tears welled in the cracks of her lips as the hollowness within engulfed her.

Chapter Twenty-Six

STEEL SAT ON the back patio drinking a cup of black coffee, absentmindedly watching the changing aspen leaves sway in the crisp breeze. His gut told him Chenoa was on a slippery slope. She smiled at dinner, laughed at his jokes, but he saw the hunger lurking in her, along with her waning strength. Whenever he asked if she wanted to talk, she would just shake her head. She'd reconnected with some of her old friends on the rez; friends who were like vultures waiting to devour her. He'd shut that down immediately, forbidding her to hang with them. She'd yelled at him, told him she hated him, and they'd had one of their biggest fights ever, but he didn't care; he'd do anything to keep her from getting sucked in. He'd known heroin addicts, and the power of the drug surpassed everything. He was certain Chenoa was fighting it hard, and he prayed the drug wouldn't lure her back.

His phone rang and he smiled when he saw Hawk's name. "Hey," he said.

"How's it going with Chenoa?" Hawk asked.

"Okay. One day at a fucking time." He took a gulp of coffee. "What's up?"

"We got the confirmation that the fuckin' Demon Riders are the supplier for smack in your county. Banger called this one. These sonsofbitches have gotta be stopped."

"Fuck! I'll call an emergency church, but I know the vote will be war." Steel exhaled.

"We've been talking at church with the brothers, and the consensus was that the Demon Riders have been a pain in our ass ever since Dustin and Shack joined up with them. The agreement is that if you want help, the Insurgents are with you all the way."

Warmth spread through him when he heard Hawk's words. Brothers coming together to fight a common evil was what the brotherhood was all about. His ties with the Insurgents went way back, and those ties would never be broken. Loyalty for the brotherhood transcended clubs and locations. Insurgents and Night Rebels would ride together.

This is why I love this fucking life. Love, respect, and loyalty were what the outlaw's world was all about.

"Thanks, brother," he said.

"Call me back when you got the details nailed down. We'll all go from Pinewood Springs."

"Sounds good. I'll be in touch."

After his call with Hawk, he texted Paco and told him to let everyone know there'd be an emergency church at five o'clock that evening. He jumped out of the chair and went inside, calling Breanna.

"Hey, baby. Can you come over earlier tonight?"

"Yeah. What's going on?"

"We got church, and I don't wanna leave Chenoa alone in the house until I get back."

"Is she doing okay?"

"She says yes, but I don't think so. I don't know if it's school, living away from the rez, or what, but I got a bad feeling."

"Do you think she's using?" Breanna asked in a hushed tone.

"Not yet. I know she's fighting it real hard, but… I don't know."

"Heroin is a powerful drug, and it's a fucking hard one to conquer. I'm not saying it can't be done, but it can be extremely difficult. Nicholas has been trying for years." She paused a moment. "I'm sorry. I shouldn't have said that. I'm supposed to be positive, and here I am making your fears worse."

"No worries. I know smack's a ruthless motherfucker. Anyway, I want you to keep an eye on her. I know I don't need to tell you, but don't let any of her friends come over except for Josie and Michela."

"Is something going on with the club?"

"Yeah."

"Something dangerous?"

He laughed. "Everything we do is dangerous, baby."

She giggled. "Okay, that was a stupid question. Is it about what's going on with the drugs in Alina?"

"Babe, you know I can't tell you. It's club business."

"All right. I'll leave work a little early and come on over."

STEEL STOOD IN front of the brothers, listening to them scream, curse, and pound their fists into anything they could find, even if it was another brother. After letting them blow off some steam, Steel slammed the gavel on the wooden block. "I'm gonna take it that we're all in agreement for war?" Voices clamored and chairs were knocked over. Again he slammed the gavel down. "To comply with the bylaws, we gotta take a vote. All in favor of declaring war on the Demon Riders of Johnstown, Iowa, say 'Aye.'"

A resounding "Aye" reverberated off the concrete walls. "Then it's settled," Paco said. "Steel's gonna name the brothers who'll go on this mission. The Insurgents are banding with us. We need some brothers here to protect the club and give the fuckin' Skull Crushers a beat-down."

"We're gonna meet up with the Insurgents in Pinewood Springs. We'll leave early in the morning. Diablo, Muerto, Sangre, Goldie, Chains, Army, Crow, Brutus, and Cueball will be coming with me. Since Paco's the VP, he'll stay behind and run things until we get back. For the brothers who are going with me to Pinewood Springs, we'll leave at three in the morning, which should get us into Pinewood at about seven. No partying or heavy boozing, but fucking's always good."

Whistles and guffaws circled around the room.

"When do we leave for Johnstown?" Sangre asked.

Steel shrugged. "I'm gonna work out the details with Hawk and Banger when we get to Pinewood, but I'd say we'll probably leave tomorrow night, rest up for a day, and then attack at night." He wiped the sheen above his upper lip. "We need to get our ammo, guns, and other weapons ready. Obviously we're taking the SUVs and pickups. Can't have our cams announcing us." He leaned against the wall, his thumbs hooked in his belt loops.

A solemnness fell over the members as they contemplated the enormity of the task ahead. Going to war was always a last resort for most MCs, and it wasn't something the Night Rebels jumped into lightly, but their backs had been forced against the wall, and they had no intention of backing down. The brothers knew that some of the ones going may not come back alive, and that many may be wounded, but it was a consequence in their world. The threat of war was omnipresent, always lurking in the shadows, waiting to appear. Violence and uncertainty were as much a part of the outlaw world as were loyalty, love, and mutual trust.

It was late when Steel got home, and the house was enshrouded in darkness. He went into the kitchen and took out a large bottled water, guzzling it down. The declaration of war weighed heavily on him. He didn't want to lose any of his brothers; they were his family more than his own brother and sister. A thrill of excitement rode down his spine as he thought of putting an end to the supply of drugs in the county. Their actions would also tell other MCs not to set up shop in Alina. *All I have to do is find out who the distributor is and fucking burn his ass.*

He climbed the stairs and stopped in front of Chenoa's bedroom door, quietly turning the handle and opening it. He heard her deep breathing and went to the side of her bed, staring down at her. She looked peaceful. Not wanting to wake her, he put his hand over her hair but didn't touch it. "May the Holy People watch over you, sunshine. The universe walks with you and you walk with it," he said under his breath before he turned away and closed her door.

When he walked into his room, he saw Breanna snuggled under the covers, a hint of vanilla and apricot wafting in the air. He took off his cut and hung it on the back of a chair, then went over to the bed and sat on the edge of it. He pulled off his boots and stripped out of his jeans and boxers, then slipped under the covers. She stirred and turned around, smiling when her sleepy gaze landed on his. She ran her fingertips up and down his arm. "Hey," she breathed.

"Hey." He slid closer to her, drawing her to him. His dick hardened when he felt her naked skin under his calloused hands. "Everything go okay tonight with Chenoa?" He skimmed his fingers across her face.

She scooted up so her face was closer to his. "It was fine. We ordered pizza and salad, went online and bought a lot of makeup with your credit card, and watched a movie."

He chuckled. "Glad my credit card entertained you." He kissed her forehead.

"Are things good at the club? Did you fix whatever problem you had?"

"Not yet, baby." He pressed her closer to him. "I gotta go outta town for a little bit."

"When?"

"Early in the morning."

"So soon?"

"Yeah. I want you to take Chenoa over to Mika's tomorrow. I don't want her staying alone while I'm gone. I'll call and talk to Mika about it. I'll call Chenoa too. I didn't mean to get home so late. I wanted to talk to her before she went to bed."

"She had so much fun spending your money that it wore her out." She laughed and peppered kisses on his throat. "I'm scared." Her breath was warm against his skin.

"I know."

"I feel that something big is going down. Am I right?"

He tilted his head down and glided his lips over hers. "It's club business, babe. You know that."

"Promise me you'll come home? I don't know what I'd do if anything happened to you."

"I'll be fine. There's no way I'm ready to pack it in." He lightly tickled her back, loving the feel of her goose bumps as they pebbled under his fingertips.

"I can stay with Chenoa if you'd like. I can come over here until you get back."

"I'd love that, babe, but Mika would shit a brick if I let that happen. She's been pissed enough over Chenoa living with me, and I don't want her saying a bunch of shit to you or Chenoa. It's only for a few days." He let his fingers skim across her rounded ass. "I love you for offering to help." The truth was that he'd much rather have Breanna with Chenoa than her staying with Mika and Roy, as he didn't trust either of them to monitor her the way he'd been doing it, but he didn't have a choice.

Her palm skated across his hardened dick.

"Touching me there is gonna bring you some rough fucking, baby," he joked as he lightly pulled her hair.

"I'm counting on it," she said as she threw off the covers and wiggled down so her face was next to his stiffening cock.

THEY HELD EACH other tightly, neither of them sleeping as they listened to one another's steady breathing. Knowing that she was scared, he covered her face with kisses, then pulled her flush to him and stroked her hair.

I'm scared too, but not for me. I'm fucking scared for Chenoa. I won't be around to catch her if she stumbles. He breathed out forcefully.

"You okay?" Breanna whispered.

"Just worried about Chenoa."

"I'll keep an eye on her. Mika loves her and wants the best for her. She'll be okay. You better get some sleep if you're leaving early in the morning."

"Yeah."

But sleep evaded him. Breanna's even breathing made him smile; he was glad she'd fallen asleep despite her worry. He needed all his energy for the mission, so he closed his eyes and soon fell into a fitful sleep.

A few hours later, his alarm went off. He sat up abruptly, waiting a few seconds for his eyes to adjust to the darkness. He looked over at Breanna and smiled. *She's a good woman. She fits into my world.* He carefully rolled out of bed, showered, and came out to dress.

She was sitting up in bed, her arms hugging her knees. "You going?" she asked in a hushed voice.

"Yeah." He looped his belt around his jeans. "Go back to sleep." He finished dressing and came over to her, running his calloused thumb over her cheek, pain tugging at him when he felt the wetness on her skin. "Don't cry, baby. It's gonna be fine. Come on now." He lowered his head and kissed her lips, the briny taste of them pricking his tongue. "No more tears, okay?" He grabbed a tissue from the box on the nightstand and gently dried her face, and then he went to the closet. Opening a strongbox, he stuffed his pockets with spare bullets, packs of razor blades, and a Glock 9.

"Call me when you get to wherever you're going, so I won't worry as much." She sniffled and grabbed another tissue, the jagged rip as it left the box filling the air.

"I'll call you when I can. Don't freak out if you don't hear from me for several days." He slipped on his leather jacket over his cut.

"I'll try not to." Her voice hitched, and it stabbed his heart.

He padded over to her again and covered her mouth with his, kissing her deeply before he pulled back and covered her face with feathery kisses. His hand skated down to her stomach and he rubbed it. "I gotta come back if I'm gonna fill your belly with a child. I love you, baby. Be brave for me."

"I love you too," she said against his ear. "Be safe."

He nodded, then pulled away and walked out of the room. When he started his Harley, a mix of love, fear, and hope flooded him as he thought of Breanna and Chenoa. *I'm not gonna be worth shit if I don't get rid of the emotions.* Emotions and war had no business sharing the same stage. In order to achieve his objective, he had to shut out all thoughts of his little girl and his woman; otherwise, one of his brothers could die.

The brotherhood looked to him to lead them, and letting feelings seep in was unacceptable.

He was a warrior, and he'd lead the Night Rebels to victory.

He looked up and saw Breanna's silhouette in the window. She waved at him. He nodded, then switched on the ignition and rode away.

It's showtime.

Chapter Twenty-Seven

THE NIGHT REBELS arrived in Pinewood Springs early that morning, stopping at Ruthie's Diner for some breakfast before going to the Insurgents' clubhouse. After Steel put his order in, he slipped out back and called Breanna. She picked up on the first ring.

"I miss you already," she said.

He pictured her twirling her hair around her finger as she usually did when she was on the phone. "I've only been gone five hours." He chuckled. "You warm me good, woman."

"I'm just getting ready to take Chenoa to school. You wanna talk to her?"

"Yeah. Put her on." Chenoa's soft voice sang through the phone. "Hey, sunshine. Did Breanna fill you in?"

"Yup. She said you're on business and will be home soon. When's soon, Dad?"

"A few days, give or take, so you're gonna stay with your mom. You good with that?"

"Yeah. That's cool."

"Remember to stay away from your reservation friends. I know it's gonna be hard 'cause they're right there, but you know their influence is bad. It's just gonna be for a few days."

"I know. I'll stay away."

"If anything comes up or you're feeling stressed or whatever the fuck it is, you call me. Don't do anything until you call me."

"Ya… sure. I gotta finish getting ready or I'll be late for school."

"Okay. Love you, sunshine."

"Me too, Dad. Bye."

"Are you still there?" Breanna asked, coming back on the line.

"Yeah. You take care of yourself. I'll call when I can."

"You take care too. Did… uh… did you mean what you said earlier about wanting a baby?"

"Fuck yeah. I want our baby growing in you." He frowned. "You don't want that?"

"I never thought about it, but I do. I'd love it." She giggled.

"Then we'll work on it when I get back. Love you, babe."

"I love you too. I better go, Chenoa's calling for me. Please come home safe."

He stared at the blank screen for a few seconds. When he'd told her he wanted her to have his baby, it had just come out of him. It'd surprised the hell out of him, but he supposed it was the impending war that made him blurt it out. He never thought he'd love another woman after Mika. It'd been so long since his heart had felt love for a woman that it took him by surprise. He'd never thought about having another child, but now that Breanna was in his life, he wanted to share it with her. He wanted them to have a child together.

He scrubbed his face with his fist, his five o'clock shadow rough against his skin. *When I get back, I'm gonna make her my old lady.* Heat radiated through his chest; he never thought he'd find a woman worthy to wear his patch. He let the moment wash over him, and then he let it go. He had to. Happiness and love wouldn't survive the war, only violence and hatred.

He pressed his lips together and called Mika next. She was thrilled Chenoa would be staying with her for a few days. He gave Mika the rules, and she was miffed but said she'd make sure Chenoa toed the line and didn't hang with her old friends.

After breakfast they went to the Insurgents' clubhouse. Banger greeted them and an hour later, Insurgents and Night Rebels were stuffed into a cramped room listening to Banger, Hawk, and Steel explain how things were going to go down in Iowa. The plan was simple: strike and retreat. Since Hawk had been in the Marines Reconnaissance and had served four tours in Afghanistan, he was instrumental in coming up with the attack plan. He had everything meticulously laid out.

Since it was an eleven-hour drive to Johnstown, Iowa, they'd leave at seven that night. Banger had some buddies in the neighboring county who'd put them up. The plan was to attack at two o'clock in the morning on the day after they arrived. The Insurgents had already sent three of their brothers—Puck, Johnnie, and Axe—to the Demon Riders clubhouse to scout it out. When the two brotherhoods arrived, they'd meet up with them to find out what they'd learned.

They would use a surprise attack, with a rush of men, smoke bombs, and machine guns. Grenades would be used as a last resort. Even though the Demon Riders' clubhouse was out in the boonies, as most outlaw clubs were, they still didn't want to attract the law. In the dead of night, in a rural community, sounds traveled a long distance.

"We've gotta get in and out quick. We find out from my brothers how many are in the clubhouse right now, how many exits, and if there're any citizens. We wanna try and eliminate the trash without hurting anyone who hasn't done us any wrong," Banger said.

Hawk stepped away from the table. "That said, this is war. There will be casualties, and some of them may be innocent. It's just the way it goes, but we'll try and minimize that consequence." The members nodded, their faces serious and taut.

"From the Insurgents' side we got me, Hawk, Throttle, Bones, Rock, Chas, Jax, Rags, Bear, Wheelie, and Jerry leaving tonight. Like I said, we got three other brothers already there." Banger wiped his hands on his jeans.

Steel leaned against the back wall. "We got ten of us, so we should be good with our numbers. Goldie's our road captain and he and yours, Throttle, will handle the vehicles that have the weapons." Hawk and Banger nodded.

"Doc's gonna ride with us," said Throttle. "He said he's got a couple suitcases full of shit to patch us up if we need it." Laughter rumbled around the room.

"He can be trusted?" Steel asked.

"Fuck yeah. He's been keeping us from dying for 'bout ten years," Throttle replied.

"And the twenty-five thousand we'll put in his fuckin' hands also helps his loyalty," Hawk said.

"And the desire to live," Crow added. Hawk laughed, nodding.

"Have a bit of relaxation, but nothing hardcore 'cause we got a lot of shit that's gonna go down. We leave tonight at seven."

Banger banged the gavel on the table and church was over.

UNDER THE CHILL of the mist that spread over the field, Steel clutched the cold metal of the assault rifle. He commando-crawled toward the Demon Riders inside the clubhouse—the enemy. In front, behind, and on the sides of him, he saw the smudgy forms of his brothers moving toward battle. Frosty puffs of vapor rose from their noses and mouths as they pushed onward.

Puck, Johnnie, and Axe's scouting had confirmed that there were fourteen members who resided in the clubhouse, plus four club girls, and that Wednesday early mornings were quiet. As far as they could tell, there were no citizens involved with the day-to-day activities of the club. They didn't have patrols except for a pack of pit bulls and German shepherds—seven in all. The pivotal element was to keep the dogs from barking.

From what the three Insurgents observed, it appeared that they weren't trained guard dogs, just vicious beasts who were kept at the point of starvation. Several MCs kept their dogs hungry in the belief that it made them meaner, so the Insurgents and the Night Rebels figured that the dogs would be entirely susceptible to an offer of food. Once Axe, Puck, and Johnnie fed the dogs, they'd shoot them with dart guns loaded with tranquillizers.

While the three brothers dealt with the dogs, the group of bikers crawling in the fields moved as one in a sea of black. Each face was grim against the chilly wind, and on every hand was a black glove. The sky was dark and gloomy without a star in sight. The clouds were so thick that only a sliver of the moon shone through.

When Axe gave the signal to Hawk that the dogs were down, Hawk flicked a lighter several times and the group jumped to their feet, crouching as they approached the dark club. The brothers easily secured the exits. Steel stepped lightly on the porch and slowly picked the lock, then carefully turned the knob and went in, four of his men in tow. He met Hawk, who'd entered from the rear, in the middle of a decent-sized room.

The clubhouse was an old two-story farmhouse with a basement. Its floorboards squeaked and they had to walk carefully and slowly to mute the sound. Between the two clubs, they outnumbered the Demon Riders by ten. Also, the club had no idea it was being invaded, so Steel figured they partied too much the night before, which would prove beneficial to the Night Rebels in claiming victory after it was all finished.

He glanced at Hawk. "My men are telling me there's no one on this floor. They must all be upstairs and downstairs." Steel motioned for five of his men to go downstairs while Hawk did the same with four of his brothers.

"Let's go upstairs," Hawk said.

Steel nodded. "Once I give the signal, all hell will break loose." Hawk tilted his chin and shined his flashlight on the staircase. All of the men had kill-lights—large industrial flashlights—which acted as both a light source and a weapon. They were legal and effective; many a rival member's head had been split open with them.

The plan was that the minute the first shots were heard, the brothers downstairs would open fire. The brothers outside would make sure to eliminate anyone who escaped the massacre in the house.

Just as Steel was ready to give the word to the men upstairs with him, he heard a loud voice boom from below, "What the fuck is goin' on?" He spun around and saw a man in his forties coming up the stairs, an assault rifle in his hands. "Get the fuck down here or I'll shoot," the man said.

Steel saw a couple of Demon Riders behind him. *Where the fuck did they come from? I thought the first floor had been secured.*

"Drop your fuckin' weapon. Nice and easy. Kick it down the stairs." The man took two more steps forward.

Steel glanced sideways at Hawk, who stood in the shadows. It seemed like the man and his cohorts thought Steel was the only intruder in the clubhouse. "I'm not dropping shit," he said through clenched teeth.

"Then your ass is gonna be filled with holes." He climbed another step. "Who the fuck are you?"

"Fuck you," Steel said as his finger tightened on the trigger. Then he heard Brutus's voice, loud and angry. "Put your fuckin' guns down or I'm gonna start shooting."

He must have come up from the basement. Perfect timing, brother.

The man pointing the gun at Steel turned around for a split second, and Steel used that opportunity to lunge at him, shoving him down the stairs. Several deep voices emerged from behind the closed doors upstairs. It was only a matter of time before all the Demon Riders would be out of their rooms.

Before he could give the signal, shots came from the basement, then the first floor, and then where he was upstairs. The gunshots cracked into the air as loud as thunder as men screamed, cursed, and cried out in pain. The violent noise filled the club and spilled outside, cracking into the startled air. The endless *rat-a-tat-tat* of assault rifles created their own harmonies as the smell of gunpowder mingled with the coppery scent of blood. More shouting. More screaming. More running. The attack was fierce, efficient, and deadly.

On the second floor, Steel went from room to room, kicking open doors and flinging rounds of bullets in rapid succession. "You secure the attic?" he asked Sangre who bolted past him, blood dripping down his arm.

"I'm headed there now. Jax and Rock are up there. I think Diablo is breaking necks with his fuckin' bare hands downstairs. He threw his weapon down a while ago."

"What the fuck?" Steel said as he entered one of the rooms.

"What can I say? The brother's fuckin' nuts. Gotta cover Jax and Rock." Sangre dashed up the stairs.

Steel glanced around the room and saw a Demon Rider lying facedown in a pool of blood on the floor. He went over and nudged him with his boot, turning him over. The man's dull eyes had the sheen of death in them, and he knew the dude was no more. Steel started to leave when he heard a small whimper and scratching on the floor. The sound was coming from the closet. He raised his weapon and flung open the door. A woman screamed and curled up in a ball as if to become invisible.

"You a club girl?" he said in a harsh voice.

Her brown head nodded. "Please don't hurt me. I won't say anything. Just pretend like you never saw me. I'll never say anything. Just please don't kill me." She caught her breath and soft sobs shook her shoulders.

"How old are you?"

"Fifteen," she said, her teeth chattering.

"What the fuck? What the hell you doing here?"

"I belong to Shack. I'm his woman for now."

Steel felt his stomach twist. *His woman. Fucking pervert. She's younger than Chenoa, and Shack's a few years older than me.* "You from around here?"

She shook her head, her face still hidden in her arms. "No. I'm from Des Moines. Shack found me at another clubhouse. I used to hang there because my friend's boyfriend was a member. They were playing poker and I was part of the bet. I lost and Shack won me."

"Fuck," he muttered under his breath. "You got family you can go home to?"

"Yeah. I never wanted to come here, but once I was here, I couldn't leave." She sniffled and raised her head slightly to wipe her nose.

"You stay in here." He took out a wad of bills and threw five hundred dollars on the ground near her. "Take the money and get your ass back home. The goddamn badges will be coming, so you can wait for them or go it alone." He backed away and walked to the door.

"Thanks." Her small voice sliced through the rage and hatred that consumed him. He walked out of the room.

"All secure in there?" Sangre asked as he, Jax, and Rock came down the stairs from the attic.

Steel nodded. "The fucker in there's dead. They all are up here. What about the attic?"

"Same," said Rock. "I'm gonna go down and see if Banger and Hawk want me to do anything else." He rushed down the stairs, taking them two at a time.

"Are any of our guys hurt?" Steel asked Sangre and Jax.

"I heard Crow and Army got hit. Don't know how bad," Sangre answered. "Not sure about the Insurgents. Did you hear anything?" He looked at Jax.

"Bones said Wheelie and Rags are in a bad way. They got them in the van with Doc." Jax wiped his forehead with his gloved hand, leaving a smear of blood on it.

"Let's get everyone together and get the fuck outta here. The badges will probably be coming soon." Steel hurried down the stairs, then stopped when he saw a circle of Insurgents and Night Rebels around Banger and Dustin. Banger was bleeding from the mouth and nose; Dustin's T-shirt was soaked in blood and he was holding his side.

"I've been waiting a fuckin' long time for this, you sonofabitch," Banger said as he stood in a fighter's stance in front of Dustin. Steel saw a long sharp knife in his hands. "I'm gonna cut the life outta you slice by slice. You've been a fuckin' pain in my ass for too goddamn long."

"The problem with you is you let the power of being president of the national chapter get to your fuckin' head." Dustin lunged at Banger, a thin wail rising as Banger cut him straight across his upper torso.

"I gotta get to my men. Two of them are down," Steel said to Hawk.

"I know. I got my brothers to take 'em to Doc. He's fixing them now, but we gotta get the fuck outta here." Hawk lifted his hand and several brothers scurried outside.

"Where's Shack?" Steel asked.

"Throttle has him. Banger wants a go at him too." Hawk chuckled. "Our prez has been waiting a long time for this day."

"Do you think Banger would mind if I kill the bastard?" Steel cracked his knuckles.

Hawk shrugged. "Banger, Steel wants to waste Shack's pathetic fuckin' ass. You down for it?"

A loud shriek bounced off the wall as Banger plunged the knife in Dustin for the final, fatal cut. "Go for it. Then we gotta move our damn asses."

Hawk pointed Steel to the back room. He went in and found Throttle leaning against a wooden table, a trussed-up Shack on the floor. "Banger comin'?" Throttle asked.

"Nah. He's given me the pleasure." Steel went over and kicked Shack full force in the face with his steel-toed boot. "That's for kidnapping and fucking a fifteen-year-old." Then he pulled out his knife, knelt down, grabbed Shack by the hair, and placed the knife against his throat. He pushed the tip of it into his flesh and a tiny red line trickled down. "And this is for bringing fucking smack to my county. For making my little girl an addict. Rot in hell, you motherfucking maggot." The gleaming knife sliced across Shack's neck. Torrents of blood flowed as he gurgled for a few seconds, then went limp.

Throttle clasped the back of Steel's neck. "I seized a bunch of paperwork from these bastards' files, as well as their computers. Hawk'll go over it all. He's a pro at this computer shit. He'll find out who the dealer is and you can gut the sonofabitch. Let's go."

They walked through the carnage as they exited the clubhouse. Several of the brothers had already left, heading back to Pinewood Springs. Doc and the wounded had left nearly twenty minutes before. Their clandestine operation was a success—all the Demon Riders dead. As far as Steel knew, the young girl crouched in the closet upstairs was the only survivor. He hoped she'd make a good life for herself, especially since she'd been given a second chance.

As they stood there, the silence returned far more thickly than it was before the attack, as if everything around them was collectively holding its breath. A few of the brothers had run off to get their SUVs and bring them closer. Steel and the others were drenched in blood, and as the frosted grass crunched under their heavy boots, they heard the very low whine of sirens. They jumped into the waiting vehicles and drove away.

They drove fast, taking the backroads and using the police scanners to track the badges. They drove on different roads, scattering so as not to draw attention from the highway patrol. Each mile they logged was one more farther from the carnage.

Steel settled back as Diablo stared straight ahead, concentrating on the road. He took out his phone but couldn't get any reception. When they stopped somewhere to refuel, he'd try again. He wanted to know how his brothers fared in Alina with their attack on the Skull Crushers; they'd planned to attack on the same night. The Skull Crushers had to be reminded who was in control of the territory, so the goal wasn't to annihilate like it'd been with the Demon Riders.

Steel put his phone away and closed his eyes, his body aching for Breanna's softness. He smiled and drifted off to sleep with her tumbling golden hair and sparkling eyes on his mind.

Chapter Twenty-Eight

C HENOA STARED AT the graffiti on her school locker as nausea assaulted her. Behind her, chuckles and whispered insults engulfed her as she felt as though she was on display. "Injun whore" in red block lettering glared at her, shattering her thoughts. Further down on her locker, "Reservation Trash" in neon yellow reached out, clawing at her. She opened her locker, took out her backpack, and slammed it shut. She turned around slowly, her hair covering her face. Through the dark strands, she spotted Hannah and Morgan smirking at her. Flashes of hate burned her, but what crushed her was the smugness on Josie's and Michela's faces, who were standing next to Chenoa's nemeses.

For the past several days, Josie and Michela had ignored her, sitting with Hannah and her clique during lunch, not acknowledging her when she'd wave or call out to them, and laughing whenever Hannah would hurl insults at her.

"What's going on here?" a deep voice asked as several students scampered away. "Chenoa?" She craned her neck and saw the principal, Mr. Alvarado, darting his eyes between her and the locker. "Who did this?" She shrugged. He glared at the students. "Who is responsible for this despicable behavior?"

All of a sudden, the amused eyes turned from her and focused on their shoes, the walls, and the drinking fountains. She pushed her hair back, her gaze meeting Josie's, who then looked down at the books in her hands. Chenoa raised her chin. "It's okay, Mr. Alvarado. Small minds do small things." She focused her gaze on Hannah, who rolled her eyes.

The principal put his hand on her shoulder. "I'll get Mr. Barkley to clean it up. And this won't be tolerated in my school. I will find out who did this and there will be consequences. Now, everyone go back to your classes or you'll all have detention."

The students cast sidelong glances at Chenoa as they shuffled away.

"I have a class," she said as she moved away from her locker.

"I'm sorry this happened, Chenoa. Do you have any idea who may have been responsible? Have you had problems with any student?"

She shook her head. "No. It's not a big deal."

"Yes, it is. I'm on this. If you have any problems, please come see me."

She nodded and walked off. Instead of going to her class, she kept walking until she was well past the school grounds. She walked all the way to Squire's Drugstore, where she went in to buy a pack of cigarettes from Jared. The clerk had a crush on her, so she used that in order to buy cigarettes.

After her purchase, she went to the alley and lit up. *The first drag always feels so good.* She leaned against the brick wall and sank down onto the cold pavement. Then the tears she'd been holding in spilled out. *I hate it there. I'm never going back. Never!* A cold sweat broke out over her and she wrapped her arms around herself to quell the trembling.

A long while later, she wiped her face and nose with her jacket sleeve and called her dad. His voicemail came on. "Dad, I need to talk to you. Call me back." She waited. No call. Again she called his number, leaving a message. For over an hour, she called and texted him repeatedly, her despair mounting. All she could see was the glaring racial slurs exposed to the whole student body, and the way they all laughed at her. No one had stood up for her.

She lit another cigarette and dialed one of her friends from the reservation. "Anthony? Hey, you wanna hang out?" A few minutes later she'd made arrangements for Anthony to pick her up. She knew her dad would be pissed at her, but she didn't give a damn. All she wanted was to be with peers who accepted her and who she felt comfortable with. *You made me go to that fuckin' school, Dad, and you're not even fuckin' picking up your phone?*

As she waited for Anthony to come, she tried her dad a few more times, to no avail. Liquid fire coursed through her veins, and by the time Anthony pulled into the alley, she was climbing the walls and feeling worthless.

"You're in a fucking bad way, sweetheart," Anthony said as Chenoa slid into the passenger's seat.

"No shit."

"You want something?" He reached out and stroked her face.

She batted his hand away. "Don't start that shit up with me."

"You liked it when we'd get high together." He laughed. "Remember?"

"Yeah, well, that was then."

"You wanna get high. I got some fuckin' good stuff. Not the shit you were taking. This is high quality. Pure. Fuckin' rocks."

She shrugged and tried her dad again. No answer. "Okay. Once won't hurt." *I need to feel better. Heroin makes me who I wish I was. Heroin makes life worth living. Heroin is better than everything else.* "Maybe I'll smoke it."

He laughed. "Sweetheart, you're so beyond that."

He was right. When she first started using over a year ago, she'd popped pills and smoked it. At that point it never seemed like a problem, because she'd used daily for weeks and had no withdrawal effects. She never had the cravings either, but then, somehow, the switch had flipped and she'd become a slave to the drug. Smoking it wasn't doing it anymore, so she went to the needle. "You got it on you?"

"Yeah, but this shit's expensive. You got money?"

"Some. How much?"

"A hundred bucks."

"Fuck. I have forty and my grandma's and mom's food stamp cards. I've been staying with them for the last two days." She had taken them "just in case."

"I know a guy who'll give cash for those cards. He owns a market near the rez. How much are they for? He pays fifty cents on the dollar."

"Is it Roy's Market?" Anthony nodded. "Fuck. I didn't know he was doing that. I wonder if my mom knows."

"What?"

"Never mind. My grandma's EBT card is for eighty bucks. Will that do it?"

"You'll still be twenty short, but I can let you slide for a blowjob."

The memory of how the drug made her feel overwhelmed her. It would chase away the shame from that morning. She could taste the peace and euphoria heroin promised her. "Fine, but I want the stuff in my hands first."

He took out the baggie and placed it in her palm. She clenched it and then slipped it into her jeans pocket. Her heart was racing a mile a minute. All she could think about was dropping into the mellow haze of love, happiness, and fucking rainbows.

He pulled over on a country road, switched off the motor, and slid his seat all the way back. As he unzipped his pants, he smiled at her. "It's been a long time. I've missed your lips."

"Let's just do it," she said as she lowered her head. She hoped he'd come fast; she needed to slip away.

FINALLY SETTLED ON the frigid floor of the abandoned warehouse, Chenoa took out her prized cellophane packet. She'd already called her mother and made up a story that she and another student were teammates and had a project to work on for one of their classes. Her mother didn't question her. She never did.

Inside the abandoned warehouse, the light was low and the people using were shuttered into the corners and against the walls of the various rooms. As she took out her spoon, needle, and lighter, a tall man approached her. Her heart raced and she shoved her packet back in her pocket. She pressed herself flush against the brick wall.

"Don't freak out. I just wanna use your lighter. I lost mine and have been searching for it for the past ten minutes. I can't find the fuckin' thing. I need a fix so damn bad." She handed him her lighter. "You good if I crash beside you so we can use it again?" She nodded but watched him warily as he hunkered down next to her. He took out a baggie, spoon, and needle from his jacket pocket. "I'm Nicholas, by the way."

"Chenoa," she said softly. She watched him melt the Mexican Mud in the spoon and then fill his syringe. He handed the lighter to her and she did the same. As she was ready to shoot into a promising vein, Anthony's warning about the fire—the potency—in the smack she'd purchased flitted through her head. She exhaled long and slow, a thread of guilt weaving through her. She knew her parents would be disappointed if they saw her, but she needed this. *I've been so good. It's just this once.* She pierced her skin with the cold, steel needle.

She glanced at Nicholas who was already in that special place that only heroin could offer, and then she leaned back and let the drug work its magic.

Chapter Twenty-Nine

THROTTLE CHUCKLED. "THE fuckin' badges think the Grave Diggers are responsible for the massacre, and knowing them, they'll take credit for it on the outlaw grapevine."

The Grave Diggers MC was a small outlaw club in Illinois that was the Demon Riders' rival. They had been sparring for years over drugs, arms, and prostitution. In the past, they'd had a war between them, but they'd called a tenuous truce three years back. There'd been rumors that the Demon Riders had dipped into Grave Diggers' territory to set up shop, just like they'd done in Alina.

"Works for us," Hawk said.

"They're that fuckin' stupid to think anyone will believe them. What a bunch of pussies," Brutus said.

"As long as it keeps the fuckin' badges outta our business, they can take all the credit they want." Banger took out a joint and lit it.

Diablo pulled the SUV into a gas station while Steel scrolled through his phone. He rubbed the back of his neck, his chest tightening when he saw the slew of missed calls and texts from Chenoa.

"What the fuck?" Diablo said from the driver's side. Hawk, Banger, Throttle, and Brutus paused their conversation. "I've never seen anything like that."

Steel looked out the windshield and darkness invaded him. About sixty black crows gathered on the tops of the gas pumps, the telephone wires, and the large rocks near the station.

"It's like a fuckin' scene from Hitchcock's movie about all the crazed birds. What the hell's the name of the movie. Damnit. I can't remember," Brutus said as he straightened from his slouched position.

"*The Birds*," said Hawk.

"Yeah. Real hard to remember that one." Diablo sniggered, and Brutus lightly punched his arm while the other brothers laughed.

Except for Steel. He stared at the black birds as the hairs on the back of his neck prickled. Iciness rode up his spine. His heart pounded. "Fuck," he muttered under his breath.

"What's up?" Hawk asked as he opened a bottled water.

"The Navajos believe crows to be bad omens. They're considered helpers of the evil spirits and the witches."

Banger laughed. "I get a kick outta all those superstitions." He turned around and looked at Steel. "You don't believe that shit, do you?"

"I've got a bad feeling. I've had it for a week now. For me, the crows are confirmation that the universe is outta balance. At least mine, or my family's. I gotta call my daughter." He opened the door as Diablo slowly pulled next to one of the pumps. He jumped out and Diablo honked the horn. The frenzied fluttering of wings filled his ears as he walked away from the station.

Several hours before, under the cover of night, they'd pulled into a rest stop, washed off the blood from their bodies, and changed their clothes. They'd burn everything when they got to the Insurgents' clubhouse. He pushed up his clean T-shirt and slid his phone out of his pocket. He plugged in Chenoa's number but she didn't pick up. Then he sent her a text. Nothing. He called again. Another text. Again, nothing. He called Mika.

"Where the fuck is Chenoa? She's not picking up her phone. She called me a bunch of times but I didn't have any goddamn reception."

"What's your problem? She's with someone from school working on a project. She just called me maybe thirty minutes ago."

"What student? And where are they studying? Is she at the student's house? I want the address."

"Fuck, Steel. Get a grip. She has a project due for her history class. She's fine."

"So you don't know where she's at?"

"I figured it was at this girl's house. I'm sure your mom didn't know where you were every second of the day when you were seventeen."

"I wasn't a fucking addict." He pinched his lips together as the tightness in his chest intensified.

"She's been doing great. She has that all behind her."

"Do you really believe that, Mika? I know you're not that fucking naïve." He blew out a loud breath. "She should've called or texted me back by now."

"Maybe she has her phone on silent or her battery's dead. She's famous for that. Don't think the worst. She's been doing great."

"Call me the minute you hear from her or she comes home. I gotta go."

He kicked the dirt under his feet as he stared numbly at the looming mountain peaks. *Call me the fuck back, sunshine.* Next, he called Breanna and got her voicemail. "Fuck!" he yelled aloud. He sent a quick text.

Steel: *Hey, baby. I've fucking missed U.*

Breanna: *Sooo good to hear from U. Was worried.*

Steel: *I'm good. Have U heard from Chenoa?*

Breanna: *Not today. Y?*

Steel: *She's not answering her phone.*

Breanna: *Probably with friends. I know she hangs with a couple of girls.*

Steel scrubbed his hand over his face. *Why the fuck isn't anyone getting this but me?*

Steel: *Ya.*

Breanna: *So sorry but with a client. Call U later?*

Steel: *K. Let me know if U hear from Chenoa.*

Breanna: *K. Love U. xxoox*

Steel: *Me too.*

A car honked and he looked over and saw Hawk motioning him over. "Ready to head out?" Steel asked as he climbed inside the vehicle. Hawk nodded and Diablo pulled back onto the freeway.

Steel watched the evergreens, aspens, and pines race past him, but his mind was a million miles away. He leaned against the door and rested his head on the window. The strains of AC/DC's "Highway to Hell" startled him. He took out his phone and saw Chenoa's name. A burst of adrenaline surged through him.

"Sunshine. I'm calling you back. When you called me earlier, I didn't have any fucking reception. What's going on?"

"I just wondered when you'd be home. I'm good. Real good."

"Your mom said that you're with a friend working on a project for school. Who's your friend?"

"School? Oh... yeah. Uh... it's Josie. We got this thing going on."

She spoke slowly, drawing out her words, and heaviness crushed down on him. "Why're you talking so funny?"

"Oh... I'm just super tired. I've been studying so much."

"You using?"

"Dad, how can you ask me that? No. I can't believe you asked me. Don't you trust me?" She acted miffed, insulted, and he didn't believe her act for a minute.

"It's not about trust. I know this is hard for you. Addiction always is. You can tell—"

"Dad. I'm good. Okay? Leave it alone. I'm so tired. I just wanna go home and sleep. I'm good. Really. I'll see you when you get back."

He clenched his jaw. "I love you, sunshine. Don't do anything stupid. I'm gonna be home real soon. Wait for me."

"Sure, Dad. I gotta go now." The phone went dead. He stared at it.

"Everything okay?" Hawk asked.

Steel shook his head. "She's using again. Fuck! I don't know what the hell to do." He pounded the window. "Fuck! I can take down rival clubs, lead my brothers, and keep the brotherhood strong, but I can't fucking help my little girl."

Banger turned around and gave Steel a joint. "That's fuckin' hard, dude. I know Belle and I been trying to get Emily straight. She's on and off with the drinking. She's been to three rehabs. She's good now, but there's always the fear and distrust for us. You feel helpless, and that's the worst part of it. I fuckin' feel your pain and worry."

Steel jerked his chin up in thanks, then lit the joint. They rode in silence for a long while. *She needed to talk to me, and I wasn't there for her. I let my sunshine down. The minute I get back, I'll check for track marks, and she goes back to rehab. We can do this. Just hang on until I get home, sunshine.*

He breathed in deeply and slowly exhaled. He couldn't wait to get back to Alina.

Chapter Thirty

STEEL DIDN'T WANT to spend the night in Pinewood Springs; he was anxious to get back to see Breanna and Chenoa. All of his brothers stayed except for Diablo, who rode back with Steel. The other brothers wanted to spend the night so they could chill out, fuck some new club girls, and talk bikes with the Insurgents.

Doc had done a damn good job patching up Crow and Army, as well as Wheelie and Rags. Crow and Army had sustained superficial wounds that only required some stiches. Crow was already sitting at the bar drinking a shot of whiskey with one of the bar girls, Lola, on his lap.

Steel chuckled as he slapped his brother on the back. "Don't fucking break open your stiches. I need you back in Alina tomorrow."

"No problem. This time, I'm gonna let the chick do all the work." He pulled Lola's head down and kissed her. "You good with that?"

"I'm good with anything," she said as she thrust her tits into his face.

Steel shook his head. "Don't kill my brother here."

"I won't. When I'm done with him, I could make you feel real good." She winked at him.

"I'm fucking sure you could, but I'm outta here. Gotta get home to my woman." He went over to Diablo, who was talking with Throttle and Hawk. "You ready? I wanna get going."

Diablo threw his shot back and nodded. "Let's go."

Steel turned to Hawk and Throttle. "Where's Banger?"

"He wanted to get home to Belle and his kids. I'm getting ready to take off too. I just called Cara. I've got an ache only she can fill." Hawk set his shot glass on the bar.

"Kimber's waiting for me too," said Throttle. "We're gonna have to come down and see you. Alina's close to the Four Corners, right?" Steel nodded. "For some fuckin' reason my woman wants to put her ass in the four states at once. Fuck if I know why, but that's what she wants. We'll probably ride down in the spring."

"Just let me know when you're coming. There's some beautiful rides around the San Juan Mountains. I heard your woman rides her own Harley."

"Yep. A pink one. I love to watch her ass when I ride behind her." Throttle wiggled his eyebrows.

Steel sniggered. "Don't see many women riding. It's cool. My woman loves holding me too much to give it up, and I like her pressed behind me." He picked up the shot of tequila Hawk handed him and let the clear liquid slide down his throat. "That was fucking good." He turned to leave.

Hawk pulled him into a bear hug. "It was epic. We gotta kick ass together more often. I hope things go well with Chenoa," he said in his ear.

Steel hugged back. "Thanks. For *everything*." They bumped fists and he and Diablo exited the Insurgents' clubhouse.

WHEN THEY ARRIVED in Alina, it was dark. He met with Paco who'd told him the beat-down of the Skull Crushers went off without a hitch. "I'm sure they won't be causing us trouble any time soon." Paco took out two joints and handed one to Steel.

"They won't be fucking with us at all now that we've eliminated the Demon Riders. I wouldn't be surprised if the pussies didn't pack up and leave." Steel lit his reefer and inhaled.

"Sounds like the best thing for them to do, 'cause next time they get in our fuckin' business, we'll destroy them. The way I see it is they've used up all their cards." Paco stretched his legs in front of him.

"That's for damn sure. I'm sick of their shit." Steel rose to his feet. "I'm gonna go over to Breanna's. We'll call church in a couple of days to get all the updates. Hawk's gonna go through all the computer shit he lifted at the fuckers' clubhouse. We should know who the local is in a few days."

"I bet the motherfucker's gonna take off once he hears about the Demon Riders."

"I doubt he's part of the outlaw pipeline. It'll take a while for the news to travel to the citizens." He pulled on his black gloves, nodded at Paco, and then stepped out into the chilly autumn air. A huge harvest moon glowed, casting a golden sheen over the tops of the trees. The stars blinked against the velvety black background as he rode to his woman's house.

The noise from his bike shattered the quiet of Breanna's neighborhood. He pulled into the driveway and walked up to the front porch. She'd given him a key a couple of weeks before, so he used it and opened her door. The scent of cinnamon, nutmeg, and vanilla curled around him as he walked to the bedroom.

She was sleeping, small noises coming from her nose. Warmth spread through him. *She's so fucking cute.* He looked at the blue numbers on the digital clock on the nightstand—1:48 a.m. *I'll call Chenoa in the morning. I don't wanna wake her.* He tugged off his leather jacket and threw it on the chair, carefully laid his cut on the top of the tall dresser, and then undressed. Not wanting to freak Breanna out, he stood over her and softly called her name. She stirred, her eyes finally flying open when he gently shook her.

"Steel!" She bolted up, her face beaming, her arms reaching for him. He climbed on the bed and she peppered his face with kisses, all the while telling him how happy she was to see him.

"It's been too fucking long, baby," he said against her lips.

"I know. I missed you so much."

He slipped the short nightgown over her head, her soft tits bouncing against him. "Fuck," he muttered as his calloused palms covered and squeezed them. Those delectable mounds teased and tempted him whenever he'd see her, and he now had them captured in his hands once more. He bent down and nibbled at their creamy swell. "Mine," he growled before pushing them up into his face and devouring them.

Whines of pleasure played in his ears, egging him on to suck and bite her hardened nipples, loving the way she arched to fuse with him. Beneath him, her legs moved as if they were ironing the sheets, and his hand roamed over her curves until it landed on her black lace panties. When his finger stroked her cotton crotch, toying with her sweet button, her legs kicked out and up. "Your panties are so fucking wet, baby."

She groaned her response then yelped when he slipped his digit under the fabric.

Her pussy was warm and wet, quivering in such a way that he was sure his fingers would be sucked into its pink folds. He pulled away, chuckling at the sigh of frustration that escaped her lips. Pushing up a bit, his lips covered hers and he kissed her gently at first. Then, with increasing pressure, his tongue dipped in, pushing farther inside, wanting her to swallow him whole. She grabbed at him, arms around his head, deep moans rising from her chest. They mingled with his breath, driving him crazy with lust and love.

She pushed him back a bit, a cranberry tint streaking her cheeks. "Wow… that was intense." She licked her lips as she gazed at him.

"You're so beautiful," he said, caressing her cheek. "I craved you so much while I was away from you. You fucking turn my world. I don't know how you do it, but all I know is that you do." As his breath slipped over her skin, he saw her shiver.

He drew a path with his tongue from her lips to her neck, sucking and nipping at her velvety skin. She'd have a mark in different shades of red in the morning; he wanted to mark her whole skin and show every man that she was off-limits. When he took her earlobe between his teeth and tugged at it, a throaty moan fell from her lips. "The sounds you make get to me," he whispered in her ear, tracing the tip of his tongue across the nape of her neck as he held the soft curves of her ass.

His desire grew and his pulse quickened as he watched her respond to his touch. He was more than ready to bury himself between her thighs, but he wanted to take it slow. Relishing her scent and the way she felt against his flesh made his cock pulse, and he reached down and pinched the base of it to ease the ache.

"I love the way you touch me. I can't get enough of you," she whispered against his shoulder before she lightly bit it.

He raised his head and locked his gaze with her heated one. When she slid her bottom lip between her teeth, he lost it. All resolve was gone as he pushed her legs apart and slid down to bury his face in her crotch, breathing her sweet almond scent in deeply.

"I fucking hunger for you, baby. I wanna taste your sweetness while I fuck you deep with my fingers." He looped his index fingers on each side of her lace panties and pulled them down slowly before his tongue dove between her puffy folds.

"Steel," she gasped, grabbing a fistful of his hair and yanking it. She kicked off her panties, bent her knees, and spread her legs wide.

He chuckled. "Anxious? Good. I am too." He brought his mouth to her pussy, hot to the touch with primal need. His tongue teased and played with her clit as he plunged his fingers in and out of her wetness. She squirmed beneath him, and he locked eyes with her desire-filled ones as he licked her like he was possessed.

"Oh shit!" Her thighs tightened against his head. "Fuck, it feels so good," she rasped while she balled the sheet in her fist.

The way she arched her back, deep moans escaping from her throat, fueled his desire and he thrust more fingers into her heat. Her breath quickened and she rocked her hips to meet his thrusts, her warm walls clenching around his digits. Then she screamed out his name, and his head was in a vise the way her thighs squeezed him as she came.

As her breathing returned to normal, he pulled out and leaned back on his knees, smiling. Locking his gaze with hers, he sucked her come off his fingers, taking each one of them slowly in his mouth. "You taste so fuckin' sweet." He scooted forward and hovered over her. "Taste how sweet you are." He captured her mouth with his, plunging his tongue inside. She moaned and gripped his hair in her hands. He kissed her passionately as his hard cock poked at her thighs. Then he pulled back.

Looking at her pink pussy, he held his cock and rubbed it up and down in her juices. "I can't wait anymore, baby." He placed the tip at her wet slit and pushed in, her warm walls encasing him like a glove. "I love how fucking tight you are." He went in deeper, her moans and gasps driving him on. Pulling out, he hammered into her, loving how she cried out while sinking her fingernails in his arms. He drove himself harder and faster inside her, and the bed began creaking. Breanna's breaths became shorter as he pounded her relentlessly.

The room was filled with her moans, his grunts, the smacking of upper bodies, and the banging bed. Steel braced his hands on the wall and hooked his knees outside her legs to drive himself deeper. "Fuck, Breanna," he growled as sweat dampened his back.

He loved the way her pussy pulsed on his cock, her juices covering him and dripping down his balls as they slapped against her ass. Then he felt her ready to come—all tight and swollen, gripping down on his cock. He kept pumping, wanting her pussy squeezing his cock as he exploded inside her.

"Breanna. Oh, baby," he grunted as he shot into her still-pulsating wetness. His seed poured out in hot, dense ropes. From the way her walls spasmed around him, he knew she was coming and he crumpled on top of her, his dick still twitching inside her. As she regained her breathing, she combed her fingers through his hair. He wanted to never move, to be entwined with her forever. He'd never felt such intensity of love or desire for any woman.

He'd claimed her, but she owned him.

"That was indescribable," she whispered in his ear. "I love you so much." She kissed the side of his temple.

He slowly moved off her and then cuddled her in his arms. "You've got all of me, baby. I've never felt this way about any other woman. It fucking blows my mind." He kissed the top of her head. She snuggled closer, shivering. "You cold?"

"A little." She burrowed even closer.

He laughed softly and reached behind him, grabbing the blanket. He flung it on top of them, tucking it under her chin.

He smiled in the darkness. *Right now, life is pretty damn good.*

He drifted off to sleep.

Three hours later, he received the call.

Chapter Thirty-One

THE ICU ROOM was as stark and bare as Steel's hope. Since he'd received the call from the hospital, he'd been sitting next to Chenoa, watching her lie there quietly, her breaths matching the beeping of the machines that surrounded the bed. It was the only indication of her heartbeat... her existence. She was in critical condition, having overdosed on a dirty concrete floor in an abandoned building.

He glanced up as Breanna walked in carrying a white Styrofoam cup in her hand. Wisps of steam rose from it. "I brought you a cup of black coffee."

Taking the cup, he brought it to his lips, blowing on the hot liquid. He took a sip and the bitterness slid down his throat.

Breanna stood behind him and slinked her arms around him, her hands resting on his chest. Light kisses peppered his neck and he placed his hands on hers. "I know this is difficult. I'm here if you need me," she whispered against his ear.

He nodded and then cleared his throat. "Her name means 'dove' in Navajo. When she was a child, she liked to pretend she was a bird soaring high above everything. She'd tell me she liked the idea of being free to go anywhere, to soar above the shit of the world. So... yeah."

Breanna didn't say anything, just squeezed him, and he leaned his head back and rested it against her stomach. Looking at Chenoa lying there was surreal. If—and it was a huge if—she pulled through this, she'd be permanently brain damaged. *I should've been there for her when she called me. I fucked this up. I couldn't protect her.* He inhaled deeply, then exhaled slowly.

The nurse came in and nodded at him as she went over to the machines and typed some information in a computer. "Do you need anything?" she asked as she turned to go.

My daughter back. He shook his head.

"If you do, please let me know." She quietly left the room.

"My baby," Mika's anguished voice filled the room as she ran in, Roy standing in the doorway. She rushed over to Chenoa and laid her head on her chest. Tears trailed down her cheeks and Steel sat rigid in the chair, taking in the scene.

He glared at Roy, who shifted his gaze to Mika. "Get the fuck outta here," Steel said.

Roy scowled at him. "I'll fuckin' stay if I want to. I'm here for Mika and Chenoa."

He leaned forward in the chair, but Breanna's firm hands on his shoulders urged him back. "I'm not gonna say it again. I don't fucking want you here."

"Roy, wait for me outside," Mika said.

"Are you gonna let him tell us what the fuck to do?"

"This isn't the place. My God, Chenoa's his daughter." Her voice cracked and she looked at Steel, catching his gaze. He gave her a weak smile and then slid his eyes back to Roy, challenging him.

"Fuck both of you." Roy spun around and stomped away.

Mika stared after him. "He'll get over it." She chewed on her bottom lip.

"What the fuck are you doing with that asshole?" Steel rose to his feet.

Before Mika answered, Breanna kissed him quickly on the cheek. "I'll let you two talk."

Steel wrapped his arm around her waist. "You don't need to go."

"I know, but I have some calls I have to make. I'll be back." She kissed him again and walked away.

"How long has *that* been going on?" Mika pulled a chair over to the side of the bed and sat down.

"A while. How did this happen, Mika? How did Chenoa end up at the warehouse? Did she sneak out of the house? What the fuck happened?"

"Are you blaming me for this? Where the hell were you? You put your club first, *again*."

A surge of fire rushed through him. Since he'd heard the news, he'd wanted to break something, hurt someone, anything to divert the pain from himself. "Don't fucking go there," he hissed. "I left her in your care. I just wanna know how the fuck she ended up at that building at five in the morning." He clenched and unclenched his fists. *I gotta calm down. I don't want to lose it in front of Chenoa.*

"She told me she was going to hang out with her friend, Josie. When she called me later that night, she said she would be home around ten. I was so tired, I fell asleep before then. I thought she'd come home, and was shocked when Breanna called me. I ran to Chenoa's room because I didn't believe that she wasn't there." She covered her face with her hands and cried softly.

Steel bent down on his haunches and put his hand on her thigh. "This fucking sucks. I'm not blaming you. If anyone's to blame, it's me. I shoulda known she was in pain. I'm talking about now, but also before she started using. I thought she was okay, but I shoulda known." He breathed out a ragged breath.

Mika shook her head. "It's the fuckin' assholes who sold her this shit. That's whose fault it is. I hate them. I hate what they did to our baby." A deep sob filled the room, and Steel put his arm around Mika's shoulder and drew her to him. As she rested her head on his shoulder, he held her as her body shook, and his daughter fought for her life.

FOR TEN DAYS he'd been by her side. She looked so small and peaceful lying in her hospital bed draped in white sheets and a blanket. Each day that passed made her death more imminent, yet he clung to the frayed thread of hope because he wasn't ready to let her go. His world at that moment was fucked up; his daughter was the one dying and he was the one living. He'd come close to death so many times—in his world of violence, the grim reaper was always lurking around the corner—yet he was okay and Chenoa wasn't. It didn't make any sense.

On a cold Tuesday night, he fell asleep in the chair he always sat in, but he woke up suddenly not long after. *Something's off here.* He glanced at Chenoa; she lay perfectly still. There was no movement from her. Nothing. The beeping on the heart monitor had been replaced with a constant whine. Frantic, he looked at the monitors and saw the jagged up and down lines were gone, replaced by a steady line covering the screen. A cold sweat broke over him as he hit the red button while yelling, "Chenoa. Breathe, sunshine. Don't leave me."

The overhead fluorescent lights glared on and numerous footsteps rushed across the linoleum floor. He moved away and watched a crew of people work on his daughter, trying to bring air back into her lungs. After several minutes, the screen still showed a flat line. The doctor covered Chenoa's face with the white sheet, forever blocking out his sunshine.

"I'm sorry," the doctor and nurses each said.

His heart shattered into pieces. For seventeen years of his life, she had been his sunshine, the good part of him. And now she was gone and his life would be forever changed.

"We'll leave you for a while with her. Do you want us to call her mother?" the nurse asked softly. He nodded, numbness killing his pain. "All right." She patted his shoulder and left.

He pulled the sheet back and gazed at her face, then bent down and kissed her, her skin still warm. Covering her hand with his, he shook his head. "For so long you flew with such grace, but then you got mixed up with the wrong crowd. They clipped your wings and you fell to the ground. The fuckers sucked up all the energy and life you could give, and then they left you to die alone on a cold cement floor. Fuck, sunshine. I wish you hadn't forgotten how to dream, how to fight. I wish I could've protected you, kept you young and close to me your whole life. Now the demons are gone and you can soar high and free. I'll love you forever, sunshine."

A desire for vengeance consumed him, and his muscles and veins strained against his skin. He threw his head back and looked upward. *I swear on my ancestors' spirits that I'll find out who sold the drugs to my sunshine and I'll obliterate them. I won't rest until I fucking kill the piece of shit who murdered my sweet Chenoa.*

He took out his phone and called Mika, and she told him she was on her way. Then he called Breanna; he needed her so much at that moment. Chenoa's death was slaying him.

He stood over her bed and stared down, his mind blank. The only thing he was aware of was the cooling of her skin under his hand. When Breanna came in, tears streaming down her face, it startled him. He'd lost track of time.

She took him in her arms and hugged him tightly. "I'm so sorry. I can't even imagine your pain." Her familiar scent comforted him, as did the soft strength of her arms.

He grunted. *I can't fucking lose it. I gotta be strong for Shimá, Mika, and my woman. I can't let this crush me.* Over Breanna's shoulder, he saw Mika standing in the doorway. He reached out and gestured her to come to him. She rushed over and he pulled her toward them. Breanna wrapped an arm around her and the three of them held onto each other, the two women crying against his T-shirt. He glanced at Chenoa, and he knew that her small body covered in white would always be etched in his mind. *I just can't believe I'll never see you smile, or hear your laugh, or ever hold you in my arms again.* He blew out a long breath and pulled Breanna and Mika closer to him.

Before they removed Chenoa's body, he bent down and whispered against her cold ear, "Thank you for being my daughter. I'll see you in the dawn of my final day. Fly high and free, sunshine." He straightened up, then jerked his head at the two men waiting to take Chenoa away. Mika had left an hour before, but he'd wanted to stay until the end. He wrapped his arm around Breanna. "Let's go home," he said.

When they got to his house, he started a fire while Breanna told him she'd make him a cup of coffee. As he sat on the couch, staring at the fire jump and crackle in the fireplace, the aroma of roasted coffee beans filled his nostrils. Her approaching footsteps made him smile.

"Here you go," Breanna said as she handed him a mug of coffee. "I couldn't find the cardamom, so I just made it black." She swept a few strands of hair from his face, then settled down next to him on the couch, drawing his back against her chest. "Is it good?"

He took a sip, the hot coffee helping to dissolve the numbness he'd felt since Chenoa died. He stretched out his arm and put the mug on the low table, then leaned back into her. She curled her arms around him, pressing him close. Kissing him softly along his forehead, cheeks, jawline, and neck, she whispered, "Just breathe. Breathe."

The feel of her, and the love and compassion she gave him, touched him like nothing ever had. When he spotted Chenoa's guitar leaning against the wall, he lost it. His chest rose and fell as grief consumed him, and his sweet woman held him tightly in her arms, stroking him.

Chapter Thirty-Two

BREANNA PACKED THE last box of dishes and looked around her kitchen. Boxes were piled on the floor and she shook her head in amazement. *I can't believe I had all these kitchen things and I don't even know how to cook.* She grabbed a bottle of water from the refrigerator and went into the living room. The following day, Steel and several of his brothers would come by and take her boxes to Steel's house.

He'd told her he wanted her with him the night Chenoa died. She'd been staying with him ever since, but all her stuff had been at her house, so she kept traipsing back and forth until he told her that he'd paid off her lease. She smiled, but then she always smiled when she thought of him.

It'd been a rough three weeks since the funeral. Because Steel was so used to being a strong leader, a man who didn't show his emotions, she had to coax his grief out of him. Her heart broke every time she thought about Chenoa's death. She couldn't begin to imagine how Mika and Steel must be feeling. Breanna knew he missed her so much, and she also knew he blamed himself for her death. She'd told him he wasn't responsible for heroin being in the county, but he just didn't see it that way. She hoped as time went by, his guilt would lessen.

A knock on her door yanked her away from her thoughts. When she opened it, Nicholas stood there, his skin a gray pallor, bruises and scabs all over. His hair was dirty and stringy, and it looked like he hadn't washed his clothes in a couple of weeks. She hadn't seen him since before Chenoa's overdose, and she was shocked at his appearance. Her fingers touched her parted lips, and her stomach twisted in knots.

"Nicholas. It's been a long time. Come in."

He brushed past her and flopped down on the sofa. "I need money real bad," he said, his eyes darting all around the room.

"Damn, you're strung out."

He glared at her. "No shit. Do you have some money? I feel like I'm gonna fuckin' die here if I don't get a shot. Fuck." He wiggled around on the couch, scratching and picking at his scabs.

"What happened to your sales job?"

"Can you leave the fuckin' questions for later?"

"How much do you need? And I still want to know what happened to your job."

"A couple hundred would be great. I still have it."

"Are you shooting up all the money you make?" She walked over to her purse on the table.

"This is a fuckin' cruel drug. I'm doing ten shots a day. I'm not making enough to support it."

"Please let me help you. I know a couple of great rehab places."

"Yeah... well... right now I need a shot. We can talk about that later. Fuck, Breanna, I'm dying here!"

She pulled out two twenty-dollar bills, and then a lightbulb went on in her head. "I have forty I can give you, but I want something from you."

"Anything."

"I want to know who the main dealer is. Who's giving you guys the drugs to sell on the street?" She laughed dryly. "Don't look so surprised. I figured you were selling when you told me about your job. And you're using the money to support your habit. But I want to know who in Alina is giving you the drugs."

He crossed and uncrossed his legs while he wrung his hands. "Candyman. Now can I have the fuckin' money? I gotta go."

"His real name."

"How the fuck should I know? He goes by Candyman."

"Call him and arrange a buy."

"He doesn't do fuckin' street sales. He's a big man."

"Tell him I want a big load for resale. Call him and you get the money."

"I can't. I'm so fuckin' strung out that he's gonna know something's up. Anyway, why do you want his number?"

"I'm doing this for a young girl who was my client and then my friend. Chenoa deserves this."

"Chenoa? I know that chick. She loaned me her lighter. She was cool. Does she want some smack? I can arrange it."

Breanna fixed her gaze on him. "Chenoa's dead. She overdosed almost a month ago." Nicholas stopped moving and his mouth opened, but no sound came out. "She was only seventeen. That could've been you."

He held his stomach and bowled over. "Fuckin' too bad. She seemed like a cool chick. Do you have the money? I gotta go."

"All right. Give me Candyman's number. I'll set something up." He balked. "If you can't do this one thing for me, then I'm done with you."

He took out his phone. "I'll call him. I'll tell him I've got a shitload of money that I stole and want to buy three pounds of Asian smack. He's got the good pure stuff, but the mixed stuff is the cheap shit that's sold the most."

"He'll be able to tell you're strung out. I'll just make the call."

"Let's get this the fuck over with! He won't meet you. He doesn't know you from shit."

She watched as he plugged in the number.

It was a quick call, and at the end of it he'd set up an appointment for that night to meet Candyman at the back of O'Riley's Market on Fifth and Grape. "Just stay in the bushes where he can't see you. You can get his fuckin' license plates on his car or something. Now give me the forty bucks."

She handed it to him. "I'll meet you at seven. Please show up."

"I will 'cause I'll need more smack by then." He ran out and slammed the door.

Sadness enveloped her as she stared at the door. *It's just a matter of time before I receive the same call Steel did. I don't know what to do anymore.* She wiped at the corners of her eyes and picked up her phone. Steel was going to come that night, and they'd planned to pick up some Mexican food and spend the night together. It would be her last night in her house. She'd lived there for several years, so the move was not without some anxiety and angst.

She wanted to tell him what was going on, but she hoped he wouldn't overreact and want to take charge of the situation. She feared it would spook Nicholas to the point where she'd never hear from him. When Steel's voicemail picked up, she remembered that he'd told her he was going for a long ride to the sacred mountains. She figured the reception probably wasn't the best around there. Since Nicholas had made the arrangement for seven thirty that night, she'd be home in plenty of time to meet up with Steel at eight thirty.

She picked up another empty box and the tape dispenser, then headed into the bedroom to pack up her shoes, clothes, and accessories.

NICHOLAS WAS LESS jittery when he came by her house that night at seven o'clock. She drove to the agreed place, parking a few blocks away.

"There's a big tree that you can stand behind. That should cover you good. Do you have any money to give me for a hit? I'm gonna need that."

"I have another forty. The money comes hard earned, Nicholas. You're shooting up my tips, and my feet are hating you for it."

He wiped his nose. "I'm just saying I'm gonna have to buy something, especially since I'm gonna have to tell him the money I stole was stolen from me when I was shooting up."

She took out the bills and handed them to him. "That's it. I'm dry for the week."

He nodded and shoved the money in his jacket pocket.

When they arrived at the location, she spotted the big tree Nicholas had told her about. The trunk was enormous, and it could easily conceal her. She glanced at the time on her phone—7:20 p.m. "We better split up. He may come early. I'm going to go behind the tree," she said in a hushed tone.

As the minutes ticked away, her skin prickled and the hairs on the nape of her neck rose. The wind had picked up a bit and it groaned through the trees as leaves swept across the pavement. It was so damn dark that the shadows of the buildings melted into blackness. She shuddered and yanked her jacket tighter around her.

"I don't think he's coming," Nicholas said in a low voice.

"Let's wait a little longer," she whispered back.

Time passed slowly. Breanna stayed hidden within the darkness, feeling every beat of her heart pounding against her hand, her pulse throbbing in her ears. Suddenly, the sound of footsteps approached, and she held her breath. Nicholas looked up from his phone. Enshrouded in the shadows, she could only see the outline of the man's form. He looked like a dark smudge against a slightly lighter background. She strained her ears to pick up the conversation.

"I didn't think you were coming," Nicholas said as he slid his phone in his jacket.

"You got the money? I wasn't sure you were serious, but I'm a greedy bastard, so I thought I'd give you the benefit of the doubt." The cackle of his laugh assaulted Breanna's ears.

"Uh... yeah... about that. Some fucker robbed me when I was shooting up at the warehouse. I've been searching for him for the last couple of hours." He scratched his neck.

Stay cool, Nicholas.

"What the fuck? I came over here for nothing? What fuckin' game are you playing?"

"No game, honest. I only got forty bucks, but I do want to buy a bag."

"I dragged my ass over here for fuckin' forty bucks. I oughta beat your ass."

I need to get a better view. Something seems familiar with this guy. She took a few steps, but because of the darkness, she didn't see the raised tree root. She stumbled and fell. "Shit" escaped her instinctively.

"Who's there?" She saw the man turn toward her; her stomach dropped.

"She's with me. She wants a hit but she's shy. First time, you know." Nicholas shoved his hands in his pocket. "So what about that baggie? I need a hit, man."

"Come out of the shadows. Don't be shy."

Breanna's leg muscles tightened as if readying her body to run. Cold sweat broke out over her forehead and under her arms. Her heartbeat racing, she fought the urge to flee and stepped out from behind the tree. She swallowed hard and walked toward Nicholas and Candyman. She had a hundred dollars in her purse, so if she handed it to him for smack, it would look believable that she was there for a buy.

"How much you got?" he whispered.

She pulled out the hundred-dollar bill from her purse. From her side view, she saw Nicholas's eyes bulge at the money. Candyman took out a cellophane bag and stepped toward her, out of the shadows. A flush of adrenaline tingled through her body as she gasped, "It's you!"

"What the fuck are you doing here?" he growled. "You playing detective, bitch?"

"You know Candyman, Breanna?" Nicholas asked.

She started to back away from him, but he grabbed her like a vise.

"Nicholas, help me!"

The man covered her mouth as she tried to scream. Her watery eyes locked on to Nicholas. He bent down and picked up the hundred-dollar bill.

Candyman threw a baggie at him. "Get the fuck outta here!"

He picked up the packet from the pavement and looked at her. "I'm sorry," he muttered, and then he ran away, disappearing into the darkness.

Her body went limp from the shock of his abandonment. Then something hard and heavy crashed down on her head and blackness engulfed her.

Chapter Thirty-Three

S TEEL LOOKED OUT the window at Breanna's house to the dark, empty street. *Where the fuck is she?*

He called her for the umpteenth time but, once again, it went to her voicemail. The wall clock in her living room said nine thirty. *She's an hour late. Fuck. Something's not right here.* Her car and purse were gone, so when he'd first arrived at her house, he figured she ran to the grocery store, or had gone to pick up some food. Then he tried calling her but there was no answer, and worry crept through him.

When he went into the kitchen, he smiled when he saw all the packed boxes. He couldn't wait for her to be with him all the time. He'd wanted her there since he rented the place, but she'd thought it better that he and Chenoa had some time together. A familiar pain tore through him when he thought of Chenoa. He shook his head, dispelling any memories; he had to focus on where the fuck Breanna was.

Deciding to ride around town and see if he could find her, he killed the light and walked toward the living room, then stopped dead in his tracks. The scraping and jiggling at the front door told him someone was trying to break in. He stepped to the side and hid himself against the wall.

The door swung open and a tall, skinny man walked in. Steel recognized him as the man he'd seen Breanna hugging on the porch that night a couple of months back. *It's her fucking brother. Why the hell is he breaking into her place?* He saw him go over to the TV set and pull on the wires. *He's fucking stealing from his own sister. What a dirtbag.* Then he remembered Breanna had told him her brother was a heroin addict.

He came out of the shadows and tackled him, the younger man

yelling, "What the fuck? Get off me!"

Steel flipped him over and straddled his chest. "Where the fuck is Breanna?"

Nicholas shook his head. "I don't know who you're talking about."

He smacked him in the face a couple of times. "I don't have time for this bullshit. I know you're her brother. Where the fuck is she?"

"Get off me and I'll tell you."

Steel got up and lifted Nicholas by the front of his shirt. "Talk."

The man scratched at his arms and neck. "Uh… she's in trouble."

His insides went taut and he narrowed his eyes. "What the fuck does that mean?"

"Candyman has her. I tried to tell her it wasn't gonna work, but she made me set up the buy. I don't know. I tried to help her, but I couldn't. I wanted—"

"Where the fuck was the buy?"

"Fifth and Grape. Behind O'Riley's. I tried to help her."

Why the fuck she'd do something so stupid, he had no clue. All he knew was that he had to get to her. He'd already lost Chenoa; he wouldn't survive if he lost her too. "Give me the fucker's phone number. Now!"

Nicholas took out his phone and fumbled with it as Steel pulled his out, calling Paco.

"Tell Goldie, Diablo, Crow, Skull, Rooster, and Chains to get to Breanna's house stat. Tell 'em to come loaded."

"Will do. Hey, Hawk called. He said he was finally able to crack the fuckin' code the Demon Riders had in their computer. He said he knows who the distributor is in Alina."

His ears pounded. "Who?"

"Richard Raley. Hawk said he's a crooked cop. FBI fucker."

Steel's face stiffened as liquid fire coursed through his veins. "I know the sonofabitch."

"The brothers are on their way."

Steel hung up and paced as he waited for the screaming cams of six

Harleys. He had to cool his rage way down; he had a job to do. Later, when he had the motherfucker strung up, he could let the rage flow through him, but now he had to be cold and calculating.

It was time to take care of business.

Chapter Thirty-Four

BREANNA'S EYES FLUTTERED open. Her head felt like she had a freight train running through it. She tugged at her arms and realized that they were handcuffed behind her. She sat on a straight-backed wooden chair in a windowless room. She looked around, her foggy mind slowly clearing. *I'm in the storage room at work. Fuck, that's right. Special Agent Raley's Candyman. How the hell is that possible?* She heard the click of the doorknob and she held her breath. Heavy footsteps approached.

"I see you've come to." Agent Raley stood in front of her.

She scowled at him. "You're Candyman?"

"I'm disappointed in you. You should've kept your nose out of this. You've caused a lot of problems. I'm going to have to kill you *and* your brother. Why the fuck did you get involved in this?"

"Me? What about you? You're a cop and you're selling this shit to people? And all the meetings we had, you seemed so concerned. You fucking asshole!"

Her head flung back when he hit her hard across the face.

"Watch it, Breanna. I'm still your superior." He chuckled. "I had to bring you to the office to buy some time. I couldn't very well take you to my hotel room."

"Is Agent Powers involved in this too?"

"Jim? Christ, no. He's as straightlaced as they come."

"What the hell do the food stamps have to do with this?"

"It's my side business. You know food stamp trafficking is a multi-million-dollar business. I just wanted a piece of the pie. The fuckin' government wastes taxpayers' money left and right. Do you realize that there are only about four investigators to handle all of Colorado and Kansas? Fuckin' insane. A definite loophole, and one that's quite lucrative."

"So you sell the EBT cards?"

"Yeah. I had a business going with Roy at Roy's Market. You were right to suspect him. After Jim finds all the paperwork on him, he'll make the arrest. I bought the cards real cheap and sold them to Roy for a 30 percent markup. He used them to buy cheap-quality shit, then sold that to the poor. See how the cycle works?"

"Was Roy involved in selling the drugs?"

"Nah. That was all me. Dustin, Shack, and I go way back to when they had a clubhouse in Nebraska. They used to be part of the Insurgents MC but got their asses kicked out. When I was stationed in Nebraska, I ran across them when we did a raid at one of their strip clubs. They had underage women stripping and giving favors to the men. When I went to their clubhouse, I found a lot of underage women, so they offered me a shitload of cash if I'd look the other way. Fuckin' easy money. I've been on their payroll ever since. I can retire with full benefits from Uncle Sam in two years. I already have the beach picked out in the Caribbean where I plan to spend my time."

Bile rose in her throat and she fought to push it down. Her head was reeling from his confession. And she also knew that it meant the end of her. *I have to get out of this. I hope Nicholas at least called the sheriff and told him what happened.* But she seriously doubted it. Addiction did that; the drug took priority over everything in life. Heroin was a potent elixir, and she could never compete with it.

"So when I was sent to investigate the food stamp fraud, I let Dustin know, and we set up shop here. I didn't know he and Shack were such dumbasses. They didn't tell me your boyfriend's club held this whole territory and had a tacit agreement with the sheriff about hard drugs in the county. Their mistake cost them big." He wiped his hands on his pants. "Don't look so surprised. We all knew you were fuckin' biker trash."

"Do you really think you're going to get away with this? You can't think Roy will roll over when he's faced with felony fraud charges."

He shrugged. "Who are they gonna believe? Me, an agent for eighteen years with an exemplary record, or some lowlife who's too cheap to pay for his own housing? Think, Breanna." He smiled.

"Steel will make sure you pay for what you did to his daughter."

"Steel? Oh yeah, your biker. I was pissed they sold to his daughter. I didn't need an outlaw on my ass, but by the time he finds out, I'll be gone. I'm planning to leave Colorado soon for another state. I got it all figured out. Except for you. You fuckin' threw a kink in my plans. And the bad thing is I liked you. You were always smiling and friendly to me. You gave me respect at work. I want you to know I appreciated it. I just wish you would've kept your fuckin' nose out of this." He rose to his feet. "I have some business I have to attend to. I'll be back for you." He tugged on her handcuffs. "Nice and secure."

The click of the door behind her made her body stiffen. *I have to get out of here.* She pulled on the cuffs, but they wouldn't budge. Looking around the room, she spotted an air vent. She sized it up and thought she may just fit. All she needed to do was crawl to the office next door, and then she could go out the window or the front door.

She tried to stand, but it was too hard. The pounding in her head was driving her crazy. *Okay, Breanna. Calm down. Just calm the fuck down. Take deep breaths. Focus. You can do this.* She closed her eyes and relaxed her body from her toes to the top of her head. She visualized herself slipping out of the handcuffs and kept breathing. When she felt ready, she took a deep breath.

Being double-jointed, she was able to collapse her thumb joint into her palm and make her hand smaller. She then folded her hand so that the ball of it touched just below the base of her small finger, her thumb tucked inside. This made her hand slightly smaller than her wrist, and the thumb bone was resting in her palm. She slid her hand out of the cuff and repeated the process with her other wrist, freeing it of the restraint.

She leapt up and searched around for her purse or phone. Nothing. Frantic, she looked up at the air vent and down at her body; she had no choice but to try it. Since she was familiar with the room, she knew there was a ladder in the closet, so she dragged it out and placed it under the vent, then pulled out a screwdriver from the toolbox in the closet. She was glad Raley had locked her in here rather than the conference room, where there was nothing but a table and chairs.

She undid the grill and pulled herself into the vent, thanking God that she only had to go a short way to the next offices where there was a window. She could escape from there.

She crawled through, her heart in her throat. "Fuck!" she yelled as a sharp edge from the sheet metal lacerated her forearm. The blood was warm as it gushed down her elbow. "Shit. Fuck you, Raley!" She drew in a breath and pushed on.

Some of the lights in the offices were on, but it wasn't enough for her to see clearly inside the vent; she had to feel her way through, and the dangerously sharp edges created a challenging obstacle course. As she crawled, the noise reverberated against the metal walls, making a lot of racket. *This definitely isn't a piece of cake like they show in the movies.*

Another sharp edge nicked her leg, stopping her in her tracks. She lowered her head and cried. Her arm was killing her; there was so much blood she was positive she'd have to get stiches. Black spots floated before her eyes and dizziness assaulted her like she was on a whirling ride at an amusement park. *Please don't let me pass out.* She took a deep breath and inched along, concentrating on getting out and having Steel's arms wrapped around her.

I should've just waited for Steel to come back. What the fuck was I thinking?

Chapter Thirty-Five

SPECIAL AGENT RALEY fumbled with the radio, trying to find a station that didn't play country music. He couldn't wait to leave the reservation and that cow town, Alina. The only thing that made his stay worth it was the money he received from selling drugs and EBT cards. He smiled widely; he'd made a shit ton of money. The residents in the county were hungry for smack, and Roy was a greedy sonofabitch, so it had worked out better than he'd imagined. He was even able to set up shop months before he'd arrived, thanks to the stupidest MC he had the displeasure of knowing, the Skull Crushers.

He snapped off the radio in frustration. "I can't wait to get the fuck back to D.C.," he said aloud. The only kink—and it was a big one—in his otherwise flawless plan was Breanna. *Why the fuck did she get involved? I ought to kill that sonofabitch junkie brother of hers for setting all this up.* A small part of him felt bad that he had to kill her; he thought she was a nice woman except for her lousy taste in men.

He slowed the car down. *Did I lock the door from the outside when I left? Damn. I can't remember.* He was positive there was no way she could get out of the handcuffs, but he was the type of man who liked to make sure all his bases were covered. *I'm only a half mile from the reservation. What the hell.* There weren't any cars on the road, so he hung a U-turn and headed back to the office.

He parked in front of the building and jumped out. When he put his key in the top lock and turned, it locked. *I forgot to lock it.* He smiled and took his key out, but as he was ready to go back to the car, he heard a loud clanging noise inside the building.

It's probably that damn AC. The fucking moron obviously didn't fix it right.

He unlocked the door and entered the building. The clanging was coming from the air vent. *The idiot was just here. It sounds awful. I'll just shut the damn thing off and call the jackass in the morning.* He walked over to the control switch and slid it to Off. Since he was there, he decided to check on Breanna.

He unlocked the door and swung it open. *What the fuck?* He stared at the empty chair and the pair of handcuffs on the floor. *How the hell did she get out of them?* The clanging noise started up again and he looked at the air vent, then saw the ladder under it and the grill on the floor. An evil smile broke out across his face. *She's in the air vent. I don't know how the fuck she did it, but she gets points for gumption. But the little bitch is causing way more trouble than she's worth.*

He walked out of the storeroom and followed the sound to the front part of the office. The repairman told him the day before that the vent to the office next to the storeroom was blocked, so he figured the little cunt had found that out and was making her way to the next vent, which was in the reception area. *Well, I'll just wait for her and give her the welcome she deserves.* He dragged a chair from behind a desk, withdrew his Glock pistol, and sat down to wait.

Chapter Thirty-Six

B REANNA DRAGGED HERSELF further, hope springing in her when she saw the glimmer of light in the distance. She'd had a setback when she ran into that damn blocked vent, but she swallowed her anger and the beginnings of despair and pushed onward. Seeing an end in sight, she caught a new burst of energy and spurred herself on. *I just have a little bit more to go, and then I can call Steel. And a paramedic.* Her legs were covered in blood, and she kept slipping in it as she crawled along.

In her haste to reach her destination, she grew careless. Another steel edge sliced her knee like a knife and she cried out in pain. Sweat stung her eyes and mixed with her tears to dampen her face. *I have to make it. You can do this, Breanna. You can. You only have a little bit more to—What the fuck?* Under her, the sheet metal separated and the fake ceiling below was creaking. Ripping. Crashing. Then she was flying, and then…

Boom! She landed on the commercial carpet with a thud. "Oomph!" She fell on her side, knocking the wind out of her. Her head was spinning. She tried to sit up but she couldn't move. All she could do was lie there groaning. It was like a semitruck had crashed into her and run her over. Her whole body ached.

I think I broke an arm or leg. With my luck, it's probably both.

"Nice of you to drop in." Raley's sinister voice chilled her. "You've caused me so much fucking trouble, you bitch." He kicked her hard in the thigh and she groaned. "I've had enough of you."

He moved into her field of vision and that's when she saw the gun. *He's fucking crazy! This is it. I'm going to die. Oh, Steel.* Tears trickled down from the corners of her eyes into her ears. She took a deep breath and a shot of pain tore through her. "Are you insane?" she croaked.

"You're going to kill me here? I thought you were a smart cop."

"Shut the fuck up, bitch!" He kicked her again, and a desire to kick him in the balls hard and then pistol whip him seized her. Bending over, he grabbed her by the hair and dragged her. She screamed out as her body spasmed from the pain, but he ignored it and kept yanking her along. He stopped and opened a cupboard, taking out a large metal box. Then he grabbed a fistful of her hair again and pulled her to the front door.

Through bleary eyes, she watched him fumble with the lock. All of a sudden, as if a tornado had hit, the door flung open with such ferocity that it knocked him to the floor, knocking the gun out of his hands. Before he could get up, she saw Steel rush in, an assault rifle in his hand and the fierceness of a warrior in his eyes. He yanked Raley up by his shirt collar. She recognized Crow, Rooster, Goldie, and Diablo as they came in behind him.

Her body relaxed. *He's come.*

"You fucking bastard! You killed my daughter. You took her from me. You're gonna pay for every needle mark she had on her skin, for every person you gave that shit to. And I'm gonna fucking enjoy watching you suffer. You hear me, motherfucker?" Steel punched Raley in the face, then threw him to Diablo. "Take this piece of shit to the cell and prep him. I want at him."

Without a word, Diablo seized him and dragged him outside as Goldie followed. Her gaze flew back to Steel, and that's when he spotted her lying on the floor. She knew she looked a mess with her clothes ripped, dirt smudges on her face, her body covered in dust and blood.

"Baby." He dashed over to her and worry laced his eyes. "You're hurt bad."

"I think I broke some ribs. And I cut the hell out of myself in the air vent. I would've escaped if the bastard hadn't come back."

He bent down and kissed her wet cheeks. "You're a fighter. You've got the spirit of a warrior woman. You make me proud." He slipped his hands under her body. "This'll hurt, but I have to take you to the

Hataɫii to heal you."

"What's that?" she whispered hoarsely.

"The Navajo medicine man." He picked her up and she bit her lip until she tasted copper. She didn't want to cry out. She wanted to show him that she was truly his warrior woman.

Chapter Thirty-Seven

A S STEEL RUSHED Breanna to the clinic on the reservation, he called and told them he had an emergency. When he'd seen the yellowish fatty tissue in her wounds and the amount of blood she'd lost, he knew the thirty miles to Alina wouldn't work, so the reservation clinic seemed the best choice. The medics were waiting at the front. They promptly transferred Breanna onto a gurney and wheeled her away.

"Park this," Steel said to Crow as he jumped out of the driver's seat and rushed into the clinic.

"May I help you?" A woman seated behind the counter looked up from her computer.

"My woman was just brought in. Breanna Quine. I'm gonna have the *Hatałii* come in."

The woman nodded. The medicine man was a common sight at the clinic. For the Navajo, they believed in the combination of western medicine with their centuries-old traditions. She typed in Breanna's name. "She's not in the system quite yet, but I'm sure she's in the emergency section."

"I need to be in there with her."

The young lady smiled. "You're Steel McVickers, aren't you?"

He looked at her more closely, but he didn't recognize her. "Yeah." He raised his eyebrows.

She laughed. "You probably don't remember me, but I'm Sam's little sister, Viola."

He scrutinized her face, then smiled. "Yeah, I can see it now. Damn, it's been a long time. Last time I saw you, you were about twelve. You grew up nicely."

Viola blushed. "Thanks. You know, I used to have a major crush on you. You grew up nicely too." She giggled.

I have to see what the fuck's going on with Breanna. "Thanks, sweetie. It's good seeing you again. I just saw Sam not that long ago. I didn't know he was in the tribal police. I gotta see my woman real bad. Can you let me go back there?"

"Normally, it's not allowed until she's in the system, but for you… sure." She pushed a button and the wooden door slowly opened. "It was good seeing you."

He winked. "Same here. Thanks."

He rushed through the doors and went up to the counter to see where Breanna was. After several minutes and a lot of people trying to help him, he finally ended up in her room. She looked pale as a ghost, and his heart twisted when she smile wanly at him. He leaned down and kissed her white lips. "How're you doing, baby?"

"Glad to be here. I really thought I was a goner."

He rubbed her shoulder. "Shh… forget about it. It's all over and you're safe."

"I'm just so tired." Her eyes slowly shut.

He kissed her again. "Rest, baby. I'm gonna have the medicine man come by after we see what the doc has to say."

At that moment, the doctor walked in. "Steel?"

Steel smiled at his mother's doctor. "Dr. Taya. Breanna's my woman. Tell me what's going on." He glanced at Breanna, whose eyes where half-opened.

She nodded. "Ms. Quine's suffered three broken ribs, which will take about two months or so to completely heal. I'll wrap them up, but she just needs to take it easy. She definitely needs stiches on her knees, elbow, and right leg, as she sustained some very deep cuts. We're going to prep her and I'll take care of that. She lost a lot of blood, so her count is low. We'll give her a pint and that should bring all the numbers back up. I'm also giving her an IV antibiotic in case of infection. I want to keep her overnight to make sure she's doing well. If not, then we'll have to transfer her to St. Joseph's in Alina."

Steel pressed his lips together and crossed his arms. "Do what you need to do. I'm gonna have the *Hatałii* come in after you're finished with her." He went back over to Breanna and kissed her. "You'll do just fine. I'll see you in a bit."

He left the room and called his mother, telling her to come to the clinic with the medicine man. Hanging up, he went out to the back of the building and lit up a joint. The cannabis mellowed him as he pressed his foot against the brick wall and smoked. After twenty minutes, he went out front and saw his mother and Herman Secody, the medicine man.

Fifteen minutes later, Steel was in Breanna's room with his mother and Herman. The staff had been told that the *Hatałii* was in the room so they would not disturb them while the ceremony took place. Steel held Breanna's hand and smiled while she watched with wide eyes as the man in beads, jewelry, and feathers set a black case on the table.

"Don't worry, baby. He's not gonna hurt you."

"Do I have to drink or eat anything gross?"

Steel burst out laughing. "You've watched too many movies. He's just gonna get things in balance again."

"Balance?"

Herman walked to the foot of her bed. "I go beyond the Western medicine. I turn to faith healing and spirituality. I'll chant and bring back the balance in your life. Since you're injured, your body is out of sync. Medicine can cure the surface, but the chants, the medicinal herbs, and the ceremony will bring Father Sky and Mother Earth together again. When there is disharmony, the tie between the sky and earth is broken."

"You know, the *Hatałii* is a tradition among the Navajo and has been for centuries. The medicine men must train and apprentice for years before they can go out on their own. They are gifted with the power," Steel said as he squeezed her hand.

"Okay. I'll open myself to it. This is important to you, isn't it?" She smiled at Steel.

"Yeah. I tried with Chenoa, but she lost her faith and the ability to hope," he said softly. "I can't lose you."

Herman took out a crystal, a large turquoise stone, two feathers, and a leather pouch. "These are my tools. I will chant as I perform the ceremony. That will heal you quicker and make your life better in the future. Your injuries were not of your choice or doing, but your life was out of balance before your injuries. Your personal injury could have been the error from lack of judgment or an unintentional contact with harmful creatures. When you are once again aligned with the universe, then you will be protected. I merely act as a facilitator that transfers power from the Holy People to you to restore balance and harmony."

"What's the crystal for?" she asked.

"It's a powerful stone that breaks through the clutter around us and shines up, so the turquoise can unite the earth and sky, bringing together male and female energies. The feather lets all your worries, all imbalance, all tension fly away as if on the wings of an eagle. After the chanting, you will drink the tea made of sage and wild buckwheats that are in the pouch. Then you will sleep deeply and peacefully as they heal your physical wounds and work in harmony with your spirit."

During the ceremony, the medicine man's clear voice sang out the words from the ancestors of the tribe. His soulful wails touched Steel, who held Breanna's hand throughout the ritual.

When it was finished, his mother went over to Steel. "I'm very happy about you and Breanna. I told you that my dreams never fail me." She hugged him quickly and then left with Herman.

"What did she mean about her dreams?" Breanna asked as she pulled the sheets under her chin.

"Get some rest. That's a story for another day." He leaned over and kissed her deeply. "I love you so much. I'm never letting you go."

She closed her eyes. "I love you too. I can't imagine what life would be like without you," she mumbled as she drifted off to sleep.

The herbal tea had kicked in; she'd be sleeping for hours. He quietly shuffled out of the room. When he jumped into his SUV, his body was on fire, fueled by hatred as he left the reservation and headed to the clubhouse. He'd make sure the crooked cop felt the intensity of his rage and the bottomless gulch of his sorrow.

Chapter Thirty-Eight

S TEEL PUSHED OPEN the metal doors and walked into the cell. Raley was tied to a chair, his face bruised and bloodied. Steel's gaze slid up to the lowered beam above. "String the fucker upside down like a pig," he said to Diablo and Goldie. They quickly looped a chain around the ropes binding Raley's ankles and fastened it to two large meat hooks, then pulled him up until his head was hanging down, chest level to Steel.

Raley's eyes bulged and a perverse pleasure snaked through Steel as he saw, sensed, and smelled the fucker's fear. He walked slowly over to a table and picked up some electric prods and two long, thin-bladed knives, watching as the crooked cop's eyes followed his every movement.

"You're the worst scum there is. You fucking sell smack to innocent people and you don't give a shit about the consequences," he said in a chillingly calm voice.

"It was the Demon Riders. They've been squeezing me for years. They had so much shit on me. They made me do this. They threatened my family. I didn't have a choice. I wanted—"

While he'd been babbling, Diablo had come closer. He slammed his knee into the agent's face. "Quit talking like a goddamn pussy. Be a fuckin' man and take responsibility for the shit you did." Diablo hit him again. "I hate a whiny-ass fucker."

Steel laughed as Goldie, Crow, Skull, and Rooster grumbled their agreement. "I hate that shit too, Diablo." Steel held the knife up so the light bounced off the blade.

With blood dripping off his face, Raley twisted and moaned. "What're you gonna do to me?"

"Show you what happens when you fuck around in our territory. And I'm gonna give you the same amount of mercy you gave my daughter and all the others."

"If you kill me, the feds will be all over you. You can't just kill an FBI agent and not have consequences."

"I never fucking cared much for badges, especially the crooked ones. Watching you die a slow, painful death will be worth whatever the feds want to bring on. Of course, that's providing they find any evidence."

"I didn't know she was your daughter. I swear. I can give you a lot of money." His words were strained as gasps and cracks interrupted him. "We can work something out. I can be very useful for your club—"

Steel glared at Raley. "Gag this piece of shit! I'm sick of hearing his pussy words."

Goldie stuffed a rag in the agent's mouth, then took the prods Steel handed him and gave Raley a couple of shocks.

"Now it's my turn." Steel locked his gaze on the FBI agent's terrified one as he approached with a knife in hand. He bent down and put his mouth close to Raley's ear. "I'm gonna skin you alive, you motherfucker. And I'm gonna do it real slow. I got a lot of time. And the shit you did to my woman? You're gonna pay for that too. In the past, some Native American tribes killed their enemies by flaying them slowly. It's been said that they could keep a man alive for six weeks."

Raley shook his head vehemently, twisting his body, tears pouring from his eyes as his deep grunts tried to push past the gag.

"Let's see if it's folklore or truth."

"He looks like a goddamn jumping bean," Rooster said, and everyone laughed.

Except for Steel. He raged inside, the pain of losing Chenoa and almost losing his woman making his hatred palpable. It was raw, honest, and jagged.

"Strip the motherfucker." Steel moved back and watched as Diablo and Crow cut off the man's clothes.

He kicked away the pile of clothes as he placed the knife on Raley's skin and began his task.

Chapter Thirty-Nine

Two months later

BREANNA STOOD WITH her hand on the doorknob, willing herself to turn it and go inside. This was the first time she'd been back to the office since the incident with Special Agent Raley. She'd followed the doctor's orders to a T, and when he gave her the green light to return to her job, she'd had mixed feelings. On one hand, she'd been bored out of her mind, but on the other, she was afraid the memories of that night would incapacitate her from doing her job.

She concentrated on breathing deeply, visualizing her body relaxing and all anxiety flowing out of her. She swallowed hard and turned the knob. A blast of frosty air covered her, and she glanced around the room. Except for new carpet, the room looked just like it had a short two months before.

"You're back," Joel's familiar voice washed over her. "I wasn't sure if you were ever coming back." He smiled weakly at her. His gaze was tentative.

"I was just waiting for the doctor to clear me. Has it been crazy busy around here?"

"Yep. Janet and I have been slammed. We're glad you're back. The department kept telling us they'd send over a temp, but they never did. So, you can see it's the same song and dance." He pulled out a paper cup from the dispenser, filled it with cold water, and drank it in one gulp. "You got a stack of cases waiting for you on your desk."

She chuckled. "It's comforting to know some things never change."

He threw the cup in the trash. "I still can't believe that Raley was the one orchestrating the drug and food stamp schemes. I never saw that one."

Breanna shook her head. "Neither did I."

"And he just took off. It's strange, though, because he left all this incriminating evidence behind. He even left his laptop."

"Really? That is strange." She rubbed her arms and looked around. "Is Agent Powers still here?"

Joel nodded. "I think he's transferring to Indiana next week. He closed the case on the food stamp fraud. It turned out that Roy's Market was involved. You called that one."

"Breanna! How are you?" Janet rushed over and hugged her warmly. "You're looking great. It's so good to have you back."

"It's good to be back. I wasn't sure at first, but now I am."

Janet gripped her hand. "I bet it's strange being here after the ordeal you went through." She lowered her voice and leaned into Breanna. "And to think Agent Raley was doing all those horrible things and acting like he was Mister Cop of the Year."

"And making us sit through all those bullshit meetings. He should get life in prison just for that," Joel said as the two of them laughed.

"Welcome back, Breanna." Agent Powers nodded at her.

"Thank you," she said as her gaze scanned his. His face looked paler and thinner than the last time she'd seen him. "I hear this is your last week."

"It is." He licked his lips, then walked over to the water cooler and filled up a paper cup. After downing it, he crushed the cup in his hands and threw it in the trash. He cleared his throat. "I'm sorry about what happened to you. You know, with Raley and all that."

She smiled. "It wasn't your fault. Anyway, I'm doing fine, and the drug and food stamp problems are finished, so that's a good thing."

"Well… they're curbed for now." He ran his fingers through his short hair. "That's the best we can hope for. I always feel angry and disgusted when a fellow officer betrays the badge." He crossed his arms, and she and her fellow coworkers watched him. He shrugged and then walked out of the room.

Breanna exhaled and straightened her shoulders. "I guess I better get to my desk and start to tackle the stack of files Joel warned me about." Janet and Joel snickered as they trailed behind her.

When she passed Raley's old office, a shiver ran down her spine. Shaking her head as if to dislodge any unpleasant images, she went to her cubicle. Eyeing the pile of manila folders, she smiled broadly. *It's sure good to be back.*

WHEN STEEL CAME out of Get Inked, his eyes landed on Sheriff Wexler reclining against the squad car, his arms folded across his chest. Steel clenched his jaw as he approached the lawman.

"How's business?" The sheriff jerked his chin toward the tattoo shop.

"Good." Steel took the keys to his Harley out of his pocket. He walked toward his bike parked in front of Wexler's SUV.

"Everything going okay with you?"

Steel narrowed his eyes. "Cut the shit, Wexler. What do you want?"

The forty-six-year-old lawman took off his sunglasses revealing fine lines around his eyes and upper cheeks. His blue gaze fixed on Steel. "I just need to ask you a few questions."

"About what?" Steel's voice had an edge to it. He didn't like or trust the law, and even though he and the sheriff had had a tacit understanding for the past several years, he still wasn't a fan of his. He figured if he didn't bother the badges, they had no reason to bother him.

"About that mess with the FBI agent, Raley, and Roy's Market." His stare bored into Steel.

"I don't know what the hell you're talking about. I got shit to do." He turned around and went to his Harley.

"We can do this civil and just chat, or I can take you in. It's your call."

"You can't take me in and you know it. You don't have shit on me."

"Doesn't your ex date that fella Roy who owns Roy's Market?"

"Yeah, she dates that asshole. What of it?"

"He was arrested a few days ago. I'm sure you knew that. Seems like Agent Powers had a sting operation going on, and he closed down the market and charged Roy with food stamp fraud."

"So? I don't give a damn what happens to him."

"Seems like the other FBI agent, Raley, was working with Roy. It also seems like that was his side business since he was the one who was distributing the heroin in the county."

Steel shrugged. "Raley? Don't know him."

"Breanna Quine did. She worked with him and he almost killed her, but she told me she got away by crawling through the air vent. Isn't she your woman?"

Steel nodded. "She's my woman."

Wexler rubbed his face with his fist. "That's what I'm having a problem with. You're telling me she's your girlfriend and that you don't know Raley. It's not adding up."

"I didn't say I didn't know *of* him. I just said I didn't know him. You got it?"

The sheriff and Steel stared at each other as the noise of the traffic on Main Street filled the gap between them. "You knew he was dealing the drugs."

"I heard that, but the fucking bastard had left by the time I found out."

"Yeah… just disappeared without a trace. His wife hasn't heard from him at all. Seems strange."

"He's probably shacking up with some chick. This has nothing to do with me." Steel took out his leather gloves and slowly put them on his hands.

"Funny thing is that the feds found accounts he had under different names, and they all had money in them. You'd think he'd want to take it out. The feds are wondering how he's living." Wexler spat on the pavement. "It's good to have the county clean again. Raley did some real bad shit and people suffered for it. I've been meaning to tell you how sorry I am about your daughter."

Steel nodded and put on his sunglasses. "I'll see you around." He swung his leg over the leather seat and switched on the engine.

"Steel?" The lawman came next to him.

"Yeah?"

"Thanks." For several seconds, the two men looked at each other as a mutual understanding passed between them. Wexler took a few steps back.

Steel jerked his chin up, then pulled away from the curb. In his side mirror he saw the sheriff walk back to his SUV, and he knew that the local investigation into the disappearance of Special Agent Richard Raley was officially closed.

Chapter Forty

S TEEL STOPPED AT the base of Mt. Hesperus and helped Breanna off his Harley. He'd been wanting to take her to the sacred mountain for a long time, but he had to wait until she was completely healed. He took her hand and led her up to the peak.

"It's so quiet here," she said. "It's simply beautiful."

"It's where the sky and the earth meet. You can hear the whispers from your ancestors, from your loved ones."

She leaned into him. "Do you hear Chenoa up here?" she asked softly.

He nodded. "Not just here. When I ride hard, the wind cries her name."

The stillness wrapped around them as the landscape of snow-peaked mountaintops, vibrant evergreen, and ribbons of streams down below surrounded them.

"She's always with me. She's in every snowflake, every raindrop, and every ray of sunshine that touches my face. She's gone but so alive."

"Oh, Steel," Breanna said as she curled her arms around him and kissed him. He tugged her closer, loving her warmth against him.

She'd been his strength since he'd lost Chenoa. He never would've believed that she'd end up being his life, his love, and his salvation when he'd first seen her at the hospital what seemed like a lifetime ago. He'd never loved a woman so completely. He'd fought falling for her, but when he'd finally let it happen, it'd been so simple.

Losing Chenoa had hit him hard. For a long time he'd lived on anger, pain, and emptiness, until Breanna had made him realize through her words, her love, and her support that he had to let his daughter go.

It was the ultimate sacrifice asked of a father, but he let her go to fly among the angels and mingle with the spirits of his ancestors.

Breanna was always there for him even though she was going through her own hell with Nicholas. After smack dried up in the county, he'd left, wandering like a nomad in the desert for the next hit. By that time, she'd told Steel that her brother was up to twelve shots a day. He felt helpless, like he had with Chenoa, in helping Nicholas. He'd offered to pay for rehab, but the two times her brother tried it, he didn't last more than a week. All Steel could do was hold her close when the fear and worry became too much for her and let her cry.

"What're you thinking about?" she asked.

"You. How happy you make me."

"Do I?"

"You know it. You've had my back." He kissed her gently.

"I'll always have your back. You're the love of my life." She buried her face in his chest and he lowered his head and kissed her, inhaling the scent of gardenias in her hair.

"We should get back. It looks like a storm's moving in." Gray clouds hung low in the distance. "We don't want to be caught in a blizzard, especially on a Harley."

By the time they arrived home, snowflakes danced in the air.

"Brrr... I'm freezing. Make a fire for us, and I'll make us some coffee."

"Put some brandy in mine." Steel chuckled. It seemed that the only thing she was good at making was coffee. He didn't mind that she couldn't cook; she pleased him more than fine in other areas of their life together. His mother minded a lot though, and she'd taken it on herself to give Breanna cooking classes two times a week. She was a good sport about it, and it gave Steel a chance to hang with some of his old buddies on the rez who he'd gotten back in contact with.

"Here you go." She handed him a steaming cup and curled up next to him. "What should we order for dinner?"

"I thought you had some of that stew you made with my mom."

"Correction—I made it on my own. Your mom gave me instructions, but it didn't work out. You know it's crap. Am I lying?" She poked him with her index finger.

A smile filled his face. "Yeah, it's shit. But you'll get better." He laughed when she rolled her eyes. "Maybe you won't. I don't give a damn. I'll love you whether you know how to cook or not. Let's just do a pizza, but not frozen. I draw the line on that."

She laughed. "That works for me." She sipped her coffee. "I ran into Mika at the rez the other day when I was at your mom's. She still seems pissed about Roy."

"In some fucking bizarre way, she blames me that he ended up in the pen for fraud."

"I can't believe she thinks it's your fault. Roy's the one who put himself there. You finding out about Raley didn't get Roy in trouble. Raley had it set up already to frame Roy for everything, including the drugs. The other agent, Powers, figured it all out when Raley skipped town. I still can't believe he didn't take his computer with all the incriminating evidence on it. And the ledgers for all the drug sales. I find it incredible that he'd leave that all behind, don't you?"

"He was desperate to get away since he knew we were all on to him. Desperation makes people do some crazy stuff."

"So after you roughed him up, you just let him go?"

He narrowed his eyes. "That's what I said when you asked me a while back. So what do you want on your pizza?" He locked eyes with her.

She swallowed noisily. "Uh… pepperoni, and whatever else you want."

AFTER DINNER HE poured them each a shot of tequila and sat on the couch, drawing her next to him. "I want us to get our own house. It's time."

"Don't you have like seven months left on your lease?"

"I'll just pay it off." He laughed at her surprised look. "How many times do I have to tell you that I don't have money issues? And that's another thing. You don't need to work so hard. You should go down to part-time."

"I need to pay off some of my debt, and since I haven't worked at Cuervos in a couple of months, I'm kind of strapped. Anyway, I like my job. Besides, what would I do if I didn't work? I'd be bored out of my mind."

"Not if you were busy with charity work, supervising the club's activities, and doing other shit an old lady has to do. Being a president's old lady is a big responsibility, with a workload that goes with it."

"An old lady? Are you asking me to wear your patch?" Her lips curled up in a smile.

He caressed her cheek. "Yeah. I want you to wear my patch and my ring."

"Your ring? Does your club give old ladies one of the club rings too? That's different."

"You're so fucking cute." As he pulled out a black box from his cut, he brushed a kiss across her lips. "I'm asking you to marry me. The ring is all yours, baby."

A small hand flew across her mouth. "Marry you? Like in a white dress and flowers?"

"I was thinking more like black leather and denim, but you get the picture."

She flung her arms around him. "Yes, I'll marry you. Of course. I never expected this. I love you." She peppered his face with kisses as she spoke.

"Maybe you better look at the ring. You may change your mind."

She pulled back and took the box from him. "You're right. If this is some wimpy-ass diamond, then forget what I just said." She winked at him and opened the box. The two-carat solitaire twinkled, picking up the amber sparks from the crackling fire. She gasped. "It's gorgeous. I love it!"

He took the ring out of the box and put it on her finger. "Breanna, you make my life complete. You are the earth to my sky. You are the harmony and balance in my life. I love you so much. I want you to be my wife, baby."

Her eyes shimmered and she bobbed her head up and down. "I haven't changed my mind. I'd love for you to be my husband. You're everything I've been looking for my whole life. I love you."

He pulled her close to him and kissed her deeply, his hand roaming down her curves until it landed on her ass, squeezing hard. "Let's get fucking naked and start on our family."

She laughed as she pushed away and slowly unbuttoned her top. He watched her, mesmerized by her sexiness, groaning when he saw her red lace bra, her pink nipples straining against it. When she stood up and shimmied out of her jeans, his cock punched at his zipper.

"Get your sexy ass over here," he growled as she bent over, her pussy peeking from under her ass cheeks.

She giggled and unfastened her bra, throwing it across the room. Her breasts bounced slightly and she cupped them, pressing them together.

"Fuck, woman. You're killing me. I'm gonna make your ass nice and pink."

"Tempting me?" She kneeled on the couch. "It worked." She kissed him hard.

He grabbed her tits and brought them to his mouth, sucking, biting, and licking them like a starving man. She threw her head back, arching her back so her breasts were deeper in his mouth. As he feasted, he ran his fingers between her legs, chuckling when they came out covered with her arousal.

She pulled away. "It's not fair that I'm nude but you're not."

"Oh yeah? What're you gonna do about it?"

"This." She tugged his shirt over his head, then pressed her hardened nipples against his chest before sliding down to his tapered waist, resting her hand on his pulsing bulge. Taking the zipper between her teeth, she locked her eyes on his and slowly unzipped his jeans.

He smiled broadly.

Fuck yeah.

Epilogue

Sixteen months later

STEEL PLOPPED HIS legs on top of the coffee table knowing his mother would lecture him when she came in. He glanced around her living room and his gaze landed on his and Breanna's wedding picture. She looked beautiful in her simple, white wedding dress, her head swept up into a messy bun. He still couldn't believe she was his forever, and whenever he saw her wearing his patch, it turned him on to no end. She was more than a wife, lover, and friend; she was his strength, his everything.

"Is Breanna with you?" his mom asked as she walked into the room. "And take your feet off the table. You're going to scratch it. Does Breanna let you do that at your house?"

He placed his feet on the floor and crossed his leg over his thigh. "I treat her real good so she *lets* me do whatever the hell I want." He chuckled when his mother placed her hands on her hips and shook her head while frowning. She didn't fool him for a minute because her eyes sparkled as she feigned displeasure.

Warmth spread through him as he looked at the curl of a smile tugging at the corners of her mouth. Since the birth of his son, his mom usually wore a smile on her face and a twinkle in her dark eyes. It'd been a long time since he'd seen her so happy, and he loved it.

"When's Breanna coming with my grandson?"

"She texted me that they're on their way. You know, we really want you to live with us. She keeps asking me if you've changed your mind. I don't understand why you're being so stubborn."

His mother came over and sat by him on the couch, her wrinkled

hand gently stroking his cheek. "I love you so much. You've been my rock since you were a young boy. You always stood up for me when I was too weak to do it."

"*Shimá*, you—"

She held up her hand. "I'm not finished. I don't want you to think for one minute that I don't love you because I'm not choosing to live with you. It's not the right time for that. You and your wife need to be alone to build your life with your son." She pulled at a loose thread in the couch. "Besides, I love being on the reservation. I've been here for most of my life. I'd miss my friends and my grandkids. They come over every day after school. It's nice. And even though Chitsa can be a handful, I'd miss your sister. Are you mad at me?"

Steel brought his mother's hand to his lips. "I'm not mad, *Shimá*. When the time is right, you'll always have a home with me and Breanna." The front door opened and he jumped up when he saw his wife and son come in. After kissing Breanna, he took Aiden from her arms and held him close. The four-month-old swung out his tiny arms and scrunched up his face. Steel laughed and kissed him on his soft, dark hair. He caught Breanna's gaze and held out his arm to her. She came next to him and he tugged her to his side. The scent of gardenias, vanilla, and apricot curled around him and he knew that for the rest of his life, those would be his favorite smells. She tilted her head and looked up at him. *She's so gorgeous.* He dipped his head down and kissed her, his tongue pushing into her mouth. It tasted of peppermint, and when she tucked her thumb in his waistband, his dick jerked.

"I can't wait to get you alone," he whispered against her ear.

She giggled. "Behave. Your mom's sitting over there on the couch."

He sucked her earlobe between his teeth. "I can't help it if you make me want to do dirty things to you. You push all my fucking buttons, baby."

"Later... I promise to make it worth the wait." She uncurled herself from under Steel's arm and walked over to the couch. "How are you, *Shimá*?" she asked.

He watched her as she sat on the couch, her hair tumbling down her back as her cute butt wiggled until she settled down on the cushion. As they spoke, he turned his eyes back to his son. He was amazed at how beautiful he was: hair as dark as midnight and skin the color of moonlight. *Chenoa would've loved to have had a brother to boss around.* He chuckled softly as he caressed Aiden's cheek with his fingertip. He walked over to his mother and placed his son in her outstretched arms. As they talked, his phone buzzed and he went outside.

"What's up, Paco?"

"Just touching base with you. Did you want Goldie to help Muerto run the pool hall? Goldie keeps saying you want him at Lust, but I thought you said you wanted him at Balls and Holes."

"No. I want Crow to help Muerto at the pool hall. Goldie's got his hands full at the bike repair shop. There's no way I'm putting him in charge over at Lust. He's fucking horny for Fiona."

Paco laughed. "I thought he had a boner for someone at Lust. He kept denying it."

"He would. He'd best keep away from her. I don't wanna have to kick his ass."

The club was adamant that the women employees were off limits to the brothers. Steel figured that the brothers had their pick of the club girls, the hang-arounds, and the citizens who liked the excitement of being in an outlaw's bed; they didn't need to sniff around the women who worked at the club's businesses. Most of the time it worked out, but occasionally he'd have to set a brother straight. It seemed like he'd have to have a talk with Goldie.

"You coming by to shoot some pool and toss back some tequila?"

"Not tonight. We're taking my mom out to dinner. I'll see you at church tomorrow. I heard that another strip bar is opening up. I want to find out who owns it. If my information is correct, Jimmy Delarosa is gonna run it. I want to know who's putting the money into it."

"I'll have Crow check it out. He's the computer geek."

"Sounds good. Anything else?"

"Is Breanna gonna take over the fundraiser we have at the fall rally for abused kids? Shannon was asking since she's done it for the last six years."

Steel quirked his lips. "Yeah, she is. Shannon's gotta understand that Breanna is the head of everything now. She's been Rooster's old lady long enough to know what the pecking order is. I'm the goddamn president, so Breanna is the number one old lady. If she has a gripe, tell her to talk to me about it. I don't want to hear that she's giving my woman a hard time."

"I'll tell Rooster. That'll do it. Later, brother," Paco said.

Steel slid his phone into his pocket and walked back inside. His mother was still holding Aiden, and Breanna sat next to her, a huge smile filling up her face. "You ready to get some food?" They nodded, their gazes never leaving Aiden's face. "Then let's go." He'd planned on taking them to a new steak house which had opened in the valley. It was Saturday night. A couple of years ago, he'd have spent it at the club, drinking hard and fucking harder, but that night, he'd planned on taking his family out to dinner, and then he and Breanna would put Aiden to bed and make love.

And he didn't want it any other way.

LATER THAT NIGHT, he sat against the headboard, his bare arms crossed behind his head. Breanna hugged him tightly around his waist, her hair covering his chest like a blanket. Moonlight spilled into their bedroom, and from the uncovered window, he could see the sprinkle of glittering stars in the dark sky.

Aiden rested peacefully in his crib in the alcove in their room. Once Aiden moved to his own room, Breanna planned to use the alcove as a sitting area complete with bookcases. They had moved into their new home six months after Breanna had healed from the injuries she'd sustained that horrible night. She'd insisted on a huge master bedroom with an alcove and fireplace, and during the wintry nights, Steel loved holding her close as the glow from the crackling fire made her hair and body shimmer gold.

"Is Shannon or Sam giving you a hard time? They've been the only two old ladies since I started the club twelve years ago."

She kissed his belly softly. "They definitely don't like giving up the throne to me, but I can handle it. Even though they're not happy I'm onboard, they respect me. I'll say that it's become easier as time has gone on. They're getting used to the idea. When are some of the other guys going to get hitched? I mean like Paco or Muerto?"

Steel busted out laughing, then turned quickly to make sure he hadn't woken up Aiden. "I can't see either of those guys having old ladies," he said in a low voice.

"Could you have seen yourself as having one?" She craned her neck and he locked his gaze with hers.

He shook his head. "Back then… no way. Now I can't imagine my life without you or Aiden." He pulled her up closer to his face and bent down to kiss her deeply, his hand grazing the side of her exposed breast. "When I hold you close, I burn raw… deep down inside. I love you so much." He pressed her flush against him, his fingers threading through her hair.

"I'm so happy we gave each other a chance. I spent so many years hating bikers and being angry at them all because of my dad. As I got to know you, I realized that being a biker wasn't the reason my dad was mean, unfaithful, and uncaring. That was just the way he was. He wasn't a good person. You've helped me to let my anger go. A big piece was missing from my life, and now I'm complete. You and Aiden make me whole. I love you more than I could ever tell you in words." She nuzzled her face against his neck. "I'm looking forward to working on the fundraiser for the charity, Bikers Against Child Abuse. It's up my alley."

"Do you miss working?"

She shook her head. "Not at all. I couldn't stand to leave Aiden with someone else. I'm happy I can stay home and be with him."

"And when you're ready, we're gonna have to give him some siblings. Maybe a sister or two." He sighed and looked at the stars. Among them, there was one that shone brighter than the others, and he liked to think it was Chenoa. He still missed her so much; he always would, but he found comfort in knowing she was free from her demons. His little girl—his sunshine—was looking down and smiling at him and her new brother.

"I know you miss her, but she's always going to be a part of you. Aiden will know about his sister. We'll both make sure of that," she said softly as she rubbed his shoulder.

"I know." He kissed the top of her head. "Have you heard from Nicholas lately?"

She shook her head. "Not in a long time."

He kissed her hair. "I know how hard it's for you not knowing where he is."

She gripped his shoulder. "I have to let it go. It is what it is," her voice hitched, and he held her tight.

Then Aiden's high-pitched cry bounced off the walls. "He's right on time," Breanna said as she looked over her shoulder. "I fed him three hours ago." She wiped her eyes and pulled away from Steel.

"Do you need any help?" he asked as he sat up straighter.

"Unless you got boobs that have milk, I have to do this alone." She bent down and picked up her robe from the floor and threw it on as she padded over to the crib.

He watched her pick up their son and kiss him on the head. She went over to the rocking chair near the window, opened her robe slightly, supported the back of Aiden's head with her hand, and brought him close to her breast. Steel smiled; he loved watching her and their son bond in such an intimate way.

After forty minutes, Breanna placed Aiden in his crib, and then climbed back into bed. She yawned and pulled the covers over her shoulders. He tugged her to him and cocooned her in his arms as she fell asleep. He kissed her temple softly. "You'll always be my passion," he whispered under his breath.

Staring at the star-filled sky, he felt his eyelids grow heavy. The trees shook as the wind weaved through them, their chaotic branches swaying in a hypnotic dance. Breanna sighed and licked her lips, and he held her tighter as sleep overtook him.

Make sure you sign up for my newsletter so you can keep up with my new releases, special sales, free short stories, and other treats only available to newsletter readers. When you sign up, you will receive a FREE hot and steamy novella. Sign up at:
http://eepurl.com/bACCL1

Visit me on Facebook
facebook.com/Chiah-Wilder-1625397261063989

Check out my other books at my Author Page
amazon.com/author/chiahwilder

Notes from Chiah

As always, I have a team behind me making sure I shine and continue on my writing journey. It is their support, encouragement, and dedication that pushes me further in my writing journey. And then, it is my wonderful readers who have supported me, laughed, cried, and understood how these outlaw men live and love in their dark and gritty world. Without you—the readers—an author's words are just letters on a page. The emotions you take away from the words breathe life into the story.

Thank you to my amazing Personal Assistant Amanda Faulkner. I don't know what I'd do without you. I value your suggestions and opinions, and my world is so much saner with you in it. You keep the non-writing part of my indie publishing world running smoothly. I so appreciate it. You are always ready to jump in and fix everything when I'm pulling my hair out. You are so cheerful, and when I hear your bubbling voice, it instantly uplifts me. So happy YOU are on my team!

Thank you to my editor, Kristin, for all your insightful edits, excitement with my new series, Night Rebels MC, and encouragement during the writing and editing process. I truly value your editorial eyes and suggestions as well as the time you spend. You're the best!

Thank you to my wonderful beta readers, Kolleen, Jessica, and Mandy. Your enthusiasm and suggestions for Steel: Night Rebels MC were spot on and helped me to put out a stronger, cleaner novel. Your insight and attention to detail was awesome.

Thank you to the bloggers for your support in reading my book, sharing it, reviewing it, and getting my name out there. I so appreciate all your efforts. You all are so invaluable. I hope you know that. Without you, the indie author would be lost.

Thank you ARC readers you have helped make all my books so much stronger. I appreciate the effort and time you put in to reading, reviewing, and getting the word out about the books. I don't know what I'd do without you. I feel so lucky to have you behind me.

Thank you to Carrie from Cheeky Covers. We were on such a tight timeline with this book because we had to work around the schedules of our model and photographer, but you pulled it off, girl. You are amazing! I can always count on you. You are the calm to my storm. You totally rock, and I love your artistic vision.

Thank you to my proofreader, Daryl, whose last set of eyes before the last once over I do, is invaluable. I appreciate the time and attention to detail you always give to my books.

Thank you to Ena and Amanda with Enticing Journeys Promotions who have helped garner attention for and visibility to the Night Rebels MC series. Couldn't do it without you! Also a big thank you to Book Club Gone Wrong Blog who is hosting and promoting *Steel*. Totally indebted to you.

Thank you to Dan Pearson for being such an awesome model. I appreciate your flexibility and work in making the cover rock.

Thank you to Al Gonzalez for taking such a great pose. Your photography skills are what made the cover stand out. A fantastic shoot.

Thank you to the readers who continue to support me and read my books. Without you, none of this would be possible. I appreciate your comments and reviews on my books, and I'm dedicated to giving you the best story that I can. I'm always thrilled when you enjoy a book as much as I have in writing it. You definitely make the hours of typing on the computer and the frustrations that come with the territory of writing books so worth it. You make it possible for writers to write because without you reading the books, we wouldn't exist. Thank you, thank you! ♥

Steel: Night Rebels Motorcycle Club (Book 1)

Dear Readers,

Thank you for reading my book. I hope you enjoyed the first book in my new Night Rebels MC series as much as I enjoyed writing Steel and Breanna's story. This gritty and rough motorcycle club has a lot more to say, so I hope you will look for the upcoming books in the series. Romance makes life so much more colorful, and a rough, sexy bad boy makes life a whole lot more interesting.

If you enjoyed the book, please consider leaving a review on Amazon. I read all of them and appreciate the time taken out of busy schedules to do that.

I love hearing from my fans, so if you have any comments or questions, please email me at chiahwilder@gmail.com or visit my facebook page.

To hear of **new releases**, **special sales**, **free short stories**, and **ARC opportunities**, please sign up for my **Newsletter** at http://eepurl.com/bACCL1.

Happy Reading,

Chiah

MUERTO
Book 2 in the Night Rebels MC Series
(Release: April 23, 2017)

Muerto is six feet of rugged, muscular danger. Secretary of the Night Rebels MC, this hot-headed biker talks with his fists then asks questions. He exudes sexiness and untamed masculinity and the women can't get enough of him. With his dark good looks, wicked tats, and sizzling lover reputation, he doesn't have to chase a woman. He never has.

He enjoys the easiness of the club girls, the variety of the hang-arounds, and the drama of the citizen women when they fight over him. But one thing is for sure… his heart doesn't belong to any of them. And he likes that just fine.

The brotherhood is where his loyalty lies. Everything after that is secondary. He'd fight to the death to defend a brother, and kill without blinking an eye if anyone disrespected him or his brothers. He's a Night Rebel through and through.

Then *she* comes into the pool hall the club owns. The black-haired woman in the tight jeans and high heels has the audacity to hustle on his watch. And when he confronts her, she gives him an attitude.

She's smart-mouthed, beautiful, and too sexy for her own good. And she doesn't want him.

The more she stays away from him, the more he wants to pursue her. He tells himself it's for the challenge, but he can't get her out of his mind.
All he wants to do is take her in his arms and devour her.

All he wants to do is claim her as his.

Raven Harris knows the good-looking outlaw is trouble the minute she sees him. He's the type of man to sweep a woman off her feet then drop her on her butt when he grows bored. No way does she need any of that in her life.

Mending from a broken heart from the betrayal of a man who'd been the love of her life, she's content with her cat and her artwork. She doesn't need a man complicating her life.

And the tatted biker is all kinds of complicated.

The only problem is each time she looks at him, her body tingles and he sets her world on fire.

But something's not right. She has the creepy feeling that someone is watching her from the shadows. Someone has targeted her and is waiting to make a move.

Can she trust Muerto enough to let him into her life? Can Muerto open his heart to her before it's too late?

This is the second book in the Night Rebels MC Romance series. This is Muerto's story. It is a standalone. This book contains violence, sexual assault (not graphic), strong language, and steamy/graphic sexual scenes. It describes the life and actions of an outlaw motorcycle club. If any of these issues offend you, please do not read the book. HEA. No cliffhangers! The book is intended for readers over the age of 18.

Chapter One

MUERTO LEANED AGAINST the bar admiring the way the woman's ass moved as she bent down low to take a shot at a ball near the left pocket on the pool table. He was surprised she could even bend in her tight as sin jeans, and her top inched up just enough to expose a glimpse of skin.

"She's got a nice ass," Crow said behind him.

"She's a looker, that's for fuckin' sure." Muerto raised his beer bottle to his lips, his eyes never leaving her tight curves.

"She's damn hot, but she doesn't know much about the game." Crow laughed. "She was in the other night and she lost her ass. Last night she did a little better, but she's got a long way to go."

"Most of the guys in here don't play so hot, except for Willy and Gator. I'm sure the guys are playing with her just to get a peek at her tits when she bends over. Hell, I'll play a game with her for that chance." Muerto pushed off the counter and went behind the bar. "How was business the last couple of nights?"

"Steady," Crow said.

Balls and Holes was the pool hall owned by the Night Rebels MC. It was a classic, dark and smoky players' hall not one of the upscale billiard rooms with loud music and video games. It was one of the last of the old-school pool halls, refusing to be muscled out by the new chic ones that had been sprouting around the county and Durango—the large neighboring city.

The pool hall had chalk-covered floors and high-backed wooden chairs against the walls so spectators could watch the game. There were six green felt pool tables at the center of the room, and an old jukebox in the corner. The place was dark with low ceilings, and the smoke from cigarettes and weed curled around the players. No one seemed to care about the law forbidding smoking in public places. They came there to play pool and watch people play as they threw back some beers. It was the gathering hole in its most basic form.

Muerto, Crow and Army ran the place, making sure the bar was stocked and the fights didn't get out of hand. The bar had a large selection of beers and hard liquor, and for friends and long-time customers, the brothers would pull out bottles of Jack Daniels No. 27 Gold and Gran Patrón Platinum. Pretzels, peanuts, and popcorn were the only food served.

"Is Zach working tonight?" Crow asked. Zach was the only citizen bartender in the place. They'd hired him about six months ago and so far the twenty-eight-year-old was working out nicely. With his fit body, he was an asset when they needed another hand to throw out an unruly group.

"Nah. He wanted the night off. I knew you and I could handle it tonight." Muerto placed the glasses he'd washed on a towel to dry.

"Two more Jacks and a couple of vodkas on the rocks. Boy, am I beat," Jaime said as she rubbed her neck.

"You need some help with that?" Crow smiled.

Jaime shook her head and turned to Muerto. "You want me to wash the rest of the glasses? That's not really man's work."

"Thanks, but I got it." He placed her drink order on the tray and watched her as she swayed her hips. She was one of two waitresses at the joint, and her jeans fit nicely around her body, but she was nothing like the blacked-haired cutie who had just lost the game.

"That's the way it rolls, baby. Look at it this way—you're doing better than you did the last two nights." A stocky man in his late twenties with a crew cut said while he swooped up the bills on the side of the pool table.

"You got me. I'm done," her dark, sultry voice washed over Muerto like velvet. He straightened up and gazed at her; she piqued his interest.

"Why don't you play another game with my buddy?" another stocky man with short hair said, placing an arm around the woman's opponent. "What do ya say, Cory?"

Cory nodded. "If you want, I'll play another game with you. Maybe you'll get lucky like you did earlier."

The slender woman glanced at the wall clock. "I don't know. How much you betting?"

"A hundred bucks?"

She whistled. "That's a lot of money. What about fifty?"

Cory grinned. "You're on."

Muerto turned away. "I'd sure like to squeeze my hand down her jeans and see how soft her pussy is," he said to Crow.

"I'll be right behind you, dude." Crow picked up a box and walked out of the bar. "I'm gonna go over our inventory. If you need me, give me a holler."

Muerto nodded and watched as Jaime approached the bar. When he'd hired her the year before, he thought she was good-looking with her shoulder-length brown hair and eyes and curvy body. But he knew she was off limits since she worked for the club. The Night Rebels never mixed pleasure with business, not even at their strip bar, Lust. He suspected she had a small crush on him, but it didn't surprise him; most women had crushes on him. The other waitress, Brandy, was always flirting with him and brushing against him whenever she had to come behind the bar. He knew he could have both of them and probably at the same time, but they were the club's employees.

Six feet of hard muscle turned a lot of women's heads. Add dark, thick hair, a strong jaw, full lips, and intense black eyes and women practically drooled when they saw him. And he loved the attention he got from them. Unlike most of the brothers, he enjoyed going out with citizens, relishing the drama that would ensue when a woman found out he was fucking another one. Whenever that happened, they'd turn on each other instead of him, and he loved that they fought over him, it made his blood boil. But when they got too possessive and started talking about relationships and marriage, he disappeared into the arms and pussies of the club girls who knew the score.

The only downside to angering so many citizen women was that he was constantly changing his phone number, and that pissed off his brothers, especially Steel, big time. He figured it was a small price to pay for the challenge of pursing a woman and getting her into his bed. The club girls were too easy, and they were always available. There wasn't any drama there except for the usual chick stuff, but they knew they were at the club for all the brothers alike, and that's what they wanted as well.

What he liked in being with a citizen was that she was his alone, and she was totally centered on him until he grew bored and moved on. When he'd go to the biker rallies the club had a couple of times a year in the San Juan Valley, he'd have a bevy of women glaring at him, wanting to tear him to pieces. He'd just wink at them and go his own way, scouting for another woman to conquer. And there was always a good supply of enamored, willing women to seduce.

The pretty chick with the cue stick was someone he'd love to seduce. Her ebony hair swayed as she twisted her sexy body to make the shots. He'd love to yank a fistful of her long hair as he slammed his cock into her from behind.

"Muerto? Did you fill my order?" Jamie asked as she placed the tray on the bar.

"What? Sorry. I don't know what the fuck's wrong with me." He grabbed several beer bottles from the refrigerated shelves and popped them open. *I got my mind on her. She's so damn hot.* He placed the beer bottles and three shots of Jack on the tray. "There you go."

"Thanks." She threw him a warm smile and headed over to the pool table where the woman was playing the game.

"I won," she said as she clapped her hands gleefully.

"See, you got lucky," Cory said as he took the beer from Jaime. "You wanna up the bet to a hundred bucks?"

Muerto jerked his chin at Army and Goldie as they walked in. He placed two shots of Jack Daniels No. 27 Gold on the bar. "I thought you guys were at Lust," Muerto said as the two brothers sat down on the barstools.

"We were, but there wasn't anything much going on there. Tuesday nights are pretty slow." Goldie finished his shot. "Fuck that's good."

"Only the best for the brothers," Muerto said as he poured him another one. "Fiona wasn't dancing tonight?"

"What difference would that make? I went there to check out the women and have a few beers with the brothers." Goldie threw back his shot.

"Fuck that. You went for Fiona. We all know you have a boner for her," Army swung around on the barstool. He whistled softly. "Talk about having a boner... check out the chick with the tight pants and luscious ass."

Anger pricked at Muerto's skin. "Cool it, dudes. She's a customer."

Army looked over his shoulder. "And why do we give a shit about that? You've fucked a few customers."

"I mean, she's a regular." *Why the fuck am I saying this lame shit?* "We kinda got a new policy in here where we don't mess with the women customers."

"When did you get that policy 'cause you didn't have it last week when you were fuckin' that blonde in the storeroom."

"Just leave it and *her* the fuck alone." Fire began to burn in Muerto's veins as he scowled at Army.

Goldie laughed. "I think what he's sayin' is that he wants to fuck her, so stay back."

Before he could reply, Crow came out and the brothers began talking about their favorite thing—Harleys. After a couple of hours of making drinks, bullshiting with the brothers, and washing what felt like his hundredth glass, loud voices pulled him away from the conversation with Goldie and Army. He looked over at the table with the hot chick and saw that a large group had formed near it.

"Watch the bar," he said to Goldie. "I wanna see what's going on." He took a few steps toward the table and saw the black-haired beauty's steely eyes as she aimed her cue stick before taking her shot. She aced the ball in the pocket, then she went around the table, balls rolling every which way, but all of them landing in the side pockets.

He quirked his lips, and as he watched her, he admired her amazing grace and accuracy as she shot down the cocky bastard who, by the looks of it, bet a wad of bills on the game. When she landed the last ball, she calmly picked up the money, counted it, and tucked it in her front pocket, although he didn't know how it fit in her skin tight jeans. *She's got fuckin' nerves of steel.*

"You hustled me, bitch!" Cory yelled.

She looked coolly at him. "You've never lost to a woman before, have you? I won the game fair and square."

"Bullshit." He glanced around the area at the men perched up on the high-backed chairs. "Am I right? You all saw it. This bitch conned me." The only ones in agreement were the player's friends. The other men stared placidly at him.

"Take it like a man, *Cory*," she said. "Next time you may be the winner and have someone accusing you. There's always a winner and a loser in every game." She shrugged on her leather jacket, guzzled the last of her beer, and walked away.

Cory jumped in front of her, his face bloated and red. "I want my money back, you fucking bitch." He grabbed her tightly around her arms.

Ready to intervene, Muerto laughed when she kicked Cory in the shin. When he raised his hand to punch her, Muerto rushed over and grabbed it in mid-air. "Hitting chicks isn't allowed," his voice was hard and gravelly.

"Do you allow stealing? The bitch hustled me. She's a goddamn pool shark."

Her throaty laugh fell over Muerto, and he liked that it made his dick twitch. It occurred to him that ever since he'd spotted her rounded ass in her jeans, his dick had been on high alert.

"You must've spent the weekend watching old movies. 'Pool shark,' what a joke." She zipped up her leather jacket.

"I've been watching you two play for the past few hours. I didn't notice anything. You play a good game, but she played better. You shouldn't bet what you can't afford to lose. Better luck next time, buddy. Go to the bar and have one on me," Muerto said.

Cory's nostrils flared, and he glanced at Muerto then back at his friends. One of them came over to him and clasped his shoulder. "Let's get another drink then go find some food."

Reluctantly he started to walk away. "This ain't over yet, bitch. Let's get outta this shithole." He marched away, his two friends in tow.

"Some guys just can't handle losing to a woman. Pathetic." She slung her large purse over her shoulder and headed to the door.

"Not so fast, sweetheart." Muerto cut her off and she bumped into him.

"What the hell?" She rubbed her head.

"We both know you hustled him." He held his hand up. "Don't fuckin' deny it. You're good. I didn't even see you slip your own cue ball in the game or out of it, but I bet if I dig in that purse of yours I'd find it."

She glowered at him.

"Even though you can wear a pair of jeans better than any woman I've seen, I don't want you back in here hustling. If you didn't have tits and curves, my fists would already be beating your ass."

She raised her chin defiantly. "You can't prove shit."

He laughed. "You better wait a while and have a beer. Pretty sure they're waiting for you outside. I'll walk you to your car when I get done sorting out the receipts. The beer's on me."

"I don't need you to play the fuckin' white knight. I can take care of myself." Her gaze went to the glass doors.

"Suit yourself." He spun around and walked to the bar. When she slinked on one of the barstools, a smile tugged at his lips. "What kind of beer do you want?"

"Give me a shot of Tequila with a twist of lime." She placed her shoulder bag on the stool next to her.

"A Tequila girl. You're full of surprises, sweetheart."

"What the fuck does that mean? And stop calling me 'sweetheart.' I'm no man's sweetheart." She propped her elbows on the counter and rested her chin in her hands.

"I believe that. Here you go." He placed the shot in front of her. "Let me tell you something, *sweetheart*. You're a shark in a sea of fish, but you keep it up, and someone's gonna run a knife right through you. Alina's a small town, and you're playing in dangerous waters." Her flashing eyes shot daggers at him. He chuckled and held his hands up. "Just sayin', that all."

"I thought the customer was supposed to ask the bartender for advice." She drank her shot. "Save your sage wisdom for someone who wants it." She twirled around on the stool, her back facing him.

"You want another?" He poured her one before she answered. "You from around here?"

She looked over her shoulder. "No." She curled her fingers around the glass.

"Where're you from?"

"Everywhere. My pop and I moved around a lot."

"Muerto, I need three shots of Tequila and six Coors and two gin and tonics," Jaime said as she half sat on the barstool next to the pool hustler.

"Sure thing." Muerto turned around and grabbed the beers then made the gin and tonics. "The guys tipping good tonight?"

"Pretty much, but those three guys stiffed me. I think they were gonna tip me but they got pissed at her," she pointed to the woman seated next to her, "for winning the game."

The woman swiveled until she was facing Jaime. "You blaming me for you getting stiffed?"

"What? No. Not at all. They could've tipped me as they drank. I loved that you put that big mouth in his place. He's always in here bragging about how great he is. He thinks he can beat anybody. Well... you showed him." Jamie giggled.

When the woman smiled, Muerto's dick jumped. He studied her face: nicely arched eyebrows, thick black lashes, a thin silver ring in her nose, and beautiful eyes. He'd never seen eyes like hers before. They were gray, not unremarkable gray like that of concrete or stone. They were the gray of the ocean an instant before dawn's first rays hit the water. And when she'd glanced his way, they'd ensnared him. She turned away quickly, and he was pretty sure he pique her interest as much as she did his. He imagined that she was a woman who wouldn't put up with any crap from a man; a feisty woman who'd give a man a real run before she tore up the sheets with him.

She turned back around, as if sensing that he was still staring at her. "Do you want something?" A frown deepened on her forehead, and her eyes looked silver like a well-sharpened knife blade.

"Depends on what you're willing to give me." He leaned forward so his face was a scant few inches from hers. The scent of leather, smoke and spice wisped around him.

She jumped off the stool and grabbed her shoulder bag. "Absolutely nothing. Thanks for the shots." She headed to the door.

It would serve her right if I let her go out alone. "I'll be right back," he muttered to Crow. Army and Crow whistled as he rushed out after her. In two long strides he caught up to her.

"You don't have to babysit me."

"I know. I just don't want something happening to a customer on my watch."

"Oh," she said.

She sounds disappointed. Maybe I got a chance of scoring after all. They walked to the parking lot, her heel clacked against the pavement. "Which car is yours?"

"The Impala." She pointed to a black car in the far corner of the lot.

As they approached it, Muerto saw two shadows in his peripheral view. He stopped and turned. "You dudes want something?" He clenched his fists in anticipation.

Cory and his friend cleared their throats. "I lost a key around here," Cory said as he dropped down to his knees and patted the asphalt.

"I think I found it," his friend said. "It was in my pocket all along." He laughed and Cory joined him as Muerto stood alert with narrowing eyes and clenched fists. "We're good, dude. Later." Cory and his buddy walked away.

"Thanks," she whispered to him.

"For what?" Muerto asked.

She nodded her head toward the two men disappearing into the night. "For that. I owe you." She slipped her hand in her purse and took out a keychain. The lights went on in her car when she opened the door.

"Yeah, I'd say you owe me. What about dinner tomorrow night?"

"I'm busy. I'll stop by again and we can figure it out."

He came up to her and pressed his body against hers, the scent from her perfume enveloping him. "You can pay me back now."

"In a parking lot? I don't think so." She placed her hands on his shoulders and pushed him back then slipped into the driver's seat. "Anyway, you only helped me out of a potentially sticky encounter, you didn't resurrect me. Maybe dinner, but that's being generous."

He shrugged nonchalantly, but a fire was building inside him. He wasn't used to women telling him no or giving him attitude. "You can come back, but if I see you hustling again, I'll throw you out on your sweet ass, and that's a promise."

"I wouldn't expect anything less from you." She simulated a kiss with her full, pouty lips and then closed the car door. All he could think about were her lips around his cock and his hand on her perfectly rounded ass spanking all the sass out of her.

After the red taillights of her car faded, he stood for a long time looking into the darkness. There was something about the smart-mouthed, tough, hustling woman that drew him, and it surprised the hell out of him. He always drew the women in, and he didn't know what to make of it.

He slowly headed back to the pool hall.

Other Books by Chiah Wilder

Insurgent MC Series:

Hawk's Property: Insurgents Motorcycle Club Book 1
Jax's Dilemma: Insurgents Motorcycle Club Book 2
Chas's Fervor: Insurgents Motorcycle Club Book 3
Axe's Fall: Insurgents Motorcycle Club Book 4
Banger's Ride: Insurgents Motorcycle Club Book 5
Jerry's Passion: Insurgents Motorcycle Club Book 6
Throttle's Seduction: Insurgents Motorcycle Club Book 7
Rock's Redemption: Insurgents Motorcycle Club Book 8
An Insurgent's Wedding: Insurgents Motorcycle Club Book 9
Insurgents MC Romance Series: Insurgents Motorcycle Club Box Set (Books 1 – 4)

Find all my books at:
amazon.com/author/chiahwilder

I love hearing from my readers. You can email me at:
chiahwilder@gmail.com

Sign up for my newsletter to receive a FREE Novella, updates on new books, special sales, free short stories, and ARC opportunities at:
http://eepurl.com/bACCL1

Visit me on facebook at:
www.facebook.com/Chiah-Wilder-1625397261063989